BINGO

BINGO

RITA MAE BROWN

BANTAM BOOKS
TORONTO · NEW YORK · LONDON · SYDNEY · AUCKLAND

BINGO

A Bantam Book / November 1988

Grateful acknowledgment is made to the following for permission to reprint the lyrics from, "Tea for Two" by Vincent Youmans and Irving Caesar. Copyright 1924 WB Music Corp. & Irving Caesar Music Corp. All rights reserved. Used by permission. "Let's Do It" by Cole Porter. Copyright Warner Bros. Inc. (Renewed). All rights reserved. Used by permission.

Illustration on page xii
copyright © 1988 by Laura (Hartman) Maestro.
Book Design by Jaye Zimet.

Library of Congress Cataloging-in-Publication Data

Brown, Rita Mae.
  Bingo / Rita Mae Brown.
     p.   cm.
  ISBN 0-553-05306-X
  I. Title.
  PS3552.R698B56   1988   88-14143
  813'.54—dc19   CIP

Published simultaneously in the United States and Canada

Bantam Books are published by Bantam Books, a division of Bantam Doubleday Dell Publishing Group, Inc. Its trademark, consisting of the words "Bantam Books" and the portrayal of a rooster, is Registered in U.S. Patent and Trademark Office and in other countries. Marca Registrada. Bantam Books, 666 Fifth Avenue, New York, New York 10103.

PRINTED IN THE UNITED STATES OF AMERICA

FG   0 9 8 7 6 5 4 3 2 1

Dedicated with Affection
And Remembered Laughter
to
The Class of 1962
Fort Lauderdale High School

AUTHOR'S NOTE

I wish to thank the following people for helping me write *Bingo*. First and foremost, my researcher, Claudia Garthwaite, deserves my appreciation. She spends a goodly portion of her time buried in the stacks of the library. My agent, Wendy Weil, does all that an agent is supposed to do and more: She makes me laugh. Noirin Lucas, Wendy's assistant, also contributes to my good spirits. Beverly Lewis, my editor, makes the work so easy for me that I can only wish an editor like her for every writer in America. Bantam's copy editor, Betsy Cenedella, keeps me in line and gives me grammar lessons. Sally Williams, Judy Hilsinger, and Sandi Mendelson take care of me on the road, and those of you in publishing know that I'm not bragging when I say these are the best publicity people in the business.

Betty Burns does her best to keep me organized.

I must also thank Susan Scott, Cynthia Cooper, Muffin Barnes, Gloria Fennell, and the gang at Darby's Folly for providing me good companionship and good riding. Special thanks to Elliwood Baxter, Carolyn and Ken Chapman, Pat and Kay Butterfield, our wonderful Master, Jill Summers, our president, Paul Summers, and the membership of Farmington Hunt Club for being themselves. Together we can escape the twentieth century.

The unsung heroes of an author's life also deserve accolades: the sales staff and the telephone sales staff of Bantam Books.

To those of you who have read other novels of mine it will come as no surprise that I must thank the animals in my life. I don't believe humans should be separate from other forms of living consciousness and I learn from animals. So I thank Cazenovia, Buddha, Sneaky Pie, Pewter, and Muggins, the cats. I thank Juts and Liška, the dogs, and I thank Freebooter and Scribble, my horses. I would also like to thank the horses of friends: Twinkie, Fetch, and Colors.

INTRODUCTION

Since this is a work of fiction, I've taken advantage of the freedom of the form. Mentioned within the text are the PTL scandal as well as the Gary Hart scandal. Both events are inaccurately dated. The PTL mess is off by one month and the Hart debacle is off by a few days. Apart from those two news stories, the other events are as found in *Facts on File*.

One of the chief joys of fiction is that to some extent the reader is a co-creator. In a film or theatrical production you see the people. In a novel or radio show you must imagine them—their voices, their gestures. Every art form has its advantages and disadvantages, and I think having the reader participate is an advantage of fiction.

Apart from the fun of participation, this effort on the reader's part forms a bond between reader and author which may be akin to the bond between audience and performer in the theater.

I have been fortunate in my readers. Not only do you faithfully buy my novels, you show up by the hundreds and sometimes even thousands to hear me speak and you send me blizzards of fan mail. I am grateful. Who could ask for anything more?

Well, I am going to ask for more. I'm going to ask you to consider carefully your own creativity. Many of you set aside your creativity for "practical" reasons. It isn't within the scope of an introduction to list painfully why and how people abandon their imaginations but it is within the scope of this introduction to encourage you to find yourself again. You haven't lost your creativity, your imagination—you've simply misplaced it.

There are as many different ways to recover that creativity as there are readers, but allow me to suggest something that will benefit each and every one of you. Keep notes on your own life. Call it a diary if you like but it's much more than that. Write down or record on tape your observations and emotions as well as the events of your time. Don't forget your sense of humor while you do this.

If you take even fifteen minutes a day to perform this labor I think your imagination will start cranking up again. For those of you who have managed to hang on to your creativity, this exercise will give you some perspective and insight into yourself and your community.

No one will ever see the world the way you see it. No one will ever have exactly the same experiences in exactly the same sequence. You are unique not just because of your genetic makeup but because of every single thing that has happened to you or that you have caused to happen. Don't let that consciousness slip off the face of the earth with your death. If you don't want to share yourself with the living, then leave something behind for those arriving on this troubled planet after you've left it.

You might wonder why I'm impassioned about your creativity. There are two reasons for this. The first is that I will be enriched by your creativity. Whether or not you publish a book or sell a painting isn't what I mean. What I mean is that activating your imagination is going to make you more exciting to yourself and to others. The second reason is that imaginative people forge new solutions to old problems. Right now we need every thinking person to step forward and contribute to a safe and sane future. You are part of that process. I celebrate your contribution.

As always,

Rita Mae Brown

February 28, 1987
Charlottesville, Virginia

BINGO

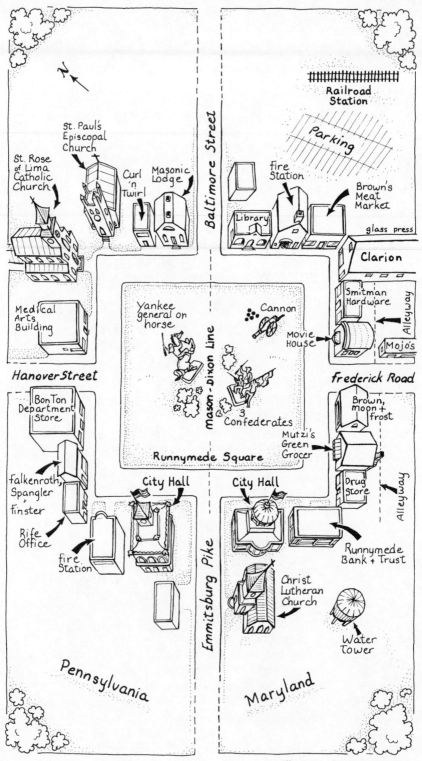

Illustration by Laura Hartman

1

FLYING A KITE

WEDNESDAY . . . 25 MARCH, 1987

"Run faster."

"I'm running as fast as I can." I was, too. "Mom, call off Goodyear and Lolly Mabel. I keep tripping over them."

"Don't blame it on the dogs. You don't know how to fly a kite." Mother did, however, order the dogs to sit by her.

Goodyear, a huge, black male Chow Chow was originally called Jet Pilot but he grew fatter and fatter, and hence the name Goodyear. Lolly Mabel, his gorgeous red daughter, was my dog, a gift for my birthday two years ago. Lolly and Pewter, my cat, were bosom companions but Pewter didn't like Goodyear. Not that Goodyear wasn't the world's second-best dog, Lolly Mabel being the first, but Mom had taught him to howl and play dead at the mention of her sister's name, Louise. We had to be careful to call Louise "Wheezie" or "Wheeze" in front of the dog lest Louise discover yet another of her baby sister's blasphemies. Well, one day I forgot. Luckily, Aunt Louise wasn't around but Pewter was. When the dreaded name Louise escaped my lips, Goodyear screamed bloody murder, then flopped down "dead." Pewter, appalled, ran under Mother's front porch and it took a good hour to coax her out.

The kite shuddered in the air but wouldn't rise. "Dammit!" I continued to pump my legs.

"Gimme that." Mother grabbed the string and ran across the lawn. At eighty-two, Julia Ellen Hunsenmeir Smith could still run, and the kite fluted upward. Mother walked backwards now,

1

jerking the string, urging the red kite, with the tail's many bow ties, higher.

A screech around the corner snapped us away from the graceful sight of the kite to the less graceful sight of Louise taking the corner on two wheels.

"I thought I was going to pick her up. You can't let her drive."

"She does what she wants." Juts observed Louise's lurching halt in front of her house.

Aunt Louise drove a 1952 Chrysler. Her deceased husband, Paul "Pearlie" Trumbull, hated General Motors, hated the auto business, and hated Detroit. He used to declare that they were nothing better than Ali Baba and the Forty Thieves and every year they'd jack up the price on cars. As it happened, he was right. "If you want to get back on your feet, miss two car payments" was one of Pearlie's favorite expressions. Well, he never missed a payment, because he drove his Model A Ford until it died around him, but during those decades he saved and saved and then he went out and bought three identical 1952 Chryslers. He drove the one, intending to use the other two for parts, and he figured that if he took good care of his car, which he did, that Chrysler would be driven by his grandchildren and Detroit be damned.

Except for the tires, which Louise wore out with alarming frequency, the black Chrysler looked spanking new. The door opened and shut with a thud. Louise emerged in her blue-haired glory.

"Well?" she demanded.

"Well, what?" Mother replied.

"Do you like it?" Louise stood motionless like a geriatric Greek statue.

"Like what?" Mother was paying more attention to her kite than to Louise.

"You getting cataracts, Julia? My hair! Do you like my hair?"

"Looks like it does every Wednesday when you hit up the Curl 'n Twirl."

"It does not! You are blind. Nickel, what do you think?"

On the spot, I fibbed. "I like it fine. It's a little shorter and more youthful-looking."

"Thank you. At least someone around here has the courtesy to pay attention to me even if it is only my adopted niece. Blood sister doesn't pay attention to anyone but herself. What are you doing out here flying a kite, anyway? You're too old for that stuff."

"It's your birthday, so I'd lay off the age jokes."

"You haven't even wished me a happy birthday!" The shadow of a pout hung on Louise's cerise lower lip.

"I was going to wait until the party." Juts reeled in her kite.

"What'd you get me?"

"Wait until the party."

"Give it to me now. I don't like presents in front of strangers."

"Strangers? You've known most of the people who'll be at your party for over eighty years."

"Not Mr. Pierre."

Mr. Pierre owned and operated the Curl 'n Twirl. His hair was tinted a delicate shade of lilac. Mr. Pierre was big on tints. "The girls" zipped into his shop on Runnymede Square and zipped out like so many pastel Easter eggs. Mother and Louise had only known Mr. Pierre for perhaps thirty years. Behind his back Mother called him "the bearded lady" but she did love him. When his companion of twenty-eight years died of throat cancer in 1981, all three drew closer together, since each was widowed. Apart from his passion for tints, Mr. Pierre was a good influence on the girls. He insisted they lower their cholesterol, he fought valiantly against refined sugar, and he encouraged them to wear shorts in the summer, old age be damned.

"Aunt . . ." I paused and looked at Goodyear, whose ears pricked up in anticipation of his trick, ". . . Wheezie, let me drive you all over to your party." Goodyear's ears drooped a little.

"No, I'll drive. I might want to stay later than you do."

Mother and I glanced at each other and decided the fight wouldn't be worth it. Everyone in Runnymede, both North and South, knew the 1952 Chrysler and they scooted off the road when they saw Louise coming. Visitors quickly learned to do the same. The novelty of a town's being divided in half by the Mason-Dixon line drew a small stream of tourists, like ants to a picnic. Once they saw the perfect town square, the statue of the Yankee general astride his horse on the Pennsylvania side and the statue of the Confederate soldiers on the Maryland side along with the cannon, they usually had a sandwich and homemade ice cream at Mojo's and then left—unless they encountered Louise behind the wheel, in which case they left immediately.

Mother put Goodyear and Lolly Mabel in the house. Usually she took Goodyear over to Saint Rose of Lima's Catholic Church, the site of her once-a-week, hotly contested bingo games and the site of tonight's birthday party. However, as the assembled friends, acquaintances, and enemies would undoubtedly sing "Happy Birthday, Louise," Goodyear would fall into his faint after the hideous howl, so Mom thought better of it.

Aunt Louise, excited to get to her party, revved her motor as

3

Mother and I slammed the doors of my Jeep. Before I could hit the ignition, she was leaving rubber on Lee Street.

"Crazy girl," Mother said. "I've tried to get her to slow down. She won't listen."

"She's amenable to money if not to reason. We could bribe her." I let up on the clutch and we were off.

"Yeah—with our many millions." Mother laughed.

By the time I pulled into the crowded parking lot at the church, Louise, her turquoise cape fluttering, was stepping through the back door.

After I parked the Jeep, Mom and I trotted through the parking lot. Wheezie, in her haste, had left her motor running. Mother reached in, turned off the car, and pocketed the keys. She shook her head and then sailed past me into the warm bosom of Saint Rose of Lima's large hall. I was a few steps behind, loaded with packages.

"Mom *cherie!*" Mr. Pierre greeted Juts. *"Ma cherie!"* He kissed me on the cheeks. Gentleman that he was, he helped me with the presents and we put them on the table, already piled high with what I knew would be junk once unwrapped.

A huge banner that read HAPPPY 39, LOUISE! hung over the little bandstand. About one hundred and fifty souls were jammed in the room and Louise was in her glory. It was going to be a long night, because not only would we live it, we would be forced to relive it almost daily hereafter.

"Aunt Wheezie's hair looks divine."

"Why, thank you, Nickel. You know she's *très chic.*" He pronounced *chic* like "chick" and winked.

Mr. Pierre always treated me with conspiratorial glee. We were the only two openly gay people in Runnymede. The other non-heterosexuals were straight in Runnymede and gay when they left it. Worse, their spouses never knew, and I thought that deception pretty rotten. Naturally, both Mr. Pierre and I suffered every excuse known to God and man when we'd run into our "friends of Bertha's" as Mr. Pierre called other gay people. They "admired" our bravery but left us to it quite alone. At any rate, being gay in Runnymede was a fairly dismal prospect and I understood everyone's circumspection or cowardice, and yet I still couldn't understand how anyone could spend a lifetime lying for the good opinion of people who also had feet of clay. In that, Mr. Pierre was my ally. If he played the part of a queen, well, he was a man and he had grown up in a different time than I did, with different pressures. No matter when he was born he would have been a naturally flamboyant character, just as I would have been a naturally detached one. If

I blended into the landscape and appeared just an average woman, Mr. Pierre glowed like neon. Together we were quite a team and we often found ourselves paired together at social functions, since we were both unmarried.

Marriage was like death in Runnymede. Everybody did it.

My boss at the paper, Charles Falkenroth, waved to me. I waved back.

"I'm surprised Louise still has this many people speaking to her."

Mr. Pierre laughed. "Do they have any choice?"

"No, I guess not."

By now Aunt Wheezie had dived into her presents. She was supposed to wait until the cake was delivered and everyone sang to her but the woman's innate greed took over. As she was wildly unwrapping a lovely package, yellow paper with cerise ribbon to match her lipstick, Mother handed her a telegram.

"This just came."

"If it just came, Julia, how come you have it?"

"Why shouldn't I have it?" Mother would have preferred that this birthday fuss be for her, but then Mother wasn't enjoying her eighty-sixth birthday. Louise was officially acknowledging this to be her eightieth birthday and no one knew for certain her exact age. If Mother knew, she kept the secret, although she was not above dropping judicious hints.

Mother made no secret of her own birthday, March 6, 1905, and it was amusing that each year Mother advanced in years while Louise fell behind. However, Aunt Wheezie would give herself away by saying things like, "You won't have me around forever," and "You're going to miss me when I'm gone." It should be noted that she had initiated these laments when she hit fifty—or more precisely, when she admitted to being fifty.

I was convinced she'd never die because she'd be afraid she'd miss something.

Furiously, Louise opened the telegram, then squealed. "Orrie Tadia!" Orrie, her best friend, was wintering in Florida. Louise raised her voice, and the congregation, feeling the effects of at least one drink, slowly quieted. "Orrie was robbed in a parking lot of seventy-eight dollars and thirty-two cents by a man armed with a coconut!" She sighed. "Orrie gets all the fun. Nothing ever happens to me." Then she looked up from the telegram, glanced around the room. "Except for tonight, of course. Thank you all for coming to my eightieth birthday party."

Ursula Yost, my nemesis and president of the local Delta Delta

Delta alumnae association, blabbed, "It's your eighty-sixth birthday, dear."

Ursie had a mouth like a manhole cover: It was large and steam came out of it.

Louise glared at her. "You have your version of reality and I have mine."

"Surely at your age it can't matter." Ursie was determined to put her foot in it.

Regina Frost, my best friend and Master of Foxhounds for the Blue and Gray Hunt, gently put her hand under Ursula's elbow and guided her away from the brewing explosion with Louise. Ursula, tottering under the weight of all her crystal fox-head jewelry, listened most times to Regina. Even Ursie had sense enough to know it's not a smart idea to cross the M.F.H. in any community.

Just then Regina's husband, Jackson Frost, the best-looking man in Runnymede, emerged from the kitchen with the cake. Winston and Randolph, his two teenaged sons, helped carry the huge confection. The room erupted into song. Louise cried. I believe half the room cried with her. There wasn't one person there who could imagine life in Runnymede without Louise, for she had preceded all of us.

The door opened and The Baker's Dozen, an a cappella singing group, burst through it in full voice.

"Who sent me this present! Who sent me this?" Louise clapped her hands like a happy child.

The lead singer, George Spangler, a lawyer in town, paused after "Silhouette" and said, "Diz Rife."

A slight pause rippled across the room; then the conversation picked up until George and company launched into "Meet Me in St. Louis, Louise."

Even Liz Rife made an appearance and apologized for Diz's—her husband's—absence. He was in New York on business. In honor of Louise, Liz wore her major jewelry. She was, however, wise enough not to let Louise wear it, even though Louise badgered Liz whenever she saw her in her "Major Stones." Back in the twenties, Aunt Louise had borrowed a Cartier necklace and earrings from Celeste Chalfonte, a great and rich lady now deceased. These same valuables were not returned until many weeks later because, Louise said, she lost them. Since Louise was so organized that even her dirty clothes were folded in the hamper, this seemed unlikely. From then on, no more loans to Louise from anyone.

Louise, cape now casually hanging off one shoulder, glittered in a

6

gorgeous bugle-bead jacket. Mr. Pierre leaned over her for another kiss. He was tremendously tall.

He nodded in Liz's direction. "Those diamonds cost her a thousand mistakes."

"Diamonds are a girl's best friend," Louise replied, "but they won't keep you warm at night."

Mother, at her sister's elbow, whispered, "Keep your voice down."

"Why should I? Everyone knows." Louise's voice boomed.

Other conversations quieted. "Everyone knows what?" people seemed to be asking themselves.

Louise noticed this. The last thing she wanted was to cross swords with the powerful Rife family. She spoke to the assemblage: "Did I ever tell you all about my twelfth birthday and Momma gave me a doll. Well, my hateful sister was so jealous she hung it as a Yankee spy."

Everyone laughed, and Aunt Wheezie, happy in the spotlight, launched into one story after another—most of them at her sister's expense. Mother must have decided to grin and bear it; either that or she was plotting an elaborate revenge. I never knew with those two.

"Nickel, you're covering this, of course?" Charles Falkenroth beamed at me. He'd edged over during Louise's story.

"You don't think it's conflict of interest?"

"Hell, everything in Runnymede is conflict of interest."

Just then Louise emitted another piercing shriek because she opened her sister's present. The card for a year's subscription to *Playgirl* magazine was attached to a lovely framed photo of Louise's heartthrob, Ronald Colman. "Julia, you pervert!"

"You get what you ask for," Mother replied.

As 1987 unfolded, this was to be oddly prophetic, but at the time I was busy stuffing myself with devil's-food birthday cake and wondering why Charles wanted to meet me for lunch tomorrow.

2

A MIGRAINE AT MOJO'S

THURSDAY . . . 26 MARCH

Little ice bits snapped at my face like the teeth of the wind as I walked around the corner of the Square and Frederick Road. Spring was dragging her feet this year; it was the grayest, longest winter I could remember. Lolly padded on ahead, oblivious to the cold. Pewter, far the wiser, stayed back in the *Clarion* office, which commanded the southeastern corner of the Square. One of the joys of living in such a small town is that your animals accompany you everywhere and folks know the beasts about as well as they know you. Chances are they like the animals better.

Charles Falkenroth had a morning meeting at Brown, Moon & Frost, the law firm on the Maryland side of the Square. The Yankee law firm almost directly opposite on the Square was Falkenroth, Spangler & Finster, that Falkenroth being Charles's cousin whom he detested. He promised he'd meet me at Mojo's for lunch and I trudged on my way, wondering why he couldn't talk to me in the office.

Our office wasn't a trip down Memory Lane; it was a gallop. The overhead light fixtures had been converted from gas at the turn of the century and that was that. The desks were the same as at the time of the War Between the States, and the oak floor laid down immediately after the Revolutionary War and never tampered with shone like a mirror. The big plate-glass window had gold letters in a semicircle blaring THE RUNNYMEDE CLARION and underneath that in smaller letters and a straight line it read, ESTABLISHED 1710.

The original *Clarion* office, on this same site, was not much more than a log cabin. When we won the war, and the publisher, Amos Falkenroth, prospered, the current building was erected. Amos was the son of founder Reuben Falkenroth, so the *Clarion* stayed in the family and in my family too. The Hunsenmeirs came to Maryland from Swabia at the end of the seventeenth century but our branch of the family didn't get to Runnymede until about 1740. They were printers and so a natural alliance was formed between Hunsenmeir and Falkenroth which lasted, more or less, down through the centuries. There were the interruptions of disease and death and sometimes we skipped a generation in our partnership but sooner or later we'd get back together at the *Clarion.* The worst time, of course, was the War Between the States, because Marble Falkenroth was a passionate Union man and he moved across the Square to found *The Runnymede Trumpet.* Tom Falkenroth, his younger brother, kept on with the *Clarion,* and they smashed at each other hammer and tongs until they both died in the 1890's, but the rupture in the family persisted and the Pennsylvania Falkenroths and the Maryland Falkenroths never did see eye to eye.

Up until the early 1960's, when I went away to college, our town enjoyed two violently opposed dailies. The *Trumpet* blasted you in the morning and the *Clarion* rang out in the late afternoon. Everyone read both papers and perhaps a story had four or five different sides but at least we got two. Then, as in so many other towns, the two papers merged to stay alive. Now Charles alternates editorials. On Monday, Wednesday, and Friday, John Hoffman writes the *Trumpet* point of view, which is to the right of Genghis Khan. On Tuesdays, Thursdays, and Saturdays, I write the *Clarion* opinion, which is moderate and reasonable. On Sundays we give it a rest.

I pushed open the door to Mojo's and Lolly danced through it.

"Lolly Mabel, where have you been?" Verna Bonneville, the blonde waitress, fussed. "Hello, Nick."

"Hi, Verna." The owner of Mojo's was a suicide blonde, dyed by her own hand. We called her Verna BonBon which suited her, since Verna was as wide as she was tall.

Charles, sprawled in a booth, wreathed in smoke from his Macanudo cigar, was reading *The Wall Street Journal.* I slid into the booth and Lolly sat down next to it as Verna brought her a Milk-Bone.

"Nickel, I'm having a club sandwich and lunch is on me." Charles put down the paper. His bow tie wiggled when he talked.

Verna called from behind the counter: "Navy bean soup today. Your favorite."

"Okay," I called back. "A big bowl."

"Gotcha."

Charles inhaled for a moment. "Oh, Jack Frost sends his regards. He said he had a wonderful time at Louise's party last night. Said you looked wonderful, too."

A twinge of guilt shot through me. "That was nice of him."

Charles shoved a handwritten article under my nose. "Check it for accuracy."

As I read, Verna slapped down the food. Lolly's tail thumped on the tile floor. "Some party last night. Think we'll make it that far?"

"You bet." Charles smiled up at her. "But only if you give me a kiss on the cheek every time I come in here. Love keeps a man young."

"Go on." Verna pushed him on the shoulder and left.

"What is this way you have with women?" I glanced up from the article.

"Ann asks me the same thing."

Ann was Charles's wife of thirty-three years. It was a good marriage; Charles was one of the lucky ones.

"This is great." I gave him back the article, which was about Louise's birthday party. He decided to cut me a break after all. "Only one tiny, tiny change. Make her eighty, not eighty-six . . . or is it eighty-five?"

"Everyone in town knows she's eighty-six if she's a day."

"Yeah, I know, but you'll give Louise heart palpitations if you tell the truth. Besides which, since everyone knows it, then everyone will know why you've made her eighty and they'll have a good laugh, courtesy of the *Clarion*."

We chitchatted throughout his sandwich and my soup and when the coffee came Charles said, "Nickel, I want you to run the paper. I'm retiring."

"What!"

"You heard me."

"I heard you. I don't believe you."

"You see before you the dubious benefits of hard labor. Time to play. As much for Ann's sake as my own."

"What about Hoffman? Does he know?"

"I'll tell him when he comes back from Baltimore tomorrow."

"I don't think he'll like it."

Charles shrugged. "He'd rather concentrate on business anyway. As long as John gets to write his editorials I don't think he'll care what you do with the paper." He paused. "The new owners should leave you alone too."

This was a crossbow bolt to the heart. "What new owners?"

10

"Well, I don't know yet. The Thurston Group has sniffed around and so has Mid-Atlantic Holding Shares."

"Rife! You can't sell the *Clarion* to the Rifes."

"Mid-Atlantic Holding Shares is far bigger than the Rife family itself."

"Come on, Charles, you know Disraeli's got the reins in his hands."

"Diz's not so bad."

"Is it progress if a cannibal uses a knife and a fork?"

Verna poured Charles another cup of coffee. She was dying to hear what this was all about but prudently withdrew to the jammed counter, where she conspicuously polished glasses. Fortunately the other luncheon customers made plenty of noise, but she strained her ears.

"Nickel, I know Brutus Rife killed your grandmother's lover but that was long before you were born. Anyway, justice was done, wasn't it? Brutus was shot between the eyes in the middle of a thunder-snow. Damnedest weather I ever saw. I was still in high school at the time. Anyway, the vendetta between Rifes and Hunsenmeirs has no reason to continue. Besides, Diz's always been friendly to you."

I wanted to say a little too friendly but I bit my lip. "You're the one to talk about vendettas. You don't like the Pennsylvania Falkenroths."

"Ah, that's family. Anyway, Mid-Atlantic Holding Shares may not buy the *Clarion*. The Thurston Group is paying careful suit."

I pushed my teacup around. Coffee made me jumpy so I preferred tea. The only time I could force coffee down my throat was before a migraine and I felt as if I was going to get a whopper right now. "Verna, can I have a cup of coffee, black?"

Charles winced. He knew what that order meant. "I don't want to upset you but I have no children. This is the end of the line for the *Clarion* and the Falkenroth family. Times change."

"But we don't have to change with them. And whoever said progress was a positive thing has never been to Florida or California."

"We're not talking about ecology."

I loved Charles. I wasn't making it any easier for him, so now I felt like a shit. "I know."

Verna put the coffee down with three aspirins on the saucer. "Right now." She pointed to her lips.

I smiled up at her and gulped down the three aspirins, which were about as effective against a migraine as charging a machine-gun nest with a rubber knife. But people need to feel useful even

11

when there's nothing they can do. "Thanks, Verna. You're a good egg to take care of me."

"Best customer!" She patted me on the back, stroked Lolly, lingered hoping for a syllable of our news, and then wandered back to the counter where Arnold Dow, the *Clarion*'s head printer, was singing "Cherry Pie." She gave him a gigantic piece of cherry pie.

"Charles, how do you know I can't be removed by the new management if I take over as editor in chief?"

"That's part of the sales contract. If they do remove you, they'll have to pay you four boxcars full of money."

"You mean, that stuff they print in Washington?"

"Your salary will increase too. Not that you're making much now."

I made $24,000 a year, and given federal and state taxes, I lived close to the bone. Still, I considered myself a lucky woman because I was doing what I love. "Nobody makes money in Runnymede. You either inherit it or make it somewhere else and retire here."

"Amen."

Verna, unbidden, came over and poured another cup of blazing coffee for me and I gulped it down. Tears welled in my eyes and I quickly swallowed my glass of water.

"Jesus!" Lolly turned her head up to inquire as to my well-being. Lolly never liked it when I raised my voice. "I guess I am afraid about my job. A title without power means nothing. I've seen what's happened to local papers when the chains get them. You have too. All they do is run AP wire stories. Hell, they don't even use local people to review books and movies. They run the damned AP wire reviews. A newspaper is a community resource. It's not only a method to generate cash. All those people care about is the bottom line. They'll slash our staff. They'll talk like accountants. Makes me sick. I want a Runnymede person to review the movies. We don't think like someone in New York City or wherever the person is who writes the damned AP review. There's news and then there's the people's response to that news through their paper. It's not a one-way street. Don't laugh but there really is such a thing as journalistic integrity and I don't want some jackleg asshole in a three-piece suit telling me how to run this show!"

As I rarely popped off, Charles stared at me in fascination. Everyone else in Mojo's was staring at me too. I took a deep breath. "Well, I'm sorry I disturbed everybody's lunch but now you all know how I think."

Verna laughed. Arnold, a furrow on his brow, went back to his pie, and people smiled and resumed their conversations.

"So much for secrets," Charles sighed.

"If you wanted to keep this a secret why tell me in Mojo's? This is Gossip Central." And it was. After the death of Noe Mojo, a Japanese gentleman, Verna and Thacker Bonneville bought the place and put up a huge blackboard by the front door with lots of colored chalk. You could write down anything you wanted, and you could draw too. Whenever I needed a source I came to Mojo's first.

"You're right. I should have had you meet me over at Brown, Moon and Frost but Jack's got a tight schedule this morning."

"Jack knows, I take it?"

"He's the paper's lawyer."

Wait until I get my hands on Jackson Frost. I sat there for a moment. "Hey, Verna, fry me up a hamburger for Pewter."

"Where is she today?"

"Office. She didn't want to get her feet wet." I turned back to Charles. "How much you want for the *Clarion?*"

"Two million plus a small percentage of the stock which will revert back to the owner upon Ann's death, since I'm certain she'll outlive me."

"May I give you my answer tomorrow morning? I want to think this through."

"I can wait an extra day. Your migraines last twelve to twenty-four hours."

"Pain doesn't stop me from thinking. It's not fair to keep you waiting."

"Okay, tomorrow morning then."

Charles was due in Hanover, Pennsylvania, so I headed back to the office without him. The sidewalk was glazed and the tiny darts of ice rained down like crystal BBs. I knew I was walking on ice, but it felt like eggshells.

After work, Lolly, Pewter, and I slipped and slid over to Mom's. Even with the Jeep in four-wheel drive the road was nasty and I dreaded the two-mile drive up Bumblebee Hill to my house. Pewter spit at Goodyear, who kept wagging his tail. After about ten minutes of feline drama, the animals settled down and I told Mother everything. Before she replied she picked up the telephone. That was Mom for you, commander of the phone call, admiral of touch dialing. She didn't reach out and touch; she reached out and grabbed you by the throat.

"Mother, don't call Aunt Wheezie just yet."

"Why not? The last time she had a good idea was in 1934. Let's give her an opportunity to come up with another one."

"Come on, Mom. This isn't funny and I've got a wicked migraine."

She put the phone down. "Say yes. You need the money."

"That thought occurred to me. I sure don't want to leave the paper. Gotta have a Hunsenmeir on the paper. It's in the blood."

"Christ, now you sound like Wheezie." She mimicked Louise: *"Blood tells."* Her voice returned to normal. "What do you care? You got your own blood."

For three decades I had heard variations on that theme. It still felt like a wasp sting on tender flesh. I don't know why I never fought back. Why did Mother and Aunt Louise have to tell me repeatedly that I was not related by blood, that I was adopted? I'm a bright person. Tell me once and I'll remember. I guess I never fought back because I didn't know how. What can you say when your mother, or the only mother you've ever known, tells you you aren't hers?

"That's not the point."

"Well, what is?"

Louise's party lingered in Mother's mind like a hangover. She was out of sorts and would stay that way until she found a way to wrest the spotlight back from her older sister. "The point is I want to buy the *Clarion.*"

"You?" Her pupils dilated.

"Me."

"You haven't got a pot to piss in."

"I've got the farm. I've got eighteen years of experience. More, if you count my work on the college and high school papers. I understand advertising. I know I can make the *Clarion* even better than it is now."

Mother got up from her rocker with the carved swan heads for armrests. She paced. Age had robbed none of her natural gracefulness. "You'd mortgage the farm?"

"If I have to. Can't be worth more than one hundred seventy-five thousand even with the fifty acres, which is good land."

"How much does Charles want?"

"Two million."

"Drop in the bucket." She laughed.

"My assets are a drop in the bucket but I'm hoping the bank will make me a business loan based on my experience and Charles's recommendation. Of course, we could drum up money by putting a mattress on your back and standing you on the Square. I'd make you a nice sign: CURB SERVICE."

"I was brought up not to make fun of my elders."

"There can't be many of them left."

"You're a fresh kid. Sometimes I wonder if I brought you up right."

"Well, I'm not exactly the girl next door."

The corner of her mouth twitched upward. "If you want to be like the girl next door, go next door."

"You'll help me?"

"I haven't got any money." She enjoyed being pursued.

"You know everybody. And you've known them forty years longer than I have. You might come up with something."

"Might."

As I opened the door to go home I heard her pick up the phone. She now had some information she could dangle in front of Louise like a fat grub in front of a grouper. Tomorrow night was bingo and the signs were ripe that those two would cut a shine.

3

A NEW MAN IN TOWN

FRIDAY . . . 27 MARCH

A thick cloud of smoke, much like the one that enveloped Pompeii when Vesuvius lost its temper, hung over the bingo parlor at Saint Rose of Lima. The large railroad clock on the wall hadn't struck eight o'clock but the consumption of cigarettes, cigars, and the occasional pipe was far ahead of schedule. Nerves were razor-sharp because Mutzi Elliott, the caller and greengrocer, was instituting new games.

Mutzi had just returned from bingo school. Up until tonight we'd played bingo the way everyone plays bingo. You get a diagonal line filled up or a straight line and you yell "Bingo." We were graduating into advanced bingo. Even Mom and Louise shut up to concentrate.

One hundred people plus Lolly, Goodyear, and Pewter, as well as Arnie Dow's cat, Louisa May Alcatt, filled the hall. Everyone knew about Goodyear's trick because Mother had shown them one by one. It was the biggest inside joke in Runnymede, and what was curious was that Louise didn't notice people calling her Wheeze, Wheezie, or even Sis. Of course, everyone had grown up with her nickname and possibly she thought it normal but I had the creeping sensation that sooner or later Goodyear would go into his fit and there'd be hell to pay. Just so he didn't do it tonight, because tension was fierce.

The Ping-Pong balls with numbers flew up in the air in a glass cage. Mutzi kept the top down because Pewter had crawled into the

16

cage once. The balls popped out one by one and he'd grab them if Pewter didn't grab them first. Usually Pewter's antics were good for a laugh but tonight not one head turned up toward Mutzi.

"Railroad tracks. Next game is railroad tracks. You remember now, you've got to get two parallel columns. Ready." He paused for effect. "Steady. Go." A ball popped up. "Number two." Mutzi sang, "Tea for two and two for tea."

Mother appeared nonchalant. She carried a little notebook with her on which she had drawn the new kinds of bingo games. Louise kept cribbing from Julia's notes.

"Keep your nose over your own card, Wheezie, or you'll get a blister on it."

"Who died and made you God?" Louise shot back.

"Darlings, we are in a house of worship." Mr. Pierre was sitting across from the Hunsenmeirs.

Louise would have come back with something but Mutzi called out, "Forty. Number forty and I tell you I didn't have sense to come in from the rain until I was forty."

A ripple of laughter rolled over the crowd. The gang was predominantly female with the men sitting along the side of the room at a bar. Truthfully, liquor should not have been sold in the church but Saint Rose's needed money. Millard Huffstetler, the church's business manager, did whatever was necessary to raise revenue. We didn't know if he informed Father Christopolous. Generating cash for the church was one's Christian duty. Louise took this to heart. She sewed raffia baskets every summer for Saint Anthony's bazaar. Louise had converted to Catholicism at age eight. Mother remained Lutheran and this proved a fruitful source of contention.

The numbers rolled on until Ricky Bonneville, one of the "Bon-Bons," screeched "Bingo." Kirk "Peepbean" Huffstetler, Millard's nephew, wearing a bib like an old-time paperboy, sauntered over and checked the card. "Got 'em. Railroad tracks straight as the C and O." He was a sign painter and still wore his spattered overalls.

"Fifteen dollars to Ricky B." Mutzi smiled. He rang a cowbell, his idea of celebrating winners.

"Verna, you have an unfair advantage," Mother shouted over. "Ten kids. You're bound to win."

"I have to pay admission for everyone. Two bucks a head, Julia. Think of that." Verna was reaching into her cavernous bag for chocolate-covered doughnuts with which to feed her brood. Even the smallest BonBon, Decca, now a first-grader, manned a card. No wonder these kids won every math award from elementary school right up through South Runnymede High.

B	I	N	G	O
5	30	33	50	62
15	17	35	47	75
2	28	FREE	60	65
13	26	39	56	71
11	20	40	58	73

INSIDE PICTURE FRAME

B	I	N	G	O
2	16	36	46	63
4	21	35	50	69
12	19	FREE	59	71
7	25	38	49	74
9	29	41	57	70

REGULAR X

B	I	N	G	O
2	16	36	46	63
4	21	35	50	69
12	19	FREE	59	71
7	25	38	49	74
9	29	41	57	70

CHAMPAGNE GLASS
Straight up or reverse

B	I	N	G	O
5	30	33	50	62
15	17	35	47	75
2	28	FREE	60	65
13	26	39	56	71
11	20	40	58	73

RAILROAD TRACKS
Any two parallel columns

B	I	N	G	O
1	18	31	46	70
6	20	41	48	64
15	16	FREE	53	71
9	25	40	55	61
14	23	35	57	68

ANY VERTICAL OR HORIZONTAL

B	I	N	G	O
1	18	31	46	70
6	20	41	48	64
15	16	FREE	53	71
9	25	40	55	61
14	23	35	57	68

BLOCK OF 9
Can be anywhere on the board, but there must be nine touching squares in a block

"Julia doesn't know anything about children. You have to be a natural mother to know. Comes with the blood." Louise, maliciously content in her wounding, cooed.

"Bullshit."

Mutzi observed the tone between the sisters. He pulled out his .38 and brandished it. "Hunsenmeir girls, take heed. I keep this gun because I never know when you all will renew hostilities." He also kept the gun because the cash was beside the Ping-Pong ball machine.

"I'm not renewing hostilities," Mother called back. "I am replying to my senile sister. She just had her eighty-sixth birthday, you know."

"Eightieth!" Louise was now on the verge of a towering rage.

"You'll never see eighty-six again. Now why don't you act your age and eat oatmeal!" Mother tossed her dab-a-dot in the air and caught it. Dab-a-dots are like Magic Markers except you press them down and they leave a perfect round colored dot over your number on the bingo card. Beans went out with the Edsel. Mother always used red and Louise blue.

"You know why your husband died, Julia? To get away from you!"

Mother smashed her dab-a-dot on Louise's forehead. Goodyear growled and Lolly stood up in front of me. Pewter stopped stealing from Verna BonBon's sandwich to watch.

The sisters attacked each other until both were covered with dots.

Mutzi blasted into the microphone: "Stop it! Girls, you stop it right this minute or I'll throw you out. I mean it."

"The hell you will," Mother bellowed. "She started it. Throw her out."

"You're lying. You know how I can tell you're lying? Because your mouth is moving."

There was another flurry of attack by dab-a-dot.

Despairingly, Mutzi called to me: "Can't you control your mother?"

"She's not my mother. I'm adopted, remember?" I laughed but I couldn't resist this small revenge for Mother's crack yesterday. It was a mistake, because now Mother turned on me with her damned dab-a-dot. Lolly, who wouldn't stand for anyone messing with me, bit Mother on the leg.

"Rabies! Rabies!"

Louise doubled over with laughter. "Ha, Lolly will catch rabies from you."

Mr. Pierre, finding his courage at last, put his arm around Louise. "Darling, you need a drink."

"I don't need a drink. I need a new sister."

"Blood! Blood! I need a transfusion," Mother yelled. She rubbed her leg. There wasn't a drop of blood on it. Lolly growled. Good-year was too confused to do anything but lick Mother's face. "You have that goddamned dog because you haven't the guts to bite me yourself," she snarled at me.

Peepbean Huffstetler helped Mother back to her seat. He brushed by me as though I were a sea slug. Peepbean had it in for me since the second grade because one time we were at the Capitol Theater watching *The Kentuckian* with Burt Lancaster and I gave him a fireball and told him it was a jawbreaker. That he could nurse a grudge that long said something about the excitement level of his life.

Louise was making her stately advance to the bar for a medicinal shot of liquor, wailing as she went. "She ruined my cards and I bought three cards."

"It's not cancer research. It's just bingo," Mr. Pierre soothed.

"You don't know anything about cancer research, Pierre," Louise chided him.

I was cleaning up the few dab-a-dots on my face. Mother wouldn't help me and I wouldn't help her and she looked like a pointillist painting. Mutzi was nervously announcing that the next game was going to be "champagne glass" and it was really hard, but this tornado of chat came to an abrupt silence as Thacker Bonneville walked in the door accompanied by a man handsome enough to be Douglas Fairbanks, Jr. Every female head in the room snapped around to look. Mother fished her compact out of her purse and aimed a blow at her cheek with the blusher. Didn't help the spots.

Verna, savoring the moment, waved to her husband. "Thackie, sugar, Ricky won the fifteen-dollar pot."

"Another one of those, Rick, and the old man retires." He cheerily waved to his boy.

"Who is that?" Mother demanded.

Airily, Verna tossed off her answer. "My mother's brother, Edgar Tutweiler Walters. From Birmingham. We call him Ed."

"I call him gorgeous," I said. Ed may have been seventy but he looked around fifty-five. He wore a silk handkerchief tied around his neck sort of like a cowboy except the scarf was shorter than a cowboy scarf. His hair glistened bright silver, catching what light there was in the smoke-filled room. He wore charcoal-gray trousers with a crease, no cuff, and his shirt was a pale-peach.

"Is he married?" Mother saw no reason to waste time.

"Widowed. Last year. Poor darling, he worshipped her. My

20

mother always says that women can live without men but men can't live without women."

"Your mother is right, but then, just because we can do something doesn't mean we have to." Mother stood up and thrust her bust forward. "Verna, introduce me."

"Julia, we're about to play the champagne glass game." In this bingo variation, the lines started at the two top corners, ran to the free space, and merged in one line to the bottom of the card, just like a champagne glass.

"Your children can play. Come on." She yanked Verna out of her chair—no easy task, since Verna tipped two hundred pounds. Verna's salvation, if not a strict diet, was navy-blue.

However, Mother wasn't fast enough because Louise, with steel in her backbone, had propelled Mr. Pierre right over to Ed Tutweiler Walters. If Ed found Mr. Pierre's lilac hair unusual he didn't let on and he spoke with rapt interest to Louise. Then he did something that froze Julia to the floor. He picked up a green dab-a-dot off one of the tables and dabbed a green dot right on the tip of Louise's nose.

"Color contrast." He laughed.

Louise laughed, too, and then went on luridly to tell him about her unstable older (yes, she said older) sister who lost her temper over something as trifling as a bingo game. Worse, she pointed out Mother and remarked that she looked as though she had leprosy with all those blue dots covering her. At least Louise, with the red dots, only looked as though she had measles.

Ed appeared charmed. Fuming, Mother returned to her seat and played out the evening with grim resolve. Louise never left the bar. Mr. Pierre came back to sit across from Mom.

"She's telling him that Mutzi has the thirty-eight to stop burglars and you."

"I'd like to serve her pork tartar." Mother could barely concentrate on her card. Maybe Louise was at first base but she wasn't going to cross home plate. You could see the wheels spinning in Mother's head as she schemed how to get even with her sister but, even more importantly, how to meet Ed Tutweiler Walters.

As Thacker BonBon had ten kids, a wife, and Ed to carry home, he couldn't take Louise to her door. I drove Mom and Aunt Louise home in silence, which was a relief.

I let out Louise first and Mother hissed, "Judas."

Louise was busy humming to herself, so she didn't notice.

4
MORE LEG
SATURDAY . . . 28 MARCH

A heavy frost coated the ground. Fox-hunting season ended a week earlier, which was a pity because the day was good for scent. Fox-hunting suffers from an erroneous reputation. Pictures of aristocrats in pink coats flash through people's minds. That's like believing that everyone who plays tennis was born with a silver knife in her back. Working at the *Clarion* had taught me that people believe what they want to believe—don't disturb them with the facts. I no longer rose to the defense of fox-hunting in particular and equine sports in general.

Kenny, my aging gelding, stood still while I brushed him. Pewter, purring madly, rested on his back. Cats love horses and horses love cats, or at least that's been my observation. Pewter meowed with delight whenever the Jeep turned into the small stable, Darby's Folly, where I kept Kenny. Lolly liked horses but she wasn't rapturous about them unless I took her on a trail ride. Lolly was rapturous about the bits of bran and grain scattered on the floor. She licked the center aisle clean.

"Hey, girl." Regina came into the stall and rubbed Kenny's chin. "Kenny, wish I had a dozen like you."

"Me, too, except younger. You know, I don't know what I'm going to do when this guy's too old to go out, and that day approaches."

"The day of the thousand-dollar field hunter is over. You'll have to pay, mmm, seven thousand at least. You could do better, Nickie,

22

if you'd take a chance on a two-year-old and start working with him."

"I haven't got the time, and truthfully, I'm not that good. Muffin should do it." Muffin was the stable's trainer.

"Got time for a quick spin. Half hour, forty-five minutes?"

"You bet."

I tacked up while Regina generously waited. For a well-coordinated woman I still fumble with my tack. Pewter bitched because she knew she was going to be left in the barn. Her swishing around my legs and Kenny's didn't help, because Kenny didn't like it when Pewter became upset. In warm weather or even crisp weather Pewter would come out too. She'd run along until she'd had enough of it and then she'd either crawl up my leg—my chaps on, thankfully—and sit in front of me on the saddle or she'd head back to the barn. But today was downright cold and Miss Pewter hated it. By the time I was ready to go, Regina had warmed up in the ring.

Also in the ring were Ursie's daughters, two unsavory specimens, Harmony, sixteen, and Tiffany, fourteen. Muffin Barnes shouted at them: "Sloppy, you're so sloppy! That jump was awful. You did everything wrong! Think of a jump as an interruption in your flat work. Now do it again, Tiff. You too, Harmony. You've done nothing to brag about today. Keep your eyes up. More leg, Tiffany. Leg! Leg! Leg!" Dutifully the girls broke into a trot and jumped again. It wasn't that Harmony and Tiffany were bad kids as much as they were unable to cope with anything except success and money. When you buy children $60,000 show horses you're bound to destroy their initiative. Tiffany and Harmony had specially made tack trunks in their favorite colors, with their initials emblazoned on the front and the top. Blue and white were Tiffany's colors and red and gold were Harmony's, which pissed me off because red and gold are my colors and Ursie well knew it too.

As Regina and I walked away from the ring, Muffin's voice faded in the background. The rolling hills of Maryland, slick with the cold, beckoned.

"I never get tired of seeing this, do you?" Regina asked me.

"No. What surprises me is that there are millions of people who can live without it."

"Be thankful. What would happen if they all left the cities?"

"Make the developers happy."

"They're happy enough." Regina scanned the skyline. "Dante?"

"Dante and Dad."

With that we cantered down into the little valley and back up the hill on the other side. We'd really made a semicircle around Darby's

Folly, because the road below us would lead us back to the stable if we wanted to go on the road, which we did not. High on the hill was Runnymede's cemetery. Celeste Chalfonte, beloved friend and employer of my grandmother, was buried there at the very top with the biggest monument I'd seen this side of the Washington Monument, that unfortunately shaped memento to our founding father. I guess they wanted to emphasize the father idea. My father was buried there, as were Grandma—Cora Hunsenmeir—and Dad's parents, the Smiths. I could walk through these stones and find ancestors dating back to the late 1600's. Someday I'd be resting up here, too, but no time soon, I hoped. Regina's family, the Clavells, as well as her husband's people, the Frosts, slumbered here. But what had fascinated us since we were children together was the beautifully carved white marble monument to Dante, the firehorse of South Runnymede and beloved of all. He was born in 1878 and died in 1907, having lived a long and useful life. Dante had a bigger stone than my father, but then Dante, at the turn of the century, benefited from lower prices. Besides, the firehouse gang took up a collection. Dad had only Mother and me to pay his final bill back in 1961. I was still in high school. I figured Dad would understand.

We dismounted to give our horses a break from our weight and to give Lolly a breather too.

Frozen flowers rested on Dante's grave.

"Kids are still bringing Dante flowers." Regina smiled. "Remember when we used to do it?"

"Maybe it was how we learned about death. And Dante's birthday is an annual firehouse celebration, so we were reminded of him, his heroics. Anyway, kids love animals, even dead ones."

"To what do I owe this burst of analysis?"

"I don't know." I shrugged.

"Paper?"

"Uh-huh." I'd told her about Charles's impending sale. What I didn't tell her about was my other preoccupations, preoccupations closer to home. Hers and mine.

"Has Wheezie recovered from her party?"

"Pretty much."

"Do you know that was one of the few times I've been in your esteemed aunt's presence when she didn't try to convert me to Catholicism."

"Mother and I want to put her on rosary methadone."

"Good luck." Regina remounted. "Let's get back before Ursie comes to pick up her munchkins. She'll start on me about our annual Tri-Delta alumnae horse show."

"That's months away." I stood on a tombstone to get up on Kenny, who was sixteen hands and too big for me to leap up on. Regina, much taller than I, could gracefully swing her leg over any animal this side of seventeen hands. I envied her that. I envied her other things, too, namely that she was our Master of Foxhounds— that and Jackson.

"You know how compulsive she is. I swear Ursie has lists and then lists of her lists. She also wants to talk hunt club business—the newsletter." Regina rolled her eyes.

"You should never have given her that job." I pushed Kenny onward.

"Given it to her! I begged you to take it."

"Come on, Gene, we've been over this *ad infinitum*. My doing the newsletter is like taking coals to Newcastle. I'm on the breakfast committee."

"You're rather bad at that."

"I am?" This surprised me. Lolly stopped for a tantalizing sniff of something. "Lolly Mabel, come on." She lifted her leonine head and hurried after me.

"You don't care much about food, Nickel, and while you're a wonderful organizer—don't get me wrong—you're terrible with menus."

"But it's not my job to plan the menus. It's only my job to get people to sponsor breakfasts after our hunts."

"Yes and no." Regina patiently continued. "You should supervise the menus to make certain there are no duplications and that the food is good."

"Let Verna BonBon do it."

"Verna's not a member of the hunt club."

I knew that. I also knew that Regina was right but one of the great advantages of having an old friend is that you can be childish and irrational. It refreshes both parties.

"Bet Ursie was the first to bitch, too, wasn't she?" I had advanced from kindergarten to junior high school in my approach.

"Actually, no. She was the second."

We trotted a bit. The frost flew from under our horses's hooves. Their breath, our breath, and Lolly's breath escaped from our mouths like billows of creamy cumulus clouds. When Regina pulled up for a walk my nose was no longer out of joint.

"I'm sorry."

"I accept your resignation. You are now appointed to the newsletter."

25

"Gene! What a sneak you are, a real sneaky pie. Ursie will never stand for it."

"Ursie is now head of the breakfast committee and all entertainments, assuming you will take over the newsletter. She thinks she has more power in the club because of it."

"Does she?"

"Of course not. Whoever controls the information and the purse strings runs the show in any organization. You know that."

In fact, I did. "Ursie's not dumb. She wants something."

"She wants to run for County Board of Supervisors and she figures if she entertains people handsomely for a year she'll be a shoo-in."

My mouth was on my chest. "You lie."

"Have I ever lied to you?"

"Give me time. I'll think of something."

"Or you'll make it up and then accuse me of a faulty memory if I don't recall the incident."

We headed toward the barn jabbering excitedly about Ursie's hidden agenda. Ursula Yost, well-heeled and well-educated, would make a good public servant in many respects. She was conscientious, hardworking, committed to no-growth, which meant she was a deadly foe to any real estate developer or chain store—a mixed blessing, but I was more with her than against her on that one. Her girls would soon be at college and she was looking for a new career, I guess. I'd vote for her, of course, when the time came. Just because I couldn't stand the ground the woman walked on didn't mean I was blind to her virtues. Politics makes strange bedfellows. The word *bedfellow* in this context gave me a shudder.

5

BUMBLEBEE HILL

SUNDAY . . . 29 MARCH

Sunday was blissfully quiet, in part because I refused to answer the telephone. If I did I would be the victim of either Mother or Aunt Louise recounting her sister's sins back to Year One. I loved my weekends because they were usually quiet. People focused on their families, which left me to focus on my little farm or my next deadline.

Today I surrendered myself to serious literature, writing checks. Why was there always so much month at the end of the money?

Money began to occupy my thoughts almost exclusively. I'd spoken to Charles about wanting to buy the *Clarion* and he didn't laugh, which was a beginning. He said he couldn't stop negotiating with the Thurston Group and Mid-Atlantic Holding Shares but that he'd help me any way he could. I suggested we have a meeting with Foster Adams at the Runnymede Bank and Trust the next week and he agreed. He also told me that John Hoffman was shocked at the news but took it with good grace. So far we were all behaving like reasonable adults. I wondered how long it would last.

Outside, a silver net enveloped us. It was as though the earth exhaled its atmosphere, like a huge beast breathing in its sleep. The earth showed no signs of waking up; there wasn't even one crocus above the ground. We'd already run three stories with meteorologists since December and I didn't want to run another one. Our staff was small and the next weather article would land in

27

my lap. Fair was fair, and that attitude kept the two young reporters who worked for the *Clarion* happy.

When I was a kid and the weather turned peculiar, Louise would say it was the result of atom bomb tests. Lately she'd revived this opinion because of the nuclear accident at Chernobyl. My own explanation was that winter lingered out of pure D ugliness. If people could personalize God, I saw no reason why I couldn't personalize winter.

I personalized my farm, but then, it was personal. Cora, my grandmother, was born and raised here, as were Mother and Louise. I inherited the farm through Mom. I had to pay off Louise. Her share's value increased dangerously until Mother put her in her place. Still, I paid the going price in 1977. Louise shopped for bargains but never gave any.

Bumblebee Hill was the name of the farm and the hill on which it was built. The elevation, seven hundred feet, afforded me views of the land, and if I walked out on my front porch I could see Runnymede twinkling below me due east.

The house, built in 1834, although simple was a good example of Federal architecture: four rooms off a center hall, upstairs and downstairs, each room with a fireplace. Electricity was added in the 1920's and indoor plumbing arrived in the late 1940's.

I put in new pipes—copper in, PVC out—in 1980, as well as rewiring. That was an expensive year. Apart from that, if Cora came back to life she'd recognize her home instantly.

The kitchen, with her butcher block in the middle of the room and a trestle table in the small nook, was as she left it. Only the appliances were new. I'd bought a red enamel stove. Why, I don't know. I can't cook but it sure was pretty.

Grandma's furniture, sturdy country pieces, dotted the various rooms. Kenny took up whatever discretionary income I had, so I never bought furniture. I made do with Cora's pieces and a few that Mother donated to the cause. I was, however, good with color and the living room was pale-peach with white trim. The kitchen was red and white. The wainscoting in the dining room was a clear, deep cream. Above that, instead of using wallpaper, Grandma had hand-painted stencils of stylized birds, silver birds on a blue background. For my thirty-third birthday, Mother repainted them for me. Like Cora, Mom was artistic and good with her hands. I was neither but I was good with my head, so things evened out.

The phone rang. I sighed. It continued to ring. I gave up and answered it.

28

"Why didn't you pick up your phone this weekend?" Mother went on the offensive.

"Slipped my mind."

"Oh, balls. How am I supposed to know if you're all right? I hate it when you go off into one of your moons. Anyway, I need you to do my books. End of the month."

"I'm not moony. I just wanted to be quiet, which is a virtual impossibility around you."

"You, of course, never open your mouth." She inhaled. "Despite you being an ungrateful brat, I've been thinking about the *Clarion.*"

"Yes." She had my attention.

"Well, what if you wrote a memoir of Runnymede and sold it? You know, in the town. Mojo's would carry it and so would the bookstore. That money could go toward buying the paper. Maybe even a big publisher would want it."

"Mother, that's a wonderful idea but I don't think I could write such a book and get it on the stands in time."

"How long would it take?"

"At least a year. Think of the research it would take."

There was a pause on the other end of the line. "Just ask Louise—she's two years older than God."

"Goodyear must be out of the room."

"He's upstairs on his hooked rug with a chewy bone." Her voice was light. "I have forgiven Lolly Mabel."

I turned from the phone. "Lolly, Grandma forgives you." Lolly couldn't have cared less. "She knows."

"Good. After all, the dog was only doing her duty. How's Kenny?"

"Kenny's fine. . . . Did you call Mutzi Elliott to apologize?"

"I called Mutzi but certainly not to apologize, since I didn't start it. Anyway, I volunteered to come in an hour early next Friday to set up, and I volunteered you too."

"Gee, thanks, Mom."

"Well, you don't have anything else to do—unless you've fallen in love."

"Very funny."

"I wish you'd meet a nice person. I hate to think of you alone—especially when I'm gone."

"You're going to live forever."

"Don't hold your breath," Mom sighed. "Honey, it took me a long time to understand this gay business but I do, kinda. I don't see that it's any different than what your father and I had, only you have it with a woman."

It's funny about Mother. She can be a self-centered bitch and then there are times when she's so sweet. "You're right but you can't invent love, Mother. It's a gift from God."

"If you want to buy the *Clarion,* I want to help, but maybe you ought to get out of this rinky-dink town. Your chances of finding a mate are better if you go to a big city. Baltimore's not so bad and they've got the Orioles. You love the Orioles."

"What would you do without me?" My voice had a teasing tone.

"Find somebody new to play gin with."

"Nobody will play with you anymore because you win all the time."

She was silent on the line for a bit. "I hope you're not staying here to take care of me. I can take care of myself."

"I'm here because I love Runnymede—and I love you."

"Don't get mushy, Nicole. I can't stand it when you get mushy." She inhaled deeply and I knew she had a Chesterfield in her hand. After she swore she'd given up smoking, too. "If you do find someone, go. No woman is going to come here to live with you. There aren't enough jobs and the town's tolerant but maybe they're tolerant because they don't have to face you having someone. Know what I mean? If you live with another woman, then it's real. As long as you're single it's an idea. They can think of you as an eccentric— which you are." She giggled.

"You really think our people are that petty?"

"Hell, yes! I've lived here since 1905 and we redefined the word *petty.*"

"I don't know what to say. Anyway, it's an academic discussion because I'm alone, but if I find someone, you'll be the first to know."

"Good. I'd die if Wheezie found out first." She took another drag and I was about to yell at her but thought better of it. Her lungs had lasted this long. "Love is all there is. Don't be one of those people who has to think about it. Go with your heart. Who cares if you look a fool? Better to make a fool of yourself than have someone else do it for you."

"Mother, how come you're on this love kick?"

"My mind inclined that way today. Well, I've got worms to turn and eggs to lay so I'm hanging up. Supper here tomorrow. What do you want?"

"Fried chicken and greens with fatback."

"You got it, and don't forget we go to bingo an hour early next Friday."

"I won't."

"Bye-bye."

"Bye."

I hung up the phone and was engulfed in a wave of guilt. How was I going to explain Jackson Frost to her? If the Fates were kind, she'd never find out. Maybe the Fates were a grand excuse, too. I didn't need the Fates to destroy me or to make me. I could do it myself.

The afternoon sun died on the windowsill, leaving remains in Pewter's dark-gray fur. She stretched and came over for a scratch. I don't know why I didn't realize it at the time—I guess I was too wound up over the *Clarion*—but in looking back I realize why Mother was talking about love. She'd fallen in love at first sight with Ed Tutweiler Walters.

6

HAIR-DO CITY

MONDAY . . . 30 MARCH

The Curl 'n Twirl reposed on the northeastern side of the Square. It was next to the Masonic Lodge, which sat on the corner of Baltimore Street. On the other side of the Curl 'n Twirl was Saint Paul's Episcopal Church. The whole north side of the Square was spiffy and bright except for the defunct Bon Ton Department Store abandoned on the valuable Hanover Street corner. Mr. Pierre grexed and groaned about Pennsylvania taxes, which were worse than Maryland taxes, although that's not saying much. However, few buildings came up for rent on the Square, so when the old Lansburg Dress Shop folded in 1957, Mr. Pierre and Bob Howard, his lover and partner, were shrewd enough to grab it. We all wondered if Mr. Pierre would be able to carry on after Bob died, but he persevered and the hair salon flourished.

In part it flourished because Mr. Pierre treated every customer as an honored guest, and in part it flourished because he shrewdly made the place exciting. Every five years he suffered a spasm of redecoration. He consumed *Architectural Digest, House and Garden,* and design magazines from Italy and France. Last year he went all-out and revamped the place. Shining high-tech, it sported a thin band of purple neon which ran around the top of the wall where molding would be. The floors were sleek pearl-gray tiles and the walls were palest pink, very flattering to his clients' complexions, some of which resembled a road map. Current music piped through-

32

out the place, George Benson, Dave Sanborn, and Al Jarreau. The music was soothing and hip at the same time.

As you entered, you encountered a receptionist behind a curving, glossy counter. The enviable task of being at the center of Runnymede's female nerve center fell to Verna's oldest daughter, Georgette. When Georgette was young she used so much spray starch on her hair it looked like lasagna. People swore she would die of scalp infection. Mr. Pierre changed all that, and Georgette's hair was worn soft and shoulder-length. Georgette, like her mother, was determined to live life as a blonde. A glorious floral arrangement commanded one corner of the counter despite the season. In the bowels of winter, Mr. Pierre could produce calla lillies. He swore he'd die before he revealed his source. It was Millard Huffstetler, Peepbean's gay uncle and Saint Rose's business manager, but possession of this secret was so important to Mr. Pierre and I guess to Millard that we let it lie.

I pushed through the door and was awash in the low buzz of neon. Goodyear, a saucy yellow bow on his collar, was flopped in the middle of the room.

"*Ma cherie!*" Pierre waved. "How'd the interview go at the bank?"

"God, Mom must have blabbed everything."

"She's in the back getting her hair washed."

"Maybe you could hold her under just a tiny bit longer."

"*Quelle honte!* Shame on you. Julia's concerned that you get the paper and I, naturally, agree. You should own the *Clarion.*"

"Why, thank you, Mr. Pierre."

"I think so too." Louise's voice boomed out from the back.

I lowered my voice. "They're back there at the same time—after Friday night?"

Sotto voce, he answered. "They're being overpoweringly polite to each other."

"I don't like it," I whispered.

"Neither do I. You remember what happened the last time they were this polite. How Julia talked Jackson Frost into letting her endorse his candidacy for mayor on television I will never, ever know."

I smiled. "Jackson's got resonance where his brains should be."

That was a trifle nasty, because Jackson wasn't really dumb but he couldn't resist a woman's entreaties. And Mother had never lost her ability to wrap men around her little finger. It wasn't that she did not give a good endorsement, playing her part as an elderly person who would benefit by Jackson's policies. It was that Louise ran into the midst of the show, loudly refuted her sister, and then wrecked the set. Well, they both wrecked the set. Jackson won in a landslide, probably because he had provided the town with such delicious entertainment. The perversity was that Louise voted for Jackson anyway. Ideology did not motivate my honorable aunt. It was always personal gain or personal animosity and she seethed with animosity because Julia, not her, was chosen for the political endorsement.

Mother emerged from the washroom, her little silver curls hanging limply around her head. Sometimes when the humidity was high it looked as though she had popcorn balls stuck over her head. Louise was on Mom's heels. Aunt Wheeze went in for the stately image. Her hair, snow-white, was long, and she'd pile it up on her head like a Gibson girl. Her hair was gorgeous and it nicely framed her face when she wore a bun on the top like that. Both sisters had lustrous gray eyes, astonishing eyes. Mother had a fuller mouth but Louise had a better chin. Of course, now she had many chins.

"What happened?" Mother clambered up on the chair.

Before I could answer she made Mr. Pierre raise and lower the chair. She enjoyed the ride. Louise, more gracefully, positioned herself in the chair next to Juts. The two eyed each other in the mirror.

I walked between them and leaned against the counter so they'd have to focus on me, not each other. Mr. Pierre skillfully began working on Mother's head while Kim Spangler, of the poor branch of the Spangler clan, came out from the back. She did the washing and gave Louise a head massage. The entire town knew of Friday's skirmish and everyone was humoring the Hunsenmeir girls.

"Charles came with me. I talked for about a half hour to Foster Adams and then I presented my financial statement."

"Did he say anything?" Wheezie's eyes were closed in pleasure.

"Bankers," Mr. Pierre sighed.

"He was friendly—"

Mother interrupted. "Of course he's friendly. He's known you since you were born."

"He's going to review my statement. He knows Charles is behind me, although Charles is free to keep talking to the other companies. It's a lot of money for him. Anyway, I'll know soon."

"I don't think he has any real power," Mother said.

Louise's eyes opened wide. "He's president of the bank. That's power."

"That used to be power." Mother was smug. "When Runnymede

Bank and Trust was bought up by Chesapeake-Potomac Bank he became a cog in a big wheel."

"He knows us better than some college-educated ass in Baltimore."

"I don't doubt that," Mother replied, "but I don't think he can approve a loan all by himself."

"You might be right but he's got some discretion."

"When you get the paper, Nickel, I've been thinking about a column. You know, something with local color." Wheezie's eyes brightened. "I'll call it 'Was My Face Red' and I'll put in there all the gossip of the town. You know, a kind of Cholly Knickerbocker of Runnymede. I know everybody and I'll get the truth. Or maybe I'll write about Runnymede the way it used to be. The good old days."

Mother turned her head to gaze directly at Louise, swooning in her literary rapture. "You can barely sign your name, much less write a column."

"Don't be nasty, Julia. I hate it when you're nasty. You know perfectly well I made A's in English and Miss Kunstler told Mother I was a star pupil."

Juts swiveled in her chair without Mr. Pierre's help. He stopped working on her. I caught a glimpse of the dreaded Chesterfield pack in her voluminous purse. So it wasn't just a puff now and then; she was back on hot and heavy. I wondered when she'd break down and smoke one in front of me. I don't smoke, drink, or take drugs, which makes me an oddity in Runnymede, possibly in America. I lashed Mother daily on the subject of tar, nicotine, and bad teeth until she gave in and stopped smoking. That was my Christmas present from her. That and a quilt, blue and white, that my great-grandmother had made way back in 1892. Mother's curls were beginning to puff up. She looked like a silver poodle.

"Miss Kunstler was scared to death of you because you threw a fake epileptic fit when you didn't know the difference between a noun and a verb."

Louise smiled. Normally she'd tear off Mom's head but her self-control was remarkable. "Who told you such a fib?"

"Orrie Tadia, your very best friend." Mother emphasized "very best friend."

"Julia, turn around. If your hair dries any more I won't be able to do a thing with it," Mr. Pierre fussed. Her vanity got the better of her anger and she obeyed.

"Orrie has imagination," came the weak retort.

"Well, I do wish she'd get back from Fort Lauderdale. Why she

35

goes there with all that riffraff I'll never know. It's not like it used to be."

"Nothing is like it used to be." Mr. Pierre's hands wrapped the curls into perfect shape.

"Mom and Wheezie are the same." I noticed in the mirror on the other side of the room that my hair could stand a trim too.

"Not the same. Older," Mother said.

"If I had known I was going to live this long I would have taken better care of myself." Louise gave a fake sigh.

"Darling, you look divine." Mr. Pierre meant it.

"Yeah, not a day over one hundred."

"Oh, Julia, you can be so childish sometimes."

"Is that so? Well, if you're so smart, tell me what is the difference between a noun and a verb?"

Louise paused. "Don't you know?"

"I asked you."

Wheezie took a deep breath, Our Lady of the Significant Sighs, and shook her hair out. "Whenever you're not the center of attention, Julia dear, you try and make me look stupid."

Mother let fly. "That's not hard."

Louise smiled a superior smile. "I think it's wonderful that you don't act the way you dress."

Mr. Pierre groaned. Georgette sat still, waiting. Kim discreetly took the scissors off the counter.

"I knew you didn't know the difference. You still haven't told me the difference between a verb and a noun." Mother was smug again and determined to keep her temper.

"Then you tell me, Smartass—Dungdot—Aspirinface!"

"Girls!" Mr. Pierre chided.

"I'll tell you." I stepped in.

"I don't want you to tell me and I don't care. What I want is my own column and I *can* write. So there. It's the least you can do for your beloved aunt."

"Ha" was all Mother said.

"If I am able to purchase the paper, Aunt Wheezie, I'll think about it. You do have the best sources of anyone I know." I hastened to add, "You and Mother."

"Julia is well connected." Louise returned to icy politeness again.

I don't know why it made me so uncomfortable. She must be holding out on us.

"Well, I've got to get back to work. I'll see you all later." I headed for the door.

Louise called out in a voice so sweet it dripped. "I won't see you for dinner tonight, Nickel. I've got a date with Ed Tutweiler Walters."

I stopped, turned around, and said, "You work fast, don't you?" I was smiling.

Mother was not.

What a relief to get out of the Curl 'n Twirl. After that bomb, and didn't Louise just know when to drop it, there would be nuclear silence in there.

I bumped into Diz Rife.

"Why, hello." His deep-brown eyes peered into mine.

"Diz, I thought you were in New York."

"Just got back. I hear you're trying to buy the *Clarion* too."

"Don't forget the Thurston Group."

"Formidable opponents." Diz's coat was vicuña. It must have cost as much as a Volkswagen.

"I guess."

"You headed back to the office?" he asked.

"Yes."

"Mind if I walk you there?"

"No."

As it was only four doors away it wasn't a long walk but Diz would take any opportunity to talk to me. He'd been that way since we were kids. The family sent him to public school up until ninth grade and then he was packed off to Exeter while his two sisters, Portia and Lucretia, were sentenced to Miss Porter's. After Exeter, Diz attended Princeton and distinguished himself academically and athletically. He got his M.B.A. from New York University.

The family had come a long way since the strong-arm days of Brutus Rife, Diz's late unlamented great-grandfather. Mother and Louise said that Disraeli was the spitting image of Brutus. Still, it's hard to relax or trust someone who can buy and sell the whole town. It was true I didn't hold Diz responsible for the phenomenal greed and illegal tactics of his forebears. But whatever the reason, he made me edgy.

"How's Liz?"

Diz and Liz, the beautiful couple of Runnymede. They'd been married for eleven years. Liz had a vast jewelry collection given to her by various admirers and corporate presidents. She was not loath to show it off. Those two didn't get married so much as they endured a merger. Liz's family, the Van der Lindes, invested in Fulton's steamship line. They'd been making money ever since. It was, as all the papers said at the time, "a brilliant match." Diz spoke of his wife only in formulaic terms. He never hinted at any problem, but then why would he say it to me? Apparently he never said anything to anybody.

"Liz is fine. She's chairman of the heart fund this year and throwing herself into it. What have you been doing—aside from trying to buy the paper?"

"Playing bingo."

"Heard about Friday night's game."

"Oh—after my meeting with Foster Adams, I interviewed the manager and employees of your very own canning plant."

"Why, what happened?"

"Two cans exploded."

He laughed. "Vegetarian terrorists."

"I don't think the two cans were sealed properly but when you consider how many cans that place turns out it's a wonder more don't blow up. At any rate, you'll feel the waves after tomorrow morning, and the health inspector will probably make a call on your manager."

"Thanks for the news." He stopped at the door to the *Clarion*. "Nickel, why do you want this paper?"

"In my blood. Why do you want it?"

"Mid-Atlantic wants to develop a communications division. Oh, I know there isn't that much money in the *Clarion* but when I heard it was available I thought, 'Why not?' I think we'll wind up buying it too. It will be the cornerstone of the division."

"Don't you own enough?"

"I don't personally own these things."

"You do."

"Just because a company is big doesn't mean it's bad. You've got to grow beyond your romantic concept of this paper in particular and business in general."

"We don't agree on this issue, Diz. Don't patronize me."

He smiled. "Maybe you're right. I did sound a little pompous. You going to start up with tennis as soon as spring arrives—if it ever does?"

I nodded. "How about you?"

"Not only am I starting, I've been taking lessons in New York. I'm going to be the best player in Runnymede this year."

"You'll have to beat Jackson Frost."

"If I do, will you be my doubles partner?"

"You never give up, do you?"

"No." He beamed.

"How much you want to bet that you'll beat Jackson?"

"Twenty dollars, and I'll do the job before July fourth."

"I'll take that bet."

We shook on it and Diz left, a lilt to his step. I pushed open the door to the *Clarion*, already spending the extra twenty dollars in my head.

Lolly and Pewter were glad to greet me. So was Roger Davis, who slapped his copy on my desk. He couldn't find the right transitions. I think Roger would kill his mother for good transitions but then that's true of most journalists.

Later that afternoon the clouds hung low, gunmetal gray. They looked ominous. When John Hoffman came back into the office he looked ominous too. He and I hadn't had any time to talk since Charles informed us of his plans.

John put his hat with the furry earflaps on his desk. At forty-six, though his hairline had receded, he remained a pleasant-looking man—clear hazel eyes, light-brown hair, clean features. He drank, so his complexion betrayed him with little red spider webs. He ate junk food and his hands shook when he drank yet another cup of roped coffee, laced with Jack Daniel's Black. Sterilized by rationality, John never cut a shine in his life or even entertained an illogical thought. We coexisted without much affection but with respect. Charles had given John increasing business and advertising responsibilities and John lived up to them. No wonder he was so good at those right-wing editorials. He was speaking directly to our advertisers, many of whom also believed that if you were poor you deserved it.

John fondled Pewter, who jumped on his desk for a kiss. He'd bring her furry catnip mice and chase her around the bullpen, as we called our quarters. I used to wonder, watching him with Pewter, if there was an entire part of his personality that got squashed when he was a kid and someone told him men don't play, they don't write poetry, they're not silly. Pewter seemed to be the only one of us who could touch his submerged and probably half-forgotten self.

He made smacking kissy sounds. "Oh, Pewter Motor Scooter. Uncle John's got a fishy for you."

He pulled out a food treat in the shape of a fish. Lolly steamed. John never brought her anything and she hotly resented his favoritism to a mere cat. After all, if robbers burst through the door to snatch our depleted coffers it wouldn't be Pewter that would save us; it would be Lolly.

John addressed me, finally. "Filthy day. Gonna snow."

"I hope not. You've been so busy I haven't had time to take your temperature about the great events around here."

He scratched Pewter at the base of her tail. She rewarded him with thunderous purring. "Yeah, the Old Guard is changing."

"Got any ideas—for yourself, I mean?"

"I could sure use a pay raise." He leaned forward over his desk. "And I like living in Runnymede. My kids like it. My wife likes it. But I've got to keep my options open."

"You've got them too. You're good, even if George Will is your hero."

The compliment got to him and I meant it.

"Truthfully, Nick, I'm kind of rocked by all this. How the hell do we know what our new owners will do once we get new owners? They'll tell Charles whatever to get him to sign on the dotted line. Now, mind you, I'm not saying they're going to be bad. In fact they might even introduce the twentieth century to this paper. Hell, we haven't even got computers yet and our wire machine is on its last legs."

The AP machine thumped and hummed as the white paper spread across the room like a crazed tapeworm. I liked the old, buggy thing but John was right. Technologically we were so far behind, we were lonesome. But when it came to solid newspaper sense, the *Clarion* was aces. A steady stream of fresh kids came to Charles Falkenroth with journalism degree and virtue intact. They left with the journalism degree. And they left real reporters. Our "graduates" worked at *The New York Times, The Wall Street Journal,* the *Kansas City Star,* both Chicago papers, both Detroit papers, the *San Jose Mercury,* the *Baltimore Sun, The Washington Post,* the *Richmond Times-Dispatch,* and my favorite, the *Louisville Courier-Journal.* People here left with bruises on their souls from Charles but they could write a story. If we'd lived in England, the Queen would have bestowed some honorary title upon Charles, but as we were Americans, what he got was the satisfaction of his work. Recognition was for rock stars or at least that's how Charles would consider it.

"Nickel—you here?" John prodded me.

"Sorry, I was just thinking about Charles. I wonder if he can stay away from the paper even if he sells it."

"He's in his seventies."

"Is he? I forget. He always looks the same to me."

"My hunch is that Ann will get him to move to Palm Springs. The desert will help his arthritis. He earned his rest."

"I can't imagine this place without him." I grabbed a blue pencil and began desecrating Michelle Saunders's puff piece on the Jewish cemetery south of town. It wasn't that I didn't like the subject matter, it was just that Michelle had obviously spent her life in a WASP cocoon. She was also a graduate of Sarah Lawrence. Her skin was so thin she could bleed in a high wind, and Charles always stuck me with her copy because he couldn't face her exhausting fits about English, her desire to be a female F. Scott Fitzgerald, her conviction that the *Clarion* staff were all trolls in the basement of literature. Well, I'd get an earful today. I scribbled in the column and spoke while editing. "Did Charles tell you I'm trying to buy the paper?"

"I was wondering when you'd get to that."

I stopped scribbling. The piece was too awful anyway. "What do you think?"

"I think you've got brass balls." He smiled broadly.

"I take it that's a compliment."

John laughed. "Hey, it's David and Goliath and I've got a ringside seat."

"You might hand me a rock."

He was thinking about the rock when Michelle scurried over. Today she wore Pappagallo shoes. This girl would be buried in Pappagallo shoes. Her disdain for my wardrobe radiated from every pore. I couldn't blame her. Shopping puts me closer to a nervous breakdown than my April fifteenth tax deadline. I wore my clothes until they were threads crossing my body. I was neat and clean but that's about all you could say for me except I looked good in jeans and sneakers.

"Have you finished with my piece? I mean, the sense of history, of cultural integrity is just stupefying, isn't it? I've just got to go to a seder." She pronounced it "cedar."

"Michelle, I'm not finished yet but I think you've got a heavy rewrite."

"The pacing is perfect." Her chin set.

Dear God, give me strength. "It does move but I think we've got to tone down sentences like this: 'A latter-day Moses, Rabbi Kahn parts the waves of societal oppression for his tiny flock.' "

"You deny the persecution of the Jews?" Her eyebrows flew into her strawberry-blond hair. Not one strand of gray in it.

"This isn't a story about persecution; it's a story about the Jewish cemetery. If you're going to talk about societal oppression, then you'd better back it up with stories of anti-Semitism in Runnymede—and we've got it."

"Here?" Michelle labored under the delusion that because the Square was quaint, our manners polished, that we were an ideal community.

John threw her a bone. "Talk to Mutzi Elliott. Ask him what happened when the Rosenbergs were brought to trial."

"Mutzi's not a Jew."

I wanted to groan. How we were ever going to make a reporter out of this one, I didn't know. I could spit at Charles for dropping her in my lap.

"Mutzi was an eyewitness," I told her. "The other principals are dead now."

John shook his head. "It's what you learn after you know it all that counts."

I got up and walked back to the press.

You can get to the press through the *Clarion* building. The press addition was built immediately after the War Between the States. Since Maryland technically was a neutral state, we didn't suffer the devastation of our great and greatly irritating neighbor, Virginia. Both the Falkenroth and the Hunsenmeir of that time invested shrewdly and added the huge press wing. They even filled it with an early linotype press. In 1924, when money was everywhere, Charles's Dad, Michael, put in the offset press. That old baby was singing today. Michael also put in a gigantic glass picture window so the citizens could stand in the wide alleyway between Brown's Meat Market and the *Clarion* and watch the paper get printed. The printers wore white overalls and white square caps. The walls were white. They were still white and so were the printers. Arnold Dow, the genius of the old machine, kept her going. I stood on the catwalk above the ponderous giant and inhaled the mossy odor of newsprint and virgin paper. I never tired of it, nor the sight of the printed page as it rolled off the press. Women, usually the wives of the printers, would bundle and tie the papers. The whole place was a ballet of activity infused with a spirit of freedom. I could write whatever I wanted in the *Clarion*. My ancestors saw to that and I, for one, wasn't going to forget it.

There was no audience today. The weather turned colder; a few flakes floated down. In the summers we drew crowds. The magic of the *Clarion* beckoned to our community, or maybe it was the magic of newspapers. Whatever, they watched. They also watched *Jeopardy* on the television but there's no accounting for taste.

When I was tiny, too small even for kindergarten, my father, Chessy Smith, would take me down to watch the paper. I think I knew even then that I'd wind up here. I think he knew too. Dad bought me a typewriter when I was six. Where he got the money I'll never know. He gave me a card of proofreading symbols. And he drilled me from behind the counter of his hardware store. I often wondered if Dad wanted to be a reporter himself. It was beyond his reach, because he didn't get past fifth grade. He had to work and help his family after his father died suddenly of a massive stroke. If this was a dream of his, and he was living it out through me, he never said. What he did say when he'd read my childhood copy was, "Where'd you get your brains? You didn't get them from me." But I did.

I didn't know Daddy when he worked as a carpenter. By the time I came into his life he had bought the long, narrow store next to the *Clarion*. He named it Smith's Hardware, today called Smitman's for the family that purchased it after Dad's death. Saturdays I worked in the store with Dad until I was big enough to be a copygirl at the *Clarion*. He taught me to be prompt, orderly, and to smile at the customers. He also taught me how to use each of the gadgets and tools in the store. I especially liked the square metal tape measure that would whoosh back into its casing if you pressed a button.

People liked Chessy Smith because he made them laugh. They'd drop by the store for a dose of amusement after they'd spilled out their troubles to Dad in hushed tones. When we'd be alone in the store, Dad would say to me: "People worry too much. They're too serious. They want answers. Well, there aren't very many answers. The secret of life is that there is no secret, you know that, kid?"

No, I didn't. Not at the time.

7

MY CHEATING HEART

TUESDAY . . . 31 MARCH

Tuesdays packed more excitement than Mondays in Runnymede but that's true everywhere. Tuesdays the Masons had their regular meeting. So did the Daughters of the Confederacy. Their rivals, the Sisters of Gettysburg, held meetings on Wednesday night in the Pennsylvania side's city hall. The Emmitsburg Pike divided the two city halls—that and taste. The Southern city hall was an echo of Jefferson, which meant it had graceful Palladian proportions and was a bitch to heat. The Yankee city hall reeked of gingerbread rococo. The architect of this edifice, Larkin Most, even went so far as to put gargoyles on the rooftop corners. On a misty night they could give you quite a start.

This night left mist far behind and embraced pea-soup fog. As I put the paper to bed on Tuesday nights, I was the last to leave. I hadn't noticed how wretched it was until I stepped outside and locked up the heavy oak doors, using a key as big as a ruler.

By ten o'clock most folks are home. By eleven they're in bed. A few hang on till midnight. Those who are still awake stay awake until dawn but those are the ones with problems. Unless a hot story came down the wire and I had to rip up the front page, I was usually out of the *Clarion* by ten. Each Tuesday I'd walk along the Square and then duck into the alleyway behind the drugstore on the southwest corner. Then I'd double back to Brown, Moon & Frost, where I'd go in the back door. I had a key. This night was no exception.

Jackson stood on a little ladder in the law library. "You've got ink on your forehead."

I looked in a convex mirror and rubbed it off. "How come you didn't tell me Charles was selling the paper?"

"Because he's my client and that's privileged information." He stepped down. "And because he wanted to tell you himself."

"What's the point of having an affair with you if I don't get the news first?"

Jackson kissed me. "That's the point."

"You'll have to do better than that."

He did. He always did. I can't even claim to have drifted into this relationship. I sailed in, damn the torpedoes, full speed ahead. And I knew better too. My parents didn't raise me to have relationships with married people but my parents also didn't take into account the slim pickings in Runnymede, especially if one is gay. Which brings me to what appears to be a flaming contradiction. What was I doing in bed with Jackson Frost? Having a good time.

I subscribe to the blue dot theory of human sexuality. Actually, I don't subscribe to it; I made it up. If on a given day every single person who has ever had homosexual sex woke up with a blue dot on his or her forehead, either three quarters of adult America would stay in bed or they'd be brazen and hit the streets, and finally all this huffing and puffing over who sleeps with whom would be *over*. Now there's more to this theory. I think the color of the dot should reflect the level of one's activity. So if you were stone gay your dot would be blue-black. If you'd once had a small experiment the dot would be such a pale blue as to be nearly white. My dot registered turquoise, somewhere in the middle but just a bit over the line.

I loathe this American obsession with sex and sexual definition. I am not who I sleep with. Actually, I was lucky to have Jackson to sleep with Tuesday nights.

Our attitude toward each other outside his office was proper. I loved his wife, Regina, and the only bad thing I could say about my best friend was she wore so much iridescent eye shadow that her lids looked like shrimp gone bad. Jackson and I had known each other since before kindergarten. Same with Regina. I guess as time went by, Regina looked like a better bet than I did. She married Jack, and if I was hurt I didn't know it at the time.

Jackson and I were doubles partners at the club but no one paid much attention. Lesbianism was etched in everyone's cerebral tentacle—*brain* may be too optimistic a noun. It never occurred to anyone that I might be sleeping with Jackson.

Lolly snored on the fake Bokhara. Pewter pulled pencils out of an embossed leather cylinder on his desk.

Afterwards he made me a strong cup of Lipton tea so I could drive home. He had only to walk around the block to Lee Street, the same street Mother lived on.

"Do you think I have a chance?"

"There are a lot of factors out of your control but if Foster Adams comes down on your side, you've got a chance. Hope so, anyway." His blond curls gleamed in the low light.

"Thanks. Oh, I ran into Diz and he made a twenty-dollar bet with me that he's going to beat you in singles before July fourth. If he does, then I'm promised as his mixed-doubles partner for the rest of the season."

"Ha! When hell freezes over. He never stops being competitive. I mean, success is a fetish with that guy." He rubbed his square jaw. "He'd be more interesting if his fetishes were sexual.'"

"Maybe. Maybe not."

"How's your mother?"

I knew why Jack was switching subjects. Anything to do with Diz generally put him in a bad mood and he didn't want to be in a bad mood. Our time together was too precious.

"I'm not sure."

"Sick?"

"No, but peculiar. She called me Sunday and talked to me about love and my future. It's not like Mom to do that. I mean, normally, anger and wit are the only way she shows emotion. Anything else—she deflects. I wonder what's going on with her?"

"It's all over town what's going on with Louise."

"I wouldn't take this date with Ed Walters too seriously."

"She is."

"'How do you know so much about it?"

"Had lunch at Mojo's, and Verna was promiscuous in her conversation."

"Everybody knows everything in this town."

"They don't know about us."

"Jack, someday they will. It's inevitable."

This thought didn't please him. "Do you ever think about leaving here? Leaving me?"

"Funny. Mom asked me that same thing. Where would I go?"

"That's not the answer I hoped for."

"Come on, Jack. I'm not fond of emotional display."

"Go live in Japan then." He smiled and continued: "You're like your mother."

"God, don't say that. That's every woman's worst fear."

"I think Julia Hunsenmeir is pretty special. She's full of fun, ready for whatever comes next, and she has a stiff upper lip. She can take whatever life hands out."

"If I want a stiff upper lip I'll grow a moustache." This was petulant.

"Wouldn't like you then." Jackson's voice was singsong, like a kid's at recess.

"Really? Truly? You wouldn't like me if I woke up tomorrow and were a man? Kind of like Kafka only with better results."

"I'd like you but I wouldn't want to go to bed with you."

"Silly boy." The cold air seeped in under the windowsill. I put on my sweater.

"Do you think about leaving?"

"Sometimes. Why do you ask? Have I said something or done something?"

"No, I just don't want to lose you, that's all." He kissed me again.

I kissed him back. "This is my home. Sometimes it gets me. The smallness. The nosiness. Christ, every new idea is perceived as an act of aggression."

He studied my face. "I know. Sometimes I feel that even the buildings are leaking nostalgia. But I don't know if I could live anywhere else. I belong here for better or for worse."

"Better." I kissed him and left, Lolly and Pewter at my heels.

8

JULIA, THE SPY

WEDNESDAY . . . 1 APRIL

The moon, a silver sickle, offered little light but the sky was crystal clear. Mother's night vision progressively deteriorated. If she wanted to go anywhere in the evening I usually drove her. I had no intention of driving her anywhere tonight but she bribed me with a huge pot of paper narcissus which she forced in her little greenhouse off the kitchen.

We headed toward Luigi's, the Italian restaurant about four miles west of town. Mark Mallory owned it and as far as I knew there never had been a Luigi in these parts. Despite the Chianti bottles with candles in them and the red-checkered tablecloths, the food was good.

"Slow down." Mother was a backseat driver.

"I'm going to park."

"No, you're not. I want to coast by."

"Okay."

The big red neon sign glowed up ahead. An Italian flag fluttered over the doorway. If we have to bring in our flag at night, Mark ought to bring in the Italian flag too. He could display it inside and get the same effect. Business was always good at Luigi's. We crawled past, craning to see into the three-over-three windows.

"See anything?" Mother asked.

"I'm driving. I can't look."

"Goddammit, I can't see at night."

"Why didn't you think of that in the first place?"

"You're the college-educated one. I thought you were smart."

"Mother, don't start."

Lolly, Goodyear, and Pewter listened from the back seat.

"I can't see."

I drove past from the other direction. Couldn't see a thing except lots of little heads. I drove by a few more times.

"I'm about to wear out my tires." I was getting testy.

"I remember you got your driver's license on a Friday. By Saturday you'd been to the filling station three times. You did wear out the tires!" She laughed.

"That's when you told me I had to get a job and buy my own car. Bet you don't even remember my first car. Ha, I bet you don't even remember your first car."

"I most certainly do." She huffed and settled like a hen on a nest. "Your first car was a 1943 two-door Mercury and it ran like a top. I'd like to have that car back. Furthermore, you paid four hundred dollars for it and it was dark-green. My first car, or the first car I drove, anyway—it was your father's car—was a Model A Ford. That was his first and last Ford product. After that he became a convert to Chrysler, so maybe it was a good thing he died before you bought that old Mercury." She paused, probably thinking about Dad. "I know a lot about cars. I kind of came into the world with them if you think about it."

"I think about Daddy every day and you know what?" I turned to Mother. "I smile every time."

"Keep your eyes on the road."

"Make up your mind. Either I stare at the road or I peer into Luigi's."

We made a few more passes with no success.

"Remember the time we played charades at the church and Chessy dressed up like Milton Berle in drag? He ruined my lipstick too. God, I'll never forget that. I believe I near to died of laughter that night. We did laugh, didn't we?"

"We still do."

"Not the same." She pulled her scarf up tighter around her neck. It was beastly cold. "But life goes on. And I mean that too. I'm not being . . . being flippant. If life doesn't go on, then you're insulting the people you loved who are dead. Know what I mean?"

"I sure do. How come you didn't remarry?" I'd asked her this a thousand times and got a thousand different answers. Mother had a fertile brain when it came to giving herself excuses or reasons.

"Who?"

"Millard Huffstetler was hot for you after he was widowed."

"Oh la! Millard is as big a lady as Mr. Pierre. He wanted a traveling companion. That's all he and Gerta did was travel."

"I think gay men and straight women can have very comfortable relationships."

"I want a real man with real balls."

"Mom."

"I mean it. I don't care if I sound anti-gay. A woman needs a man who wants her. It isn't enough to be needed. Millard needed me but he didn't want me. Hell, I don't care if he wants some man. That's his business, but my life is my business and I deserve better than that. After all, I had the best in your father."

Wasn't much I could say to that. I drove around some more.

"I have an idea," Mother piped in.

Inwardly I moaned. "Yes." My voice was bright.

"Park in the parking lot. Let's sneak up and peek in the window."

"What if someone sees us? You'll look a fool."

"What else is new?"

I did as I was told. The girls were told to stay in the back seat, which didn't go over well but they did it. Mom and I tiptoed to the first window by the parking lot. The tiptoeing itself was pretty funny. Who was going to hear us inside Luigi's? The place was a clutter of plates, cups, saucers, and talk. The photo of the Colosseum beckoned us. I never did like eating at Luigi's and facing the Colosseum. Rivers of blood soaked into that Colosseum sand. Of course, maybe we'd be better off if we got honest about football and let them kill one another out there too. They sure are trying. At least the Romans were up front about their bloodlust.

"There they are," Mother whispered.

Louise, dressed to the nines, sat opposite Ed Tutweiler Walters, also beautifully turned out. Accompanying them on this hot date were Verna and Thacker Bonneville along with the ten BonBons. As two of the oldest children were married, their spouses were there as well.

Mother put her hand over her mouth and hurried back to the car. I ran after her. We got in, closed the doors, and howled.

When I got my breath I asked, "Do you think she knew?"

Mother shrugged. "Even if she did she'd lie though her teeth about it. 'The date of the decade' was how your aunt put it."

"Well, it's beyond decade—there're more than the ten BonBons." We laughed some more. "What are you going to do tomorrow? Nail her?"

"And spoil my fun? I'm not going to do anything."

I cranked up the Jeep and thought to myself: "And after that, everything!"

We sang, "Row, row, row your boat" the whole way to Mom's house, even though it made Lolly bark. Lolly hates the sound of the human voice in song. We're even, because I won't give you much for the canine voice.

9

THE STATIONS OF THE CROSS: A MOMENT WITH AUNT LOUISE

THURSDAY . . . 2 APRIL

What a surprise. The temperature climbed into the mid-fifties and at lunch hour hoards of people poured into Runnymede Square. A brave crocus popped her head up under the Confederate statue. I was glad no blossom came up by the Yankee statue, although you could see the green shoots breaking the ground.

Mutzi Elliott was sitting on a bench with Michelle Saunders. Her notebook was open, so she was working. Mutzi wore a pink string tie. That was his official spring tie. People tend to simplify one another. We all knew Mutzi liked string ties and cowboy boots. Every Christmas the man was inundated with string ties. By now they've probably taken over his garage and are threatening the house next door. As our greengrocer—not to mention bingo caller—he saw most of us once or twice a week and the diehards, like Mom, every day. Mother insisted on fresh vegetables.

I was wondering where she was, since the first warm day had been eagerly anticipated. Careful scanning of the grounds revealed her escorted by Verna, coming up Frederick Street toward the Square. No wonder I didn't notice her. Verna obscured my view. It's ugly to call Verna fat, so I'll say she was generously nourished, and when she had her appendectomy it did take four orderlies to lift her off the gurney. Even at a distance I could see Mother was working her magic act. She was animated. Verna stopped every few steps to hold her sides in laughter. No one would ever accuse my mother of being dull but they'd sure accuse Julia Hunsenmeir Smith of plenty else. Mother had a reputation for being viciously witty. She wasn't one to cross, because she'd slice you and dice you publicly. She was also accused of being vain. Now I didn't agree with that. I looked at Mother again, coming toward the Square. There she was, eighty-two, and her step had the resilience of a young woman's.

Health was Julia's religion. She exercised for one hour every day and had done so since she was a teenager. She did jumping jacks, push-ups, and sit-ups, followed by her walking three to five miles. Winters messed up the walking. Five years ago I saved my pennies and gave her a treadmill for Christmas so she could keep up with her walking. She also did her own housework, which, as any woman can tell you, is exercise. So while her wrinkles had wrinkles and her skin had lost elasticity, she had the body of a healthy fifty-year-old. Mother always said that age was a disease and you can fight it. I don't think Mom is vain. I think she's smart. Except for the cigarettes. The other thing that ticks people off about Mother is that she's on the cutting edge of fashion. Granted, we're talking about fashion for Runnymede but given TV we aren't that far behind. Julia was the first woman to bob her hair, the first to wear pants, the first to wear a miniskirt, and she was in her fifties then. She loved the wolf whistles. She never relinquished her position as fashion leader and I think it was her self-confidence that got people. The Rifes had more money than God, and Mom still looked better than those women. If she'd had the money for a face lift, she could have fooled everyone.

At any rate, I couldn't keep up with her when it came to fashion. I spent my money on books and Kenny's board at the stable. But I worked out: one and a half hours every day with weights—not the sissy stuff, the heavy stuff—and then I'd run. The crow's-feet took hold around my eyes and I had a streak of gray right off my widow's peak, but other than that I was also living proof that Mother was right about aging: It's up to you.

If Mom was on her way to the Square, where was Aunt Wheezie? I decided to stroll around the whole Square. As it was large, that was a pleasant half-hour task. Also, one has to pass and repass. That's Southern for talking the first time you see someone and then when you run into them again you talk some more. Passing and repassing.

"Nick!"

I turned to see Regina. She was wearing a pink shirt, a khaki skirt, and a light-green shirt jacket. Her light hair was pulled back in a chic ponytail complete with ribbon. The eyeshadow glowed green today. Regina was an attractive woman out of her barn clothes. Lolly ran up to her. I would have moved a little faster but Pewter picked that moment to bitch. She wanted to be carried. Pewter was a hairy gray cannonball, the Verna of cats. I put her on my shoulder.

"What are you doing downtown today? I thought you had a meeting with the vet."

"I did. Didn't take long. The mare's got a stone bruise—that's a relief." She breathed deeply. "A few more days like this and we can get out on the courts."

"One of these years we are going to have to raise money for indoor courts. It's torture not playing in the winter."

"I couldn't agree more." Her teeth sparkled, perfectly capped.

I knew they were capped but I was jolted one time in college when we'd gotten fake IDs and hit up a bar in Baltimore. The dance floor was illuminated with ultraviolet light and it made Regina's teeth black. Regina, like me, was a Delta Delta Delta, and in those days that meant something. These days it meant alumnae meetings hosted by Ursula Yost, who still insisted we practice our secret handshake.

"We could try and hit some on Saturday if the weather holds."

"Sure. Oh, it's official. You are editor of the Blue and Gray Hunt Club Newsletter. Ursie wants you to call her and pick up her files."

"What a con you are."

"Don't complain. I had to listen to her complain about the cost of Vogel boots. One half hour on boots!" She spied Mother coming into the Square. "I get older and Juts gets younger."

"Do tell her."

"I will." She started off and called over her shoulder. "Portia Rife is back in town. Bet she stops by your office."

"It'll be good to see her."

Smiling, she continued on her way. "What a rotten liar you are."

I smiled, too, but for entirely different reasons. Mother waved at Regina and then me.

"See you later, Mom!" I hollered.

"If you're lucky" came the reply and soon she was engulfed in conversation with Regina.

Georgette BonBon and Louise came out of the Curl 'n Twirl. Louise had her I'll-buy-lunch look on her face. My family was certainly working over the Bonnevilles.

"Pewter, honey, it's time to get down." We were in front of the

Pennsylvania side's city hall. As I was going up the steps Mr. Pierre came down.

"Sweet love." He kissed one cheek and then the other. "This is what's meant by turn the other cheek." Then he patted Lolly and told Pewter she was the cat's meow. He thought that was wildly funny. "What riches might our city hall hold for you?"

"Have you been reading the papers?"

"Breathlessly."

"Then you know we're about to go through another zoning fight."

"Oh, those zoning unpleasantries recur like malaria."

"But the struggle is tougher on your side of the line. I don't know why."

"I do. We've got more rich people per capita than you do."

"All twenty of them," I remarked.

"And most of them Rifes, but they get what they want. Anyway, I don't care if Rife converts the old shoe factory into a mini-mall or whatever they call it. Those jobs went to the Third World ages ago. If it creates jobs, I'm for it. I wish he'd buy the old Bon Ton."

"Me, too, except I don't want a zoning variance that can be used again and again. It will be used like a law without ever being voted on by the public. Diz is smart enough to know what to do when he gets his foot in the door."

"True." Mr. Pierre's eyes swept the Square. "But Diz isn't going to ruin the Square."

"Hope not. Anyway, I need to read those laws again."

"Ah, there's Julia." He kissed me on the cheek again and dashed off.

Mr. Pierre and Mother were very matey. There was something conspiratorial about them.

"Put your back into it."

"Aunt Wheeze, if you'd hold the light steady I could do a better job."

She shined the powerful flashlight over the garden beds which I was mulching at nine-thirty at night.

"How come you haven't written an editorial about Jim Bakker resigning from the PTL Club?"

"Because Charles Falkenroth says he smells a bigger story. He wants us to wait. John's raring to go, of course."

"Sometimes I agree with John's opinions."

"You do it to spite me." I heaved the last load of mulch onto her pachysandra bed and spread it around. "Once spring is here to stay, this will be perfect."

"Come on in. I'll give you a cup of tea and a pickled egg for your labors."

"Two pickled eggs."

Aunt Louise's house glittered with religious artifacts. I had long become accustomed to the suffering poses of Christ hanging in each room. The one I couldn't abide was an enormous picture of Jesus with his crown of thorns. The eyes opened and closed while the blood dripped from the thorns. The picture was electric, and when Wheezie turned on the lights you got the full, horrific effect. I'm quite sorry that Jesus endured the unleashed evil of the human race. Jesus suffered and was made man. I suffered and was made angry.

On this subject Aunt Louise and I differed. My Aunt Louise hasn't missed a tragedy since B.C. If she isn't experiencing one herself or watching someone else she'll read about historical trage-dies. She loves suffering. I can't decide if she does this because she wants to be a Catholic martyr or if she really likes pain. She's the only person I know who will feel guilty about resting in peace.

Her pickled eggs bit into my tongue with the right mixture of vinegar and sugar.

"Better than Julia's?"

"You know I can't say yes."

"But you know that I know it's true." She picked up a copy of the *Clarion*. A photo of the heavily mascaraed Tammy Bakker glared back at her. Tammy's eyelashes must precede her into the room by five minutes. Wheezie put on her glasses and studied the photo. "If I looked like that my Mother wouldn't have let me go to church."

"The woman's tear ducts must be connected to her bladder. I've never seen anyone cry so much."

"If they'd stayed within the True Church, none of this would have happened."

"Bull, Wheezie. Catholics are wearing out sin same as Protestants."

"Maybe, maybe not, but we have a system for forgiveness."

"No, you've got a system for relieving guilt. You confess, get slapped with a few extra Hail Marys, and go out and do it again."

She drew her breath in sharply. "I've done the Stations of the Cross in my time."

"You know, I've been considering starting my own church. It appears to be a growth industry. I'll call it the Church of Your Redeemer Not Necessarily Mine." I took another bite of delicious egg. "Or how about A Couple of Saints Cathedral?" I warmed up. "First Church of Christ Electrician."

Louise chuckled despite herself. "You're a blasphemer, Nickel." She regarded me through her bifocals. "Your mind doesn't work like a Hunsenmeir mind."

"I'm grateful."

"Don't be smart. We haven't done so bad."

"Neither have I."

"That's a matter of opinion."

"I just mulched your flower beds. Don't start your lesbian lament."

Her hand made a dismissive sign. "I gave up on you years ago on that one. No, I meant you can be sarcastic and airy. Above it all."

"I prefer to think of myself as detached. My profession encourages it."

"You can't live separate from people. Maybe you can be detached on the job but not off of it. You only go around once on terra cotta."

"Terra firma."

"That's what I said."

I knew Mother would kill me but I couldn't control myself. "How was your date with Ed Walters?"

"Too, too wonderful."

"Tell me."

"Some emotions are best kept to oneself."

"Now who's being detached?"

"Nick, sometimes you can be too clever by half."

As I drove away from the house, Louise turned out the light shining on the Virgin Mary in half a bathtub on the front lawn. Then she turned out the lights throughout the house and I could see her climbing the stairs. Who knows what dreams Louise had in her bed, the bed she'd slept in since her wedding day, June 14, 1918, when she'd been seventeen. Most of the people old enough to remember her wedding were dead, so she didn't even have to lie and call herself a child bride. These days, seventeen is a child bride. The marriage worked. Whatever Louise's faults, she accomplished something most of my generation couldn't: a successful first marriage. Louise had lost her older daughter to death in a fire at age twenty-nine. She used the sorrow shamelessly but she survived it, even if I did still have to hear about it. Worse, in some ways, she'd lost her younger daughter, Maizie, to insanity. When Mother and I were feeling beneath contempt we would say to ourselves that she drove Maizie to it. Realistically, I think the problem was chemical and Maizie's brain was like an alarm clock. In her forty-seventh year the bell went off and so did Maizie. Runnymede was a small town but Louise lived a full life. I'll never know what her dreams are or were but I knew I couldn't discount her as a contentious old lady. My aunt had more to her than that. The question has always been, which side of her would win out: the good or the bad. I never knew, but then I never knew that about myself either.

THE NEW MADONNA AT SAINT ROSE OF LIMA'S

FRIDAY . . . 3 APRIL

My desk sat in front of the big *Clarion* window. I could survey the
entire Square. I started coveting this desk when I was fourteen years
old and began working at the *Clarion* as a copy girl. Back then the
reporter who occupied the desk was one Isaac Cooper. Apart from
the papers covering the desk it was loaded down with Isaac's cheap
cigars. Isaac was drafted by the wire service to go to Vietnam. I was
already in college when that happened. Unfortunately, Isaac never
came back. People forget that a journalist will die to get the story. I
keep a cigar in my desk drawer so I won't forget. John says I'm
grotesquely sentimental but he forgets I've seen his face when one
of our profession is killed in Central America or Lebanon.

I didn't get his desk for my very own until 1979. I can't imagine
not wanting to sit here and see the Square while the Square sees you
but Charles has an inner sanctum, cherry wood, too, which is
unusual, and he holds court in there so when the desk became free
he gave it to me.

Michelle's copy, much improved, rested before me. Michelle,
however, did not rest. She paced by her desk. She made phone calls
and paced some more. I couldn't edit this copy fast enough for her.
As I knocked out one adjective too many on the last page, I noticed
Goodyear streak across the park. The local fury, Bucky Nordness,
was in hot pursuit. Bucky was the northern side's chief of police.
On our side we had a sheriff, David Wheeler. Bucky took his duties
seriously. David got the job done but had fun while he was doing it.

58

"Michelle, answer my phone." I shot out of my chair and was through the door before Pewter could raise her head.

"Goodyear! Goodyear."

The black chow with his purple tongue shot over to greet me. So did Bucky.

"You know there's a public ordinance about dogs being on a leash."

"Well, Goodyear's on the Maryland side now and so are you, Bucky." I crooned this with buckets of good nature.

"I don't give a damn, Nickel. We can't have dogs doing as they please."

"Goodyear's not my dog."

"I know that." He thought. "I wanted to remind you, that's all. You ought to print an update about the leash law in the paper."

"I'll take it up with Charles. I apologize for Goodyear. Mother probably forgot."

"Forgot, hell. Julia flagrantly disobeys the law. She thinks the rules apply to everyone but herself."

I didn't appreciate this assessment of Mother's character but there was a grain of truth in it. "I'll take Goodyear over to the Curl 'n Twirl. I'm sure that's where she is. Mind if I take him without a leash? Haven't got one."

"Yeah, okay," he grumbled. "Nickel, someday those Hunsenmeir girls are going to push me over the line."

I nodded sympathetically and Goodyear followed me to the Curl 'n Twirl.

Georgette smiled as we zipped through the door.

"Hi, George." Mom was in the chair with a conditioning cap on. "Hi, Mom. Hi, Mr. Pierre. Bucky Nordness is ass over tit about Goodyear being in the Square without his leash."

"From the waist down, Bucky Nordness resembles an umbrella." Mr. Pierre was sly.

"Ha!" Mother put down the magazine she was avidly reading.

"Be that as it may"—and it was an apt description—"you can't let Goodyear run as he pleases. What if Wheezie were coming around the Square in her Chrysler?"

"The vehicle of doom," Mr. Pierre intoned.

"You're right." Mother held up the magazine for me to see. "I'm going to redo my living room just like this."

This was one of those house magazines where the decoration job in every room cost about $150,000.

"Mother, the coffee table is made of marble. You can build an addition on your house for what it would cost."

"Mr. Pierre and I have it all figured out. We'll do a fake marble—"

"*Faux,* my precious," Mr. Pierre interjected.

"And you can help me paint. I want pale-apricot."

The trapdoor in the pit of my stomach opened up. Not only would I paint, I'd spackle, put up dry wall, sand, plane, and break every fingernail I had. Mother's improvement schemes came out of my hide. By now I was experienced enough to start my own construction company and hated it. There are women out there who want to be electricians, plumbers, carpenters. Not Miss Smith. That butch crap just tears my ass with boredom. The fact that I never liked to get my hands dirty with anything but ink didn't stop Mother from pressing me into service with bribes, guilt, or outright threats to my physical well-being. I was heartily sorry that she and Dad hadn't adopted more children so I could spread this burden among my siblings. And when she was done with me, Louise would start up.

I left the hair salon with a heavy tread, remembered I hadn't told Mom when I'd pick her up tonight, and whirled back through the door.

"Mother, we go an hour early to bingo tonight."

The mouth that wouldn't die was strangely closed. Mr. Pierre busied himself cleaning his spotless counter.

"Mother?" I spied the small glass ashtray in her lap. That old trick. I came up behind her and smacked her between the shoulder blades. Billows of smoke poured out of her mouth.

"You little shit!" She coughed.

"If I'm a shit, you're a liar."

"*Tumulte.*" Mr. Pierre threw up his hands. That meant bedlam in French but I never knew if he was pronouncing the stuff correctly. I thought of French as the venereal disease of the tongue.

"Call your own mother a liar."

"You promised to give up smoking."

"The spirit is willing but the flesh is weak."

"Not your flesh." I relented. "If you smoke, you smoke. I just don't like you being a sneak about it. And what are you doing in here so early anyway?"

"Full schedule." She inhaled gratefully and blew the smoke as Bette Davis would have done it.

"Mildred Adams was in at the crack of dawn." Mr. Pierre volunteered this information. He also called her "Mildew" behind her back.

Mrs. Adams, as the wife of the bank president, had a high opinion of herself which was not shared by the rest of the community. Charles said she was that way because she was shy. If it was shyness it was effectively disguised.

"And how is Mrs. Adams?"

"She says that Foster is going to appraise your farm, the *Clarion* building, and the lot, too, as well as the equipment, press, type, the whole nine yards."

"That's standard, isn't it? I mean, if a business is on the market and the bank may carry a loan on it, they would need to know what things are worth."

"Bloodsuckers." Mother didn't like bankers.

"They're just conservative, Mom."

"You didn't live through the Depression!"

"Hear! Hear!" Mr. Pierre agreed.

Even Kim Spangler, washing hair in the back, called out from behind the curtain. "You tell her. I remember too."

"It's standard operating procedure. There's nothing wrong with Foster doing his due diligence," I said.

"Mrs. A. says you don't have a snowball's chance in hell. You have few assets except what's in your head. You're a woman perilously close to middle age, and furthermore, you're a lesbian. Her very words." Mr. Pierre's eyes darted dangerously.

"Did she say that?" Mother stabbed out her cigarette. "I'll give her a piece of my mind. And today, too, that stuck-up bitch."

"Mom, don't you dare. That would really put an end to the loan." I turned to Mr. Pierre. "In those words?"

"Close to it."

"Damn, I hate everyone knowing my business."

"Get out of Runnymede then." Mr. Pierre's voice was far more kind than the statement.

"But financial stuff. The sex bullroar I can take but she can't be blabbing about my finances. It's unethical."

"If we picked our friends on ethics, who'd be left?" Georgette called out from the reception desk.

Funny, Georgette was so quiet I made the mistake of thinking she wasn't very smart. I was revising my opinion.

I sighed and collected myself. "Let's keep this to ourselves. If she wants to run her mouth we can't stop her and maybe she'll make Foster so damned mad he'll approve the loan to spite her."

"I told you your problem is in Baltimore." Mother's eyes looked at mine from the mirror.

"Let's take it a step at a time."

Mr. Pierre put his arm around my shoulder. "I took revenge. Attack a Friend of Bertha's and you attack me, *n'est-ce pas?* I gave her hair a poisonous rinse. Her change-of-life red has a definite greenish cast to it."

"Bless you." I laughed and kissed him.

I no sooner got through the door of the *Clarion* than Michelle leapt at my desk. "Well?"

"Check my changes. I think we can run it."

She leaned over me. Lolly lifted her head to observe this. Lolly didn't like people getting too close. "I have this terrific idea for our Sunday supplement."

"Shoot."

Just then, a lumbering compositor—one of the guys who compose the page form, which is almost solid lead—moved through the front office. He winked at Michelle and made her blush. "Nick!" he called at me.

"Yes, Hans."

"Tell Arnie if you see him that I'm taking an early lunch." He winked at Michelle again and pushed open the front door.

Her face was red. "He makes me nervous."

"He likes you."

She blushed again. "I'm not used to working-class men."

"Hans?" I'd never once thought of the typesetters, the compositors, the proofreaders, and that back-room gang as working-class people. They were the muscle of the *Clarion* family, kind of like stokers in a battleship. "Hans is Hans. Now what's your idea?"

"I want to do an article that's different. What if each of us were to write a letter to ourselves as children?"

"I don't get it."

"You write a letter to yourself at five or eight or whatever."

"That's a little too vague for me."

"You put down every idea I have that is psychological!" Her lower lip jutted out.

"I guess I do." I didn't want to be nasty. "To me, it's not news. It doesn't even belong in the living section."

"You're wrong. The Lifestyles section generates a lot of reader interest with self-help psychology."

"Okay, Michelle, bring me a better idea and I'll consider it."

"I have a piece about the bombing of the synagogue after the Rosenberg trials."

"That's not current news."

"You can put it in as a history piece, a remembering. Passover is April fourteenth. Run it then."

"Let me see it."

She smacked the pages in front of me, then hovered.

"Michelle, let me read in peace."

When Michelle arrived at the *Clarion,* she'd displayed a breathtaking willingness to turn guesswork into fact. You've got to get eyewitness reports. You've got to go to the original documents. You've got to spend hours, wear and tear on your car engine, and wear and tear on your feet to get those facts. There's no shortcut. She'd done her homework on this piece. I knocked out a few florid sentences, but otherwise it was clean.

I put it on her desk. "Not bad."

"You'll run it?"

"Unless Charles has an objection, yes."

Michelle smiled from ear to ear and didn't bug me the rest of the day.

Louise planned her grand entrance to bingo. She arrived ferociously rouged. As Ed was her escort, she wanted to make sure everyone would notice. Mother knew that. Poor Louise. She thought she was going to be the center of attention, and once again her younger sister held the trump card.

When she saw Mom she screeched, "What have you done?"

"You like it?" Mother patted her silver-white curls.

"My finest creation." Mr. Pierre framed Mom's head with his hands.

Over her ears, sweeping back like graceful wings, were two streaks of violent magenta. I'd had time to adjust to it. I'd picked Mother up at her home. Once I recovered from the shock I liked it. As every person entered the bingo hall they reacted either pro or con.

"You look like Madonna." Louise's spite illuminated her face.

"I don't know what Madonna's got that I haven't, only I've had it longer."

Ed Tutweiler Walters laughed. This further inflamed Louise but since Ed sat down next to Julia, my aunt had no choice but to sit on the other side of him and make the best of it. The BonBons minus Thacker clogged the remainder of our table.

"Where's Goodyear?" Aunt Wheeze bent and searched under the table. I could hear the thump of Lolly's tail.

"He wasn't up for bingo tonight," Mother replied.

This was a bald lie. The wretched animal bawled his head off when we pulled out of the driveway but Mother was firm. Ed hadn't seen Goodyear's trick yet and she figured he'd call Louise "Louise." Damned if she was going to have her show ruined. An extra

Milk-Bone did not take the sting away for Goodyear as he witnessed Lolly and Pewter get into the car.

Mutzi called out, "Inside picture frame. Now you remember, you must complete a square around your free space. Exactly like a picture frame. Okay, here we go." He reached into the bouncing Ping-Pong balls. "Number seventy-one, let's have some fun."

"I am. How about you?" Mother turned to Ed.

"Yeah. Never a dull moment in this town." His voice, a light baritone, suited his person.

I was sitting opposite this volatile threesome. I didn't want to miss anything. Also, I wanted to be able to run if necessary. Mr. Pierre sat next to me.

"Forty-seven. Forty-seven. If I were forty-seven I'd be in heaven," Mutzi sang out and the older members of our bingo crew laughed.

"Where were you when you were forty-seven, Mr. Walters?" Mother's teeth gleamed in the light.

"Birmingham, Julia. Don't be dense. You know he's from Birmingham." Louise tried to cut her off at the pass.

"Yes, I know that but I was thinking he might say that he just turned forty-seven." That was laying it on a little thick.

"Bless you, Mrs. Smith, and please call me Ed."

"And you'll call me Juts, of course."

"Give it a little time, Ed, and you'll call her plenty else," Louise dug.

"I hope so." Mother glowed.

No matter how many times I watched my Mother cast her net over a man she found attractive, it fascinated me. Sometimes I thought it was the mongoose and the cobra. Other times I thought it was her wacky humor. You never knew what Julia would do or say. I'd known her from the cradle and I still couldn't tell you which way she'd cut. The hair, for instance. She fooled me with the magenta streaks.

Mr. Pierre was on my wavelength. He whispered to me: "There goes another one."

"What'd you say?" Louise's eyebrows came to a point over her nose.

"That I wished I were in Geneva tonight." Mr. Pierre dabbed number seventeen, which Mutzi called out. "Finally! I've been sitting here with a nude card."

"What's in Geneva?" Wheezie asked.

"They are auctioning off the Duchess of Windsor's jewelry," Mr. Pierre answered.

"Were you going to buy something for me?" Louise was the coquette.

"No, I thought I'd wear it myself. Just a simple tiara with diamond drop earrings." Mr. Pierre's eyes danced.

Ed started to laugh. A shadow of fear raced across Louise's face. She was sitting opposite two queers. What would Ed think?

"We nourish our eccentrics. Sometime I must tell you about Celeste Chalfonte, who died on Nickel's birthday, November twenty-eighth." Mother dabbed a number.

"He doesn't want to hear about Celeste." Louise was close to an inside picture frame.

"Oh, I'd like to know everything about you two beautiful ladies and about Runnymede too," Ed gallantly offered.

"We operate on the principle that boredom corrupts," I piped up.

"Number twenty-three for thee-e and me-e-e." Mutzi was singing again and smacking at Pewter, who was fishing in the glass cage because he took the top off.

I continued, "See, people think that drugs are the sorrow of America, or drink, or . . . well, take your pick."

"Where do I start?" Ed smiled at me. I was beginning to like him.

"I think people get into trouble when they're bored. The mind needs problems and puzzles and issues. If someone lets his mind go, he'll get into trouble." I noticed Mother's bosoms seemed a bit large. I'd noticed that when I picked her up but then I thought it might be the cut of her dress. Now upon further study I decided it wasn't just illusion. They were bigger.

"We are never bored in Runnymede." Mr. Pierre picked up the conversation. "Although I'm not sure our stimulation, as Nickel would wish, is intellectual. Sometimes our stimulation is pure D spite." He was skating close to the edge.

"We have our fair share of that in Birmingham."

"Bingo!" Louise's hand shot up.

The sullen Peepbean, Mutzi's lieutenant, came over and counted Louise's numbers. "A winner."

"Goody, goody. What do I get?"

"Twenty-five dollars." Mutzi rang a big cowbell. "Nickel."

"What?"

"Get Pewter."

"How come you've got the top off the ball machine?"

"Because the feed isn't working right so I've got to reach in and get the balls."

"All right." I picked up Pewter, who grumbled furiously.

"This'll shut her up." Verna brought out some baloney. Pewter accepted this.

Decca, the smallest BonBon, watched the cat eat the baloney and then tried to eat her own sandwich without hands. Verna gave her a light smack. "No fressen."

In Runnymede, "fressen" meant to eat like an animal. Maybe it meant that in other parts of the country, too, but I'd never heard the word in my travels. Decca knew what it meant because she stopped. Georgette, next to her youngest sister, young enough to be her own child, wiped Decca's mouth with a napkin.

Mother pulled out another bingo card. "Ed, one time when Nickel was a little girl she behaved very badly. She still behaves badly but I can't do anything about it now. I told her she was a little animal and I put her food in the dog bowl and made her eat it on the floor just like a dog. She didn't give me any trouble for a few weeks after that."

I laughed. "Mr. Walters, she was a witchy mother."

"You turned out all right," Ed complimented me.

"You don't know the half of it." Louise was really working on my mood.

Mutzi raised his hands. "Okay, we're doing a regular game of bingo. Regular game. And I want you to know that if we keep doing as well as we've been doing, we can play blackout bingo in a couple of weeks."

"This sounds like fun." Mr. Pierre brought back drinks from the bar for everyone.

"Now pay attention. We're putting up a sample on the board here. Peepbean!"

"Huh?" Peepbean hadn't been paying attention.

Mutzi said in a nice voice, "Put up the blackout sheet."

"Oh."

The blackout sheet was a special four cards printed on one sheet of paper. You paid for four cards. A regular bingo card cost one or two dollars depending on the game but the blackout sheet was going to cost us eight dollars. The pot would depend on how many people showed up. The limit was one blackout sheet to a player per blackout game. This differed sharply from our regular games where you could play as many cards as you wanted. Verna built herself a little shelf to hold her cards upright so she could keep track of them and she could play up to ten at a time. Mutzi kept explaining to us that *all* twenty-five numbers on one of the cards had to be blacked out, or called. The pot was also determined by how many numbers it took to get the blackout. So if fewer than fifty-five numbers were called, the pot would be pretty big, a couple thousand dollars on a big weekend. If more than fifty-five numbers were called, the pot was reduced.

Half the proceeds of every pot went to Saint Rose of Lima. Without the income the church couldn't have continued its Meals on Wheels for the shut-ins and elderly. And the church was in constant need of renovation. The first part of Saint Rose's had been built in 1680. The only church older was Christ Lutheran Church on Emmitsburg Pike right off the Square. As the Germans came here first, they built a church before anyone else. The cornerstone was laid in 1662. Saint Paul's Episcopal, catty-cornered from Saint Rose's, wasn't established until 1707. They made up for being Johnny-come-lately by being richer than the rest of us. The Chalfontes, Rifes, and Yosts endowed Saint Paul's. Bingo endowed Saint Rose's. Christ Lutheran missed the boat and kept mounting funding drives which exhausted its membership, of which I was one. We'd have been better off with gambling. I was in favor of craps myself, but the pastor frowned upon my idea. Actually, the pastor frowned upon me. I tried not to let it interfere with my sporadic attendance.

"Peepbean will pass out blackout sheets so you can study them at home and get the idea. We'll have a dry run in a couple of weeks and see how we do." Mutzi cranked up the Ping-Pong ball machine again.

"Do you get it?" Mr. Pierre inquired of me.

"Kind of."

Louise was turning puce-faced as Mother wove her web around Ed. Bingo couldn't end soon enough for me. I wanted no part of a fight tonight. I was exhausted. The *Clarion* sale preyed on my mind more than I realized. When Mutzi banged the cowbell to close the evening I could feel the tension ebb out between my shoulder blades. We'd made it. Mr. Pierre seemed relieved too.

Mother invited me in for a late-night snack. That meant a hot fudge sundae with pretzels. I can't eat late at night or I have nightmares, but I came in anyway and watched her devour a monstrous sundae. I had a cup of Sleepytime tea while an ecstatic Goodyear played with Lolly. Pewter ignored the dogs.

"He'll call me before Wednesday. Want to bet on it?"

"I'm not betting with you, Mom."

"Where's your sporting blood?"

"Any woman who's trying to buy a newspaper and makes twenty-four thousand dollars a year has sporting blood."

"Mmm." She licked the last heaping mound of fudge off her spoon. "Whenever I have religious doubts I remember the hot fudge sundae." She leaned back in her chair. "There's something I want to get off my chest." She reached in her bra, pulled out her falsies, and threw them on the floor. She whooped with laughter. So did I.

"I thought you looked packed."

"I want Ed Tutweiler Walters to ask me out. Better a girl has tits than brains, because boys see better than they think."

11

LOUISE MUSCLES NICKEL

SATURDAY . . . 4 APRIL

Bright but cool, the morning invigorated me. I was awake at six-thirty, fed the animals, and endured a fit of home improvement. I painted the kickboards on my stairwell white. Sometime during World War I the stairs themselves had been painted sky-blue by Cora. I kept them sky-blue. Then I really lost my head and painted the baseboards and quarter-rounds in the kitchen. By now it was nine A.M. and I figured I'd buzz by the *Clarion* before going to the stable. Roger Davis had weekend duty this week and I thought I'd pop in and see if he needed any help.

It turned out he didn't but I did. When I got to the *Clarion* office Roger was embroiled in a huge discussion about the Homearama ad placed by one of our odious local developers. This commercial worthy paid for an Easter insert. The layout, color, and copy were terrific. What Nils Nordness wanted now were little Easter bunnies on the corners of the pages. I winked at Roger and he winked back.

Bucky Nordness, Nils's brother, sauntered through the door. Bucky, North Runnymede's chief of police, painted little cars on his fender—like notches on a gun. This was Bucky's idea of humor. His other peculiarity was that he was much given to conspiracy theories.

"Just the woman I wanted to see."

"Hello, Bucky. What can we do for you?"

"I'm investigating a weapons incident of March twenty-seventh. That's Friday a week ago at Saint Rose of Lima's."

"Someone steal the collection plate?" I hadn't heard about it.

"I have it from a reliable source that Mutzi Elliott threatened your mother and aunt with a thirty-eight."

"Oh, that." I'd completely forgotten. "Bucky, he didn't really brandish the gun. He only displayed it."

"I've warned him before about that thing."

"Mutzi has a permit. He's very responsible. Besides that, he was a marksman in the Korean War, so he knows what he's doing."

"He shouldn't oughta have it." Bucky shifted his weight. "I know he's got a permit but the way you all carry on over there, someone's liable to get hurt."

"Have you talked to Mutzi?"

"Yes, I have. He was not cooperative."

"Sorry to hear that." Actually, I was thrilled to hear it. Mutzi probably wanted to wrap a string tie around Bucky's neck and slide the clasp up until his eyes bugged out.

"The pots are getting larger and we're going to have a giant one for blackout bingo. It's not such a bad idea for Mutzi to be armed."

This didn't go down well with Bucky. After giving me a lecture on the use of firearms and what might happen if they fell into the wrong hands, he wanted to know about blackout bingo. I told him what I could. He allowed as how he'd better be there for that game and I, lying, said that was a wonderful idea. Why, he might even win. Then I tactfully suggested that he drop his inquiry lest Saint Rose of Lima's suffer undue embarrassment. He grunted and went over to Nils. I left for the stables. Regina wasn't there, so I drove over to the club.

The club's proper name is South Runnymede Tennis and Racquet Club. There aren't enough people here with money to pay for a golf course but we have a lively group of tennis, squash, and platform-tennis players. The real country club, Willow Bend, is north of town. They've got a beautiful eighteen-hole golf course, an Olympic-size pool, and composition tennis courts. However, we've got true red clay courts—twelve—and two grass courts, so people who care for the old game come to South Runnymede Tennis and Racquet. We've also got two outdoor and four indoor squash courts. Indoor squash and fox-hunting keep us sane in the winters, which seem to be getting worse or else I'm minding them more.

Each clay court is divided from every other court by lovely boxwoods. Every court is also fenced, and great tubs of geraniums and petunias blossom during the summer. The little clubhouse, a cottage really, contains bathrooms, a Coke machine, and a pro shop. Adirondack chairs with cushions dot the outside of the court areas and the grass courts have bleachers surrounding them. Court one, of the clay courts, also has bleachers. Because of the grass courts, fine players from Maryland and Pennsylvania make their way to South Runnymede T & R. During the peak of the season, competition can be fierce, with Jackson usually triumphant, especially on grass.

South Runnymede High practices at T & R. I was captain of the team my junior and senior years in high school, and occasionally when a coach cannot be found within the school, I am pressed into service. North Runnymede High, called The Other Runnymede High by us, practices at Willow Bend, which means they can't do jack shit on clay. We contrive to play them at T & R but last year the heads of the athletic department put their empty heads together and decided to rotate the matches. Since The Other Runnymede High, colors blue and white, is in another state, these matches are off the books. We do it with football, baseball, basketball, every sport. It's important to win state in your division but victory means we beat North Runnymede. When I was captain we not only beat them, we annihilated them. How could we lose? Regina and I were number one doubles, I was one singles, she was two. Ursie was three singles and she would have played one at any other school. So it went. Regina and I will occasionally wear our black letter sweaters with our orange "R" in the center to matches against Lodi Spangler and Frances Finster, the reigning queens over at Willow Bend and before that at North Runnymede.

Many times I would find myself lingering at the club or driving by at sunrise. Perhaps that was because it never changed, while we changed constantly even if we didn't know it. Or maybe some of us changed and others stayed the same. I was never quite sure, because a person can change inside and if there is no external manifestation, how would I know? Perhaps it was enough that I was changing. I was beginning to measure my life, because now I knew there was an end point to it and I didn't want to waste my time. As Charles Falkenroth was ready to retire (even though I still didn't believe it), I was getting ready for more responsibility, for more power in my community. I liked the feeling.

Regina and I finished three sets. We were both terrible, as it was the first time we'd hit since November. As we walked back to the clubhouse I heard a familiar screech. Aunt Wheeze shot up the hill, caromed into the parking lot, and nearly sideswiped Diz Rife's Aston-Martin Volante. He must have driven in while Regina and I were playing. Normally discreet when it came to his millions, Diz lost his restraint with cars. Louise slammed the door of her Chrysler and inspected the Volante.

"Aunt Wheeze, what are you doing here?"

Regina whispered in my ear: "I'm going in for a Coke. See you later."

Louise continued to examine the car. "I like this. I could drive this and be happy."

"For one hundred and forty thousand dollars you should be very happy."

Her curiosity changed to reverence. "That's worth more than my house!"

"Mine too."

"I want to talk to you."

We sat on a bench on one side of a clay court. Behind me I could hear hitting, grunting, and the familiar sound of tennis shoes sliding on clay.

Aunt Louise wasted no time. "I don't want you saying anything to Ed Tutweiler Walters about your carryings-on with women."

If only I had someone to carry on with. If only I had done everything I was accused of doing!

"I'm not going to bring up the subject, Aunt Wheeze. But I'm sure one of the multitudinous BonBons has told him."

"Verna wouldn't talk about something like that."

"Someone will."

"Well, I don't want it to be you." Her voice rose. "This was a respectable family until you came into it."

"You, of course, walk on water." I knew she was an old lady but sometimes Wheezie could get my goat.

"That's another thing. I overheard you making fun of the Pope's bull about Mary. I'll thank you to keep your opinions to yourself. You aren't Catholic and you don't know what Mary means."

"I do know what Mary means. I read the encyclical when it came over the wire. John Paul referred to her as the 'common mother,' he reinforced the concept of the immaculate conception and the virgin birth, and he stated that when Mary died she was taken up into heaven so her body wouldn't be committed to earth. I also know it was another way to keep women from being ordained."

Louise cast a cold stare. "You're sacrilegious."

"Why? Just because I happen to think Jews invented guilt and Christians refined it?"

"Are you telling me you don't believe in Jesus?" Her lips compressed.

"No. I never said that."

"Good. These are craven times."

"Yeah, well, Americans want a Jesus who doesn't suffer, much less die. He should have bright white teeth, smile a lot, and say, 'Go for it.' Also, he shouldn't look Jewish."

This stopped her for a moment. "You are sacrilegious." She took a new tack. "And I don't appreciate you talking my impressionable sister into that ridiculous hairdo. Purple hair!"

"Magenta."

"Never heard of that color."

"Like a deep, hot purple-pink."

"Oh." Wheeze crossed her legs. She was wearing support hose today. "I don't care what you call it. You stop putting her up to things. She's too old for that stuff."

"She's not too old for anything. And you know as well as I do that no one on this earth can talk Julia Ellen Hunsenmeir into anything."

"You always take her part!"

"She's my mother. What do you expect?"

"She raised you. She's not your mother."

"She's the only mother I've ever known."

"Well, sometimes I wish we could find the real one so she could take you back! Now I don't want you ruining my romance, you hear me?"

"I'm not saying anything about anything."

She stood up to leave. "Don't forget my column either. If you get the paper."

"What did you want to call it?"

"Golden Memories. Silver Thoughts."

"I thought you were going to write a column of social embarrassments called 'Was My Face Red.' "

"I want to do something with class," she replied.

"You?"

"You're such a smartypants. Since you were tiny." With that parting shot she walked over to her car, got in, and once again endangered the citizens of our fair town. Even mad she was a lady. She wouldn't call me a smartass.

I sat there feeling as if my psychological carburetor needed repair. I didn't notice Diz until he sat down on the bench next to me. He was wearing a Fila warm-up suit. In cold weather I played in gray sweat pants and sweat shirt. Those fancy suits like Fila and Ellesse cost two hundred to three hundred dollars. I can eat for a month on that.

Diz twirled his racquet.

"Nice warm-up," I said.

"Thanks. Bought it in New York. Nice sweat suit." Diz smiled. "I think it's the same one you wore in high school."

"A descendant." I laughed.

"Don't you ever get tired of it?" His voice lowered.

"Of my sweat suit?"

"Of Louise, of Juts, of everyone reminding you—"

"Oh, that. Goes in one ear and out the other. Anyway, I remind myself that Moses was found in the bullrushes. I think I was just found in the bull."

Diz laughed. "Don't go on any mountaintops."

"I promise. How's your game?"

"Getting better. Yours?"

"Rusty."

"I couldn't help overhearing. I was in the next court. I hope you don't think I'm rude," he apologized, returning to our former subject.

"Actually, I can't recall one time that you have ever been rude, even when you were a boy."

"I must be doing something wrong."

Since he was being honest with me, I thought I'd be honest with him. "You've always been under scrutiny, under pressure. Thank God you do have impeccable manners."

"Got to make up for my bandit ancestors. You don't know how lucky you are, Nickel, not knowing your people."

"Yeah, you might be right."

"Did it ever occur to you that we're the two most misunderstood people in Runnymede?"

NICKEL MAKES A PROMISE TO MR. PIERRE

SUNDAY . . . 5 APRIL

"What'd you say?" Mr. Pierre was breathless with anticipation.

" 'No. I never thought of that.' That's what I said."

Having finished my story about Louise, Diz, and tennis, I grabbed another *crème caramel*. Tea with Mr. Pierre sent shivers of delight down my spine. Cooking was his third-favorite pastime, after gossip and decorating.

This Sunday afternoon, cozily protected from the drizzle, the two of us chatted. Lolly and Pewter slept at our feet. Usually tea meant the gang at the Curl 'n Twirl plus whomever else Mr. Pierre found amusing that week. He kept a hit list and a shit list. Once even I plummeted to his shit list, barred from tea for a month. I remember it well because I'd come home from my first semester at college and used "fucking" in every other sentence. The praise word was "far-fucking out." Mr. Pierre steamed with indignation. Mother refused to talk to me but he tore into me. First he said it was plain rude. Second, he said it bespoke a paucity of imagination. The English language contains the largest word pool in the world. If a person can't find the correct word, then that person is a dolt, lazy, and not fit for society. One should seek to be amusing in one's speech and if one cannot be amusing—after all, not everyone is entertaining—then one can at least be accurate. Further, he blasted me about invoking a word for the sex act which cheapened the user *and* the sex act. By the time he was finished I agreed with him but I was eighteen and refused to give in. I defiantly stalked out. I soon altered my ridiculous posture. Living without tea and Mr. Pierre was like being banished to Siberia.

We oohed and aahed about the jewelry sale wire story which I brought over. Mr. Pierre loved the AP printouts. At the auction, one ring of the Duchess of Windsor's, a thirty-one carat diamond, was bought by a Japanese dealer for $3.15 million.

"I desperately wanted her flamingo pin," he sighed. "Flamingoes are in this year."

"Oh, God, don't camp it up in front of Ed when we're at bingo."

"Louise can't tell me what to do. I'm not her niece. *Jamais!* Never. And if he can't tolerate an old queen, he's not worth knowing. She's getting potty about this so-called romance. I think that spending time with Ed Tutweiler W. is a form of sensory deprivation, that's what I think."

"He's the strong silent type."

"Puleeze. Why does being a man mean not communicating?"

"Maybe he's shy. What would you do if you were caught between Julia and Louise?"

"Run!" He poured more tea.

The steam curled upward while the logs settled in his art deco fireplace. I felt happy in this house. Upon reflection I realize that I felt loved. He loved me for me, not for services rendered.

"But then, you're between them every day."

"Honey, I'm just one of the girls. They're not going to snatch one another bald over me."

"If they do, it will be a bad advertisement for the Curl 'n Twirl."

"Why do you think I'm forever mediating their spats? My business depends upon it." He laughed and picked out a wicked, tiny toffee cake, bitter chocolate over toffee over a graham-cracker crust. Biting into it, he moaned with pleasure. "Since Bob's gone, my pleasures have been oral. I must go on a diet. Nickel, you heard it here first. Tomorrow."

"Let tomorrow take care of itself." I reached for one too.

"Darling, I've been meaning to tell you, but I haven't had any time, that there's a lady in town who finds you smashing. Yes, that's the word—smashing."

"Go on."

"Don't believe me?"

"Is she under seventy?"

"Yes."

"Who? Don't make me guess."

"It's more fun if you do."

"Come on."

"Regina Frost." A flicker played on his lips.

"I don't believe it. She's like my sister."

"Truly?"

"Yes."

"Then you're a beastly little shit, Nickel." He said this without rancor.

"Why? What did I do now?"

He played with his teacup. "I wanted to hear what you'd say about Regina. I'm very fond of her. She's a lovely girl, lovely, except for that glaring eye shadow, and she adores you. Absolutely adores you."

"Not sexually."

"No, but as I said, I wanted to hear your response to her."

"Why?" I thought this most peculiar.

"Because you're sleeping with her husband."

I'm a useless liar. No point even trying. "Does anyone else know?"

"What kind of answer is that? No, I'm the only one who knows. Let's just say some nights I've worked late or taken a midnight stroll, and I put two and two together. You're safe, for now."

I exhaled audibly.

"It's wrong," he continued.

"I know." The words rolled out of me. "I do know and I hate it but I . . . I don't know. He makes me happy."

"He's the husband of your best friend."

I astonished myself. I started to cry. Mr. Pierre got up out of his chair and sat next to me on the love seat. He put his arms around me.

"Oh, Mr. Pierre, I feel awful."

"I know. You're alone. You've been alone for a long time. But this is not right. This isn't the way."

"I'd die if Regina found out."

"True. She might kill you." He hugged me. "People make mistakes. I myself made such a mistake. That's why I'm beseeching you to end the relationship before more harm is done. Everyone gets hurt in a situation like this."

Once I collected myself I promised Mr. Pierre that I would make a clean break with Jackson. Driving home, I told myself it wouldn't be so bad. Desire would become a memory. After all, I wasn't going to be ruled by my hormones.

13

HIGH FASHION COMES TO THE *CLARION*

MONDAY . . . 6 APRIL

Baseball season opened today. Roger Davis turned in a good piece about Jack Kemp declaring his candidacy for President on the Republican ticket, and Michelle was finishing a snappy follow-up piece on the closing of the Peach Bottom nuclear plant.

The Nuclear Regulatory Commission shut down the plant on March 31 because operators were found sleeping at the controls. Peach Bottom is in Delta, Pennsylvania, safely far away from the northern side of Runnymede. However, when Three Mile Island cooked, Runnymede found itself in the third zone of danger. Since then our readership has wanted to know everything about nuclear plants.

Tonight was the much-ballyhooed Hagler versus Leonard fight. Charles decided to do a column on that himself once he knew the outcome.

Hectic, harried and hurried, this Monday ran true to form. David Wheeler, our sheriff, rolled in and wanted to know if Bucky Nordness was the biggest douche bag in Runnymede. I said I didn't know about that but he was having a running fit about Mutzi and the .38. I suggested that David come to bingo on the blackout night. As yet we didn't have a date but I promised to tell him the minute I knew.

Then I got a brainstorm and assigned the blackout bingo story to Michelle.

"Bingo? You want me to write a color piece on bingo?"

"Yes. I expect the blackout game will be a few weeks off, so you have plenty of time to learn the rules."

"You give Roger an assignment on the Republican race, and me bingo. That's sexist." Her painted fingernails, misty mauve, drummed the corner of my desk.

"I also gave you the Peach Bottom job and that's hard news."

"I don't want fluff pieces."

"Goddammit, this is a small paper and you'll take what I give you. Last summer I covered a brush fire near Emmitsburg. You're no better than I am!" As I didn't usually get edgy, heads turned.

"All right, all right, but I never heard of anything so low-rent and boring as bingo."

"I happen to go every Friday night. Do you find me low-rent and boring?" This surprised her and she hesitated. I pressed on. "Taking the fifth? Fine, but I promise you this, blackout bingo isn't going to be boring. It will be the fattest prize money anyone has ever seen here and"—I paused—"you might even enjoy it. Now get out of my face."

Michelle, sensitive when it came to herself, withered away. I opened my desk drawer, picked up Isaac's cherished cigar, had half a mind to smoke it, and put it back. Fate wasn't with me. Portia Rife, breathing New York sophistication and flair, swung open the door. Under her arm rested her portfolio, her huge portfolio. She cheerily smashed it on my desk, making Pewter jump. I shrank under the glare of her fierce insincerity.

"Nicole, precious, it's been eons." Portia had the effrontery to kiss both my cheeks.

"How nice to see you," I flatly fibbed. "How is life north of Forty-second Street?"

Portia's childhood heroine was Marilyn Monroe. She spoke with a breathy quality that drove me bats. Maybe men like it. She also leaned over me, and as her bosoms were well developed, I was in danger of losing an eye. "What a joy to know someone in Runnymede who's cosmopolitan."

Ha. The last thing I was, was cosmopolitan. I was a Maryland small-town hick, albeit a well-educated one.

"You flatter me."

Damn right she was flattering me. She wanted her photographs in the Lifestyle section. In the bad old days it was called the Women's Pages. I liked that term better. These days it was all style and no life.

Portia flipped open the black portfolio. An array of fuzzy photos greeted me. On some she had superimposed geometric drawings, triangles, trapezoids, in Day-Glo colors. This was high-fashion stuff. I considered giving her an assignment in Nicaragua. And here is a high-fashion corpse and over there is a darling machine gun. I kept my thoughts to myself as she breathed in my right ear. I was certain condensation was forming in there, and if not condensation, then condescension.

Charles hung up the phone and stood up in his office, imploring me with his eyes. The Rifes' various industries were steady, fat advertisers.

In the middle of an aria about low bodices and high hemlines I capitulated. "Portia, might you leave me these?" I picked out four. "I think the others are very"—I searched—"outré and daring, but you know, sugar, Runnymede is pink and green and Pappagallo."

Portia stuck her finger in her mouth and mimicked a gag. Michelle's face registered her feelings. I'd forgotten that Michelle was the preppy queen of the *Clarion*. Even though she'd pissed me off, sniffing at bingo, I felt bad. Portia never noticed, but then, other people's feelings were not high on Portia's list of priorities.

I carefully slid out the least-offensive photographs. "I'll send you tear sheets."

"You're terrific, Nick." More kisses on the cheek and then she tactfully left us in a cloud of Giorgio, a perfume of suffocating intensity.

Charles sauntered over. He held up the photos. "Give this to Michelle?" he wondered.

"No, I just assigned her blackout bingo."

Michelle pitched a verbal horseshoe at my head. "Yes, and I'll wear pink and green and even my Pappagallos."

"Oh, Michelle, can't you take a joke?"

"You meant it."

"Well . . ." I waffled, then took charge. "Charles, let me do the fashion piece. I'll make the Rifes happy."

"Whatever you say." He returned to his office and shut the door.

Michelle glowered while Roger fought to keep from laughing. He put his feet on his desk, too, so we'd notice his shoes, very sensible ones with thick rubber soles—glamorous combat boots.

The phone rang. Mother. "Guess what?"

"Elizabeth the Second of England called to chew the rag."

Mother's voice deepened. "That kind of day?"

"Umm."

"Get over it! Now listen to my news. Ed asked me out! You owe me a hot fudge sundae."

"No, I don't. I didn't take the bet, remember? You were eating a hot fudge sundae when you wanted to make it."

"Oh." She sounded so disappointed.

"Hey, want to meet me at Mojo's for a hot fudge sundae?"

"Whoopee." She hung up the phone. She'd put on her lipstick. Throw on her coat. Within five minutes she'd be around the corner at Mojo's.

"Michelle, hold the fort. I'm meeting my mother. Be at Mojo's if you want me."

"I don't want you," she half-snarled.

"No, but we might need you." Roger beamed.

"Come on, Pewter." She jumped into my arms. "You, too, Lolly."

I left the *Clarion* for Mojo's with my little family. I even remembered to bring Mother the Orioles' schedule we'd printed up on heavy paper. Mom turned onto Frederick Road from the opposite direction. Lolly surged forward to greet her and Goodyear. I did too. My spirits were lifting.

I was happy that Mother got her date and I was happy to see her. When the rest of the world faded to black-and-white, Julia remained in Technicolor.

NICKEL BREAKS HER PROMISE

TUESDAY . . . 7 APRIL

Ray Leonard won the middleweight fight. Charles swooned in his column.

Michelle showed up for work in black Reeboks and jeans. Wisely, I said nothing.

Mother called three times asking me what to wear for her date tomorrow. On the third try she hung up the phone saying, "Why am I asking you? You don't know anything about clothes, anyway." As I was scrambling for copy to match Portia's photographs, I agreed with her. Why were rich women in New York and Los Angeles spending a fortune to look like migrant workers? Obviously, I was ignorant about fashion. From the evidence I wanted to keep it that way.

John Hoffman read the wire stories on the Iran-Contra affair. Conservative though he was, he did not believe in public officials' violating the law. If you can't obey the law, then resign your post and work from the outside to change it. I knew his editorial would be a zinger because he was pounding on his IBM like a concert pianist.

Roger leafed through magazines for tidbits. The *Clarion* would stick pieces of information and funny stories in the odd spaces. Our layout, old-fashioned but quite beautiful, would mark these off with a graceful device, a thin black line with a slender ellipse in the middle of it.

"We ought to run an article on breast-feeding." Roger held up the article so I could see the photos.

"No," I replied.

"Why not?" Michelle wanted to know.

"Because breast-feeding is greatly overrated unless you're over twenty-one." I couldn't resist.

Roger whooped.

Michelle blushed crimson.

John stopped flailing away at his typewriter and smiled at me. "At least we have that in common."

I laughed. John, like so many men, probably entertained lesbian fantasies. He shivered with delight on those occasions when I'd say something outrageous. I myself didn't think it was a big deal, but then I've never thought sex was anything worth getting exercised about. Live and let live.

My phone rang or I would have thought of something else to torment him. "Hello."

"What's so funny?" It was Aunt Wheeze and she could hear the laughter in the background.

"Nothing much. What can I do for you?"

"I ran into my sister. You know, the one who's suffering her second childhood or senility—take your pick. You'd think she was the only person in the world to have a date, and, Nickie, it's not like she's going out with him by herself. She's going to the movies with Ed Tutweiler Walters and various BonBons. Well, he only asked her so she wouldn't feel left out. After all, he knows how close I am to my sister and he could see how she was feeling. He's a very sensitive man. He knows all the lyrics to love songs and not just Cole Porter but country-and-western. He also studies religions. Like I said, he's very sensitive. I suggested we go together—the more the merrier, you know, that's my motto—and that sister of mine flew all over me like a wet hen. You have to do something with her and—"

I interrupted. "Aunt Wheezie, I'm at work and I've got a deadline. Why don't I stop by about six and you can tell me everything?"

"I'm on the flower committee at church and we have a meeting then. Let me tell you why I called."

At last.

She launched another verbal missile. "I'm sick and tired of Juts with her outlandish costumes and the hair. A woman her age should look dignified. I tell her but she goes out and buys more flaming-red lipstick. It goes up the cracks in her lip. Makes her look like an old bag. You don't see me wearing that color, do you?"

"Can you come to the point?"

"Rude! You are rude, crude, and unaffected."

"I've got a deadline."

"I'm driving over to the big shopping mall in Emmitsburg and if I don't find what I want I'm going up to York."

"No, you're not."

"You can't tell me what to do or how to do it. My 1952 Chrysler runs better than any car in this town. And I'm only on the second one for parts. The third one sits in my garage brand-new and I start it every day like Pearlie told me. I can go anywhere. I can go to California in my car."

"I thought you were afraid of earthquakes."

"I am. The entire state of California will fall into the Pacific Ocean."

"Don't worry about it. The fish will reject it. There will always be a California."

This stopped her for a moment. She recharged her batteries. "Well, I am going to the Emmitsburg Mall and I only called because I like someone to know where I am at all times. Just in case."

"You called me because you want me to take you to the mall."

"Would you?" Her voice dripped with honey.

"Yes." I was resigned. It wasn't just that I didn't want her to die on the way to the mall. Think of the innocent people she'd kill along the way.

"I can be ready in an hour."

"You can wait until Saturday. I have to work."

"Oh, I forgot about that. What time?"

"Pick you up at ten."

"Let's take my car. It rides better than that Jeep. Besides which I don't want to look like a field hand. Ladies don't drive Jeeps."

"We'll see, Aunt Louise. Bye now." I hung up. At least she respected my work.

"The last thing to die on your Aunt Louise will be her mouth." John's shoulders started to heave up and down. He laughed hardest at his own cracks.

"This is a rare day of agreement for us, John."

A pink glow on the Confederate statue turned to red, then mauve and finally purple. Sunset produces such a sadness in me. Deep down I wonder if I'll live to see the sun come up again. I have never taken life for granted. Today, as the staff left, one by one, bundling up, for the temperature was falling again, I watched them cross the

Square or walk around the corner. The changing light seemed to change them too. Their features became softer and as they walked away they reminded me of a tintype, of people frozen in time.

Daylight savings would be here in another week and then sunset would be pushed further and further back until June 21, a Midsummer's Night, my favorite day of the year.

By nine I was in Jackson's office. Pewter ran up and down his library shelves but she wasn't destructive. Lolly worried her rawhide chew and Jackson worried me.

"You've got to think the way they think."

"Jackson, I can't think like a banker. I can't sink that low."

"Very funny. I prepared your forms and financial statement. We've done the best we can do."

"What do you mean, exactly, when you say think like Foster Adams?"

"Don't personalize it."

"Okay, okay."

"When a banker examines a loan application, he or she has a checklist of items. They want the financial statements of the *Clarion*. They've got those so they can project income. They know that the circulation can be improved. But what they really think about is a worst-case scenario. What can they grab to support the debt if—"

"The *Clarion*'s been around since before the Revolutionary War. She's never going under."

"That's not their viewpoint."

"Well, what the hell do they want to know?"

"First and foremost, how will they be repaid. Can the collateral cover the debt if there's a fire sale."

"A fire sale! I don't like this, you know."

"You need to know what you're up against."

"Diz Rife. I think he'll outmaneuver the Thurston Group in the twinkling of an eye."

"We'll get to Diz later. Let's put ourselves in Foster Adams's shoes. He wants to support your application."

"He does?" I was happy.

"Yes, but he has to take it to Baltimore. He might need more collateral than you've got. He's got to sell you and the *Clarion* to people who don't even see small towns anymore. They fly, or drive on the Beltway."

"Figures are figures whether they know us or whether they don't."

"Right. That's why I'm providing you with this rundown. A bank will lend seventy-five to eighty percent of the current appraised value of property. You're in good shape there because the *Clarion* is prime real estate in a prime spot and your farm's good too. Where you run into difficulty is on the printing press. Usually a bank will lend fifty percent of book value on used equipment depending on the condition—"

I interrupted, which I rarely do. But I was excited. "Arnie Dow keeps that machine running. He loves that baby. It might as well be new."

"I don't doubt it, but Chesapeake and Potomac isn't going to see it that way. That equipment is both so specialized and so old that the bank won't lend you anything on it. Zero."

"Zero?" I was aghast.

He nodded his curly head. "I don't know if everything else we've got will cover it."

"Jack, are you serious? They'll not value the press at all? It's a beauty, that press. I mean, we do papers the old way, the real way, with lead and grease and—"

"I know, but from their viewpoint there is a limited resale market. It's worthless to them."

"Goddammit, what do they know about newspapers?"

"They know the industry's computerized now and that the *Clarion* could reduce its workforce by one third, easily one third, if it would go to cold type."

"I don't believe in putting people out of work just so you can have new machines."

He kicked off his shoes. "I don't either. I'm starting to agree with you about full employment versus constant technological replacement of people. I guess it's the spinning-jenny argument all over again." He sighed. "But there has to be a middle ground."

"Societally, yes. Where the *Clarion* is concerned, no. I'd die before I'd fire Arnie and the guys in the back room. So there's an easier way to print a paper. Is it more fun? Does it serve the community any better? What we've got is plenty good enough and as time goes by people can visit us the way they visit Williamsburg."

"No doubt they will." He took off my shoes and rubbed my feet. He sat on the sofa while I lay across him. "Have you any stocks or bonds or anything else of value you may have overlooked?"

"Pewter and Lolly."

"Worth their weight in rubies." He rubbed between my toes and on the ball of my foot. "Feel good?"

"Very relaxing."

"There's one other thing that the bank will examine. That's the integrity of the borrower. You're blue chip there, honey." He moved from my feet up my leg.

"What is there about massage that's so wonderful?"

"Depends on who's tickling your fancy." He kneaded my calves. "Hard from riding. Are you going out Saturday?"

"If I get back from Emmitsburg in time, I think I'll take a long, languid ride."

"Hey, while you're over there pick me up some polo shirts, the stone-washed kind."

I pulled my leg away. "Buy them yourself. I'm not your wife."

He laughed. "You could have been."

"Surely you jest." I put my leg back into his hands.

"No, I don't. I bounced between you and Gene like a pinball."

"This is historical revisionism on a par with Stalin erasing Trotsky's name from the history books. You liked me, Jackson. You always liked me, but when Regina fully flowered, shall we say, you went wild. You wanted to hump your parts raw."

"It wasn't like that at all."

"You were crazy about her. Well, who wouldn't be? Raging lust, that's how I remember you way back when."

"You make me sound pretty superficial."

"Weren't you? I was. Isn't that what being young is all about?" He smiled and kept rubbing. "You weren't as superficial as you make out and neither was I. You have to learn to forgive yourself for being ignorant. We were all terribly smart when we were in our twenties but we were ignorant."

I knew what he meant. "Maybe so. But I look back on the young me and I am embarrassed, if not mortified, sometimes."

"You make me feel young right now." He began rubbing my thigh.

"Bull. A man thinks he's only as old as the woman he's sleeping with, and I'm not but three years younger than you."

"Nick, do I ever get through to you? You keep me at arm's length. You do make me feel young. Why do you have to push me away when I say something like that? I have feelings. I'm not a block of wood, and contrary to what you and your women friends think, I'm in touch with my emotions and I'm willing to bet there are other men who are too."

I could feel the crimson on my cheeks. "Goddammit, I hate phrases like 'in touch with my emotions,' I hate the whole phony psychological claptrap of our times, and I really hate it from you. You have feelings. I'm glad. I have them myself but I have the good sense to keep them to myself."

"You wouldn't keep them to yourself if I were a woman. I thought about what you said last week. Remember? You twitted me about what if you woke up a male, what would I do? What if the metamorphosis worked on me? What if I woke up female? What would you do then?"

"It would be the same."

"No, it wouldn't. You'd take me seriously then."

"I take you seriously now and I'm guilty as hell."

"You don't think I'm not? But I can't help myself. I think about you all the time, Nickie. I want to be with you. Don't you ever think about me?"

"I do." I lowered my eyes. This wasn't going as I had hoped.

"Well, what do you think? Why don't you talk to me?" The little muscles around his jaw tightened.

"Does it make it any easier if I do? For me it only makes it harder. It's difficult enough to feel something. Having to talk about it only makes it more painful. Maybe talking about emotions releases them for some people—most of them on talk shows, I might add—but it sure doesn't do it for me. It makes them worse."

Jack smiled. "So our relationship is that painful." It was a sad smile.

"Yes." I breathed deeply. "How many times have I kissed you since we were children? Social kisses. Hi and goodbye. Glad to see you. Why was the kiss under the mistletoe at the hunt club Christmas party the kiss that did me in?"

"I felt it, too."

"Were you as surprised as I was?"

"Uh—probably not." Jack's smile was brighter. "I'd thought about you that way before. I don't think you focus much on romance or sex. Actually, Nickie, sometimes I think you clean forget about sex."

"Yeah, you're right, but I'm your favorite info-maniac."

"You never stop—maybe that's why I love you." He put his arms around me.

I hugged him in return. "You're right. Everything you say about me is right. My eye is on the target. I really do forget about the mush stuff but—you made me remember. Some day years from now I'll remember that Christmas party with fondness but right now, honey, it's hard. I'm torn. Do you know what I mean?"

"Yes. I know what you mean." He stroked my hair. "But I'm not sorry about what you call the mush stuff. I've complicated my life and I've complicated yours and I love my wife and—" he paused, "you make me feel wonderful. I'm not sorry."

I did feel sorry and I intended to tell him. I meant to break it off but he was so defenseless, or that's what I told myself. This wasn't the night. He was on my team. He did care about me and what happened to me and he wanted me to get the *Clarion* as much as I did. I needed him. I guess I needed him far more than I knew.

MR. PIERRE IS PISSED
AND URSIE PAYS A CALL

WEDNESDAY . . . 8 APRIL

The American Society of Newspaper Editors, meeting in San Francisco yesterday, elected its first woman president, Katherine Fanning, editor of *The Christian Science Monitor*. Happy though I was about this, I recalled that once, ten years ago, I'd written an editorial in which I indiscreetly made a reference to Mary Baker Eddy. I said she was responsible for more death than Hitler. I thought it was funny. Christian Scientists did not. Apart from the incensed letters to the *Clarion* received from our readership, I was subject to a stinging rebuke from the then editor of *The Christian Science Monitor*.

That taught me two things: The press does have power. Who would have thought a reporter on a tiny newspaper would reach into the inner counsels of one of the most powerful papers in America? And one of the best, too. Second, I learned that while I believed nothing was sacred, most people did not share my irreverence. These sensitive beliefs are a little bit like the human ego: You think it's hidden but it's easily reached with an insult.

Charles appreciated the volume of mail even as he didn't appreciate the tone of it. Charles took the middle course, which meant few feathers were ruffled. Being a proponent of free speech I utilized this precious amendment perhaps once too often in my youth but it stirred the readership. It began to stir Charles. Instead of reining me in, he gave me more latitude. He enjoyed the spectacle without having to face it emotionally. I was left to confront whatever hornet's nests I stirred. But that's as it should be. Charles was my editor, not my protector. I was proving so successful in my ability to rough up the conservatives of our area that he lured John Hoffman to the *Clarion*. Now John could rile the liberals and me, too, on occasion. Attacking personalities was off limits. We had to stick to issues and so we did. Our readership grew by 1,722 subscriptions over that period. Our rough readership statistics put us somewhere around 5,000. That doesn't seem like much, but consider how small Runnymede is. I knew, in my heart, that if I could buy this paper I could double our readership. I was full of ideas, energy, and passion. As the owner I would have to be more circumspect than as a reporter or editor. After all, if businesses don't place ads, we go broke.

We did lose an ad once and it wasn't my fault. John came out guns ablazing against abortion. He so offended Trixie Shellenberger, M.D., over at the Medical Arts Center that they pulled their ads for three months. To Charles's credit he made no excuses for John nor did he tell him to tone down.

To me befell the task of the rebuttal. As I couldn't have an abortion myself but feel every woman has the right to make her own decision, my rebuttal was half-hearted. I think I offended almost as many people as John, because I wasn't championing their cause. I didn't get mad at John; I got mad at Charles for sticking me with the damned rebuttal. That was one of the few times I've lost my temper with him.

Blue pencil smeared all over the page in front of me. I gave up. This article was without salvation. I wondered how many blue pencils I'd used up in my lifetime. Would they girdle the globe or merely stretch to Des Moines, Iowa, and back?

"Roger."

"Yo!"

I handed him his article. "Are you trying to make this as illiterate as possible?"

"No, it comes naturally." He grinned with good nature.

"How about another try? You don't have to dazzle me with transitions. Just tell me the story."

"Okay."

I glanced out the window and beheld Mr. Pierre bearing down on the office. Before I had time to marvel at his haste or make my escape to the back, he was inside the door.

"Bellissima!" He kissed me. His voice lowered; his right eyebrow shot up conspiratorially. "Well?"

"Uh—I'm working up to it."

91

"Lâche!" He evaporated as quickly as he had materialized.

I think he said that I chickened out in French.

Apart from my disappointing Mr. Pierre and myself, the day was tolerable. I stopped off at Darby's Folly to groom Kenny and ride him for a too-brief half hour.

Then I went home and cooked spaghetti. I don't like spaghetti but I like cooking even less. It was easy. Pewter stole half of it off my plate. That habit was my fault because I'd set a place for her and we'd eat together. As Pewter matured she decided my food was better than cat food. So I'd put some of my food on her plate. But she ate so much faster than I did she'd have her face in my food within minutes of being served.

Ursie breezed in as we were finishing. No one ever knocked in Runnymede. She didn't say hello.

"You let that cat eat with you?" Her upper lip curled.

"Want some?"

"Certainly not." She paused before sitting at the trestle table. "It's unhygienic."

"Oh, hell, Ursie, my cat is cleaner than most people—and better company too." Dig. Dig.

"I missed you at the stable so I brought you this." She dumped a gargantuan pile of file folders on the table. My china rattled. "Blue and Gray Hunt Club newsletter files. Everything's there. I keep concise records and I hope you will too."

"You're a hard act to follow."

This pleased her. "Thank you but I know you'll do your best." Ursie took in the kitchen. "Why don't you let Mr. Pierre redecorate for you? Those people have such a flair. Remarkable, really."

Fortunately, I am disciplined. I did not punch her out. "Just like blacks have rhythm."

"I didn't mean it like that at all. That's the problem with you minorities. You're too sensitive."

Actually, I agreed with Ursie on that but I didn't feel agreeable at that moment. "If you want to run for public office you'd best be aware of those sensitivities."

Her perfectly coiffed hair shook for a second. Her eyes narrowed. "Me? Run for public office? Whatever or *whoever* gave you that idea?" A pause. "Has Harmony or Tiffany said anything?"

"Your daughters are blameless."

"Well, where'd you get such a thought? Me. The very idea. How absurd."

"Methinks the lady doth protest too much." I shoved the plate away from me. "You're highly intelligent, the kids are close to leaving home, and you're getting bored, bored, bored with volunteer work."

"I am not." She shifted in her seat.

"Yes, you are. You didn't run for president of the Garden Club this year and you also stepped aside so Carolyn Chapman would be elected vice-president of the Hunt Club."

"Circumstantial evidence."

Of course it was, but I wasn't going to tell her of my conversation with Regina. It was too much fun to hook her and reel her in, the blowfish.

Ursie tapped her long (fake) fingernails on the dark wood. Her curiosity overwhelmed her denial of ambition. "Do you think I'd make a good, uh, public servant?"

"I do. I'll vote for you."

"You will? You don't like me."

Ursie, direct. Well, this was interesting.

"We're the best of enemies then." I smiled a Chessy Smith smile. Dad could charm a dog off a meat wagon. My charm was not so potent but at least I had some.

Ursie smiled back. "So we are. Who's to say how it will all turn out?"

She left as she arrived, unescorted by me. Lolly Mabel saw her to the door. I snatched the phone off the hook the instant Ursie backed her new Volvo station wagon out the driveway. The license plates read H. BEAR for "Honey Bear."

Regina picked up on the other end and I succumbed to the cheap thrill of gossip. I told her every syllable of my conversation with Ursie, every nuance, every pause.

We giggled and when I hung up, my heart knocked against my ribs. I loved Regina. Absolute, unqualified love. My tawdry, low-rent behavior, my damned affair, hurt me.

I saw my ideas tarnish in the corrosive air of the outside world, or maybe it was my ideals. Well, I wasn't ready to throw in the towel but my nose was bloodied. Maybe after thirty everyone feels that way. Maybe, but Regina shouldn't get her nose bloodied on my account.

The other event of the day was that Mother, Ed, Verna, Ricky, Georgette, Max, and Decca went to the movies. Max was not a BonBon but Georgette's steady, although not steady enough to suit Verna.

After the show Mother invited eveyone back to her house, where she concocted dripping banana splits and ice cream sundaes. Then she spoke aloud the magic "Louise" and Goodyear howled, rolled over, and played dead. This was a big hit with Ed.

The BonBons and Ed left at midnight. By 12:01 she called to give me a full report. When I mentioned that I was asleep she informed me that I needed more night life; I was turning into a grind. Ed, like everyone else, was sworn to secrecy about Goodyear, and I was sworn to secrecy too. I couldn't tell Aunt Wheezie about Mother's date. Mother reserved that form of enlightened sadism for herself.

16

APPOMATTOX AND LUNCH WITH MICHELLE

THURSDAY . . . 9 APRIL

"You're a flaming asshole." David Wheeler threw his sheriff's hat on the ground.

"You're setting a bad example for young people." Bucky Nordness pointed to a child pulled along by her mother. "Now get back on your side of the line. This is my jurisdiction, remember!"

David walked across the Mason-Dixon line to the Dixon side.

"Is it always like this?" Michelle asked me.

"Yes and no. It's been like this since Bucky's been police chief of North Runnymede."

As we spoke Bucky fired his revolver in a loud salute, and his two deputies did likewise. A fife and drum corps, out of step, emerged from the Fire Station on the northwestern corner of the Square. Fortunately, their compass was shortened because they could only march on the northern side. To cross the line would have been foolhardy under the circumstances.

"I hate that wall-eyed son of a bitch." David picked up his hat and brushed it off.

"So, fire our cannon April twelfth. If it was good enough for Fort Sumter, it ought to be good enough for South Runnymede."

David regarded me with a bright eye. "By God, you're right. I'll load it with a cannister of paint and hit their goddamned city hall. Gray paint!"

This thought pleased him and he headed for Frederick Street. As it was lunchtime, he'd go to Mojo's and give everyone a detailed account of Bucky Nordness's every shortcoming, real and imagined. Bucky was one of those men who doesn't seem to realize that by following the letter of the law you can do almost as much damage as by breaking it.

As for his celebrating Lee's surrender at Appomattox on April 9, 1865, it was in questionable taste.

"Why do people care?" Michelle mused as we walked to Mojo's ourselves.

"Come on, Lolly, you can move faster than that." Lolly found a Pekinese belonging to Mutzi alluring. Pewter thought its little face looked as though it had been flattened with a frying pan. On the whole, Pewter didn't have much good to say about dogs. I returned to the question. "People care because it's within memory. My mother's grandfather fought in the war. When you consider, that's close in time."

"Seems silly."

"I don't set much store by it, Michelle, but it's part of our culture. The trauma of that loss can never be overestimated. Why is it any sillier than Hopi Indian dances? That's their culture. This is part of ours."

She decided to let it drop. "I'm glad we're having lunch."

"Good."

Folded under my arm was *The New York Times Book Review*. It took me a week to read every article. I would also read every article in *The New Yorker*.

When we were seated at Mojo's, Michelle borrowed the *Book Review*. She scanned the best-seller lists. "Someday I'm going to write a book."

Maybe I should have taken this seriously but I didn't. Every newspaperman thinks he's got a novel in him. Best that it stay there.

"Fiction or nonfiction?" I tried to sound interested.

"I'll start with nonfiction because it's closer to what I know and then I'll work my way up to fiction."

"Hey, I've got your first nonfiction hit. *Vaginal Care in the Nuclear Age*."

"Don't you ever take anything seriously?" A petulant shadow crossed her face.

"Not if I can help it."

"You ought to."

"Mizz Saunders, I buried my father. I took my lumps in the antiwar movement and the civil rights movement. Harder to bear was the treatment those same men, our 'brothers,' handed out to us when we started the women's movement. As we say in Runnymede,

I've been up the road and I've been down the road. I learned I'd rather laugh than cry. Whenever possible I'll laugh. I also figure that other people have their fair share of pain, problems, and the heartbreak of psoriasis. If I have any compassion at all for them, I'll try to make them laugh too."

She simply stared at me as Verna carefully placed two huge bowls of navy bean soup in front of us. If there truly is a heaven, Verna's navy bean soup will be served there too.

Michelle ate three spoonfuls before she answered my small but controlled outburst. "I never thought of it that way."

"How do you like your soup?"

"It's delicious. Nickel, how come you don't bring up gay issues? Like at the paper?"

Was this going to be a deeply boring lunch? "Honey, everyone will bring it up for me. You'd think I was the only goddamned lesbian in America."

"Other people are afraid."

"So what! You either have guts or you don't. You either tell the truth or lie. I've done about all I can do. I'm telling the truth as best I know it. Everyone else can hang on their own hook. Anyway, I'm tired of being used by people too afraid to do their own fighting."

This must have hit her hard. Her eyes watered but it could have been the soup. She found her voice. "A lot of people have more to lose than you do."

"What?"

"Well, you haven't much money and you're not going to inherit any."

"Is money the absolute value?" I smiled. "Money is pictures of dead people. At least Canadians put the picture of a living person on their bills." I smiled some more. She seemed so tense, but then Michelle probably didn't relax in her sleep. "And since when do you measure your life in money? Are you that cheap?"

"No. Well, I guess I'm finding excuses for those people, aren't I?"

Verna called, "More?"

"How about half a bowl? Really, Verna. Not another whole one. I'll be fat as a tick."

"Not the way you exercise." A huge bowl appeared before me.

"May I have more too?"

"Why sure, sugar." Verna brought another one for Michelle, who was again wearing her black Reeboks.

"I asked you to lunch because I want to know what the company policy is about seeing someone on the paper." Finally, Michelle got to it.

"No policy. This is a small town. If you can find anyone still breathing who interests you, everyone understands."

"Roger Davis asked me out. I'm a little uncomfortable."

"Roger's a good man." I adored him.

"Oh, I know that. I don't want to mislead him or get in too deep or—"

"Hey, it's one date. You like it, you'll have two." I could tell this logic wasn't convincing to her but she dropped the subject.

"I have another question."

"Uh-huh."

"I'd like to do film reviews. I know you do them and I don't want to impose upon your turf, so to speak, but I think I could learn."

"Fine with me. We'll divide up movies as they come to town. Want to divide up the revivals too?"

"Sure!"

We ate in happy silence for a few moments.

"Oh, Michelle, one thing."

"What?"

"About film—it's no accident it comes in a can."

17

A LOVE TRIANGLE AT BINGO

FRIDAY . . . 10 APRIL

"Thirty-six, thirty-six. Have some fun. Play some tricks," Mutzi sang.

Peepbean, attended by his relentlessly devoted fiancée, strolled around the large room. His engagement would be announced in next week's *Clarion*. His fiancée couldn't help being born ugly but she could have stayed home.

Ed Tutweiler Walters, sandwiched between Julia and Louise, flourished from their attentions. Louise became Chatty Cathy and Mom resorted to flashes of wit. Mr. Pierre, although disappointed in me, nestled next to me.

The Saint Rose regulars were there, as were Michelle and Roger. It's doubtful that Michelle could get any further from her background even if she landed in Tunis. Bingo's charms would conquer even her.

"Seventy-five, seventy-five, three cheers, you're still alive." Mutzi yanked another ball out of the hopper.

"Watch it!" Mom cupped her hands to her mouth. The room laughed.

"Julia, it's unfeminine to yell," Louise scolded.

"Hey, I won. Bingo!" Ed jumped up. "Bingo."

"So, he isn't Gary Cooper," Mr. Pierre whispered.

Being straight versus being gay has little effect on a gentleman's appreciation, even need, for being the center of female attention.

Mr. Pierre detested being displaced by a man he regarded as a

99

Birmingham ruffian. On the other hand, he wished for one of the sisters to have a mate again. Which one, and was Ed the right material?

Louise, mesmerized by her sister's expanded bosom, toyed with a dab-a-dot. You could see the thought cross her mind. It didn't cross—it trespassed.

"Aunt Wheeze." I broke her concentration. "Are you ready for block of nine?"

"I've got every new way memorized. Block of nine is easy: You fill in a solid block of nine numbers, three, three, three. I like to think of it as a mini-blackout bingo."

"Pretty smart." I polished the apple.

"I was smart before you were born."

"Yeah, and you've been in more laps than a napkin."

"Juts, I wish you'd desist from this sexual banter. Never in the anals of history has it been proper for ladies of quality to resort to such innuendo."

"*Annals* of history." I covered up my smirk.

"That's what I said," Wheezie came back at me.

"Innuendo . . . is he related to impetigo?" Mother was getting wound up.

"Impetigo's a disease." Ed was joyfully folding the bingo money into his wallet.

"Think of it as light leprosy." Mr. Pierre continued to take the cap off his dab-a-dot and then replace it.

Mutzi began calling the next game, the block of nine.

"Ed, have I ever told you the story about me and Chessy the first week we were married?"

"No, I don't believe you have." His pleasant voice soothed the nerves.

"Can it, Juts. We've heard that story since B.C."

"I don't spoil your stories." Mother sounded calm. I doubted that she was.

"That's because I don't repeat them." Louise smiled.

"Right, once was enough."

"Mother." I butted in. "Number eight. On your card."

"Oh." She dabbed a dot. "Well, Ed, Chessy and I had been married one week."

Louise moaned.

"Shut up, Wheezie," Mother commanded. "As I was saying, we were enjoying marital bliss. I cooked breakfast. We ate it. Chessy drank milk with his breakfast. He emptied his glass, put it back on the table, and pointed to it. I said, 'What?' My brand-new husband replied, 'My Momma always filled the glass when I lived at home.' I stared at him. 'What time is it?' Chessy checked his watch. 'Eight-fifteen.' 'Good,' I said. 'By eight twenty-five you can be back home. I don't care one way or the other.' Well, Ed, that closed his mouth and the marriage lasted for thirty-six years."

"You shoulda filled his glass. Marabel Morgan would have." Wheezie had half a block of nine.

"Marabel Morgan is a twit." Julia bent over her card.

"Just what is a twit?" Louise appeared impassive.

"The present tense of twat."

"How disgusting!" Aunt Wheeze threw down her dab-a-dot. "And in mixed company."

"Girls! This is your first warning," Mutzi boomed. He was too close to the microphone.

Michelle, only a table away, observed the sisters raising their voices. I could hear Roger tell her: "They're always like that. That's half the reason people come to bingo." Michelle's glance traveled from Mom to Wheeze to me. What was going through her head?

"I think it's a funny story." Ed put the lid on it and now Louise was frying.

Mr. Pierre and I spent the remainder of the evening so close to our bingo cards we may have fostered nearsightedness. We got the giggles every time we caught each other's eye and that made Louise angrier. She beamed for Ed but to the rest of us—Lolly, Pewter, and Goodyear included—she glowered.

On the odd occasion Mother and Aunt Wheeze could do the mature, responsible thing. That didn't mean they wanted to. When it came to each other they refused to grow up. They'd compete over a cheese straw if it were the only thing in the room to fight about. I wanted to believe that people could change, and that included change the dynamic between them. Maybe some things or some people couldn't change. I wasn't so sure anymore. I wasn't even sure if changing their relationship of constant bickering and out-right war would even be good. Maybe it kept them young.

18

LOUISE IS ABDUCTED

SATURDAY . . . 11 APRIL

Rain lashed at the windshield. In bad weather the Jeep gave me confidence. It must have given Louise confidence, too, because she wasn't backseat driving. Creeping along the Emmitsburg Pike, I figured it would take us twice as long to get to the mall.

"I want to buy me some cigarette pants."

"That'll be nice." The road was disappearing again.

"Canary-yellow. No, maybe sunbird-yellow, and I want a dragonfly-blue top to go with it. And then I want big earrings, something enameled and bright."

"Going all-out, aren't you?" I was wrapped over my steering wheel.

"Take parts when tarts are passed." Louise said this in a knowing tone of voice.

"I beg your pardon."

"Take parts when tarts—"

"What's it mean?"

"You don't know what that means? It means when a tray of tarts is passed at a party, you take as many as you can because you don't know when the tray will come around again. Don't you have sense?"

I decided not to answer. Although the deluge continued, the color of the sky lightened from anthracite to putty. Aunt Wheeze twittered about one thing and another. We passed a fifty-five-mile-an-hour speed limit sign.

"Sign's going to be changed. They raised the speed limit to

102

sixty-five. Well, I'm sixty-five and accelerating. I'm picking up speed. At my age that's all I'm picking up." She breathed deeply. "How old do you think I look?"

"That's hard for me to say, since I see you every day and I've known you since I was born."

"Don't weasel me. Do I look seventy?"

"Uh—yeah, I guess you do."

"Eighty?"

The road wasn't the only thing dangerous. "That's maybe the upper limit." I sounded convincing, I thought.

"Liar. You're a terrible liar. Tell me this"—a sharp intake of breath—"do I look older than Julia?"

"Do you know that song, Aunt Wheezie—it has the line in it: 'Let there be peace on earth and let it begin with me'? Maybe we could practice that."

"No, I don't know that song. I never heard such a thing and I could care less. I want some answers to my questions. Do I look older than my sister?"

"A tad."

"I knew it! Well—I have a better chin." She rapped her fingers on the dash. "Of course, you could be taking her part again. I don't think you are, though. Not this time. What do I do? I've never been old before. How do I know what it's like to be old? I don't know where the time went. Do you know that sometimes I wake up in the morning and it takes me a second to remember that Momma's dead and I don't have to go to school? I know that sounds silly to you but it's true. Where did the time go?"

I couldn't answer, because I was beginning to have those feelings myself. The more I lived, the more I wanted to live. Every day I learned something new; maybe it was something bad, but it was new and I loved learning—except when it was something bad about myself. I tended to undercut that. Anyway, since others were anxious to point out my shortcomings, I saw no reason to dwell on them.

Aunt Wheezie continued. "If I got a face lift, you think it would take twenty years off my face? Ten?"

"Sure. Those plastic surgeons are artists if you go to the right one."

"Those magazines at the Curl 'n Twirl write about face lifts all the time." Her voice dropped a half octave. "Remember the time Mr. Pierre told us he went to Rio?"

"He did. He brought back pictures of Carnival."

"I believe, I truly believe, that he had a face lift. He has to be fifty if he's a day and he looks—what do you think—forty something?"

"He looks pretty good but he's fanatical about what he eats and how much he sleeps. He's like Mom that way."

"Oh, her. She's showing her age plenty, I can tell you. I swear Mr. Pierre had a nip and a tuck."

"Ask him."

"I could never." A beat. "You could though."

"Me?"

"He'll tell you anything."

"I'm not going to ask him. If he didn't tell anyone when he came back from Brazil, beautifully rested, why would he tell now?"

"That's a fact." She nestled back in her bucket seat. "So how can I find a good doctor? I don't want some quack."

"You don't want a face lift either." I bit my tongue to keep from saying she was too old for major surgery.

"Why not?"

"It costs a fortune."

"How much?"

"At least five thousand dollars."

That information created a solid silence that lasted five minutes, an eternity for Aunt Louise.

"I could sell the third Chrysler."

"Don't you dare. What's the fuss? You've never worried about your face before."

"Ed Tutweiler Walters pays more attention to Juts than to me."

"He does not."

"Yes, he does. You're not around him. You don't know him. She's weaving her web again. Damn her!"

"Don't let her get your goat. Relax."

"Easy for you to say. She gets her witty face on. Her let-me-entertain-you face. Men are so dumb. Fall for it every time."

"You're making too much of it."

As we drove into the mall the rain stopped and the sun popped up like golden toast from behind the clouds. The abrupt change lifted Wheezie's spirits. I parked the Jeep and we found cigarette pants and a suitable blouse but she couldn't find her earrings. We decided to try a jewelry store in the town of Emmitsburg itself. We climbed back into the Jeep and I remembered there was a sale on tennis balls—Wilson's, my favorite—at the sporting goods store. I drove up to the curb, left the motor running with Aunt Wheeze in the passenger seat, and hopped into the store. As I was standing at the counter, six cans of balls in my arms, I glanced out the front door and saw two young men get into the Jeep. They drove off.

I dropped the balls and ran out of the store. I could see Wheezie hollering and I could hear her, too, since her window was down.

"Thief!"

The Jeep accelerated. Stupidly, I ran after the car. It began to swerve. Aunt Louise had her shoe off and was hitting the driver about the head for all she was worth.

Now she was bellowing, "Rape!"

A few drivers in their cars noticed the weaving pattern of the Jeep. They got out of the way. I kept running. One smart soul, a teenaged boy, raced his car up behind the Jeep. He honked his horn. The Jeep circled, fast, around the huge parking lot. People leapt out of the way. One lady dashed into a store and I hoped she had the brains to call the police—which is what I should have done but I didn't want to lose sight of Wheezie. Finally, these two bozos, the driver and the one in the back seat, found the way out of the parking lot, but the light was red and traffic was heavy so they couldn't shoot against the light. The next thing I saw was my Aunt Louise being kicked out of the car. She skidded across the asphalt. The light changed and the Jeep tore down the Pike. Aunt Louise hobbled to a phone booth there on the corner. I was impressed with her presence of mind. My lungs, searing with pain, about gave out by the time I sprinted up to the phone booth. I was just in time to hear Wheezie say, "Juts, you'll never guess what happened to me!"

19
FORT SUMTER REMEMBERED

SUNDAY . . . 12 APRIL

At noon the church doors open in Runnymede and we buzz out like bees from various hives. Christ Lutheran, Mom's and my church, reposes on the Emmitsburg Pike, immediately off the Square on the Maryland side of the line. Christ Lutheran is one of those Georgian gems found only along the Eastern Seaboard of our nation. The warm brick, offset by creamy white lintels, a gilded and white steeple, and the white of the marble steps glistened in the spring light. The gardening committee of the church planted thousands of daffodils and tulips. The daffs rolled like a yellow tide in the wind, and the tulips were breaking the surface of the earth. As Easter was next Sunday, they might open if the weather held, which would make it a perfect Easter.

As we did most Sundays unless it was brutally cold, Mother and I turned right after leaving church and walked past both city halls on the Emmitsburg corner only to plunge into the Square. Everyone else did the same, so Sundays became a grand promenade.

The doors of Saint Rose of Lima opened. We could see Louise, assisted by the statuesque Shirley McConnell, hobbling down the steps of the Gothic church. Mom and I called Shirley "Attila the Nun" because she had been a Dominican sister for years, finally renouncing her vows because she discovered love in the form of O. Logan McConnell. The "O" stood for Orion, but Logan sure wouldn't stand for it.

Bruised and scraped from her ordeal yesterday, Aunt Wheeze

flourished as the center of attention. Given the amount of bandages swathed about her person, she resembled a mummy. Aunt Wheeze had pitched a fit yesterday when the police wanted to take her to the Emmitsburg Hospital. A squad car dropped us off at Trixie Shellenberger's. Aunt Louise encouraged the good doctor to exaggerate her injuries. Clear across the Square we observed the unusual attentions bestowed upon Wheeze. She lapped up the sympathy. I could have used some myself, because the police had quickly recovered my Jeep but found it totaled.

We strolled past Runnymede Bank and Trust; the drugstore, open for business now that church was out; Mutzi's greengrocer stand; and Brown, Moon & Frost.

I knew God would forgive me for my adultery with Jackson Frost but I wondered if I would forgive myself. I guessed I loved Jack. No, I didn't guess. I did love him but I saw no reason to burden him with this knowledge, since our affair was doomed. In a funny way I loved Regina more. I was never attracted to her, so my love was free from lust. Maybe because of that or in spite of it, I'd never know, I could open up and let the love grow. Everything that Mr. Pierre said preyed on my mind, especially after church. I saw Regina and Jack with their boys, Winston and Randolph, gracefully descend the steps of Saint Paul's Episcopal, and seeing Louise, they hastened to her.

A crowd was gathering on the South part of the Square but Mom and I couldn't see why. I wondered what Mother would say if I told her about Jackson. She'd probably be angry with me. I wasn't in the mood for anger today. I rarely was. I'm one of those people who will avoid a fight if possible. If not, watch out.

The more I thought about Jackson and Regina the more I realized how much closer I was to her. This was a continuing theme of my life, my detachment on my deepest level from men. Jackson wasn't my first long-term affair with a man. I lived with a man throughout college and for a year afterwards. I'd had a few crushes in between him and Jackson. Yet it never failed. I would reach a place emotionally with them, and I could go no further. I felt as though they shut a door on me, or maybe the door was closed to them as well. I was beginning to half-believe that men's deepest emotions were inaccessible to them. I used to think I felt this way because I'm more gay than straight, but my women friends who are more straight than gay (and probably never thought of making love to another woman, silly girls) say the same thing. We feel much closer to women than to men. Even my friends in good marriages have confessed that there are things they'd tell their closest women friends that they wouldn't dream of telling their husbands. Because he's not interested? Because he doesn't know how to handle it? Because he'd be threatened? I sure don't know but I do know we do something terrible to men in our culture. We take them away from themselves and we substitute money, power, and toys.

Mother spoke up. "You're quiet."

"It's not the company."

A young woman walking along the Square with her family was in navy-blue. Mother sniffed, "People don't know anything anymore. Look at her. Navy-blue and it's not even Easter."

"I think the dress code went the way of the whale-oil lamp."

"A pity."

"Well, Mom, what we've gained in informality and comfort we've lost in drama and beauty, so I guess I have to agree with you. If people don't know what colors are appropriate, then they could at least learn to write a good thank-you note. Nowadays they pick up the phone instead. It's tacky."

"I'll tell you what's tacky. There's Liz Rife shooting out of Saint Paul's in chinchilla."

"It might be tacky but I'd like to have it. I expect she's got a fur coat for every day of the week. I'd settle for one," I replied.

"What kind?"

"A full-length Russian sable with shawl collar—I guess that's what you call those collars that aren't really collars with no notches on them."

"In cloth I think you call it a polo coat."

"Well, that's the one I want. In fact, I think I'd kill for sable."

"I'll help you bury the body." Mother laughed. "Nickel, something's really going on over there."

We buzzed into the Square. The small crowd we had initially observed swelled until it must have included everyone leaving church. We squeezed our way into the mass and beheld David Wheeler, already deep in the grape. Mutzi Elliott, in no better condition, stood next to him and had a long artillery swab, the long pole used to jam down the cannonball. They must have been drinking throughout the night.

Mutzi waved the swab and David launched into a tirade about Bucky Nordness and the firing upon of Fort Sumter—which were intertwined. Not that it made any sense. I suddenly remembered that I was the dolt who suggested David celebrate April twelfth to spite Bucky.

"Ready, Mutzi?"

"Ready." Mutzi patted the Confederate cannon.

David touched the wick, and boom. Except it wasn't a can of gray paint that flew out of there. It was a real cannonball. Nor did it hit city hall, the intended target according to David's garbled account. The ball whined across the Square, tore off a branch of maple tree on the North side, and crashed into the front window of Falkenroth, Spangler & Finster.

A hush fell over us. Louise's eyes bugged out of her head. Mr. Pierre's mouth hung open. Regina's hand flew to her face and David was coughing from the smoke.

As soon as he could breathe, his first words were, "Jesus H. Christ on a raft."

Mutzi giggled. The giggling turned into uncontrollable laughter.

Mr. Pierre dryly commented, "A little more to the left, David, and you can take out Rife's offices too."

Mutzi was now rolling on the ground. "You know that T-shirt: 'First, we kill all the lawyers'?"

The law firm of Falkenroth, Spangler & Finster had suffered an eclipse on the South side of Runnymede. Those of us in Maryland used Brown, Moon & Frost, while those on the Pennsylvania side used Falkenroth, Spangler & Finster. You might say no love was lost on either side.

"Except it's Sunday. Nobody's in there," Aunt Wheezie blurted out, then bumbled on. "I didn't mean that the way it came out."

David was fast sobering up. Jackson, our mayor, stepped forward. "David, I'm afraid there will be legal repercussions."

In the distance we could hear Bucky's siren. Father Christopolous, in his vestments, hurried down the steps of Saint Rose's. He observed the situation and ran toward the offices to see if anyone was hurt. At the sight of him, Mr. Pierre started off to join him.

"Wait a goddamned minute, Pierre!" David growled at the fifty or so of us crowding around. "You all, every one of you, just stand still. Here's the drill. Ain't no one telling what happened. You tell and you will get parking tickets and speeding tickets until death do us part. Got it? Mutzi and I were cleaning the cannon and it went off."

Jackson, perplexed, raised his hands for silence because the murmur of the crowd became a roar. "Ladies and gentlemen, let us review the facts."

"No facts to review, Jack."

"What you're suggesting is a lie."

"I'm not suggesting. I'm telling!" The veins bulged out on David's neck.

"At the very least you are distorting evidence."

"They do it in Washington all the time." David's belligerence was accelerating and so was the sound of the siren.

"If Oliver North can lie and get away with it, why can't David?" Mother's voice carried over the burst of chatter.

"Right." Mutzi, still on the ground, agreed, but Mutzi would have agreed with anybody at that point.

"I'm defending my country by fair means or foul." David had the bit in his teeth. "That asshole with the gift of speech, that jerk—and I refer to Bucky Nordness, who is so bad he could screw up a wet dream—that Yankee had the gall to celebrate our surrender at Appomattox this week. I won't stand for it!"

"That was 1865." Jackson wanted to get David out of there before Bucky and company pulled up in front of Falkenroth, Spangler & Finster.

"Tell that to Nordness. He's rubbing our noses in it!" David shouted. Then he turned to me. "Nickel, you promise not to write the story?"

"You mean I can't use my headline: 'War Not Over'?" I smiled and it relaxed David a little. "I shall use discretion, David." You bet I would or he'd beat my ass then and there.

"What about the rest of you?" David scanned the crowd.

"Oh, we won't tell," Aunt Wheezie vowed. "Why see David put through the wringer because he got sloshed?"

"I am not sloshed, Mrs. Trumbull," David vigorously defended himself, referring to my aunt by her married name.

The crowd talked but a consensus was brewing. We wouldn't give Bucky Nordness the satisfaction of a big stink and possibly lawsuits flying like confetti. David should not have gotten drunk and Mutzi should not have jammed down a real cannonball, but they did. Best for them quietly to pay the repair bill of Falkenroth, Spangler, and Finster and be done with it. David's dislike of Bucky exceeded that of the rest of us but it was felt that Bucky did become overzealous in his duties and it was also felt that his jubilation each and every April ninth was in poor taste. As the squad car careened around the Square, coming down from the Hanover Road, the crowd dispersed. Jackson had David firmly under the elbow. David shook his arm off but did leave. Regina and I pulled Mutzi out of there with the help of Randolph and Winston Frost. Mom, Louise and Mrs. McConnell walked three abreast behind Regina and me so that no one on the other side of the Square could see exactly what we were doing. We dumped Mutzi in his shop and figured he could sober up by himself. His wife was out of town—a good thing, because she was more to be feared than Bucky Nordness when it came to Mutzi's drinking.

Mr. Pierre offered an impromptu party, and Mother, Louise, and Mr. and Mrs. McConnell, about half of the BonBons, Jackson and Regina and David crammed into his house. No one would allow David any more alcohol but he was becoming good-natured. Mr. Pierre shot me hot stares every now and then. I weakly smiled and tried not to stand too close to Jackson because I'd want to touch him.

Mother came over. "Are you going to write about it?"

"I'll use David's story. I guess that makes me corrupt but Aunt Wheezie's right. Speaking of which, I was surprised when you said what you did about Oliver North."

"He's lying and people think he's a hero."

"Wait until he testifies."

"What difference will it make?"

I said, "Maybe we'll get the truth."

"If Oliver North were your friend and told you to write a false story to protect him and you believed in what he was doing—would you?"

"No."

"You're doing it for David." Mother knew how to get me.

"Oh, come on! That's such a little thing and David would get dragged through the mud. We're not talking about violating the Constitution or lying to the American people about foreign policy."

"The principle is the same."

Mr. Pierre was now standing next to Mom, having overheard the conversation. "Integrity is built on many small things."

"Thanks a lot!"

"Don't get peevish, Nickie," Mother warned. "You're always ready to point out to me, God, and everybody what's right and what's wrong. Now you get a taste of your own medicine."

"I do not go about telling people how to live their lives."

"You do in your column," Mother said.

I certainly didn't think my column was as proscriptive as she was making it out to be, and furthermore this grilling was unfair even if they were right—in principle. To make matters worse, Mr. Pierre kept treating me, nonverbally, of course, as though my life were a heterosexual extravaganza. When Jackson came over to join the argument—excuse me, discussion—I wanted the floor to open so I could drop through it.

"What's going on over here?" Regina came up behind Jackson.

"These two are giving me rat week."

Mother pounced. "I am not and neither is Mr. Pierre. I asked her about Oliver North—"

"Actually, I heard the whole thing." Jackson saved her her breath.

"So?" Now Mom was on guard.

Regina came to my side. "Why are you getting on Nickel's case? We're all complicit in this, as I see it."

"But she represents the press. If the press doesn't tell us the truth, how can we make sound judgments about our community?" Mr. Pierre didn't sound hostile to me but I still didn't like being under attack.

"Well, I'm the mayor and I'm covering up. What about me?"

"Jackson, we expect our politicians to lie. We don't expect it of the press." Mother cut to the bone—mine and Jackson's.

Jackson's face went white. "Julia, do you think I lie to you?"

"Not you. But you're the only politician I do have faith in and maybe it's because I can watch you. I can't watch those slick toads in Washington. I don't know them."

"Somebody knows them. Their families. Their communities," Regina said.

"Yes, and if they got in Dutch, I bet their families and their communities would cover up for them." Mr. Pierre was on a tack.

Nobody said anything for a minute. We didn't know what to say.

I finally broke the silence. "You're right. I am violating my own ethics as a reporter. But David's my friend and I have to balance the story with its effect on his life. Nobody was hurt, thank God. David used poor judgment but who hasn't at one time or another? Maybe I'm using poor judgment now but if the story comes out in the paper there will be repercussions all the way to Baltimore and to Harrisburg. Then we won't have the opportunity to correct this ourselves. The state legislators could conceivably get in the act, since this problem involves two elected public servants. What purpose does that serve? And I get to watch the team from Eyewitless News make an ass of my friend, of us in general? I guess if I have to pick between a professional code of honor and my friend, I'm going to pick my friend, at least this time, and I'm going to try and solve this mess among ourselves."

"If everyone does that, then we haven't evolved beyond tribal behavior." Mr. Pierre handed around another tray of goodies.

"We haven't." Regina smiled, easing the tension. "The United States is a culture but not a civilization. We're still too new."

"Well, that's what Charles Falkenroth says, in a way. He says the United States is an unfinished democracy." Jackson was enjoying the discussion.

"So, I guess we keep trying," Mother replied.

It should be noted that my mother has never missed voting, whether in a local, state or national election. Being born in 1905, she remembered when women couldn't vote, and a hurricane couldn't keep her out of the voting booth.

Maybe Jackson was enjoying the discussion but I wasn't. I was shown up as an unevolved tribal person—an unevolved tribal person standing next to her best friend and her best friend's husband, with whom she was having an affair. Surely tribal people are smarter.

NICKEL FIGHTS WITH JUTS

MONDAY . . . 13 APRIL

"I don't understand how you could be standing right there and not get the story." Charles Falkenroth stood over me as I sat at my desk playing with my razor-point pen.

"First of all it was Palm Sunday and Aunt Wheezie had her palm frond in front of my face. Second, it was very confusing because it happened so fast."

"Bullshit, Nickel." Charles let me have it. "You're a trained observer."

"Tell me what Bucky Nordness said when he called you up." I fudged for time. Surely I could come up with a better excuse.

"He said that David Wheeler, out of pure D meanness, fired a cannonball into the offices of Falkenroth, Spangler, and Finster but he is certain the ball was meant for him."

"Sorry your cousin wasn't working that Sunday." A malicious flicker appeared in my eyes.

"Me too. That son of a bitch is off on another vacation."

Countless reasons sprang to mind as to why Charles detested his cousin but one reason overshadowed the others. William Falkenroth had contested their grandmother's will concerning the disposition of 720 acres of good land. This issue took five years to settle and cost Charles many thousands of dollars in legal fees. Through the Falkenroths as well as through Mother and Louise, I learned that a family is a bizarre combination of people with conflicting interests united by blood.

"Here." I handed Charles the story I wrote Sunday concerning the cannon incident.

He grabbed it from me. "You'll have this back in five minutes." Charles walked into his office. Pewter followed. He let her in, then shut the door.

Michelle called out from her desk: "Is he going to run my Passover piece?"

"Yes." I thought she was enjoying my discomfort the tiniest bit too much.

Roger was out of the bullpen, so I called back to her: "How was your date?"

"Okay." She sounded noncommittal. "How long has your mother had purple hair?"

"It's not purple, it's magenta, and it's only on the sides."

"Are they always like that . . . your mother and her sister?"

"I told you about them and so has everyone else here."

"But I've never seen them go at it."

"That was nothing."

"I guess I'll have to get used to it if I stay in Runnymede. I think I'll keep going to bingo at least until the blackout game."

"Did you like it?"

She thought about that. "Yes."

Charles emerged from his den, Pewter at his heels. He stopped by the AP wire. "Gary Hart declared his candidacy in a speech at Red Rocks Park above Denver. Another one." He tore off the wire story and put it on Michelle's desk. "How many have we got now?"

"Biden; Gore, except they haven't formally announced; Jesse Jackson, who hasn't stopped running since 1984; Dukakis; Babbitt; Gephardt; and who knows who else on the Democratic side? Cuomo? We don't know what's cooking there, even though he said he isn't going to run," Michelle answered brightly. "Want the list of the Republicans?"

"No, it's too depressing." Charles came over to my desk and placed the story in front of me. "Well written, Nickel, but I don't believe a word of it."

My face burned. "That's the best I can do."

"You'd better do better or you're not fit to own a newspaper." He twirled and left me in my misery. "Michelle, any of those men got your vote?"

"Only Pat Schroeder would have my vote."

I glanced at Michelle. That was a new note or maybe I never heard it before. I hadn't expected her to support someone like

Representative Schroeder. I figured Michelle for a misplaced Yuppie languishing in the backwaters of Runnymede, where you watch the population progress from fetus to fossil.

"The reason so many men are running for president is they want to make sure they have a job," Charles said.

I roused myself. "You say that every four years."

"Every four years it's true." Charles went back into his office and Pewter came over to console me. She also took Lolly's rawhide chew away from her.

"What are you going to do about the story?" A note of sympathy crept into Michelle's voice.

"Make the rounds. I'll go over to the law offices, I'll talk to Bucky, and I'll talk to David. Better get on it." The phone rang. Foster Adams's clear voice snapped me to attention. Could I come over to the bank?

I hung up the phone. "Michelle, I'm on the trail. Will you answer my phone?"

"Sure."

Foster's walnut paneling surrounded him. Somehow the office seemed more imposing than Foster. I listened carefully to him, imposing or not.

". . . so you see, Nickel, that press is two years older than God." He smiled with that turn of phrase. "To say nothing of the other equipment—hopelessly outdated, all of it. I can't put a value on it. Now the lot and the building, that's different. Gone up handsomely. Same with your farm."

"I certainly appreciate your thoroughness, Foster."

"Thank you." He swiveled in his chair, got up and came over to the edge of the huge desk. He sat on it and beamed down at me. "The bottom line is, you're short. I wanted to tell you before I took this down to Baltimore. Maybe you can come up with more assets, something you've overlooked, or maybe you can find a partner or investor. I want to present a strong application. I think you should get the *Clarion*." He emphasized "should" which was sweet of him.

"I appreciate your support." I swallowed hard. "How much am I shy?"

"Right about two hundred and fifty thousand dollars." He still beamed at me.

I guess to a banker $250,000 is chicken feed unless it's owed to them and the creditor bellies-up.

I tried not to let my voice crack. "Let me see what I can do."

"I'll be going down to Baltimore April twenty-third. Talk to me before then."

He ushered me out of his office. As I walked through the main part of the bank building with the huge brass swinging lamps overhead, the brass bars in front of the tellers, the polished marble floor over which my grandmother and my great-grandmother and great-great grandmother trod, the only sound inside my head was "two hundred and fifty thousand dollars!"

My feet headed across the Square toward the Curl 'n Twirl. I wasn't conscious of my direction. I managed to come back to earth by the time I passed the Confederate statue. I also managed to see my mother rapidly light a cigarette and swoop into the Curl 'n Twirl. She hadn't even grabbed a magazine when I came through the door. The cigarette looked stapled to her lip. She and Georgette Bonneville were rehashing the events of yesterday.

"Mother, I wish you'd stop smoking."

"It's my duty to support the great states of Virginia and Maryland." She twirled the cigarette between her fingers. "Now that you've been a dutiful daughter tell me what's the matter."

"Huh?"

"You can't fool me. What's cooking?"

"Oh, Foster Adams called me into his office. He couldn't have been nicer but he told me I'm two hundred and fifty thousand dollars short. I've got until April twenty-third to find the money or an investor."

Mr. Pierre yelled out from the back room. "Piece of cake. *Gateau.*"

Georgette offered an idea. "Maybe you'll win the Publishers Clearing House Sweepstakes. Then you could buy the town along with the paper."

What struck me was that Georgette was serious. "I'll look for the envelope in the mail." I sat down on a chair.

Pierre strode out from the back and hovered over me. "Trim, trim, trim."

"Go ahead." What the hell. I could go over to Bill Falkenroth and Company after a haircut.

The snip, snip of scissors accented Mother's comments. She sat in the next chair. As she talked I noticed with mounting alarm the number of silver hairs mixed in with black. They piled up in my lap. Was he trimming me or giving me a crew cut?

"This isn't your day, honey. Louise won't let you use her third Chrysler, the perfect one." She hit on "perfect." "She's sorry your Jeep is wrecked. She knows it will take some time to get the insurance money for it but she doesn't want one scratch on her car."

"How much?" Simon Legree Hunsenmeir, I thought.

"One hundred dollars a week." Mother's reply was swift.

"That old bandit." Mr. Pierre cut away.

"It's still cheaper than a rent-a-car." I sighed. "Tell her seventy-five a week is my absolute top offer. Take it or leave it."

My entire life was boiling down to my net worth. Why was money in sight but never in hand?

"I'll tell her. You can pick up the car after work." Mother switched gears. "Where are you going to get two hundred and fifty thousand dollars?"

"Damned if I know."

"Why can't Charles hold a second? Like a second mortgage on a house," Mr. Pierre suggested.

"He could but I don't think he would. He and Ann want to take the money and run to Palm Springs. Can't say that I blame them. Also, right now I wouldn't ask him for a paper clip. He's pissed at me because he knows I'm not telling the whole story about David Wheeler and the cannon."

"Yeah, Mutzi rolled in today looking like death warmed over. Anyway, he wanted to make sure we'd keep our traps shut," Georgette called out from behind the lilies on the counter.

"Poor Mutzi can't afford the legal wrath of Bill, Kevin, and Tinker any more than David can." Mr. Pierre critically appraised my face.

Bill, Kevin, and Tinker were Falkenroth, Spangler, and Finster, respectively. There was also young George Spangler working in his father's company.

"I'll believe it when I see it," Georgette said.

"How about some coral rouge? You need a pickup." Without waiting for a reply Mr. Pierre was brushing my face.

"Reminds me of Nickel's little paint box when she was a girl." Mother played with Mr. Pierre's tray of rouges and eye shadows.

Anger swirled up through me like lava. "You're the last person I thought who would bring that up. You threw my paints away."

A scarlet flash hit Mom's cheeks. "They were used up."

"The hell they were!" I was out of the chair.

Both Mr. Pierre and Georgette were astonished. Frankly, I was too.

"You're soft as a grape."

How typical of Mother to shrug this off.

"I am not. You threw the paint set out and you knew I loved to

118

paint. More than anything I loved it. I wanted to grow up to be a painter."

"You used colors wrong."

"I was seven years old!"

"You're too sensitive." She emphatically shut Mr. Pierre's makeup tray.

"One day I'm too sensitive and the next day you tell me I'm too remote. Make up your mind. I know why you threw out my paints. Because my natural mother was a painter. Still is, for all I know!"

Mother's voice became quiet, frighteningly quiet. "I didn't want you to turn out like her."

"Well, I didn't!" I jumped out of the chair and stormed out of the Curl 'n Twirl. I was behaving like an adolescent and even though I knew it I couldn't stop myself. I'd even forgotten to pay Mr. Pierre.

Kenny neighed when Lolly, Pewter, and I entered his stall. He was clean for a change, no rolling in the mud today, so grooming sped along. In the background I heard Harmony Yost command her mother to bring her a running martingale. Ursie said, "I'll be right there, dear." If a kid of mine ordered me about like that I'd smack her face into next week. Ursie puzzled me. The trivial nature of her ambition drove her constantly. She longed to be a social leader, and failing that, she would get around it by becoming a political leader. Her sublime lack of tact insured that she would singe nerve endings whenever she opened her mouth. She never understood this failing in herself. And how she loved to be in command, secure in the mantle of petty authority. She'd bark out orders like a D.I. on Parris Island, yet she'd let those status-conscious little horrors of hers push her around like a chambermaid. Mom used to say, "If you don't discipline your children, someone else will do it for you." Harmony and Tiffany Yost might coast through college but once out in the real world those two girls were in for a nasty surprise: people did not exist to kiss their ass. The only person they listened to was Muffin Barnes, perhaps because Muffin had what they wanted: riding knowledge.

A further uproar engulfed me as Tiffany discovered her saddle pad was dirty and her hoof pick was missing. Ursie's head appeared over the stall's Dutch door.

"Nickel, may I borrow your hoof pick?"

"Sure." I handed her the instrument.

"Elliwood Baxter's coming back from Palm Beach today."

"Great. I'll be glad to see her."

Elliwood wintered at the Palm Beach Polo Club west of West Palm, where she knocked the ball when she wasn't knocking other people out of the saddle. The woman had nerves of ice.

"Hear the rest of the news?"

"No."

Ursie glowed. "Her eldest daughter joined one of those Eastern religious sects. Guess she'll shave her head."

"That's the men. The woman walk around with little cymbals on their forefinger and thumbs, chanting to Krishna. The cult leader's name is Raj Cohen."

"How do you know that?" Ursie missed the joke.

"Uh, I made it up. Anyway, I'm sorry to hear that Catherine feels the need to make a flagrant display of her spiritual beliefs."

"Mother," Tiffany wailed in the background.

"Just a minute, precious." Ursie turned back to me. "Notice anything about Regina lately?"

"No. Why?"

"Oh—nothing."

"Ursie, don't do that. If you've got something on your mind, out with it."

"I don't like to gossip." Said by one who lives for it.

"Anything that concerns Regina concerns me. I have no idea what you're talking about because she looks wonderful."

"Always will, that one. I don't know, I get a feeling. Maybe something's not quite right at home. You know how restless Jackson gets."

"Sure. Every four years he wants to move, or buy a second home, or he goes over to the Porsche dealer in Baltimore and drives cars. It makes Gene crazy. They aren't poor but they have only so much money. No Porsches for Jack."

"Yes." She dragged out the *yes* into four syllables. "His periodic restlessness manifests itself in a roving eye."

I stood bolt upright and dropped my brush. "Jackson Frost? Come on, Ursie, you don't know that, and I've never heard anything like that about him."

"You wouldn't," she sniffed.

A trickle of sweat rolled down my armpits. "What?"

"You're practically family. Nobody would tell you or Regina if he was up to something. But I have it on good authority that three years ago he indulged himself in a little fling over in New York, Pennsylvania. Regina didn't know a thing about it but a wife senses those things, don't you think?"

What if her insinuation was true. I wasn't the first. I'd kill him.

"Like I said, Gene seems fine to me and I can't imagine Jack doing anything like that."

Her voice rose, redolent with false warmth and humor. "Well, dear, of course you can't imagine anything like that. You have no sense of what goes on between a man and a woman. Blue Angels." She made a motion over her head imitating the jets. "Goes right over your head."

I didn't know whether to laugh, cry, or choke her.

NICKEL BITES THE BULLET

TUESDAY . . . 14 APRIL

The South is finally forgiving Lincoln and registering Republican. I, however, will remain staunchly Democratic. As for Abraham Lincoln, regardless of his sins committed against the South, I never wished him assassinated and today was the anniversary of that wretched day in 1865. Why that stupid joke kept running through my head I didn't know. You know the one: "Aside from that, Mrs. Lincoln, how did you like the show?" Also on April 14, fourteen years later, Alexander Solovieff tried to kill Czar Alexander the Second. April 14 must be the day for assassinations.

I was feeling a bit of an assassin myself because I knew I was going to end my relationship with Jackson tonight. I tried not to think about it as I drove Aunt Wheezie's Chrysler to the Square. Cars skidded to a halt. Others pulled over on the side of the road and waited for me to pass. At first, this behavior alarmed me. Then it got funny. I'd come up behind someone, toot my horn and watch them go ape-shit. Then I'd pass and wave and they'd realize it was me. Thacker BonBon just missed a telephone pole, but when he saw it was me he had the good grace to laugh at both of us. Lolly found this exciting. Pewter hid under the seat and ten minutes of coaxing finally convinced her to come out. For a fat cat she could move fast and she burnt the wind getting out of the car. When I reached the steps of the *Clarion* she was washing herself as though nothing had happened.

The sun flooded the Square with soft morning light. Goodyear was sitting in front of Brown's Meat Market patiently waiting for Ralph Brown to open for business this lovely day. Mr. Brown was generous with juicy joint bones; shrewd, too, because everyone with a dog shopped at the meat market. Which was to say everyone. The only people who didn't own dogs were those with allergies and we were suspicious that they invented the allergies. Not to have a pet was to court gossip that you didn't like animals, and if you didn't like animals it was but a short step to not liking children and after that not liking people, the worst offense imaginable.

I knew Mother was loitering somewhere around the Square or in one of the shops but I didn't see her. So I pushed open the door to the *Clarion* and found Michelle at her desk.

"What are you doing here so early?"

She held up the paper. "I wanted to see my Passover piece."

I picked up the paper on my desk. Arnie Dow or one of the compositors put fresh copies on our desks each morning. No one told him to do it; he just did.

"Looks good in type, doesn't it?" I read the paper as I stood over the hot plate waiting for the water to boil for my tea.

Michelle wiped out her Garfield cup with a paper towel. "I'm going to send a copy to Mom and Dad. This is my best piece, so far." She paused. "I think, anyway."

"I do too." I smiled.

Michelle glanced out the window. "Here comes Goodyear with a huge bone. Should I let Lolly out?"

"No, they'll fight over it."

"And here comes your mother."

I turned from the coffee machine in time to see Mother in her jogging outfit and her nifty Nike shoes, striding along the sidewalk. She passed the *Clarion*, saw me, and waved. I waved back. Between us this would amount to an apology. I held up my teacup and pointed to it. She shook her head and continued on her walk.

"She's got miles to go before she sleeps," I said.

"What?"

"She likes to walk between two and five miles a day depending on the weather."

Michelle's eyes got bigger. "My God, she's in her eighties."

"Eighty-two chronologically. Her emotional age is something else again."

"That could be said of anyone." Michelle heaped milk substitute in her cup. "She doesn't look like she's in her eighties. If I didn't know her or you, I'd guess that your Mother was in her early sixties."

"She really is proof that if you take care of yourself you can look good a long, long time."

"So are you."

This caught me off guard. "Oh—thank you."

"Did you work out this morning?"

"I did." I gulped down my tea. Through the steam I beheld a familiar figure coming down the library steps. Aunt Louise was tottering under the weight of books. As she hadn't cracked a book since fourth grade, this was a revolution. "Michelle, do you see what I see?"

She peered out the window. "Your aunt plans to read a lot."

"That's impossible. I mean, she hates to read."

"No kidding."

"She says there are those who read between the lines and those who don't read at all and she qualifies for the latter."

"How can anyone not want to read?"

"Beats me." I finished my cup and poured more. I needed an extra shot this morning. "I'd better go help the old girl, even though she's a bandit."

"Bandit?"

"I'll tell you when I get back."

I reached Wheezie as she spilled her books on the sidewalk. Her greeting was not one of gratitude.

"Where are the Southern gentlemen when you need them!"

"Buried at Gettysburg and Sharpsburg, Aunt Wheeze." I bent over and gathered up her books. The titles intrigued me: *Karma and You, The Way of Little Feather, The Path to Higher Consciousness, Psychic Healing,* and the *I Ching.* "Aunt Wheeze, what are you doing with this stuff?"

"I'm studying Eastern religions."

"Why? Aren't Western ones bad enough?"

Her cerise lipstick appeared even brighter in the dewy light. "I'm broadening my horizons."

"Father Christopolous won't like it."

"What he doesn't know won't hurt him. Besides, these books teach me how lucky I am to be a Christian. After all, it takes a Christian to truly understand and appreciate sin. Christians believe in progress. These people just walk around in sandals."

"Is that a fact?" I carried the books around the back of the library to the parking lot. Her 1952 Chrysler shone like a black waterbug.

"I'm sure I'll learn a lot."

"Does this have anything to do with your beau—your contested beau?" I put the books in the front seat. The door wasn't locked. Nobody locked their doors in Runnymede. The locksmith didn't live who could build a lock strong enough to keep out a cat or a lover. As to thieves, we didn't have any, other than those we elected to public office.

"Ed's quite interested in religion. He believes there is a collective mind."

"Is this collective mind sane or insane?"

She crawled up into the driver's seat. She had a crocheted cover on the seat plus a pillow so she could see up over the steering wheel. Aunt Louise was shrinking with age. "I intend to find out." She started the motor. "Don't tell my sister about this."

"I won't."

"She thinks she's making headway with Ed because she's reeking of charm. She'll probably carry on that I'm older than she is, too, even though I told Ed I'm the younger one. Well, I don't care what she says, because I'm going to be well-read and well-rounded. I'm going to know things she doesn't know. See."

"I do."

"Besides, all the sugar's in the bottom of the cup." She winked and laid rubber as she left the parking lot.

A goodly portion of our taxes went toward repairing the damage Aunt Louise did to our parking lots and highways.

A light fog curled around the statues in the Square. Twilight imparted to it a silvery glow. Roger filed his story on Maryland's response to front-runner Gary Hart. We were the last two in the *Clarion* office.

"Good. You did your homework."

"I like the political stuff." He hesitated. "Nickel, what do you think of Michelle?"

"Got a lot to learn but not without talent. But then I think I could say the same about myself. The more I learn, the more I know I don't know."

His warm brown eyes gazed directly into mine. "I mean, what do you think about her apart from work?"

"Oh." I'd never once given it a thought. "Uh—she seems nice, well-bred, smart."

"They say women know more about women than a man does." He took a breath. "Maybe you know things about her I don't."

"I'm not being very helpful. I don't think I have any special insights into Michelle other than that if you can get her to lighten up I figure you'll be halfway home."

"Thanks." He smiled, grabbed his coat, and whistled his way out the door.

Alone in the office, I put the paper to bed and made a few calls on behalf of our Blue and Gray Hunt Club newsletter. I typed up an item about Elliwood Baxter's polo handicap. I called Ursie to double-check a local tack sale date and then I shot an hour over the light box, heroically trying to lay out the newsletter. Both Pewter and I were covered in paste.

The animals and I left once twilight turned to black velvet. I doubled back on the alleyway, hesitated, and then entered Brown, Moon & Frost.

Jackson happily greeted me and immediately got to business. I was glad of this because it delayed the inevitable.

"Not much time." Jackson sat next to me on his office sofa. "You have some choices though. You can try and put together an investor package between now and the twenty-third. You don't need anything on paper except for a profit-and-loss statement. Everybody in Runnymede knows you, and what they'd be investing in is the paper and you. The problem is there isn't much money here. Rife and Chalfonte are the big bucks. The Yosts have some money but I doubt you'll get any. You'd be lucky to scare up twenty-five people at ten thousand apiece."

"I'm afraid to go to Spots Chalfonte."

"She's out of town more than in it." He grabbed a tennis ball and squeezed it, a habit of his to improve his grip. "Mizz Chalfonte likes you, though. Apart from real estate, as far as I know, Chalfonte money has not gone into town businesses since they moved their own company to Texas in 1969. No state taxes."

"Texas teeters on the brink of a state tax. Maybe the factory will move back."

"Nah." He looped the ball over me.

"There's George Spangler."

"Son to Kevin and you're on Kevin's shit list right now. So am I."

"What for? I haven't done jack shit to Kevin or George Spangler."

"He knows we know the real story about David Wheeler and the cannon. As the two most responsible citizens observing the debacle—in his mind, anyway—we're culprits for not coming forth with the facts that will help him and Bucky nail David."

"I'm on Charles Falkenroth's shit list too."

"Story?"

I nodded. "Yes."

Jackson spoke again. "The investor route, well—" He threw up his hands.

"Damn." I felt horrible. "There's got to be a way. I wonder if I could put together a package and make the rounds of Baltimore people with money." I paused. "Except I only know about three rich people there."

"There is another way. You won't like it." Jackson patted my knee. "You can come to terms with Diz Rife. Work out an arrangement where you own a percent of the paper. If the *Clarion* maintains continuity throughout the transfer it will be because of you. And Diz likes you."

"John Hoffman could run the *Clarion*."

"But he won't."

"Why not?"

"He has bigger fish to fry."

"John Hoffman?" I was incredulous.

"Why do you think he's spending so much time in Washington?"

"I don't know."

"He's been interviewing like mad for jobs. It's do or die for John. He's not getting any younger."

I was stunned. How could something like this go on without my knowing about it? "How'd you find out?"

"He interviewed at the *National Geographic* and at the *Washington Star* and I have an old friend there. Called me for the scoop and I told him John's a good man so long as you don't talk politics."

"Did you really say that?" I smiled.

"Yes. Now what about Diz?"

"I don't know if I could work with him. I don't want to be the hired help. Why would he split fifty-fifty with me on ownership?"

"Because he likes you and he needs you. He doesn't have to own the *Clarion* one hundred percent."

"Does he know that?"

"Ask him."

"Why don't you ask him? You're my lawyer."

"He hates me and I hate him. You know that."

"Oh, Jackson, that's in your imagination. Just because you both courted Regina doesn't mean he still carries a grudge or a torch. That was a long time ago."

"Then why does he want to beat me at singles? Why does he want to take you away from me as a doubles partner? Whatever I have Diz wants. He's the most covetous man I know. You'll go a lot further if you approach him directly." A light blond stubble covered Jack's face. It made him look tougher when he spoke of Diz.

I walked around the room. This was a new thought for me. I

wanted time to digest it, and time was one thing I didn't have. "Okay. I'll give it a shot."

"I knew you would. Now get back down here on this sofa."

"There's another item we need to discuss." I sat next to him. "Mr. Pierre knows."

Jackson's face blanched. "If he tells your aunt we're sunk."

"If he tells my mother she'll wring my neck." I had my priorities straight. "But he's not going to tell."

"Good." He reached up and massaged the back of my neck.

"Did you have an affair with a woman in York a few years ago?"

Jack was caught off guard. His hand gripped my neck. I removed it. "Where'd you hear that?"

"Don't answer a question with a question. Did you or didn't you?"

He slumped back on the sofa. "Yes."

My heart stopped for a split second. I was stunned at the power he had to hurt me. I pressed on. "Were there others?"

"It's not what you think, Nickie."

"What is it then? I can't believe what a blind fool I am. I really thought I was the first. I thought you loved me."

"I do love you! It's hard being married. It's hard being faithful. I made some mistakes."

Now I was a mistake. "I'm sorry I was one of them." My voice could have cut steel.

"You're not. You're different." He took a deep breath. "I'm different. I know your worth. Maybe a few years ago this would have been a sporting affair—fun, lighthearted, an escape from routine. But it's not that. I love you."

"You have a funny way of showing it." This was unfair and I knew it the minute the words were out of my mouth. Fair or not, I was gathering my courage, bolstered by his confession. "We're through. We had no future anyway. I've been consumed by worry over Regina. So now I'm out."

"Don't do this! Don't hold my past against me. Hell, why am I defending myself? I'm not a promiscuous man. I'm sorry. I had two affairs in my life and I learned from them."

"Does Gene know about them?"

"No."

"You're still my lawyer. We'll go on as we were before this."

"The hell we will. We'll never be the same. Do you think love is a faucet and I can turn it on and off?"

"You'd better try."

I left. He didn't run after me, for which I was grateful. Lolly and

Pewter stuck close to me. Funny how animals know when you're upset.

I got in the old Chrysler and drove away. The fog was so thick I crept along at twenty miles an hour, which only gave me time to think. To think about Jackson's warm, deep baritone, his well-muscled body, his odd laugh like a catch in his breath. I also thought about his infidelities. I felt as though I had a spear lodged in my chest and what made it excruciating was thinking, This is how Regina would feel if she found out. Only for Gene, it would be worse. She would be betrayed by two people she loved, not just one.

I sank into an ornate gloom. My sense of my own self was taking a beating. I wasn't the kind of person to have an affair with a married person, much less my best friend's husband. Ending the affair didn't change the fact that I'd done it. I thought about going into therapy, but therapy won't cure a character defect or make the immoral moral. What I had done was profoundly immoral and no amount of self-understanding was going to make my action less reprehensible.

I could barely make out my house as I searched for the driveway. A heavily diffused light over the front porch was my guide.

I went upstairs and crawled into bed. I was almost as miserable as I was on the day Dad died. Pewter snuggled in next to me.

The Greeks wrote, "Whom the gods wish to destroy they first make mad." I would amend that to "Whom the gods wish to destroy they first make fall in love." I used to think romantic love was a neurosis shared by two, a supreme foolishness. I no longer thought that. There's nothing foolish in loving anyone. Thinking you'll be loved in return is what's foolish.

POPCORN

WEDNESDAY . . . 15 APRIL

"Are you happy? I'm miserable."

"It's April fifteenth. The entire population of the United States is miserable." Mr. Pierre sighed, then leaned over and kissed my cheek. "*Ma cherie,* you did the right thing and I'm proud of you."

Although I still felt miserable I had the comfort of knowing that he recognized my sacrifice. "I wasn't exactly out marching with the Seven Deadly Sins and I don't think I'm going straight to hell—but I am relieved."

"How'd Jack like it?" He placed a sizzling omelet before me.

"He didn't." I took a bite of the omelet and felt sick. "Don't be angry with me if I can't eat your cooking. You're the best cook in Runnymede but I'm not hungry."

"Nonsense. I've seen you in the depths before, remember? You don't eat. Now I am going to make certain that you keep your strength up." He waved his hand at me to eat up; the gold family-crest ring on his third finger seemed more worn than I remembered. "Nickel, do your duty."

"Duty is something you expect other people to do." However, I consumed the entire omelet and did not feel the better for it.

"Know what you need, darling?" He buttered cornbread for me.

"I need two hundred and fifty thousand dollars."

"You need a mate. Not a lover but a mate. Someone who is just for you. I know Jack loves you. Who doesn't?"

I could think of scores of people who didn't love me, including the loonies who wrote in response to the editorial columns, but I decided to pretend I was universally loved this morning and let Mr. Pierre continue.

"You need to be someone's Number One and vice versa. Do you realize that your entire life—and I am generously not counting the years—you've played solitaire. I mean, Jack loves you, yes, but Regina is his Number One. That's what marriage means—even if one does stray off the reservation. And as for Julia, well, she loves you but Chessy was her Number One and that's as it should be."

"I think Mother is her own Number One." Much as I loved my mother, I considered her self-centered, a thought I'd kept to myself until now.

"Piffle. She's constructively selfish. She lets you know where she stands."

"On my neck and quite close to her self-interest."

"Doesn't everybody? You're being hard on her because she's your mother, ungrateful child, and you had that silly argument over the paint box. And don't get off the subject. You do that all the time when you don't want to discuss something emotional, and I emphasize the word *emotional*. Detachment is fine for your profession but not so fine for your life."

"I've heard that before."

"But have you listened?"

Obviously I had not. I became respectfully silent, ate the cornbread, and then spoke. "When I find my true love you'll be the first to know."

"I certainly hope so. What are friends for?" He checked himself in the mirror across the room. "Time for a rinse." He patted his hair.

"Losing your lilac tint, are you? Actually, why do you do that to your hair? It's beautiful, thick, wavy hair."

"I do it because if I'm going to be hung for a sheep I might as well be hung for a wolf."

I understood perfectly. What a pity some people needed to call him a faggot behind his back and what a pity he needed to waste energy responding to them. Tinting his hair lilac was his response, and like the man, it was assertive, funny, and oddly touching. Maybe I loved Mr. Pierre at that moment more than I loved even myself. I kissed him and braced myself for my interview at Racedown, the ancestral home of the Rifes.

As I put my hand on the doorknob, Mr. Pierre called out to me: "Until you have a mate, I have another suggestion."

"What's that?"

"Buy a little retreat up in the mountains away from here. You need a getaway, a place to restoreth one's soul."

"I haven't got the money."

"You don't need much money for a cabin with no running water. You could call it Uncle Tom's Cabinet."

The countryside surrounding Racedown embraced me. Soft, rolling hills with patches of thick woods imparted a sense that God was in her heaven and all was right with the world. The willows sported their spring green while the buds on other trees glowed with that dark red prior to bursting open. Racedown, a huge stone mansion added to over the centuries, commanded a ridge running roughly parallel to the west. If you continued to drive west you would run into the mountains called a variety of names according to the locale. Probably the name by which these mountains are best known is their Virginia appellation, the Blue Ridge. From Racedown you couldn't see the mountains but you could see the foothills grow in size as you gazed west, and if you turned around and looked east, the land slowly became calmer and flatter, a sea of rich grass.

Upon seeing the Chrysler, other drivers got off the road the entire four miles to Racedown. The driveway into Racedown was a mile long and a huge loop ran in front of the mansion, so I pulled the 1952 Chrysler in front of the distinguished door with the graceful fan window over it, unusual in a stone house.

The door swung open before I could knock. Portia, in tiger-striped leotard, opened the door. She crimped little tendrils in her hair and wore a scarf around her neck. The scarf resembled a knitted sock. I had thought she was back in New York.

"Nickel Smith, come right in. Diz is in the study. I liked the copy you wrote for my fashion photos but tell your art director to make the photos larger next time."

"I thought the layout was good."

She dismissed this. "For a paper that decided to use photographs in 1955, yes."

We still ran no photos on our front page, although the first page of the other sections ran photos. I loved the *Clarion*'s austere front page. I wanted a newspaper to look like a newspaper, not a god-damned comic book. While I debated whether to tell her or not, I found myself at Diz's study and was spared my own opinions.

The study, lined with old bound books, was my favorite room in Racedown, but then studies and libraries are my favorite rooms in any house, I think. The unusual cherry wood glowed with a deep red light. Most paneling in our part of the world was done in walnut or, if built somewhat after the colonial period, mahogany. This cherry wood was spectacular and it suited Racedown, a dwelling of angles and surprises, filled with the usual quota of fine Hepplewhites, Sheratons, and Chippendales. George III silver gleamed in nooks and crannies. While I recognized these furnishings for what they were—superb pieces, priceless pieces—I was becoming bored by them. If Runnymede had a prime sin it was best seen in her decor: The whole town, not just Racedown, trembled at the thought of anything new.

Diz jumped up to greet me. I sat down across from him in front of the finely detailed fireplace, where a fire crackled to ward off the morning's chill.

"I'm delighted you've called upon me." He sounded genuine.

"I'm delighted you would take the time from your busy schedule."

"Now that we're both delighted, let's talk." The firelight was reflected in his eyes.

"The *Clarion,* that's why I'm here. I want to buy it and you want to buy it and I'm short of cash."

"I expected you might be." He smiled but it wasn't a triumphant smile.

"I wondered if we might do this together—if we could come to terms."

"What's your offer?"

"Fifty-fifty but I run the paper. I know there are myriad ways to cut a deal like this but that's the deal I want—that and the option to buy you out if you ever tire of the paper."

"What's to prevent me from buying the *Clarion* and hiring you?"

"Not a thing." I leaned back in the cushy wing chair. "Except I'll leave. Nothing personal, Diz. I just don't want to be the hired help."

His eyes twinkled. "No, I don't guess you would."

"Jackson Frost will be happy to give you my financial statement because I will be shouldering half the liability."

"All right." He reached for a humidor on a table next to his chair and retrieved a cigar. "Montecristo." He held it up before lighting it. "I have a secret stash."

"At the end of his life I think Dad would have killed for a Cuban cigar."

Diz inhaled, his head wreathed in expensive smoke. "Your dad was the best man I ever met. You know when I'd come into the store . . . When did he open the store?"

"Same year Pearlie bought the three Chryslers, 1952."

"God, my father couldn't get over that." Diz laughed. "Turned out that old man Trumbull was smarter than all of us. I could retire half of the national debt on what Rifes have squandered on automobiles. Well, anyway, when your Dad stopped hiring out as a carpenter and started the hardware store on the Square, I'd go in for odds and ends. You know, he always gave me something for free—a tape measure, a pocket flashlight, the kind of things that little boys treasure. Chessy Smith was the only merchant in Runnymede who gave me things for free and didn't charge me double."

"He liked you."

"Well, I loved him. I don't guess he was the smartest businessman in the world, because he gave away too much for free." Diz laughed. "But he sure knew how to make people happy." He sucked in a long sweet draw. "Maybe that's why I think your offer has some merit."

I hung on the edge of my seat before I realized what I was doing. I shimmied back as surreptitiously as I could manage. "You'll think about it?"

"I will, but you have to think about a few things. I can accept Jackson as your lawyer for this transaction but if we become partners, you find another lawyer, because he rubs me the wrong way."

"I think you're wrong about Jack."

"You would." A stream of hot blue smoke came out of his flared nostrils. "Since third grade you've thought he was something special—because he was the best-looking boy in the class. I think the man is full of fine conscience and rude egotism. And I can't stand the way he preens in front of women—most notably you."

I swallowed hard. How to play this? I didn't want to wreck our as-yet-unformed partnership but even if I was mad at Jackson, I didn't want him insulted by Diz. "Let me talk to him. In view of our long frienship I think he would step aside for the good of my future but I can't do anything so rash as discharge him—should we come to terms—without discussing it with him."

"That's fair enough, but tell me this." He paused dramatically. "What do you see in him?"

"He's my doubles partner." I slid into second gear.

"Not for long." He poised on the edge of another question and then let it go. "Okay, the future of the *Clarion*. It's antiquated, inefficient, and overstaffed. You can pump up your profit by forty percent before taxes if you know what you're doing."

"Such as." My mouth turned sand dry.

"Modernize the equipment, drastically trim the staff, including editorial. You don't need four reporters plus the editor in chief for this small town. Raise the advertising revenues just a little. The

Clarion is too cheap. Aggressively seek new advertising in the surrounding area."

"This modernization—it would cost Arnie Dow and the boys in the back their jobs, wouldn't it?"

"Yes, but we would be generous with our severance pay and they have pensions."

"The *Clarion* is their life."

"Nickel, profit is what runs this country. I'm not suggesting we throw these laborers in the street. They will be compensated."

"You don't understand, Diz. A newspaper is more than a business. It's a community resource. If we don't guard that resource, the press will soon become indistinguishable from General Motors or any other industry. We're the lifeblood of a free country. No press, no democracy. Profit is secondary to that function."

He simply stared at me. "Nickel, I admire your passion but you haven't got the sense God gave a goose."

My voice cracked, an unfortunate giveaway to my distress. "I guess we aren't cut out to be partners."

"I don't want to fight with you. I'd like it if we could work together." He stood up because I did. "So maybe you aren't good at business. You write a column and you can sure get the story when you've a mind to—"

I interrupted. "You know what I wish? I wish you had started out like me. I wish I knew how far you could get on your own. You and I would be better off."

He came close to me. "You don't think I've never wished the same thing? No matter what I do in this world no one will ever give me credit for it. Not even you."

I moved a half step closer to him. I was maybe three inches from his face. "You're right. It's hard to separate the man from the money but I can try. What I can't do is give up the *Clarion*. She may be inefficient, as you have pointed out. She may be overstaffed. But she's ours. She's the voice of our little, unimportant town and I don't want her any other way. Maybe individuality is a luxury but I'm willing to fight for it."

I walked out of the room, and to my surprise, Diz followed me. "Nickel, think about it."

"No."

He opened the door for me and lightly touched my forearm. It had the effect of holding me. "Why do we always wind up on the opposite sides of the fence?"

I placed my hand over his hand. "I don't know."

Driving back to Runnymede, I forced myself to concentrate on the road. My mind scattered like buckshot. I thought of Diz's intense eyes. I thought of Jackson. I thought of my stomach, which the last few days had been throwing a nervous hissy every time I ate. I thought of Aunt Louise's Chrysler, which felt solid under my hands like my own past. I soon thought of Aunt Wheezie's own car, because a mile out of town she zoomed at me from the opposite direction. What I remember is she had huge light-pink plastic bags in the back and Ed Tutweiler Walters in the front. She swerved away from me at the last minute and went off the road onto the shoulder. I slammed on my brakes, and as I did, I heard a popping sound. I rushed out of the car to see Aunt Wheezie fighting her way out of her car, which had mysteriously filled with popcorn. As there was a lot of static electricity in the air, my illustrious aunt had popcorn stuck over her body. So did Ed T. Walters. I know I shouldn't have but I laughed. I bent over, I was laughing so hard.

"I coulda been killed!" Aunt Louise shrieked at me—this coming from a woman who braved two car thieves in Emmitsburg and didn't bat an eye.

I hastened over to the car and the be-popcorned Ed. "Does that thing still run?" I indicated the car.

"No, but I do." To my shock, Ed began running down the road away from us. This only made me laugh harder.

Aunt Wheeze took her purse, also white, from the car. She had to dig for it and she hit me hard over the head. Then she started hitting me everywhere. Well, by now Ed came back. That was his idea of a joke and my idea as well. Louise saw things in a different light. "Don't you laugh at me."

"Stop hitting me!"

"When you stop laughing, you ungrateful brat."

"Look at Ed."

She got her first hard look at Ed. The purse went slack in her hands. She glared at me. She glanced back at Ed. It was a valiant fight but Aunt Wheezie lost to her own sense of humor. She began to laugh. We laughed so hard we had to sit down by the side of the road.

I caught my breath. "What were you doing with a car full of popcorn?"

"Taking it out to Sonny and Sister Bonneville. They're having a church party for Grandma and Grandpa Bonneville. I cooked up a mess of it and I put it in those thin big plastic bags, the see-through garbage kind. When I went off the road they ripped and went all over the place."

Ed picked popcorn off of him. "Do you know I haven't had this much fun since I was a kid? I'm sure glad I came up here to visit my family."

Aunt Louise melted and appeared suddenly grateful for the accident.

"How come you swerved when you saw me?" I knew her driving was atrocious but there wasn't another car on the road.

"I didn't know if I was coming or going. I saw the Chrysler bearing down on me, you see, but I forgot I gave it to you—just for an instant. Well, it blocked my bowels." She blushed. "Excuse me, Ed. A turn of phrase."

"It may have blocked your bowels, Louise, but it damn near scared the shit out of me."

If I'd said that, she would have swatted me again. Instead she started to laugh and then he laughed and I laughed and for a few moments I forgot about the paper and remembered to be glad I was alive on this spring day with my loony old aunt and her boyfriend— well, kind of her boyfriend.

SECRETS

THURSDAY . . . 16 APRIL

Maundy Thursday has been one of my favorite days since I read *The Divine Comedy*. I was fifteen at the time. Dante, writing at age thirty-five, feels he has reached the halfway point of his life and this happens on Maundy Thursday. Also, I know that Easter is only three days away, and I'm one of those people who likes Easter far more than I like Christmas. Surely the Devil invented the Christmas card.

This Maundy Thursday, I rose at six-thirty, fed Pewter and Lolly, worked out, and prepared my approach to Charles Falkenroth, who was still displeased with me. By the time I returned to the office yesterday Charles had left and although my concern was of dire importance to me it might not be of dire importance to him. I am a great respecter of other people's priorities and schedules.

Mother is not, and at seven-thirty she called. "Work out yet?"

"Just finished."

"Steer clear of my sister today. She's been so mean that she'll break a stick just because it has two ends."

This Southern expression seems to make no sense except to other Southerners.

"Thanks for the warning—and what did you do to her?"

"I like that! I did nothing. You know how irrational she can get. I think she's still addled from her episode in the car yesterday."

"Maybe she's trying to be good but having one of her bad days."

"I don't care if she can fart popcorn! Wheeze is childish and I don't want to be bothered with her. I'm not even sure I want to be bothered with you." Mother hung up.

In her mind I had taken Louise's part against her by suggesting Louise was not the lowest wormfucker that ever lived. So now Mother was mad at me and my aunt was lurking out there in Runnymede with her own grudge. It wasn't even seven forty-five yet, and I prayed this beginning was not an indication of things to come.

Fortunately the morning picked up steam. I caught Charles the minute he strolled into his office. I told him everything that happened between Diz and me concerning the *Clarion*. Then I flat-out asked him to carry a note for $250,000. I explained that he'd be walking away with a great deal of cash, and holding a note was not such a bad investment at eleven percent interest for ten years with a balloon at the end. After I exhausted what I thought were good reasons, Charles stood up and put on his hat and coat.

"Let's go."

"Where?" I asked.

"Foster Adams. I don't know what your chances are but I'm willing to take a shot at it, even if you did fudge on a story to save a friend."

Foster accepted our idea and promised to make a strong presentation in Baltimore on April 23. The day appeared to be leveling off into a solid, productive one. When we got back to the office my phone rang and I picked it up. It was Louise, burning. I flatly told her I could not talk to her and I would call her after work.

We were in our daily editorial meeting. John was ripping up Roger's idea about an article on taxing church property. Most people don't know why church property is exempt from the rolls and Roger thought it might be interesting to explain, again, what our founding fathers had in mind. I didn't think John's criticism was fair but I tempered my desire to get even with him when he outlined his proposed series on real estate developers and alleged kickbacks to zoning board members. Charles, as usual, leaned back in his chair, his bow tie untied, and offered suggestions or politely batted down ideas. Michelle had become fascinated by bingo and wanted to expand her piece.

In the middle of this, Aunt Louise charged through the front door. "Nickel Smith, get out here!"

She startled us.

I stuck my head out of Charles's door. "I'm in an editorial meeting. You'll have to wait."

"Family is more important than work." The veins in her neck bulged.

Lolly barked and Pewter scampered out of sight. My aunt was on the verge of a rampage. I turned around and Charles made a shooing motion with his hands. I was excused from the meeting and Aunt Louise was all mine.

I closed the door behind me and walked over to her. "Now, Aunt Wheezie, you can't do this to me."

"I can do anything I want." She swung at me with her purse, her favorite lethal weapon. "Ed's taking Julia out tonight by herself and it's your fault."

"Put that purse down. I am not talking to you about anything until you put it *down!*"

The purse, bald in spots from wear, was placed on my desk but, I might add, within easy reach should she want to whack at me again. "Now tell me what this is about."

"Ed doesn't want to go out with me. Not since I ran off the road yesterday and that was your fault."

"There wasn't another car on the road."

"I don't care." She pouted. "I saw myself coming and going. I told you that. It scared me. I thought I was in the twilight zone."

"Hey, I'll take you over to Mojo's for an early lunch. You'll feel better."

"No. Half the BonBons are there and they know Ed's going out with Juts. I'll be humiliated."

"Aunt Wheezie, he's being courtly to both you and Mom. You're making too much of it and you certainly aren't being humiliated."

"Ha! You weren't the one with popcorn covering you head to foot. I tell you the lights were on in the kitchens of Runnymede over that story."

"Come on, it's not that bad. He laughed."

"At me!"

"At the situation." I scribbled a note and put it on Michelle's desk telling her that I was at the drugstore with Wheezie. "We'll get a fountain Coke."

"I'd like a strawberry ice cream soda." She was weakening.

"Okay." I handed her her purse.

She said in a small voice, "It's because she's younger and prettier. Julia's the pretty one."

"That's nonsense." I suspected that Mother *was* a bit prettier than Louise. "Besides which you told Ed you were younger than Mom."

As I escorted her to the drugstore I wondered about Ed Tutweiler

Walters. Both Mother and Louise worried me. I liked Ed. He sure was handsome, and in his youth he must have been devastating. They were nuts about this guy who showered them with politeness, but I didn't take his attentions seriously. They did. I don't know what it's like to be old. I hope I get to find out but I think being an old heterosexual woman can be very painful. This volcano of emotion over Ed showed me how lonesome the Hunsenmeir girls were. After a certain age—maybe the middle forties or fifties, I don't really know—men turn to younger women, and their own generation of women is left out in the cold. It's cruel but it's a fact. I never thought of Mom or Wheezie as old or unattractive but I saw them nearly every day of my life and I had learned to love—and occasionally hate—them for what they were, for the unique individuals they were. An outsider, a man, saw a package, not the person. How many years had they felt snubbed or pushed aside? Mother generated more male attention than Louise, but in Runnymede people went two by two like the animals toward Noah's ark. There weren't any men available to either of them, except Mr. Pierre, and I was grateful he was gay. Had he been straight I think they would have killed each other over him. What were they going to do to each other over Ed? Half of me wanted to laugh at Louise for displacing her fury on me and half of me wanted to cry, it was all so desperate.

After lunch I went back to work, calling for quotes on zoning variances on both sides of the Mason-Dixon line. I'd wanted to write a time-frame breakdown of the alleged Iran-Contra deals but gave it to Michelle instead. She deserved the plum and I can't say that I wasn't interested in zoning.

Ursie, wearing a chocolate-brown suede skirt, high suede boots, and a suede jacket to match her skirt, swept through the front door. I was afflicted by her presence as she towered over me.

"Give me a second here, I've got Tinker Finster on the line for a zoning quote."

She dumped papers on my desk as Tinker, a true lawyer, hedged his bets by saying that we had to maintain our town's integrity while fostering growth.

The receiver was not in the cradle before she started. "I forgot to give you these."

"What are they?"

"The scores, division by division, of the Hanover 'A' show." An A-rated show was more important than a B-rated show, and riders wanting to move up in the world of hunter-jumpers needed points from "A" shows to do so. Many of our hunt club members or their children rode in these shows.

"Ursie, why'd you wait until now to give this to me? The newsletter gets printed tomorrow."

"Because Harmony's music recital was Monday and then Tiffany's horse threw a shoe and I had to spend hours on the phone with the caterer for our alumnae meeting. I forgot. It won't happen again."

"It can't happen again, because I'm the person now collecting the information. Dammit, I did the layout last night too."

She feigned sympathy but I suspected she was enjoying my predicament. After all, wasn't she saddled with the hunt club newsletter for the last three years? As she evacuated the *Clarion* her Joy perfume left a trace of her presence.

"I'd help you if I could," Michelle offered, "but I've got to drive over to Baltimore to pick up Mom. She's flying in for a one-day visit."

"It's nice of you to offer but you don't have to—I'll give you good assignments anyway, because you're getting good."

"I didn't think of it as a trade." Her voice was dry.

"Sorry. The sight of Ursie makes me cynical."

John Hoffman emerged from the back room. I wanted to say the sight of him made me cynical, too, but I didn't.

"Michelle, let me know if I can help you. Lot of facts to juggle."

"Thanks, John." Michelle didn't mean it. She thought she could do fine by herself.

"I've got some theories about this Iran caper." He leaned over her desk. "This is a perfect example of national security being more important than our domestic laws, *if* the law was broken."

"Bull." I had the number dialed for my next quote and put the phone down.

"Just what I expected from a bleeding-heart liberal."

"I'm no bleeding-heart liberal, John, and I don't much appreciate your label. I'm a realist, especially where politics are concerned, and I don't expect people to act like saints and I don't expect them to scuttle their self-interest, but I do expect government officials to abide by the Constitution. We can't have one set of rules inside the U.S. and another set outside the U.S."

"Fortunately, you are not a national security adviser." He smirked. "Morality has nothing to do with international relations."

"Nor national ones," Michelle volleyed. I was proud of her.

"You'll agree with anything Nickel says. Female solidarity."

The sight of Michelle taking on John brought Charles out of his office. He leaned against his door, and Roger wandered in from the morgue—the name every newspaper uses for its storage of back issues and pertinent information. The exchange mushroomed in intensity until John accused Michelle of being a dyke, at which point I blew up.

"That's it, Hoffman. Right now. Shut your fucking face!"

He surmised I was bordering on the violent and decided to pull in his horns. "Don't take it personally."

"I'm taking it very personally. Just because she has an opinion of her own and is becoming competent in our profession and, more to the point, does not agree with you, you call her a dyke."

"It was an unfortunate choice of words," John replied.

"I think so too." Charles puffed on his pipe. He hadn't moved from the door but I knew when he clenched his pipe hard between his teeth he was furious.

"I'm sorry."

This calmed our group somewhat and we returned to our tasks. I called Regina and begged her to come down after supper and help me. I also got a quote from her on zoning. I identified her in my article as a lifelong resident and concerned citizen. Her quote was: "The Zoning Commissions for both North and South Runnymede have made inconsistent decisions concerning land use. We need to revamp those commissions or to hold a referendum on the issue."

When she danced through the door, I showed her her own quote set in type. Then we got to work. We typed the show information in columns, then took turns at layout. Breaking off the affair with Jackson made me feel quasi-virtuous. I wasn't but I was relieved. I didn't want a barrier between me and Regina. I also told her about Michelle's sparring match with John and we batted opinions back and forth.

"There, what do you think of that?" She held up our front page. Our masthead ran the hunt club's logo: crossed swords in front of a fox mask.

"Better than what I'm doing. I've got zip talent for layout."

"What if we dumped the 'out'?" She laughed.

"Thanks, Gene. I appreciate that and how would you know?"

"Wouldn't." She walked over to the hot plate and boiled water to make instant coffee for her and tea for me. "It's odd, isn't it, that people can be as close as we are but not know intimate things about each other?"

"I don't think it's odd. You can't sleep with everyone."

"You could try." She laughed again.

Regina enjoyed a robust sense of humor but I was now on guard and I didn't like feeling that way, even if it was my own fault. "I haven't time. I mean, how would this newsletter get printed?"

"Maybe human relationships are like a clock. With most people the relationship is maybe fifteen minutes or ninety degrees on the dial. Just a quarter of what the relationship could be. Call it a social relationship. Sex would be part of that circle, part of that three hundred and sixty degrees. And what's so strange is, you can sleep with someone and not complete the circle. Sex isn't enough. It's necessary for a full understanding but not enough. Get it?"

"I don't know." I was standing next to her now, dunking my tea bag to make the tea strong. Pewter rubbed up against my legs. Whenever I was near food she became sticky-affectionate. "What are we?"

"We're forty-five minutes, three-quarters of the clock. Close, but I don't know everything and neither do you."

"Are you sixty minutes, three hundred sixty degrees with Jack?"

"No. I don't know if any woman ever gets the whole circle with a man. Maybe. But I've got forty-five minutes with Jack—a different part of the circle, though. He has what you miss and you have what he misses. Ironic."

"Have you ever slept with another man since you've been married?" Why did I ask that?

"Nickie, I tell you everything—well, almost everything. Everyone has to have some secrets . . . and the answer is 'no'."

I opened Hoffman's desk drawer and gave Pewter a treat. Lolly wanted one too. The feeding hid my confusion. "Yeah, I guess, but maybe secrets are like stomach acid. They give you pyschic indigestion."

"Ha. You make the truth a sacrament. Because you've told the truth about your sexual orientation you don't have to tell it about everything else you know. Sometimes a secret can be rejuvenating and it doesn't have to be sexual. Just"—she paused and her voice sounded like Regina as a girl—"private."

"Secrets make me feel dirty. You are as sick as you are secret. That's what I used to say to closet queers."

"That's different. You're talking about cultural oppression and I'm talking about individual liberty, or the cultivation of secret gardens, if you will. Of course, I don't expect you to keep secrets from me." She laughed.

I glanced at the time and walked back to the layout table. Regina didn't follow. She slowly drank her coffee before she joined me.

"What do you think of this page?" I handed her another one.

She didn't inspect it. "Nickie, you are so incredibly repressed that sometimes it hurts me."

"Huh?"

"You share your ideas but you don't share yourself. Your emotions are locked away somewhere. Even I don't know where they are, and I want to. Your mother and I talk about it sometimes."

"Behind my back."

"Where else?"

"I figure that people have enough to handle with their own emotions. They haven't time for mine."

"That's not true. You do this because you're gay and because you're open about it. Sounds like a contradiction but it's true. You know and I know that you're outside the approved social order. You're well-mannered and thoughtful but you're distant. What is it that you don't want us to know?"

"Me. I don't want you to know me," I blurted.

"I love you. I want to know you."

"Straight people only want to know gay people if they act according to straight people's rules. People don't want to hear what I think about women—or men, for that matter. They don't want to see the heat or feel the passion, although they're perfectly happy to celebrate it in one another. But because I feel that for a woman, it makes them uncomfortable. Can you imagine if I walked through Runnymede Square holding a woman's hand? It seems such a small thing and yet the cumulative effect of these chilling conventions is to drive you back into yourself, or at least it's driven me back to myself. Hell, I'm not stupid. I know I'm repressed, to use your word."

"I'm not a straight person. I'm me. How do I know I couldn't be in love with a woman? I met Jackson first and I didn't think about it. Don't lump me with the others and don't sell your friends short."

"Oh, Gene." I put my arm around her shoulders. "You're such a romantic. My friends like me in spite of the fact that I'm gay, not because of it."

"You're wrong. You are who and what you are because of everything that's happened to you and everything you are inside. Loving a woman is part of that. It's what has made you you and we love you."

Tears stung my eyes. I very much did not want to cry. "Thanks."

She hugged me back. "Anyway, why should you carry the weight of the world on your shoulders? Frances wasn't worth it." She referred to the one woman I had loved, so long ago I was in danger of forgetting.

"Evolution is the hope of the immature. I'll try and be more open. Might be in another life, though."

We laughed. We didn't finish the newsletter until twelve-thirty that night but the time flew. I knew that someday I would tell Regina what I had done, because I couldn't keep a secret from her. On the one hand I knew she should shoot me, and yet oddly enough, on the other hand, sleeping with Jack had made me much closer to her. I didn't know if she would ever feel that way about me once she knew. What I did know was that Regina was worth ten of me.

24

RENEGADE BINGO

FRIDAY . . . 17 APRIL

Winter gave us a backhanded slap. A cutting wind under dull skies reminded me that we weren't out of the woods yet. As it was Good Friday, the weather added to the dolorous nature of the day. I have never understood the Christian fascination with suffering and death. The crucifix makes me ill and I find it painful even to contemplate a mutilated man, much less worship one.

Mother, devout in her off-center way, would be singed if I told her my thoughts. Aunt Louise would light so many candles for me she'd burn down Saint Rose's. Silence on the issues that concerned me the most was becoming my *modus operandi*. Regina was right. I was reaching the point where I began to fear I couldn't open myself up to anyone.

This is not to say that I don't love Jesus Christ or his message; I do. I don't love what's sprung up around him, and in the office we received rumblings of strange goings-on in the PTL Club. Roger and I dubbed it Pass the Loot, but the official name is Praise the Lord. If I made as much nontaxable income as those TV preachers, I'd be praising the Lord too. Since when does Jesus need a press agent? If God is so smart, you'd think he'd hire better help.

Good Friday services start at two o'clock but I dashed into church for an early morning service, as I knew I'd be in the bullpen today. It was my turn to cover for everyone else when they went to service. Not much crackled on the AP wire.

Mother called to tell me about her date. She and Ed drove over

147

to Emmitsburg for a good dinner. She said he reminded her of Dad. He didn't remind me of Dad. She said to be sure to come to her house tonight for renegade bingo. Saint Rose of Lima's did not run the bingo game or any other form of festivity or fund-raising on Good Friday. Mother's rationale was that as Jesus died at three in the afternoon, what we did at night was our own business. Also, she felt it her civic responsibility to keep people off the streets. I allowed as how I would come this evening, armed with dab-a-dots.

After that conversation I began thinking about The Last Supper. I bet it was fettucine Alfredo.

Mother's house, luxurious in landscaping, displayed what real estate agents call curb appeal. The curbs were loaded tonight. I had to park two blocks away and I was glad I'd taken Lolly and Pewter home, because there'd be too many people in a small space.

When I opened the door Mom shot right up to me. "Two dollars. Price of admission."

I dug into my jeans. "Here, but where is the money going?"

"A charity of my choice." She put the money in the apron she wore.

I walked into the room and Mutzi was calling. The BonBons were out in full force, including Sonny and Sister, Verna's twin brother and sister. These were the people to whom Louise was to have delivered the popcorn. Their real names were Cleota and Leota. Why Verna's mother called a boy Cleota we will never know, but they circumvented this problem with the nicknames Sonny and Sister. Most of the gang was there, including Michelle and Roger— their second date.

Aunt Wheeze, disapproving of a party on Good Friday, sat in the kitchen with Goodyear. She made up a batch of pickled eggs. One of the good things about my aunt was that she hated to be idle. She whizzed in and out of the kitchen with her eggs and other dishes. Finally she alighted next to Ed.

"How are you doing?"

He pressed his dab-a-dot on number nineteen. "Just fine. You work too hard. Why don't you sit down here next to me? Let one of these other girls pass around the horse's dubers."

"Horse's dubers'" was another name for hors-d'oeuvres.

"For a minute." Louise nestled in.

Mother noticed this and hurried behind her. She kept her hands in her apron, jingling the money.

Louise, irritated, reached around and grasped Julia's wrists. "I can't hear the numbers."

"Who cares. You aren't playing."

"Ed is." Wheezie's voice contained a reverential ring.

"I think I'll pass around the tidbits." Mr. Pierre abandoned his card.

I sat down and took it over. "I'll split the winnings with you if this card is a goody."

He smoothed his hair. "I just love the way us girls stick together."

"Pierre!" Louise reprimanded.

"Ah, the voice of the Virgin Mary. Or is it Divergent Mary?" Mr. Pierre winked at me.

A martini preceded bingo for Mr. Pierre. Tonight I sensed he might have indulged ever so slightly and downed two in quick succession.

"Don't talk like that in front of Ed," Wheezie scolded, the voice of propriety.

"It's better than hearing you blab." Mother remained behind Ed and Louise.

"I don't mind." Ed smiled at Mr. Pierre. "I wasn't born yesterday. But can I ask you a question?"

"Anything you want." Mr. Pierre's hand circled his head with a flourish.

"Did you ever—uh—were you ever with a woman?"

For a moment the people around our makeshift table became quiet.

"When I was twenty-one I was violently in love with Theodora Weigle—we called her Teddy. One evening I knew it would be *the* evening. Naturally, I would have married Teddy, you understand. This was not a superficial attachment. When the time came to— came to—" He paused, collected himself. "When the time came to, I couldn't. I couldn't do anything as undignified as lie on top of her."

With that he skipped into the kitchen, leaving Ed to ponder this story. Wheezie was crimson. Mother smiled and jingled her money as she prowled behind other tables.

"Bingo!" Millard Huffstetler shouted.

Millard rarely attended bingo. I was glad to see him. You can spend too much time with your orchids, and Millard did. He'd brought corsages for Mom and Louise and a tasteful arrangement of hot coral tulips. Mother inclined to bright colors. Sometimes a little too bright. Her shoes, for example, were see-through jellies, pink, and she wore mint-green socks too. The colors were muted but then she threw on the vibrating pink apron, and with the magenta streaks in her hair I thought it was a bit much. Mother was Mother, though.

Other than that short flurry between Mom and Louise, the evening unfolded pleasantly. I have often thought that if I live to be as old as my Aunt Louise what I will remember is the laughter. When I was a kid, Daddy, Mom, and I would laugh at breakfast, lunch, and dinner as well as in between. Tonight was one of those nights when everyone was in a great mood; one joke followed another; one good crack was topped with another. The big surprise was when the game was over. Mother gave me the profit.

"Mom, I can't take this."

"Sure you can," Mutzi yelled. "And David Wheeler says if he could have come tonight he'd have tossed in fifty bucks just for you."

"Why?"

"We want you to get the *Clarion*." Verna smiled.

"How else will I write my column? Did you all know that Nickel is giving me my own column? Just like Cholly Knickerbocker and it's going to be called 'Looking Over My Shoulder,' so you all better watch your P's and Q's around me."

Aunt Wheezie had changed the name of her column again. On the basis of this imaginary column she foresaw a great literary career.

"That's enough, Sis." Mother cut her off at the pass because Louise had gulped another mouthful of air and would have continued in her journalistic fantasy.

"You're not a bad boss." Roger folded up his bingo card.

"I notice Michelle is conspicuously silent," I teased.

"Tough—you're the meanest thing to adjectives I've ever seen—but you're fair," Michelle replied.

"Thank you." I turned to Mother. "Was this your idea?"

She swept her hand across the room. "We came up with it together. Mr. Pierre and Wheezie and Georgette and Ed and I were over at Mojo's for lunch and one thing led to another. Verna gave us the food for the party, and Millard, the flowers. Peepbean wouldn't come but then what else is new? He never will like you but"—she beamed—"everyone else does. So you get that paper, honey."

My throat hurt. "Thank you all very much. I'll try to live up to your confidence in me." That was that. I couldn't get out another word.

"Okay, let's play 'Crap on Your Neighbor'!" Mother gleefully announced.

The card decks were smacked on the table. Mr. Pierre cruised through with another round of food before the game. "Crap on Your Neighbor" is a card game whose rules defy explanation. Suffice it to say you can cheat; if you see someone's card you can holler it out to everyone else; you can bribe your neighbor to get up and spy on other hands. Anything goes.

As Jesus was sleeping in his tomb, half of Runnymede stayed up until one o'clock in the morning. That's late for us. The shouting rattled the rooftop but since everyone on the block was also at the party, no one called David Wheeler to complain of noise.

I didn't get back to the farm until two because I stayed to help Mother clean up. Apart from anger or good humor, Julia disdained extravagant displays of emotion. I had thanked her and the others— that was enough. As far as she was concerned the thanks was in the work itself. I'd damn well better do a good job with the *Clarion*.

Exhausted, I emptied pockets on the bird's-eye maple dresser that was Grandma's. The bingo pot was $372.49, a lot of money to everyone playing bingo and a lot of money to me. I took off my clothes, didn't hang them up, and collapsed in bed. Before falling asleep I decided the first day I ran the *Clarion* under my own masthead, I'd run an ad thanking everyone who was at Mother's tonight.

URSIE HAS THE BIT
IN HER TEETH

SATURDAY . . . 18 APRIL

".. . now we need a fence crew. You don't have to be big and brawny, merely willing to get dirty."

Regina and I started whispering to each other and Ursula snapped, but in that polite make-you-want-to-gag tone: "Nickel, I don't think you take our annual Delta Delta Delta horse show seriously because you haven't any children." Ursula's tinted lenses, emerald-green, clouded over. "We do this every year for our scholarship and every year you obstruct the show."

There are dumber ways to raise money then a horse show but right at this moment I can't think of any. Our alumnae chapter rents an indoor riding ring. The participants van their horses and ponies to the show, pay a stall fee if they come in the night before, and then spend the day combing, braiding the manes, and spiffing up their animals, only to have the beast roll in the dirt immediately before its class. Owners of light-colored horses especially suffer. Little girls flood horse shows along with their parents, a species devoted to their offspring and hostile to show judges. Given that Ursie organizes the show, she also determines what kind of classes we sponsor. Events are cleverly arranged so that Tiffany and Harmony win some kind of ribbon, even if it happens to be for the chug-a-Coke race. This race has the children lined up. They ride to the other end of the ring, dismount, chug a Coca-Cola, mount up, and ride back to the finish line.

As long as Ursula Yost was president of our sorority alumnae association, we'd endure the horse shows.

"You're the strongest, Nickel. You can man the fence committee." Ursula bared her fangs on the word "man."

She had tried to prevent me from joining the alumnae association
on the basis of morals: mine. She cast upon me the dirtiest jobs,
hoping to drive me out even after fifteen years of membership.
Ursula believed one could not be a Tri-Delta and a lesbian. How
wrong she was, but then Ursula never did have a sense of fun. Her
heyday was the early 1960s, the years of Tuesday Weld and Sandra
Dee. She was a woman who took Ralph Lauren seriously. She also
insisted that women should wear derbies in the hunt field. What
could be classier than a derby and what could offer less protection?
Besides, what we wore was up to Regina as M.F.H., not Ursie. I
wore a hunt cap. One more strike against me in Ursie's book. And
then, dear old Kenny was a paint, and Ursie turned her nose up at
any animal not the "right color." Perhaps tradition made her feel
secure.

"Okay, I'll run the fence committee but only if you remember not
to start the classes until I get out of the ring." Last year she set out
a child along the course, and I hit the dirt as 16.2 hands of animal
bore down on me.

Running the fence committee consists of browbeating your more
muscular friends to help you actually pick up the bars, standard
posts, logs, and cut brush and move them. The brush is put on the
tops of some jumps to give them the appearance of what one might
have to clear in the hunt field. The classes are divided between
those outdoorsy obstacles and the show-jumping courses: painted
rails, in-and-out jumps, and the like. Often pretty potted plants are
placed in front of some of these jumps. Not only does the fence
committee have to alter the course completely under the direction
of the course designer, we must also rapidly raise the fences as each
class becomes more difficult. If you forget to wear gloves, your
hands get full of splinters and cuts. If your partner, in moving a log
or coop—a triangular-shaped jump—drops his end before you drop
yours, there goes your back.

Any animal that strays into the ring is my responsibility to catch
and remove. As everyone brings their Jack Russell terriers, I offer to
the public the spectacle of myself being outwitted by a dog.

The best part of being on the fence crew is driving the tractor.
The soft loam in the ring needs to be raked between divisions.
There are usually three classes to a division, and if a class is
particularly popular—e.g., 180 entries—then I would rake even
between the classes.

Driving the tractor is *très* butch and I can't resist playing into the stereotype. I always put on my Baltimore Orioles baseball hat and wave to the spectators. Of course, I wear my earrings and lipstick too.

This year our illustrious Master of Foxhounds, Regina, was the course designer. We'd gone over the plans. She laid out a tough course. I had a feeling we'd have spills aplenty and I suspected Regina hoped Tiffany and Harmony might provide us with a few.

"Last year we experienced regrettable delays due to slowness of the fence crew." Ursie stared at me. "This year I want course changes to run like clockwork. Nickel, you bring your people out before the show for a dry run."

"Come on, Ursie, it's hard enough to get there for the show," I protested.

"You have wonderful powers of persuasion." She flashed a false smile. "Clockwork! Clockwork! Clockwork!"

Regina piped up: "Don't get crazed with this. Nickel doesn't persuade people, she bribes them. You'll bankrupt her."

The other alums laughed.

Ursie did not. "I refuse to endure the number of complaints I did last year. Nick, a rehearsal. Don't try to elude your responsibilities to our chapter. Remember Jonah and the whale."

"What's a big fish got to do with it?" I wanted to know.

Her voice was clipped. "Stop obstructing this meeting. I've said all I've got to say on the subject."

I shut up, not because I agreed but because I didn't feel like a fight. I'd ridden an emotional roller coaster the last few days and I had no emotions left for Ursie.

I fidgeted because I wanted the meeting to be over. I also couldn't wait to tell Ursie that my friends who owned Kalarama Farms in Kentucky had offered to sell me a gelding by their great stud, Harlem Globetrotter. Harlem is a saddlebred. Hunter-jumper people call them shaky-tail horses but a saddlebred is a sturdy, multipurpose animal. If I worked with this boy I was hopeful I could turn him into a real hunting horse. They provided me with generous terms but I still didn't know if I could do it, given my financial situation. Then, too, how was I going to board two horses? But I wanted that gelding. He exuded a dark glamour and a sweet disposition.

"Is that it?" Regina demanded of Ursie. She wanted to play tennis even though it stayed cool.

"Yes. Meeting adjourned."

The ladies, ranging in age from twenty-four to sixty-nine, romped for the buffet while Regina and I sped for the door. Driving over to the barn, I excitedly told her about the saddlebred and we schemed to come up with money.

After our three sets of tennis we sat in the little cottage. Regina packed turkey sandwiches and Perrier.

"Another year on the fence committee. Who are you going to press into service this time?"

"Guess I'll round up a crew at the last minute."

"If it weren't for the last minute, nothing would get done." Regina polished off her sandwich.

"That's what Wheezie says."

"That's where I heard it."

My face must have registered how I felt because Regina said, "What's wrong with you?"

"I feel sick."

"Gee, the sandwiches taste good to me."

"They're delicious. Excuse me." I went into the bathroom and threw up. As soon as I did I felt fine. I returned to Regina. "I don't know what's going on with me, Gene. Nerves. I'm trying not to let this *Clarion* sale rattle me but—well, I guess it is."

"Jack said you'd know by next Friday."

"Looks that way. Foster's going to Baltimore on Thursday. Since Charles has agreed to hold a note for the two hundred and fifty thousand dollars, I'm in a better position vis-à-vis the bank. None of this portends what Diz will do, since he has more money than God."

"If the bank gives you the loan he might back off. He likes you."

"Not that much." I reached for another sandwich because now I was starving.

"Won't that make you sick?"

"No. I toss once and then I'm great. I ought to go to Trixie and get something to coat the lining of my stomach, probably."

"What about tranquilizers?"

"Couldn't work."

Regina opened a bag of Wise's potato chips. "Yeah, I couldn't do it either. They say millions of people are hooked on them too. Somehow it's cleaner than booze."

"True. You support your physician, you support your pharmacist, and you support the big drug companies who produce the stuff. Taking tranquilizers is All-American."

"Yeah, snorting cocaine only makes Colombians rich."

We laughed and finished our lunch. Then we went out and played doubles. I felt terrific.

26

BLESSED EASTER

SUNDAY . . . 19 APRIL

Easter dawned radiant and fresh. We each cherish personal rituals, and rising with the sun on Easter Sunday is one of mine. Easter remains my favorite holiday except for my birthday. Christmas I have to share with Jesus but my birthday is all my own. However, for public holidays and high holy days, Easter wins. Who can resist the soft spring light, the hymns, the hope of resurrection—except that the Resurrection only applies to one of us. Easter's also a terrific opportunity to display one's wardrobe.

Runnymede Square, a moving kaleidoscope of people, proved that point. Pinks, yellows, smart navy-blues, mint-greens, polka-dotted dresses, every color, stripe, and combination imaginable paraded through the Square after services. Portia and Lucretia Rife, home for the holiday, competed with each other as well as with Liz, Diz's wife. As none of the rest of us could drape ourselves in Valentino, Versace, and Kenzo, those three battled it out in a class by themselves. Among our group, Verna BonBon traipsed down the steps of Saint Rose of Lima wearing a silk dress with a scalloped cape. She wisely chose a deep periwinkle color. Louise indulged in the Victorian look and this was for Ed's benefit, since he attended mass with the Bonnevilles. What only Mother and I knew was that her dress belonged to Grandma Hunsenmeir. Louise's hair, atop her head in that becoming fashion, was wreathed with a ribbon plus one palest-pink rosebud. The rosebud about gagged Mother.

Mother wore a light-yellow dress with teal accents, gloves, shoes, hat, and purse to match. The veil of her hat was pale-yellow and the little dots on the veil were teal. I pulled myself together in a decent blue skirt and a cashmere sweater. My heels were killing me.

Together Mother and I tottered about the Square, where we passed and repassed. David Wheeler and Bucky Nordness coolly walked by each other, families in tow, and did not speak. The wives did. This was duly noted by everyone.

Aunt Wheeze put up Christmas dinner and Mother cooked Easter dinner. They'd divided up the holidays long before I was born. Mr. Pierre came for dinner, bringing with him a spectacular salad to complement Mom's ham.

Goodyear and Lolly behaved but Pewter did not. The lure of ham tested her willpower. After three mad leaps onto the table and a dash from one end to the other, Mother shut her up in the kitchen, where she wailed her fury and hurt feelings. My repeated trips in with ham calmed her not a bit and finally Lolly sat on the other side of the kitchen door and cried.

I broke down and put Pewter on my lap so she could eat with me. Aunt Wheezie grimaced about cat hair in my food but by this time I had hair balls myself. It shut up the cat and she purred through the rest of the meal, even enjoying a bit or two of white cake. The dogs and Pewter got bowls of ice cream too.

The best part of Easter or any holiday with Mother and Louise was open house after the meal. Anyone could visit up until ten at night. As it was warm enough to open the windows, we could hear our friends coming up the walk.

Mother organized an Easter egg hunt for the kids. Little Decca BonBon found the most. Children from the neighborhood adored Mom's Easter egg hunts because they were testing. Mother would climb trees and stick eggs in the hollows where limbs joined. Her attitude was, if this old lady can get up there, so can a kid.

As the light faded we prepared cold cuts, even though everyone moaned about how full they were and how fat.

Ed Tutweiler Walters played kick-the-can with the children while we laid out the table.

"Food!" Mother opened her front door as Regina and Jackson strolled up the walk.

Jack and I avoided each other as much as we could. We were cordial. The sight of him cut through me like a knife. I wanted to touch him, to smell his hair, to run my hands over his bulging pecs. He had the most beautiful chest. Even though that one affair before me had dented my pride, I wanted him. The power of attraction, whether it's chemistry or fate, fries your brain cells. I was determined to make it mind over matter.

Mr. Pierre entertained us at supper with a story we'd heard before but Ed hadn't. This was the tale of Penny Pfeiffer, who lived in Greenville, South Carolina, where Mr. Pierre was born and raised. As the children also had not heard it, we fell into a casual silence.

"When I got out of the service after Korea, I wanted a trade I could take anywhere. In the service I was your basic infantryman so I didn't learn anything there that would carry over into civilian life, and what I learned I will not repeat in mixed company." He smiled at the ladies.

Thatcher Bonneville, a Vietnam vet, chimed in. "Hear, hear."

As the men nodded agreement, Mr. Pierre continued. "So I said to myself, 'What can I do where I can be my own boss, not get a lot of money tied up in inventory and yet make a good living, meet interesting people?' I thought about being a diesel mechanic but one gets so filthy. Also, I didn't like the diesel mechanics I'd met. That was out. I thought about being a florist but you can lose your flowers if the power goes off on a cold winter's day. That wasn't for me. Why, I even thought about farming but then I'd never be able to travel. I'd seen too much blood in the war to want to be a doctor and I certainly don't have the temperament to be a lawyer—forgive me, Jackson. I don't know how you do it. After a lengthy process of elimination I hit upon hairdressing. Hairdressers have been the intimates of nobility for centuries. They know the trends first. They are able to exercise some artistic flourish, particularly with progressive clients, those chic women on the cutting edge." He glanced toward Mother.

"I went to school and studied and discovered I had a flair for it. One of my teachers—I'll never forget her, Mrs. Penny Pfeiffer—taught us about hair health. Every Saturday, Penny would go to the old folks' home and do the ladies' hair. She performed this service out of the goodness of her heart because the pensioners could not have afforded even a wash and rinse. One Saturday she asked me to accompany her. I did and when we got there I watched her work on the residents and I, too, styled a few ladies' hair. In particular, I remember two girls advanced in their years who thought they were on a boat to Halifax. I had to speak to them as though I were the captain. What I noticed was that Penny only styled the front and the sides of heads. Never the back. As we left I asked her why and she said she used to work for an undertaker, and given the occupants of the home, she was doing the local funeral parlor a favor."

He loved that story. I don't know why. I never thought it was that funny but because he laughed, the kids laughed, and then we laughed at the kids.

"Did I tell you that last week Regina and I went to a party over at the rectory of Saint Paul's? Tim Deane was there handing out business cards—I kid you not," Jackson said.

Tim Deane was our local funeral director. I don't believe undertakers should network.

We giggled about that, then conversation veered toward Nordness versus Wheeler, the *Clarion,* the question of whether Charles could really retire, the Hunt Club, tennis, school, the basketball scandal at the University of Maryland due to the death of Len Bias, drugs, lack of discipline, the weakening of moral fiber, and pass the dessert.

Except for my turmoil over Jack, it was one of the nicest holidays I can remember, the calm before the storm.

27

LOVE LIFTED ME

MONDAY . . . 20 APRIL

I passed Mildew Adams, wife of Foster, on my way into town. She pulled over by the side of the road, saw it was me in the Chrysler, waved, and rolled back on the road. Mr. Pierre's rinse shone with a greenish cast on her hair. It did my heart good to see it, and while harboring ugly thoughts against Mildred might not have been the way to heaven, she deserved it. Pillow talk between her and Foster included my financial statement and she had no right to blab it around town. However, now that Charles was holding a second for me on the paper buy-out, her lips were sealed. Actually, I'd like to staple them shut.

A whiff of coolness hung over Michelle and Roger. Both were diligently bent over their typewriters but looked up to greet me, Pewter, and Lolly. John was on the phone and hung up with a bang, scaring Pewter.

"That's the sorriest son of a bitch that ever shit behind good shoes," John exploded.

"Who?"

"Nils Nordness."

"So what else is new?" I said.

Roger called out, "Yeah, there are two douche bags in Runnymede. Nils Nordness and Nils Nordness."

"What's Bucky then?" I asked.

"An enema bag." Roger returned to his story. "Nils operates under the erroneous impression that because his

160

brother is chief of police for North Runnymede, the rules don't apply to him," John fumed.

"He was that way before Bucky became the chief of police." I offered this small historical insight.

"Hey, I don't care if the guy is a terrible developer, a suck developer. I wouldn't live in that crap he throws up out there on the Baltimore Road. But to each his own. Right?" John laced his coffee. It was ten past nine in the morning. "I wanted to know if the rumor I'd heard was true: that the old Bon Ton Department Store had been bought by Mid-Atlantic Holding Shares and Nordness put in a bid for reconstruction."

"Where'd you hear that?" I sat down with a bump.

"I've got my protected sources. Mid-Atlantic's been successful in keeping it quiet but the deed transfer is next week. Then it's a matter of public record." John drank his coffee.

"Diz Rife bought the Bon Ton?" Michelle, silent but attentive until now, spoke.

Roger stopped typing. "Why?"

John leaned back in his chair. "My hunch is that if he buys this paper he's going to modernize. What good is this old building with the huge press under glass, a dead duck as opposed to a pheasant under glass." He faced me. "I give you a fifty-fifty chance to get this paper now with Charles's cooperation, but Diz is going to do something with the old Bon Ton even if he doesn't get the *Clarion*."

"Like what?" Michelle, out of her seat now, brought me a cup of tea. I'd had not time to make it yet.

"Thank you, Michelle." I gulped the tea, trying to focus my meager mental abilities. I'm not much good in the morning and my detractors would extend that to the remainder of the day.

"I say he'll mount a frontal offense." John left no doubt in his tone of voice.

"Are you telling us Diz will start a paper whether he gets the *Clarion* or not?" Roger was incredulous.

"Exactly." John sounded triumphant.

"Can this little town support two newspapers?" Michelle wanted to know.

"Who knows?" John shrugged.

"We can." I was firm. "We used to and I don't see why we couldn't do it again.

"No way." John disagreed, as I knew he would. "You can't compete for the advertising dollar. Two papers flourished here before television but they flourished everywhere. Hell, New York City had more newspapers than the fingers on my hand once upon a time. The fact that two papers lasted here as long as they did is testimony to how backward this place is."

"Or testimony to the fact that we don't watch television," Roger said. "I don't watch it."

"Me neither," Michelle supported him.

"It's beneath contempt. The pabulum of the mind." John fixed another cup of coffee. If this kept up he'd fall asleep or get belligerent, and he was leaning toward belligerent.

"I like it," I piped up.

"What?" They all looked at me as though I were a sea slug.

"No, I really do. I don't watch much of it because I'm busy and because we know each other here."

John cut me off. "I don't get the connection."

"I mean we make our own fun. If I lived in a big city and lacked the close friends that I have here, I know I'd watch TV a lot. The characters on the shows would become fantasy friends, kind of."

The AP wire coughed then and began chugging. Paper spewed out on the floor. Roger got up to check the news as John, Michelle, and I continued a spirited discussion of TV and the concept of pitching to the lowest common denominator, since that was John's view of how networks choose programming and people get to be stars. Roger appeared spellbound by the AP machine.

"Roger, what are you doing?"

He couldn't lift his eyes off the copy. "You're not going to believe this."

We bumped into one another racing to the wire. He was right. We couldn't believe it. The PTL Club story blew apart into sex, sin, and seduction. It was scandal too good to be true. Jim Bakker, head of the PTL Club, was accused by another TV preacher of practicing oral sex in a Florida motel room with a secretary, of having homosexual encounters and group sex.

I grabbed the phone off Roger's desk, since his was the closest to the AP machine. "Mother. Get down here."

"You're a dutiful daughter." John laughed. He knew this news would be like cayenne on Mother's brain.

Within minutes she and Goodyear burst into the room, having dashed through the alleyway and entered through the back press entrance. Her Adidas running shoes were grass-stained, so Mom must have cut across the neighbors' yards.

"What?" She was breathless.

Michelle, Roger, and John respectfully stood aside while I took Mother to the machine and handed her the copy, some of which had spilled onto the floor. She pushed her glasses up on the bridge of her nose and read. And read. We watched. She was silent. Then she smiled. This was followed by a girlish giggle, overcome by a laugh, until Mother was leaning against the machine helpless with laughter. I fetched her a cup of coffee while Roger, a gentleman, gave her his chair.

She recovered enough to talk. "There is a God!"

Surprised, I said, "You had doubts?"

She nodded. "Every now and then, like when Wheezie got that first date with Ed." She wiped her eyes. She'd been laughing so hard she had tears in them. "I guess Jim Bakker turned 'Love Lifted Me' into a porno song." She sang a few bars.

"You have a lovely voice, Mrs. Smith," Michelle complimented her.

"Oh, honey, you'll have to go to lunch with me so I can tell you how Celeste Chalfonte, Ramelle, Fairy Thatcher and Fannie Jump Creighton, Ev Most, and myself went across the county singing that very song. Why wait for lunch? Come on and I'll buy you an omelet."

Michelle looked beguiled.

"You can go, Michelle." I okayed the defection and turned to Mom. "Why aren't you calling Wheezie?"

"Because I'm going to wait until fifteen minutes before the noon news. Then I'll call. It'll drive her up the walls. Which reminds me. Mr. Pierre and I settled on a frothy apricot, so you figure out when you can paint. Come on, dear." She touched Michelle's elbow and off they went.

I'd forgotten about painting Mother's living room. I dialed Mr. Pierre.

"Bon soir."

"Mr. Pierre, it's morning."

"Bon morning," he replied.

"What's this I hear about a frothy apricot?"

"Ma cherie, light as an anemic peach. We'll do the woodwork in a linen-white and I've ordered teal pillows and even a magenta one to accent Mama's hair."

I groaned to myself. "She doesn't have enough money for that."

"Discount. I motored up to York and hit the fabric discount house that Bob and I found years ago. Better than that, my precious Nickel, I've found someone to paint a coffee table faux marble."

"Who?"

"Peepbean."

"Peepbean!"

"He's very good. Millard has developed in his nephew an aesthetic impulse."

Millard had developed little else in Peepbean.

"All right, how much to I have to lend her?" *Lend* was a euphemism for cough up cold cash.

"Umm, maybe three hundred dollars—if we're careful. Maybe a tee-ninesy bit more."

Well, there went my renegade bingo pot. "Okay, but you've got to watch her every minute. Mother has never heard of the word *restraint* in these matters."

"You may depend upon me. And might I remind you, Nickel, that if it weren't for me she would have rushed out and purchased these things retail?"

"And might I remind you, Mr. Pierre, that if you didn't keep those fancy interior decorating magazines in your shop she would never know the difference?"

"How wrong you are. Your mother is naturally creative."

"My mother is naturally nuts."

"I shall strike that from my memory. I do have customers, you know."

"I know. I see the results daily. One more small thing. I believe you should take a coffee break and come over here."

"Why?" His voice rose.

"Why not?" My voice was playful.

He was by my side before I blinked. I showed him the AP wire and swore him to say nothing, not so much as a syllable until fifteen minutes before the noon news when Mother would be telling Wheezie.

"What I sacrifice for you." He mocked sorrow and then maliciously, with a smile, said to John: "This will go down as the most expensive blow job in history."

John could not bear gay men but he did laugh. So did Roger. By now Arnie and the guys from the back were stooped over the machine, too, all of them laughing.

Mr. Pierre kissed me on the cheek. "You are a true friend, darling, to give me such pleasure. I shan't forget this."

"Good. You can be on my fence committee for the Tri-Delta horse show." I pushed him toward the door as he sputtered a refusal, which settled into a rancorous agreement.

He paused at the door and dramatically threw his bottle-green scarf with thin yellow strips around his neck. To those assembled he said, "The Bakkers are a good example of why some animals eat their young." He exited amidst laughter.

LOVE LIFTED ME HIGHER

TUESDAY . . . 21 APRIL

Orrie Tadia blew back into town today at noon. Although her airplane touched down in Baltimore at nine-thirty A.M. and it couldn't have taken more than an hour and a half to reach Runnymede with her son-in-law, Mac Marshall, driving, she lurked on the edges of town until noon. Noon, even in bad weather, meant the Square would be filled with anybody who was anybody and Orrie would not be denied her entrance.

Lolly Mabel, Pewter, Michelle, and I were cutting across the Square to peek inside the old Bon Ton building, since we couldn't believe what John told us about Diz buying the thing. No sooner had we reached the midpoint of the Square—now a riot of blooms, since both sides competed even in gardening—than we heard a horn honk. Then another one. Soon the horns were honking around the Square. Mutzi Elliott dashed out of his greengrocer store with his cowbell. Lolly started barking and Pewter growled. The girls hate loud noises.

Mother and Mr. Pierre ran out of Daddy's hardware store. Louise was coming down the steps of the library, without books this time. Aunt Wheezie, her devout Catholicism notwithstanding, had lectured Mother and me the night before at dinner on the meaning of karma. She hated being behind her sister in hearing the PTL news and covered up with a burst of religious mysticism and refinement. She also told me more than I ever wanted to know about soul travel. She said she would be practicing leaving her body tonight

when she went to sleep. I asked her if she would come visit me at
the farm and she said no, she'd always had a hankering to see Paris.
Mother wanted to know what happened to Louise's body during
her travels and Louise replied that her body stayed in the bed.
Mother suggested that while Wheezie's soul was out there in the
Great Beyond, she might want to pick up a new body, a younger
model. This didn't go down with Aunt Louise, and dinner at Luigi's
plunged into recrimination.

Whether or not that affected my aunt's reading habits, I don't
know. But when she saw Orrie in the front seat of Mac's convertible, heard the horns, heard the cowbell, she hurried down the steps
as fast as she could.

Orrie, like an aged and hefty prom queen, waved to us and we
waved back.

Michelle was curious. "Does she usally get this kind of greeting
upon her return?"

"No. We're glad to see her, of course, but this is unusual."

We walked toward the library. The Bon Ton could wait. Orrie
and Mac headed, with majesty, for the library. When the convertible
pulled up next to the curb there was a joyous screaming and
hugging known only to Southern women. Mother and Mr. Pierre
were also heading toward Orrie.

As Michelle and I came up behind the car we saw on the rear
bumper this sticker: HONK IF YOU'VE BEEN MARRIED TO MAC MAR-
SHALL. Mom and Mr. Pierre saw it about the same time we did.

Orrie, after more hugs from Louise, sharply turned. "Nickel
Smith, what's so funny? I haven't seen you since Christmas and this
is the greeting I get?"

"Orrie, you look tanned and wonderful." The truth.

"We're laughing because of your sticker." Mother smiled but
with a tart edge.

"What sticker?" Orrie flounced in her seat, bathing in the attention.

Louise trundled up behind the car. "Oh, Orrie, you'd better see
this yourself."

"I don't want to get out of the car. Mac, what are they talking
about?"

Mac's trim moustache twitched. "I don't know."

As mothers-in-law go, Orrie wasn't so bad but Mac wisely decided to check out the back of his car. He sauntered up and
observed his bumper. We were quiet. Mac's face turned red.

"Well?" Orrie demanded.

"Mother Tadia, it says, 'Honk if you've been married to Mac
Marshall.' "

"It does not. You're making this up." She heaved herself out of the car and came around. "It does!" Without blinking she wheeled on Mother. "Julia, you're behind this."

"Orrie, now why would I drive all the way to Baltimore to put a sticker on Mac's car? Be reasonable."

"Orrie, darling, so chic and, well, tropical, look at it this way—the only time there was more celebration in this town was Armistice Day in 1918." Mr. Pierre charmed her.

"You weren't here in 1918," Louise corrected him.

I couldn't resist. "No, but you were."

Before Louise could hot up, Mr. Pierre returned his attentions to Orrie. "I shall expect you at my establishment at your earliest convenience. You look so youthful, Orrie, we need to change your hairstyle. Away with the old. Banish age. Let's say hello to youth."

Orrie ate it up. "See you tomorrow morning." She waved to Mutzi. "Hey, Mutzi, I want pattypan squash!"

"Too early," Mutzi hollered back.

"Start thinking about it." She climbed back in the convertible. Mac obediently followed. "Now, ladies and gentlemen, I must unpack and settle myself after my long journey. I'll be receiving tomorrow."

Off they drove.

Michelle and I stayed on the sidewalk and walked around the Square over to the Bon Ton.

"Orrie's after-dinner drink is Kaopectate and she sneaks gin in it." I sighed, thinking of the Orrie of my childhood and the Orrie of today, the same delightful person with the addition of a few decades.

"What's the meaning of the bumper sticker?"

"That? Mac's been married three times and two of those times to Orrie's daughters. She has four, you know."

"I forgot, if I did know. Trying to remember everyone's genealogies is difficult."

"I know. I've lived here all my life and I can't keep them straight either, what with second cousins, third cousins, and shirttail cousins. Anyway, Mac lives in Baltimore with the daughter to whom he is currently married, and let's hope it lasts. Orrie'll kill him if it doesn't."

"Where's his ex—the other sister?"

"Jackson Hole, Wyoming. After the divorce, that girl slingshotted out of here. Wife Number One, ex-wife, I mean, lives in Red Lion, Pennsylvania."

We stood in front of the Bon Ton, peeking in the windows.

"Looks the same." Michelle pressed her nose against the window.

"Sure does. Let's go over to Falkenroth, Spangler, and Finster for a minute."

She obediently followed. A new window had been installed immediately after the cannon episode. Looked like Falkenroth, Spangler & Finster had better relations with their insurance company than I did. Not a word yet on my Jeep or a penny either. The sign painter, Peepbean Huffstetler, carefully outlined the "R" in Spangler as we opened the front door.

"Hello, Peepbean."

He grunted. That was hello.

The place seemed vacant, as it was lunch hour, but we heard a rustle in the back.

"Yo," I called out.

George Spangler, in lime-green pants, answered. "Who is it?"

"Nickel and Michelle."

He softly walked down the little hallway. "To what do I owe this unexpected pleasure, ladies?"

"You were practicing your putting, weren't you, George? The Willow Bend championship's coming up in June." I hoped that would disarm him a bit. It did.

"Well—"

"This is going to be your year, George." I glided on to my next subject. "Do you know the closing date for the sale of the Bon Ton?"

"Friday."

"Good for the town. Line up those putts, buddy." I smiled and left, and as I went through the door it hit George what he'd done.

"Nickel—" He trotted after us. "Diz doesn't want anyone to know."

"Why? It's good news."

"He's funny that way. Wait until the deed is recorded."

"George, I'm a reporter. I won't use your name, okay?"

His face registered relief and dismay simultaneously, " 'Preciate that."

I liked George but I didn't respect him. He had inherited just enough money to make a bum out of him. His only effort was in obtaining his law degree from the University of Virginia back in 1971. If he drew up a will or a deed a month, that was sweat for him. It's hard for me to believe a man without a vocation has balls. Since he rarely worked, he was a great source of gossip because his whole life was one long social exchange. You might say that George was the original party boy. The road map of broken veins on his face was proof of that.

*   *   *

As Michelle, Lolly, Pewter, and I cut across the Square the talons of fear gripped my gut. I didn't want the *Clarion* to go to Diz. I didn't want it to go to anybody but me.

"How are things with Roger?" I asked Michelle.

"He's a nice guy."

"That sounds noncommittal."

"What's it to you?"

"Don't get testy. I'm being friendly, not nosy. I think the world of Roger and I'm even starting to like you too."

She changed the subject. "Do you think your Mother was behind that bumper sticker?"

"Yep. She must have paid someone to do it. Orrie is Louise's best friend. Now that she's back Mother will need me as an ally."

"What's going on with Ed Tutweiler Walters?"

"Michelle, I believe you might turn into a Runny yet. You're evidencing an interest in gossip."

"I prefer to think of it as news." She picked up a stick and threw it for Lolly.

"As far as I know, Ed divides his time between them when he isn't with the BonBons."

"Wonder when he's going back to Birmingham?"

"I don't know. It must be fun to be retired—and have a little money, you know? Ed can come and go as he pleases. I can't imagine that."

"Me neither. I don't think I want to stop working. My Dad retired at sixty-five last year. He built and ran a window treatment plant."

"What?"

"He made blinds, shades, window treatments."

"Oh."

"Ever since he retired he's been sick, one complaint after another. Mother's irritated because he's underfoot, and much as he loves sailing, how much can he sail? I told him to start another business or to get involved with young people starting businesses. Be a consultant. I think the reason for Mom's brief visit was less to see me than to get away from Dad."

Out of the corner of my eye I noticed Jackson Frost bearing down on me. Jackson paid his respects to Michelle and then said in a too casual voice, "You putting the paper to bed tonight?"

"I do every Tuesday." I tried to be casual myself.

"Might see you later." He bid us good-day and left.

"He really is the best-looking man in Runnymede," Michelle chirped.

"Yep." I had a lump in my throat.

True to his word Jackson came over to the *Clarion* at nine-thirty. Lolly greeted him by rubbing her head against his legs. Pewter waited for Jack to come to her.

"Hi."

"Hi," I answered.

"I got used to seeing you Tuesday night." I didn't reply, so he continued. "I'm sorry, Nickel."

"Me too."

His white teeth gleamed in a half smile. "What was it you said to me once? 'Monogomy is contrary to nature but necessary for the greater social good.' I don't know whether I believe it or not."

"I don't know if I do either but there isn't an alternative, or if there is one I don't know about it."

He sat opposite me. "Whatever happened to the sixties?"

"We got married and had children, I guess."

"You didn't." He stuck his finger in a cup on my desk filled with blue pencils and he rattled them around. "Sometimes I envy you and sometimes I think you missed the boat."

"I think that too—sometimes."

"Do you miss me?"

"Of course I miss you, but what good does it do to talk about it? I have to admit that I'm relieved."

"I'm not," he said matter-of-factly.

"Weren't you ever worried about Regina finding out?"

"Not as much as you were."

"Sometimes I don't understand you."

"I don't want you to understand me—I want you to love me." His beautiful blue eyes lit up.

"Please, let's give the word *love* a rest."

"Gene and I have been married for twenty-two years. Your relationship changes over those years. I think I'm blessed with a good marriage, but to tell you the God's honest truth, if she went out and had herself a rip-roaring affair I wouldn't be jealous."

"No, you'd feel justified for what you've done." I didn't feel like being generous.

"Maybe, but you haven't been married for decades. You don't know how it feels. And furthermore, don't tell me how I feel or what I feel. I know I wouldn't be jealous. We're so close, Gene and I, but that heady, lusty, can't-live-without-you stuff is gone. I think she feels the same way about me. In a funny way, she and I have a friendship somewhat like the two of you have."

I remembered that Regina had said something similar when we were slaving over the Blue and Gray Hunt Club newsletter but she also noted the differences. But then, no two friendships are identical. If they were, people would be interchangeable parts, with no individuality. Death would lose its sting. If someone is replaceable, you wouldn't care if you lost her.

"I believe you as much as I can. And you're right, I haven't been married for twenty-two years. I don't know what it feels like."

"I want us to be friends. If we lose that, then I've lost a lot."

"We'll always be friends. Until death us do part." I smiled bigger than I should have.

"Maybe there is a Cupid with a bow and arrow," he mused. "Last Christmas he let fly, and that was that."

"People would be better off if we had a mating season like animals. At least our troubles would be confined."

"Was it trouble?"

"Yes and no. You know what I mean. If you were single I wouldn't have a minute's guilt." I sighed. "One of the great things about living alone is that I have so much time to think. I often wonder what society would be like if we did have a mating season, or else, to take the opposite tack, if we dispensed with the sexual codes we have and let 'er rip."

"Lot of fucking and killing."

"We have enough already."

"You're the strangest soul, Nickie. One way or the other, you'll move away from the emotional to ideas."

"That's me. I'm tired of hearing how repressed I am."

"Did I say that?"

"No, you didn't," I grumbled, "but it's been a hot topic of conversation of late and I don't think I'm wildly repressed. We each have a distinctive way of approaching life and I'm a person who will try and use my head first. The heart follows the head for me, not the reverse. Dammit, that really is the way I am and I'm not going to change."

This seemed to ring a bell or at least a distant wind chime.

"I'll buy that." Jackson leaned back in the chair. "You're obviously dying to spring on me your latest theory which has to do with sex. Now, mind you, I'd rather be having sex with you than hearing about it but I'm in your company, so I'm happy."

I wanted to hug him. Sometimes he could be so sweet he reminded me of Dad, but like every woman past the age of puberty I knew no adult male ever loved you the way your father did. After puberty it's quid pro quo. I rubbed my hands together. "Humans can mate at any time. We're always ready. Agreed?"

"Agreed."

"Okay, one way that cultures past and present try to settle this confusion is to harness sex. If we made love to anyone who caught our fancy, whenever we wanted, nothing would get done."

"I agree to that, too, and wouldn't it be glorious." A grin illuminated his handsome features.

"Don't be a pig. I'm serious." He laughed and I continued. "Marriage was a good way to limit our sexual expression. Even if a culture allows one man to have many wives, or one woman to have many husbands, there's been a restriction imposed that limits sexual energy and breeding. That way we have energy left over for agriculture, the arts, building, war—whatever. We can create true communities because we've stabilized the sex drive. Different cultures stabilize that drive differently but they all stabilize it."

"I'm still with you."

"So, one of the first rules of any society has to be that married people are off limits to other people. It's vital for a community to know and to advertise who is taken and who is available."

"I don't like this part of the theory quite as much."

"I didn't say I liked it either but that doesn't make it any less true. The human race can't afford to have everyone running after everyone else. Apart from the confusion that would create, it foments disease. Especially now. I mean, Jack, sex has never been private and it never will be. We perform the act in private but we must be public about the connection. Sex is how we pass down worldly goods. It's how we create the primary unit of our society, the couple. Other societies have larger primary units but sex is still part of it."

"I see what you mean, honey, but I will always believe what I do with my body is nobody's business but my own."

"But it is. Look at it from another angle." I got up to make tea for myself and coffee for Jackson. "This rule applies to gay people as well as straight people. If a person is gay, then he or she is not a suitable mate for someone who is straight. We each need to find a suitable mate who will not only love us but protect us and help us become productive, useful members of our community. Think of the energy expended to find a suitable mate. Our entire culture is obsessed with the romantic phase of mating. No wonder we're so backward. Well, anyway, I got off the track. When a gay person marries a straight person, there's heartache. The community absolutely must know who is straight, who is gay, who is married, and who is single. Without that information we make painful mistakes and lose time."

He sipped his coffee while I knocked back my tea and made another cup. "I never thought of it that way."

"If you accept my theory, then coming out is not an issue of individual liberty; it is a matter of community responsibility. Communities must have truth and trust. Not understanding that sexual information is crucial to our building communities is going to weaken the community as well as harm the individual. So it's actually in everyone's self-interest to make coming out easy for gay people. Gotta accept them for what they are because they are a permanent part of every society on earth and have been from B.C. to the present. Doesn't it make sense to find a way to include them in our community and make them useful? The burden really is on straight people. Hell, if the price of honesty is getting your head bashed in or losing your job, who but the brave are going to tell the truth?"

He reached over and took the second cup of tea out of my hand. "Don't drink another cup of tea, Nickie."

"Why?"

"You'll talk all night."

I laughed. "Sorry."

"Not as sorry as I am. I think your ideas are pretty interesting. If I lived with you I'd hear them every day. Christ, why can't you, Regina, the kids, and me just push the boundaries of the family a little further? Sometimes I feel locked in and I hear the clock ticking." He touched my hand. "I have little to complain about and yet I'm in love with two women at the same time. In our society there's no more room for me than there is for the gay person."

I'd never thought of that. I put my teacup back on the counter. I wanted to kiss him but I didn't. His frustration was my frustration but I didn't have an answer for either of us. There comes a time in one's life when you no longer subscribe to relative pain. Homosexual or heterosexual, black or white, man or woman, we suffered, we cried, we bled. Did it matter how? What mattered was, could we give one another comfort and perhaps even laughter? Could we make this journey of life with some tolerance and grace? Could we grasp the simple, splendid truth that we are all part of one another? I was part of Jackson and he was part of me but I couldn't have him.

Before he left I asked him to be on my fence crew.

He shook his head and then started laughing at me. "From social theory to horseshit."

"Maybe social theory is horseshit."

"Maybe everything is." he had his hand on the huge doorknob. "Eventually all things are known and few matter."

"Who said that?"

"Gore Vidal."

"He did not, did he?" I questioned.

"If he didn't, he should have." Jackson blew me a kiss as he opened the door. "And yes, you weasel, I'll be on your fence crew."

His curly blond hair caught the light outside the door and then he disappeared into the Square. I loved him. I could not longer fool myself about how much I did love him. I gazed out at the statues and the cannon. Night caressed the Square with her black velvet glove. A surge of euphoria shot through my body. Sorrowing as I was at not being able to make a life with Jack, at no longer being able to sleep with him, the purity of that love made me human. It's the only force that might possibly save our pitiful race.

LOUISE LEARNS
THE ROPES

WEDNESDAY . . . 22 APRIL

The day started with a tiff in the composing room between Pewter and Louisa May Alcatt. Arnie Dow brought his cat to work that morning because he would be taking her to the vet's on his lunch hour. His wife worked up in Hanover, so she couldn't do it. Louisa May, hale and hearty, needed her rabies shot. By the time I reached the composing room, ugly words had been exchanged and suspicious hair tufts were lodged in Pewter's claws.

Arnie, a good-natured man, kept his temper about the cat argument. As I heaved Pewter's ever-increasing bulk over my shoulder he wished me luck. Said he and the boys were rooting for me.

Staggering under the weight of Pewter, whom I considered renaming Godzilla, I ran into Ann Falkenroth. She rarely visited the paper, so seeing her was a pleasant surprise. Ann belonged to that generation of white women of a certain class who were trained to take care of a home, a man, and children, beautifully. The idea of working in the outside world was both frightening and repugnant. In fact, it was Ann Falkenroth née Lansburg who cut Spots Chalfonte to the bone back in 1932. Spots landed a minor role in a Ronald Colman movie and on a visit home Ann said, "Spots, you look ravishing. I'm so sorry you're still working." Now whether Ann said any such thing is up for question. I'm not going to ask her. Apart from that moment, if it happened, Ann was a good woman.

"That cat is on a seafood diet. Everything she sees." Ann petted Pewter's head.

175

"How nice to see you. I wish you'd come by more often." I was sincere.

"Charles has his bailiwick and I have mine. Did he tell you we found exactly the right place for us in Palm Springs?"

"No. But he's been flying in and out of the office like a hummingbird."

"I know." She rolled her eyes. "Well, we did find the right community for us. It's called Morningside and oh, Nickel, it's scrumptious. The walls of the place are serpentine, the lighting is fabulous, and the golf course is going to tax my slender abilities. I tell you it's something to be standing on an emerald-green fairway staring up at the San Jacinto Mountains, and we even found the right model home for us, the Oakmont Four! We thought about the Pinehurst but decided we needed more space if for nothing else than for Charles's books. You must come visit us."

"I'd love to." I could easily adapt to Palm Springs and I vaguely remembered a brochure for Morningside that Charles once left lying around the office. I could get used to that too.

"Well, dear, I've got to run. Garden Club and you know what a witch Mildred Adams can be if one is late. Notice I said 'witch.' "

"I admire your restraint."

Ann giggled and slipped out the back door. She possessed a bubbling energy, a genuine sense of optimism. I could understand why Charles loved his wife.

As she went out the back door Ed Tutweiler Walters came in the front. This was a day of surprises and the noon church bells hadn't rung yet. He was waiting by my desk as I carried in Pewter from the back.

"Hello." Ed never used more words than he had to use.

"Ed, how good to see you. Won't you sit down?"

He took the wooden captain's chair next to my desk. "Read your article this morning about the Bon Ton. Town's talking."

Good. That's what they were supposed to do. "You're kind to mention it."

He leaned forward. "Nickel, if you hear of a place to rent, will you call me out at Verna's or leave a message at the restaurant?"

"Sure. What are you looking for?"

"Nothing fancy. In town." He smiled. "I like it here. I need a change."

"Runnymede would be lucky to have you. I know my mother"—this killed me but I had to say it—"and my aunt will be very happy if you live among us."

He flushed at this but it opened him a bit. "Birmingham is full of memories. Time for a change." He paused. "You know, I haven't had fun like this since my wife was alive."

Memories and a sense of the future keep us alive. I was sure that Ed's memories of his wife drove him forward. I was equally sure that neither I nor any other human being would know those memories.

"I'll tell the gang if they get a promising ad for the classified, to let me know."

"Thanks."

As Ed rose, in rolled Nils Nordness, and was he pissed. John, languishing at his desk, did not bother to take his feet off it as Nils hovered over him.

"You misquoted me, you sorry son of a bitch!"

"Nils, I have my notes right here." John handed them up to the real estate developer.

Ed sat back down.

Nils read them for two seconds. "This isn't English."

"Shorthand." John smiled.

Nils threw the note pad on the ground. "Hoffman, I'm never giving you an interview—I'm never giving anyone from this god-damned paper an interview again. And I'm pulling my advertising."

Lolly scrambled out from under my desk. I held her by the collar as she growled.

"Suit yourself." John smiled again, bloodlessly.

Charles, up from the press in time for the last exchange, walked over. "Nils, what's the problem here? No need to be threatening."

"This jackass misquoted me."

"I didn't misquote you. I can't print everything you said. No reporter can do that. I picked out the salient points."

"Stick to your column." Nils turned to me. "At least those are better than Miss Bleeding Heart here."

"Nils, I'll thank you not to come into my newspaper and insult my staff." Charles's bow tie hopped up and down.

"It won't be your newspaper for long, thank God. Diz Rife has respect for businessmen. Things'll perk up around here."

"Maybe he'll buy it and maybe he won't," I piped up.

"You don't have a snowball's chance in hell." Nils's gaze circled the room. "So you all better start kissing Diz Rife's ass."

"You're doing a good enough job on that already." John still kept his feet on his desk.

Nils clenched his fists, swayed a moment, and then charged out.

"You'll drown in a sea of parking tickets if you go north of the line," Roger said to John.

"He was born a twin, you know—Nils and a turd? They threw

out Nils and kept the turd." John finally took his shoes off the desk. "Thanks for the support." He spoke to Charles.

"Every species of authority or rich man has had it in for the press since Peter Zenger." Charles slapped John on the back, heard his phone ring, and returned to his office.

Ed whispered to me. "Is it always like this?"

"Only on Wednesdays." I smiled.

After Ed left, dazed by the outburst and somewhat excited, we started talking at once. I don't know what it is about a fight but my blood gets up and my mood rises with it. I could twist the beginning of *A Tale of Two Cities* to say it was the worst of times and I was at my best.

After we finished hooting and hollering I called out to Michelle: "Got an assignment for you."

"What?"

"I want a feature on airport art and I want you on my fence crew for the horse show."

She stopped for a moment and then said, "You lie."

"Michelle, pretty soon you'll be one of the boys." I smiled broadly at her. She wasn't sure how to take that, but Roger laughed and so did John. She allowed as how it might be a compliment.

Orrie Tadia perched in the high chair at the Curl 'n Twirl. Georgette BonBon pored over an issue of *Cosmopolitan* with a half-naked woman on the cover. The cover girl appeal confused me. Wouldn't a half-naked woman do better on a magazine for men? Yet *Cosmo* sold like hotcakes. Was there something buried deep in the psyches of women that I didn't understand?

"What are you doing here?" Orrie asked me.

"Lunch hour. Came to see if Mom was about."

"She's at the paint store." Mr. Pierre, deeply concentrating on Orrie's new color, champagne blond, never removed his gaze from her hair.

I started to leave but Orrie said, "Well?"

"Very becoming. And Mr. Pierre knows exactly how to frame your face, Orrie. With the tan, you look, well, you look like you did when I was a girl."

I don't know about soul travel but Orrie was so happy she might have floated off her chair. "Aren't you the sweetest thing. Honey, did I tell you about Lauderdale-by-the-Sea? Cirrhosis-by-the-Sea, I call it. Apart from the tidal wave of alcohol consumed at the nightly cocktail parties the weather was splendid and I was robbed by a man armed with a coconut—"

"We learned that at Wheezie's birthday party."

She settled in her chair. "So you did. I don't know how you can bear the winter. Or Louise. She's two years older than God. She needs heat."

"I ran into Ann Falkenroth and they've found a place they love in Palm Springs. Heat made me think of it."

"They did?" Orrie loved gossip—pardon me, information—as much as Mother and Wheezie.

And myself, although I hate to admit it.

"Place called Morningside. I saw the brochure and the cheapest place is four hundred and fifty thousand dollars. The one they're buying isn't cheap."

Orrie waved her hand, the fingernails painted a fresh coat of Plum Fantasy. "After he sells the *Clarion* they can buy a city block."

"Keep your head still, darling. I want to get this right." Mr. Pierre pushed her head back.

"I'm on your side, Nickel."

"Thank you, Aunt Orrie." I called her "aunt" sometimes because I did when I was little. In those days I thought every woman or man not my mother and father were my aunt or uncle. I imagined myself the center of a large family.

Her voice dropped to the sotto voce range. "Precious lamb, what is this about Ed Tutweiler Walters?"

"Jungle lust." Mr. Pierre winked at me.

"Stop." She slapped at him but her tone said *More, More.*

"I've never seen anything like it." I was by her ear.

Georgette put down her magazine. "Nickel, speak up."

"This is private," Orrie sniffed.

"He's my uncle." Georgette was right.

"Darling, you have so many," Mr. Pierre chortled.

"Georgette, what do you know? I mean, all I know is Mother and Aunt Wheezie shoot daggers at each other at the mere mention of his name."

Orrie moved her head and Mr. Pierre pushed it back again. A Jack Russell after a groundhog couldn't have been more attentive.

"He doesn't say much," Georgette volunteered, "but I know he knows he's between them. He's not stupid."

"Does he have any money?" Orrie blurted.

"Orrie, *très* subtle."

"Pierre, you want to know as well as I do," Orrie said.

"He has a pension from work. Uncle Eddie isn't tight but he isn't a big spender. I reckon he's set. If he sells the house in Birmingham he'll be pretty well off."

"Think he'd like a champagne blonde with a deep Florida tan?"

"Do you want to have both Louise and Juts mad at you?" Mr. Pierre shook a curling iron in front of her face.

"Now that you put it that way . . ." Orrie slumped back in the chair and let Mr. Pierre work his will upon her.

That evening I accompanied Aunt Wheezie over to Saint Rose of Lima's. First she entered the parish, genuflected, and whispered some prayer under her breath. She stuck her elbow in my ribs because I didn't genuflect nor did I make the sign of the cross. My being a Lutheran mattered not a bit to her. I bent my knee and made the sign of the cross, speaking in Latin. Changing to the vernacular was the dumbest thing the Catholic Church ever did.

Our shoes clicked on the old wooden stairway as we descended into the hall.

"Nickel, I wish you'd come back to church."

"I go to church."

"The True Church. I hate to think of your soul wandering in Purgatory because you're a Lutheran."

"Maybe my soul can travel out of Purgatory like yours does when you sleep."

"Don't make light of anything so serious."

"Aunt Wheezie, I think piety is like garlic: a little goes a long way."

"You do this to me every time I try to save your soul."

We snapped on the lights. How lonesome the place appeared without the bingo tables set up, Mutzi, the Ping-Pong balls.

"Fuse box or circuit breakers?" I asked.

"Circuit breakers."

We wandered around until we found the circuit breakers in metal boxes right inside the kitchen, which was at the far end of the hall. I opened the boxes and Louise studied their contents.

"See one circuit breaker, you've seen 'em all."

"I have to know what controls what." She pointed to a number on the switch and a corresponding number on the inside of the metal box door. Written on the door was the section of the church to which each fuse supplied power. For instance, number sixteen had written beside it: FATHER'S OFFICE AND SMALL PANTRY, FIRST FLOOR.

My aunt's dedication to the church was genuine but a small part of her ferocity had to do with the fact that she thought being a good woman meant being religious. Ed's appearance in our midst had toned down her Catholic fever. I wondered if her temperature was climbing again.

"Why isn't Millard here to show you himself?"

"Oh, he's very busy tonight. Knights of Columbus, you know. He told me he wanted me and Verna to know how to run things around here like a sexton. In case he's sick or something."

"What's the matter with Peepbean?"

"Nothing's the matter with Peepbean except he's got the personality of a gargoyle. Isn't that what you call those things atop Yankee city hall?"

"Yes."

"Anyway, if there's a family emergency Peepbean can't help us at church. After all, they're from the same family."

I had the strangest feeling Aunt Louise was lying to me but for the life of me I couldn't imagine why. Tempted as I was to tell her I was changing my life, I would become Shirley of Nazareth, specializing in foot washings, I bit my tongue. The charge I would get from her outrage would be vitiated by the subsequent lecture. Was I growing up at last?

30

A VISIT TO DAD

THURSDAY . . . 23 APRIL

My father's grave, rosy in the dawn, was smothered in pink-throated tulips. Mother brought him a steady stream of flowers, wreaths, and occasionally something funny like a plastic pink flamingo. Her diligence in tending his resting place was admirable. I wasn't so diligent, but cemeteries make me feel as if I'm in a marble quarry. The graveyard covered the slope of a wide hill, facing east. Dad's grave nestled under a huge black gum tree at the top of the hill. Dante's grave—the firehorse—was at the bottom of the hill. In summers Mom and I would picnic up here both for the view and to be close to Daddy. Today I came up to put a horseshoe on his grave. It seemed more appropriate for Dad than flowers—from me anyway.

His tombstone read:

CHESTER CLIFFORD SMITH
BORN AUGUST 7, 1905
DIED JULY 13, 1961

We didn't go in for sentiment. The world didn't need to know how we felt about him so long as we knew. What astonished me about my father's death was that I never stopped loving him. Here it was almost twenty-six years later and each year I loved Dad more. Each year I realized on a deeper level how much he gave me. Love doesn't die. It keeps growing. Perhaps someone you love has to die before you can believe that.

Knowing that love doesn't die makes me oddly brave. I don't want to die. I think death is a greatly overrated experience. I disliked experiencing my father's death and I have absolutely no desire to experience my own. But die I must and in some corner of my being I'm not too afraid. Because those people who love me—there are a few scattered about—they'll keep loving me. Maybe someday they'll learn what Dad has taught me and they'll become a little braver themselves. What the hell, you might as well do what you want to do. You're going to be dead a long time.

The biggest chance Dad took was to marry Mom. The second-biggest chance he took was to adopt me. The third-biggest chance he took was to open the hardware store, since it plunged him into debt. For Dad, the risks yielded rewards. I'm not saying that Mom couldn't be a pain in the ass or that I didn't wear the poor man out, since I tagged at his heels like a penny dog. And I know the hardware store provided him with a healthy share of headaches, yet when you tallied it all up, his asset column won.

The sun, a ball of scarlet fire, illuminated the tombstones. I could believe graves would open in such a light and the earth offer up her dead to the Kingdom Come. Dad would crawl out of the ground, dust himself off, and hurry forward, worrying that he'd overslept. I wondered if the soul did outlive the body, because if it did, I knew my father's soul was somewhere out there trying to be useful. Dad abhorred negative thinking, laziness, and waste. "You're here to do the best you can and you're here to give. Any fool can take." Bet I heard that one a thousand times. Bet I'd give everything I had to hear him say it one more time too.

Under the sod lay Runnymede's other Protestant souls and our Jews in a special section compliant with their religious rules. The Catholics remained separate from us even in death, but their cemetery was only a mile away. The thought of Louise being buried next to Pearlie, and Mom being buried next to Dad, gave me a pang. Seemed the Hunsenmeir girls ought to be buried together. In a snit Louise once suggested that Mother's tombstone read "Laid Out Again" and Mother replied, lightning fast, "Yours ought to read 'At Last She Sleeps Alone.'" Wheezie pitched a hissy and smacked Mother with her purse over that one.

Aunt Wheezie did not sleep around but I do think she gave herself up to the thrill of infidelity once in the 1920's. Mother swears to this and then Wheezie swears at Mother. It's a subject best not discussed.

In my own will I set down that my tombstone will read "Now I'll Really Raise Hell." Jackson thought it was funny and he told Billy

Moon, his partner, who told someone, who told Aunt Wheezie, who came after me and said that was sacrilegious and just like me. If I didn't change my will and show it to her she would never speak to me again. Boy, was I tempted. Eventually I gave in and changed the damned will. Now the stone's supposed to read: "She Did the Best She Could." Wheezie still doesn't like it but she agrees that this epitaph isn't sacrilegious.

The temperature, at about fifty-four now, would reach into the high sixties or low seventies today, our warmest day so far. A brilliant cardinal swept by my head, his mate not far behind him. Then I noticed two chipmunks chasing each other like mad. Spring. In my mourning over Jackson, I'd nearly missed spring, the mating season. The animals celebrated for me. The next round was about to begin. A new generation of robins, deer, raccoons, chipmunks, cats, possums, and grasshoppers and butterflies was about to enter the party. I breathed in the moist air. How fitting that this cemetery should be a scene of renewed life. And how fitting that the robins, deer, raccoons, and other animals erected no monuments to their dead. They were too busy living. Only humans hid away their dead so the remains couldn't replenish the earth, so the flesh could not go to keep alive another animal. Were we honoring our dead or were we selfish? Dad would say selfish.

In this necropolis moldered people who squandered their lives. They pissed away their money, pissed away yours if they could get their hands on it, drank, fornicated, and got dizzy on their own senseless carrousel. Providing a meal for a bobcat might have been the only productive thing they ever did.

Not every dead person here was a wastrel but there were enough of them to give me pause. As I walked down the hill I paused at Grandma's grave. Mom put daffodils on Cora's grave. Grandma loved yellow. Tubs of black-eyed susans, daffodils, jonquils, anything yellow surrounded Bumblebee Hill. Cora put them down and I saw no reason to pull them up. I faithfully fertilized them too. And I added a picket fence with an arbor. I trained yellow tea roses to climb over the arbor and along the fence. She would have liked it.

A car crept up the hill. I must have been standing at Grandma's grave longer than I realized. I hopped in the Chrysler and coasted down into town. Today was the day Foster Adams would present my loan application to the lending officers of Chesapeake and Potomac. By the time I pulled into the *Clarion* parking lot I realized I must have visited my ancestors to ask for their help. I know I'm not related by blood, if you want to get technical about this ancestor stuff, but I don't think the spirits of Dad or Cora care. They never cared while they were alive.

Mother was running around the Square. She wore a regular sweat suit, like my old gray one except hers was pink, and she had a mallard-green towel wrapped around her neck. Nice combination. Goodyear paddled at her heels. I let Lolly out to get exercise with them and shouted good morning.

Charles, hands on hips, stood beside me to watch Mom. "Eternal Julia."

"Between the two of us we keep the manufacturers of amino acids in business."

"Nickel, do those things work?" he wondered.

I pointed to Mom. "Need more proof? Exercise, sleep, eat right, and gobble amino acids."

He shook his head in admiration. "Hear Ann told you about Morningside."

"I'd never hear it from you."

"I forget. I walk through that door and my mind focuses on the paper. Drives poor Ann nuts. She says I'd forget my head if it weren't on my shoulders."

"Did you find the house last time you were in Palm Springs?"

"Well, we looked. I didn't think we could afford it but the house is a dream come true. There's even a button by the bed so you can summon help if there's a medical emergency. The houses are on one level. Be nice for Ann not to have to go up and down stairs anymore."

It would be nice for Charles not to go up and down stairs anymore. He was the one with arthritis.

"I hope you both will be very happy there."

"Hey, got another hot one!" Roger and Michelle were huddled before a small TV by the AP wire machine.

We hurried over in time to see Jim Bakker resign from the PTL Club. Tammy was crying her eyes out, but then she usually did. She said she wanted to get a job and she thought she might like to work in a doctor's office.

"A proctologist, no doubt."

Charles threw back his head and laughed. Every now and then I come up with a good one.

Other than a call from Regina telling me that Diz and Jackson decided to play their tennis match Sunday at the club, it was a quiet day, which was disquieting. Gave me more time to think about tomorrow.

THE BIG DAY

FRIDAY . . . 24 APRIL

Jackson and I said little to each other on the way over to Foster's office. We longed for each other's company and we were both nervous about this meeting.

The minute we hit the door to Foster's inner sanctum I smelled trouble. For one thing Foster looked stricken. After we sat down and pleasantries were exchanged he got to it.

"Nickel, Chesapeake and Potomac felt you were a bit too much of a risk. I'm sorry."

"Can you give me the reason for their denial?"

"You don't have enough assets."

"Even with Charles's help?" Jackson had an edge to his voice.

"Yes." Foster was struggling, but with what I didn't yet know. "I don't expect you or anybody to have sympathy with a banker or the bank. But let me give you a few things to think about which may put this in perspective. If a bank shows a return on assets of one and a quarter percent, that's a banner year. Because we have the money, the public's attitude seems to be 'screw 'em.' We get one bad loan application after another, and I hasten to add that your application wasn't bad, but it was a squeaker. Bankers are by nature conservative because people are conservative when it comes to their money. Notice the distinction, 'their money,' yet when they go to borrow money it's 'the bank's money.' I am terribly sorry. I think you're a good risk."

Jackson dropped his charm. "How's it feel being jerked around

186

like a teller by Chesapeake and Potomac? You're supposed to be president of this bank."

Foster, taken aback, sputtered.

"Jackson, I'm sure Foster did all he could." I felt like the bottom of my stomach had fallen out. I would have thrown up except I forgot to eat breakfast this morning.

"Thank you, Nickel. I did."

"Let me ask you one thing." Jackson was like a dog worrying a bone. "Did they inquire into Nickel's marital status?"

Foster became wary. "It was mentioned."

"And if the single woman also happens to be a lesbian I imagine it's even more of a minus, isn't it?"

"That never came up. I absolutely promise you it never did."

"Come off it, Foster. It didn't have to. Anyone who isn't married by age thirty looks suspicious these days."

"Jack, I resent your tone of voice. I have known this girl all her life."

He didn't mean to be rude in calling me a girl. To Foster I was a girl, I was so much younger than he was.

"So what?" Jackson bored in on him.

"So I vouched for her character. You asked me a question and I told you the truth. I do not want you to get the idea you can sue Chesapeake and Potomac because of Nickel's being denied a loan. Yes, being a single woman is a detriment. In the best of all possible worlds it wouldn't be a detriment but it is today. I don't know if she would have gotten this loan if she were a man. It was shaky as it was."

"But she would have had a better chance." Jack's voice rose.

"Yes, goddammit, yes! What do you want me to do about it? These things don't seem very important until they hurt someone you care about. I never thought about it. Hell, Jack, when I grew up there were no women in business around here except for Celeste and she was a law unto herself. I'm sorry as hell about this."

Foster, not a man to speak from the heart, was exhausted by his efforts. He seized the handkerchief in his breast pocket and mopped his brow.

"Foster, I thank you for going to bat for me."

"Don't be so accommodating and nice," Jack snarled at me. "There's a community reinvestment act and the *Clarion* fits the bill. The banks, taking the money out of the community, are required by law to put a certain amount back, to stimulate the local economy. I'll find an angle because the *Clarion* belongs to you!"

Foster's voice was heavy. "You can slice it any way you want to,

Jack. Chesapeake and Potomac isn't going to give her the cash. They don't care what goes on in Runnymede. They'll do the minimum to comply with the reinvestment act."

"That's what we're fighting," I said. "That's why we don't want the Thurston Group or Mid-Atlantic Holding Shares to get the *Clarion,* because once the paper slips out of the control of the community it no longer serves the community as effectively."

"I understand," Foster said.

"You sure do, because if you really ran Runnymede Bank and Trust, the *Clarion* would be Nickel's. We're being devoured by corporate giants who don't see our faces, hear our voices, or pass us in the streets. People have got to fight back." Jack stood up.

"I don't know what to do." Foster wiped his forehead again.

"Jack, come on." I tugged at Jack's arm. "Foster, no hard feelings on my part."

As we dragged ourselves across the Square I dreaded telling the gang. Right now my life was a potato chip in the maw of big corporations. Yesterday I'd gotten a call from my local insurance company, Richards, Hilton, and Richards, telling me they'd referred my Jeep claim to the wrong company, Maryland Accident Protection. The claim belonged to the giant firm of First Eagle Insurance. The Eagle lady called and grilled me. Christ, you would have thought I'd had the Jeep stolen on purpose. She hinted darkly that I shouldn't have authorized any repairs, but of course I was doing what the Maryland Accident Protection claim adjuster told me to do. In the mean time, Eagle had two decades of insurance payments from me and not one claim until now. What was the difference if it was Eagle or Chesapeake and Potomac? They were out to screw me. To them we existed as walking pocketbooks to be emptied. I felt very hateful at that moment.

Jackson left me at the *Clarion* steps. He was as downcast as I was.

"Nickel, don't give up. There's got to be a way."

"I don't know, honey. Let me digest this first and then if we have room for a legal fight, I'll think about it. I figure the minute you commit a problem to the judicial system you just tripled it."

"I can't fault you there." He kissed me on the cheek, a social kiss but it burned my cheek.

I walked straight into Charles's office and told him everything. I said if he was going to sell, he might as well give it to Diz Rife because better the devil you know than the devil you don't, not that Diz himself was a devil. As I left he picked up the phone. Can't blame Charles. He has to look out for himself.

As I walked to my desk Lolly whimpered. She could read my mood like a weathercaster.

"The worst?" Michelle asked.

I nodded.

John rose. "This is as good a time as any. I'm quitting. I took a job with *National Geographic.* Guess I'll tell Charles." He squared off in front of me. "Nick, I give you credit for trying. Maybe it's time for you to move on too." He lightly rapped on the door to Charles's office and went in.

Roger broke a pencil.

"Hey, it's not a funeral. Charles will fight for your jobs."

"We wanted you to have it," Michelle said.

Within minutes the news spread through the plant. Arnie and Hans came out to verify the story. Arnie, speechless, walked back to the printing press. I followed him. When I reached the big press, quiet because we'd run off the paper for the day, Arnie had his hands smacked against the feed. He was crying.

I tiptoed over to him and put my arm around him. "They say all good things must come to an end."

He sobbed, "They'll junk my baby. They'll fire us."

Tears welled up in my eyes. I patted the sleeping machine. I loved her too. "I reckon they will."

"You'll be okay," he said.

"You go, I go. A bunch of goddamned computers and a pay raise aren't enough for me. This is the paper. We're the paper."

He wiped his eyes and I wiped mine. I noticed that Hans was misty-eyed, too, and the other guys in the back stood dumbfounded with misery.

"Hey, let's go smoke Isaac's cigar." Why I thought of this I still don't know.

We trooped back into the editorial room. I opened my drawer, grabbed the little penknife my Dad had given me when I was in sixth grade. I cut off the end of the cigar and lit her up. We passed it around like a peace pipe. Even Michelle took a puff.

Then Arnie produced a full bottle of Johnnie Walker Black. I don't drink but I took a pull. We cried and drank and smoked and sang and one by one we crept away. John outdrank everyone. Two drinks and I was a basket case. Roger hiccupped. Michelle drank Hans under the table, to everyone's surprise. Even Charles got snookered.

I stumbled over to bingo that night. If Lolly and Pewter hadn't been with me I'm not sure I would have found my way to Saint Rose's. I bought a card, sat down next to Mr. Pierre, who sniffed the air suspiciously, and Mother tells me that my head hit the card. Somebody got me home. I don't remember a thing although Mother said that even Peepbean was sympathetic when I moaned before I passed out that the loan was denied. Imagine that, Peepbean being sympathetic.

THE HAIR OF THE DOG

SATURDAY . . . 25 APRIL

My mouth felt like cotton, my head throbbed, and an intruder was in my kitchen. I hauled myself out of bed, disturbing Pewter, who slept on the pillow next to me. It was eight in the morning, late for me. I stood at the top of the stairs straining my ears. There definitely was someone in my kitchen. I couldn't understand why Lolly hadn't barked.

Click, click, click, her claws tapped on the floor downstairs. A second set of clicks ballooned in my ears. If I called my dog, the thief would know I was awake. I didn't know what to do so I hastened to the bathroom and threw up. Why did people drink if this was the result? After the purge I felt somewhat restored, although my headache continued unabated but at least it didn't feel like a migraine. This was a new-model headache.

I tiptoed back to the top of the stairs and slowly, one careful step at a time, crept down. Suddenly Lolly Mabel skidded around the corner. Chows smile a lot and Lolly's wrinkled red face registered pure joy at seeing me and at being chased, because right on her tail was Goodyear. I relaxed and sat on the stairs. Lolly licked me. Goodyear kissed me too.

Mother was bending over the big butcher block in the center of the kitchen. "You look like the dogs got at you under the porch."

I moaned. "You're all heart."

"And a lot of liver too. Here, drink this."

She handed me a foul concoction. "What's in here?"

191

"Trust your old mother. It's the cure for your ills."

I gulped it down. My throat caught fire. My eyes watered. My hand shook and Mother snatched the glass from my fingers before I could drop it. She then pried open my mouth once I stopped shaking and poured down black coffee. My body was too assaulted even to puke again. In about five minutes I decided I would live. Pewter, on the butcher block, purred at me.

"Well?" Mother demanded.

"Very effective."

"Sit down. I'm going to feed you."

"No. I couldn't possibly."

"Your blood sugar is in your toes. You need to eat. By noon you'll feel like yourself again." She pulled out my cast-iron skillet.

A small nook with a bay window overlooked the meadows to the west. That's where I ate my breakfasts and my dinners if I was home for dinner. The big dining room had Grandma's formal dining table but I bet I used that room less than five times a year. I lived in the kitchen, but then I think everyone does. I rested my head on my hand and gazed out on the meadows. My pink and white azaleas blossomed at the edge of the yard, and in the woods at the edge of the meadow I could see the pink and white dogwoods at the peak of blooming. The whole world was pink and white. Even my tongue was pink and white.

Lolly and Goodyear tore back into the kitchen. This time Lolly was chasing Goodyear.

"All right, kids," Mother warned them, "slow it down or no treaties."

The dogs recognized the word "treaties" and the angelic expressions that came over those furry faces made me laugh and then my head hurt again.

"Oh." I put my head in my hands.

"Try not to think about it and take these." She tossed two B.C. powders at me.

B.C. powders, manufactured in Memphis, are a remedy known to Southerners. B.C. cures a headache, arthritis, neuralgia, rheumatism, maybe even bad temper. This wonder drug has but one drawback. It tastes violently awful. You can swallow it in pill form like an aspirin but that's for weak-asses. If you want the substance to slam into your bloodstream at full speed you take the little packet of powder, knock it back in your throat, then drink whatever is at hand as fast as you can.

I fetched myself a Coke, steadied on my feet, threw back two packets of B.C. powder, and chugged the co-cola.

I sat down with a thump. "I've got so much liquid in me my stomach will rise and fall with the tide."

"Don't worry, the coffee and Coke will go through you in no time."

She fried up some eggs, the butter sizzling in the pan, as she looked out the big kitchen window.

"Oh, no."

"What?" I need not have asked because I heard the screech outside.

The dogs barked.

"That's enough," Mother said.

Goodyear stopped but Lolly didn't.

"Lolly, I can't bear it." Lolly turned to study my expression. She decided to growl instead.

With a voice that would waken the dead, Aunt Wheezie stuck her head in the back door: "Yoo hoo."

"We're in the kitchen," Mother replied.

Louise stomped through the mud room, which was right off the kitchen. She cheerfully burst upon us, prepared to improve my lot despotically. A bag of groceries nestled in her arm.

"Gonna fix you up." She placed the groceries on the butcher block.

Pewter stuck her head in the bag which prompted Aunt Wheezie to unpack it quickly and toss the bag on the floor. Pewter jumped off the butcher block—the thud was deafening—and shot into the bag. Her rattling around in there sounded like defective machine-gun fire.

"Pewter, let Mommie bribe you with some catnip."

"Sit down. I'll do it." Mother fetched some catnip, fresh, out of the pantry where it was sequestered in a shiny Italian cracker tin.

Pewter vacated her bag and pounced on the catnip. Her eyes rolled in her head. She abandoned herself to pleasure.

"Better living through chemistry," I laughed. "Kitty drugs."

"Here." Mother set a plate before me.

She set one down for herself and Aunt Wheezie, too, and we ate a calm breakfast. Wheezie didn't let me clear the table. She did it. Mother washed. Wheezie dried and I began to feel much better.

"Eagle Insurance trying to screw you?" Mother asked.

"Yeah. Another job for Jackson."

"You pay these people thousands of dollars over the years, you need them once, and they do everything they can to evade their responsibility." Louise snapped the dish towel.

"And we have to put up with it because one company is about as bad as another," Mother added.

"You can't even buy the car you want anymore. What's the difference if it's insurance or cars or bowel cleaners like Comet," Louise said.

"Bowl cleaners," I corrected her.

"No, I mean bowel." Her voice rose.

"Fleet, then, not Comet." I smiled.

"Wonder what Comet would do up there?" Mother splashed around in the water. "Bet you'd have the cleanest intestines known to man."

"Remember Packards?" Louise got a dreamy expression. "Now there was a car. They don't build 'em like that anymore."

"*They* don't even build 'em. Robots do it," I said.

"Rolls-Royces and Bentleys are still made by people, people who aren't afraid to have their names on the car. I read that." Mother pulled the plug and the water spiraled down into the drain.

If we lived in New Zealand it would spiral in the opposite direction. If I ever visit New Zealand or Australia I'll probably spend too much time staring into drains and toilets. The natives will fear I have a nasty fixation on fluids.

"I'd like to own a great car and keep it for the rest of my life." I gazed out at the beautiful dogwoods again.

"Me too," Mother said.

"Think about it. If you buy a Bentley Turbo for a hundred and twenty thousand dollars and you run it for thirty years—and I think I'll live for thirty more years if I don't have a night like last night again—well, that's four thousand dollars a year for that car. If I live forty more years it's—let me think a minute—it's three thousand dollars a year. Just maintaining a piece of American junk will cost you that, plus think of the number of cheap cars we go through in our lifetimes. It's more economical to buy the Bentley."

"If you can get the money in the first place." Mother wiped her hands. "That's what gets me about the rich. They can afford to buy quality, so dollar for dollar they're getting much more for their money than we are."

"I have the best deal." Louise sat back across from me. "My hubby knew what he was doing."

"He did, but it's not a Bentley, Wheezie." Mother sat down too.

"What do you know about cars?"

"I know a lot about cars."

"Oh, ha! Chessy wouldn't let you near his machine. Not after your first driving lesson right up here at this house. She rammed into the porch, Nickel. The piano slid off the porch. Momma always put the piano on the porch in the summertime. The porch splintered up like a toothpick. Fannie Jump Creighton climbed onto the roof and shimmied up the pole. People flew off that porch like rats off a sinking ship.

"You exaggerate."

"I most certainly do not! You nearly killed me."

"Don't tempt me, Wheeze." Mother's foot wiggled.

I was trapped on the inside of the trestle table and couldn't get out.

"Well, your sense of history seems to suit yourself." Louise sniffed. "But you don't know beans about cars. You turn on the ignition key and that's it."

"I remember Ev Most's father had a Rochester Steam Runabout," Mom said.

Ev Most was Mother's best friend in childhood and throughout life. She died after a long illness in 1978 and since then Mother had drawn closer to me. Ev's grandfather built the Yankee city hall. The Mosts contributed a lot to our town, and sadly, her son left for the big city, so there wasn't one Most left in Runnymede.

"Steam engines were good. Don't know why they didn't catch on. There was a Hudson Steamer and the Stanley Steamer. Everyone knows about that one."

"Make a bet."

"What?" Louise rose to the bait.

"Set aside steamers. I bet I can name more cars that are no longer manufactured than you can."

"That's an easy bet. Ford Model T. Ford Model A," she chirped, then paused. "What's the prize?"

"Trip to Orioles game."

"No deal. You like baseball better then I do and you have tickets anyway. Make it a gift certificate for"—she thought—"fifty dollars at Young Sophisticates."

Young Sophisticates was on the Emmitsburg Pike and specialized in clothes that do well in areas where the population is overpoweringly WASP.

"You should go to Old Sophisticates," Mother said.

"Don't get fresh and don't think you can throw me off the track by being snide, little sister. Either you take the bet or not."

"I'll take it." Mother reached across the table and shook Louise's hand.

"Wouldn't this be easier if you weren't allowed to name different models of the same brand? For instance, Ford Model A and Model T, Cadillac Fleetwood and Osceola," I said.

"There was never a Cadillac Osceola." Wheezie sounded dismissive.

"Yes, there was," Mother said, "in 1905. I knew you wouldn't win this game."

"We haven't started yet!" Louise snapped.

"Do you each accept those terms?" I persisted. "No model names, just brand names, and the cars must be extinct today."

They nodded in unison.

"How many chances do I have?" Louise wanted to know.

"We should go until we run out. Order doesn't matter."

I assumed the task of being the referee. "No, doesn't matter at all. Now I happen to have in my pocket a quarter. I'll flip it and, Wheezie, you call it in the air. If you get the toss you go first. Okay?"

"Okay." Wheezie's excitement sparkled on her face. I flicked up the quarter.

"Heads!"

"Heads" it was and Aunt Louise had the ball.

She savored the moment by enjoying a sip of coffee. "I'm ready. Nickel, write these down."

Pencils and pads of paper littered my house. A legal-size yellow pad rested on the window ledge. I picked it up, poised the pencil, and said, "Go."

"The Morris Electric—"

"No fair!"

"We agreed no steamers. We didn't say anything about electric cars." Wheezie grinned like the Cheshire cat.

"Mother," I intervened, "as there are so few electric cars, I think you're safe."

Mother wasn't having any. "How do you know?"

"A hunch."

"I say it's out of bounds."

Louise leaned back in her chair, a superior air wreathing her face. "I knew you'd crawfish out of the game. I know more about cars than you do."

"Bullshit. Keep your old electric cars. Go on, bigmouth."

Wheezie nodded to me and began anew. "Nash, Rambler, DeSoto, Kaiser, Hudson, and hmm, the car invented by that poor man they drove bankrupt." She placed her finger to her temple. "I know, Tucker, and LaSalle."

A long silence ensued.

"Running out of gas?" Mother smirked. "You keep thinking. I get a turn now."

"I won the toss."

"Yeah, but you're taking too long. It's my turn."

"Aunt Wheeze, you have been quiet for a few minutes."

"Can you believe it?" Mother tormented. "The last thing to die on Wheezie will be her mouth."

"You always say that. Be original." Louise glared.

"My turn." Mother inhaled and rattled off names, "Pierce-Arrow, Willys Jeepster, Studebaker, Packard—"

"I said that!" Louise trumpeted.

"You said it at the kitchen sink. You didn't say it in the contest."

"You slutbunny!"

"Where'd you hear that one, Aunt Wheezie?"

She lifted one shoulder. "Overheard Ursula Yost's daughter Tiffany at Mojo's. And I say Packard is mine."

"You didn't name it during the contest. I'm sorry," I said.

"You take her part. You two are ganging up against me!"

"I am not!"

"Why not?" Mother turned on me now.

"I'm not going to referee if you all act like this. I made a ruling that I think is impartial.

They stared at each other.

"Since Julia is wasting time, let me go."

"I'm not finished. We had to settle a dispute. Don't get so slick."

"Go right ahead. Be my guest. Probably only know two more cars, anyway, and I know a hundred. Hundreds." Her voice rose on the second "hundreds."

"Opel." Mother clenched her teeth.

I held up my hand. "Made today."

"No, it isn't. The Opel Admiral was an old car."

"Mom, there's a car on the road today called an Opel."

"It's not the same people."

"They were bought out, Juts, so it doesn't matter because the name is alive. I'm taking a turn. You shut up and suffer." Louise folded her hands. "Reo Flying Cloud. Bet you don't remember that one. In the twenties."

"I was going to say it next."

"Tough." Louise continued. "Cord."

"Auburn!" Mother shouted.

I wrote down her entry but warned her: "Aunt Wheeze has the floor."

"Thank you, Nickel." Wheezie pressed forward. "Duesenberg."

197

"That's not an American car," Mother said.

"Who said anything about American cars? Anyway, it is an American car." Louise lifted her hands to heaven.

"We'll be here all day. Remember Celeste's Hispano-Suiza and the old Rife sisters' big Graf-whatever it was called? We'd better stick to American cars. Bugatti. Hey, I saw one once in the early thirties in Baltimore."

"I'll go along with you, Julia, in the interests of time but I want it clearly understood that if we included foreign cars I'd still win."

"Oh la!" Mom tossed her head.

"Pencil to paper," Louise ordered. "The Essex Four."

After this came a short pause, and her eyebrows knitted together.

"I'm going." Mom dived in. "The Stutz Bearcat. The Franklin—there were a lot of those around when I was a kid. Saxon and the little Imp."

"Doesn't count. That was a cycle-car."

"Count it." Mother pushed the pencil in my hand. "We didn't say word one about how many wheels the machine could have."

"Maxwell and the Brewster," Louise shouted.

By now a quiet hung over the table. Both were straining.

"Oakland," Mom said.

Another long silence.

This time Louise broke it. "White, and Peerless."

"Damn," Mother muttered under her breath.

More silence.

Mom jumped up. "Columbia."

Louise fired off. "The Henry J and the Frazer Manhattan. I win!"

I tallied up the cars during the next long silence.

Louise spoke again. "I win, Julia."

"But I know there were more cars."

"So what? You can't remember them. I told you I know more about cars than you do. But you never believe me. You think you know everything."

"Oh, shut up." Mother desperately wanted to think of more cars. Nothing came to mind.

"Mother, do you concede victory?"

"Not yet."

"Juts, give up. I win fair and square."

Mom grabbed the tablet. Louise's column was longer than her column. "You win." She grumbled.

"Gimme my fifty dollars."

"I don't carry that much money on me. I'll write you a check Monday."

"Cash. You might get spiteful and cancel the check."

"Wheeze, I wonder how your mind works. I wouldn't even think of doing such a thing."

"Oh la." Louise imitated Mother.

"Cash. Monday." Mother hated to lose at anything.

"Fine. Money earned is good but money won is sweet. And, Julia, I've been meaning to tell you those falsies look dreadful. You might be fooling Ed Tutweiler Walters but you certainly aren't fooling anyone else."

"Watch it."

"Well, you've been sticking to him like a lamprey. I suppose wiggling one's bosoms might be considered sexy in some circles."

"Do you want your fifty dollars or don't you?"

"Trying to help. I mean, experience doesn't seem to teach some people anything and you've had plenty."

"What's that supposed to mean?"

I scanned the horizon for a way out of the nook.

"Oh—nothing."

"What experience?"

I admired my hanging ferns. I like ferns. Their fuzziness reminds me of split infinitives, and I like split infinitives because they make me laugh.

"I do recall, Julia, that in 1960 you wore an inflatable bra to that party Verna gave."

"You stuck me with my corsage pin."

"Purely by accident but I should think you'd learn not to waddle around with big—bosoms."

"Ladies, I feel one hundred percent better. I'm just marinated in sociability. Why don't we walk outside?"

"I don't want to walk outside." Louise dipped close to a deep alto register.

"I do." Mother hopped up and sped into the mud room before Louise could protest.

"She can't stand to lose. She even cries sometimes, as old as she is," Louise whispered. "She's running away. If she stayed here there'd be a big fight. What a baby."

A reply would have been like taking nitroglycerin over the mountains. I weakly smiled and shot out the door myself. The dogs shot out with me.

Mother was strolling through my flower beds. I caught up with her.

"You've been working out here."

"Yeah."

Mother stopped at my tulip bed. "She can be a real nosebleed."

"Ignore her."

"Can you?"

"Mmm, sometimes."

Grandma's tubs, scrubbed and bright, showed little tips of flowers ready to greet me in May.

"I'm so sorry you never had a sister—or a brother, too, for that matter. You'd know what I go through if you did."

Mother and Louise had two brothers. One died of spinal meningitis as a baby. He was born in 1897. The other lived into his teens and was killed building a house. He fell off the roof and died of internal injuries.

"I never think about it. Anyway, seeing you and Aunt Wheezie makes me kind of glad I don't have a sister. You fight constantly."

A big grin crossed Mother's face. "I love the way she brings out the worst in me."

33

JACKSON *VS.* DIZ

SUNDAY . . . 26 APRIL

World War II raged in front of us. Jackson and Diz used their tennis racquets like bazookas. The match started in a gentlemanly fashion. Diz wore his Fila outfit and Jackson appeared in Tacchini. At South Runnymede Tennis and Racquet Club white prevails, so while there were splashes of color on both men, they were more white than not. The match was on grass too.

At first, those of us in the gallery thought: another rout by Jackson. He skunked Diz for the first set. The second set teeter-tottered but Jack kept his serve and took that 6–4. The third set, a brutal tie-breaker, was won by Diz. The fourth set also went to Diz in another squeaker. The fifth set was neck and neck.

Those lessons in Manhattan must have paid off because Diz shortened his backswing to compensate for the speed of grass. You haven't got the time for a lovely preparation arc as you do on clay. His serve also was much improved and twisted into Jackson's body or skidded away on the outside corner.

Regina, Mr. Pierre, Mom, Wheezie, Orrie, Georgette BonBon, and Max, her boyfriend, huddled on the left side of the bleachers. Liz and Portia Rife, Bill Falkenroth, Kevin and George Spangler, Tinker Finster, Ursula Yost, and Frances Finster sat on the right side of the bleachers. David Wheeler and his wife wandered over after their game and sat in the middle. Sides were clearly drawn.

During the changeover at 5–4 we picked up a piece of the

201

exchange between Jackson and Diz. Their conversation did not run a charitable course.

Diz served and held. Frustration marked Jackson's face. He was so accustomed to wiping the courts up with Diz that the equality of the struggle offended him. Jackson, powerful and smart, battled the slighter but quicker man. Diz used the whole court and he kept Jackson off balance by mixing up his shots. He'd slam a forehand topspin into the back court and then on Jackson's return he'd take the pace off the ball. Nor was he adverse to the lob, that most heartbreaking stroke in tennis if you're on the receiving end of it.

When the fifth set heaved over into a tie-breaker, those of us in the stands collectively held our breath. This was tantamount to a palace revolution. None of us could believe how hard these men were fighting. This was more than a tennis match. No money would change hands at the conclusion. No trophy would be given. The results would not be printed in the *Clarion* despite the fact that one of the participants was soon to be the new owner. The end shocked everyone. The tie-breaker, a recent invention in tennis, must be won by two points. They'd blasted each other to 9–9, a comment in itself. Jackson turned over service to Diz. The next point, a long one, swung to Diz when he hit a backhand down the line that caught the chalk, spraying it upward in a fountain of white. On Diz's next point he served an ace. Jackson could have lied and said "wide" because it was close and it's pretty easy to cheat if you're that kind of person. But Jack wasn't. He stared at the spot, rooted to the court. Nobody said a word. Then he called, "Good." Still he couldn't move.

The stands erupted and Diz trotted to the net, happy in his victory. He leaned his racquet up against the net and waited. Jackson strode up to shake hands. That part was okay but Jack muttered something and Diz, Jack's hand still in his, smacked him upside the head with his left hand. Jack dropped his racquet and in a flash they were pounding each other, the net between them until Jack vaulted the net and the two of them fought and rolled in the grass like bad boys.

David Wheeler and Mr. Pierre rushed out to separate them but couldn't do it. Eventually Max, Bill, Kevin, and George supplied their services and the two contestants were dragged apart. Jack yelled that Diz couldn't be satisfied being the richest man in the county, he had to win at everything. Diz retorted that Jack was a bad loser and always had been and that Jack's days of being Runnymede's peacock were over.

Cooling down took about five minutes, and the men finally let

Diz and Jack out of their respective grasps. Jackson stalked off, hopped in the car, and drove away. Diz retreated to the locker room.

"I'll run you home," I told Regina, since she'd been left high and dry.

"Tell you what"—she watched Jack drive off—"let's play three sets of singles and then round up victims for two sets of doubles. I am not going home to that until sundown."

"Sounds good to me."

Our three sets supplied us both with chills and spills. Regina won the second set, so she started playing out of her head. I couldn't let up for a minute in the third or she'd have snatched it from me.

"Now that was fun." Regina toweled off.

I dropped into an Adirondack chair and bribed one of the court kids to bring me a Coke. Regina was sitting on a bench. Diz walked over to her.

"Regina, I hope you harbor no ill feelings toward me. I think emotions ran high our there and I want to apologize."

She wiped her face again. "I know that."

He turned to me. "I bought the paper."

"I know."

"Reconsider?"

"You going to stick to your plan?"

"Yes. The Bon Ton will be ready in about a week. The wiring is what takes the most time. There isn't much else to do but put up partitions."

"Even Nils Nordness can do that." I shouldn't have said that.

"I don't think much of his construction firm either but this is a simple job and it's good to patronize local business. What do you say?"

"Thank you—but no."

"You're still going to be my doubles partner, aren't you? Remember our bargain." He sounded disappointed that I wouldn't be sticking with the *Clarion*.

"I don't renege on promises—and I think we'll make a good team." I dug into my purse and gave him the twenty dollars I'd bet him weeks ago.

"Hardest money I ever earned." He folded the bill and stuck it in his jacket pocket. "Would you ladies like to give it a try now?" He jerked his head behind him. "I bet we can talk Bill Falkenroth into being Regina's partner."

Regina stood up and cupped her hands to her mouth. "Bill Falkenroth, this is your big chance."

We had so much fun we played four sets and nobody wanted to give up until our legs got wobbly.

Driving Regina home, I chose the long way around town, and the keen gold of late afternoon light slanted across the macadam road. Before our eyes Nature rose up in her glory and her might: most of the trees now bore their new bright-green leaves, the grass deepened to vibrating emerald, and bluebirds darted in between the swallow-tails. This was the spring of springs, the apotheosis of spring.

Curious that in the depths of my sorrow over losing the *Clarion*—and it really hit me full-force today, because yesterday I'd concentrated on my hangover—I felt rejuvenated by spring; I felt young, strong, and invincible. So intoxicating is Nature that she can lure us away from the artifice of being human and remind us that we are animals. The conquest of winter must be celebrated in the blood. It still remains our greatest victory.

Regina and I motored along in the happy silence of old friends. Whenever I entertain doubts about the existence of the Almighty, I remember that through my friends God has loved me.

A SEX STORY BREAKS
AT THE *CLARION*

MONDAY . . . 27 APRIL

Being a woman is a huge natural advantage for many reasons, one of the most important being that on the average we live longer than men. This advantage, for me, dwindles each year when I have a physical and endure the pelvic exam. I feel as though I've been in the stirrups more times than Princess Anne. At least Trixie Shellenberger warms up her speculum.

As I put my clothes back on she asked the usual questions. I gave the usual answers except that I admitted I was worried about my nervous stomach. She asked a few sex questions and I wouldn't talk. I thought her attitude was strange. She'd been my doctor since she started practicing here in 1971. She knew better than to press me on such matters.

She said the blood work would take about a week but the other tests would be finished by the end of this week and she'd give me a ring.

I liked my doctor. I didn't like it when she stuck that needle in my arm to get blood, but apart from that, I liked her. The fact that she was an early riser helped.

By eight-thirty I was out of her office at the Medical Arts Building across from the Bon Ton on Hanover Street. Lolly, Pewter, and I tacked on a diagonal over to the Curl 'n Twirl but no one was in yet. So I rounded the Square as opposed to squaring the circle and arrived at the steps of the *Clarion*. The morning sun spread over the west side of the building. I decided to go around to the back and watch the press. Arnie, in his white hat, marched up and down the catwalk. Papers, in orderly fashion, rolled off the press. Hypnotized by the sound and the sight I must have been there for ten or fifteen minutes. I didn't notice Mother until Goodyear leapt up to greet me—and with dirty paws too. Pewter, full of catitude, refused to move aside for Goodyear. Goodyear thought better of running around my feet, where Pewter had stationed herself in defiance.

Mom came alongside me. "Remember when your Daddy used to bring you down here?"

"Yep."

"He'd sit you on his shoulder and tell you about the headlines and the news of the day. You thought the men inside were ice cream people because they were in white. Everytime your Dad would bring you here he'd have to take you over to Mojo's for a hot fudge sundae because you couldn't get it out of your head that the *Clarion* didn't serve ice cream."

"I'd forgotten about that."

"Remember the time you started your own newspaper and wrote it in crayons?"

I did remember. "I must have been six."

"I think you came out of the womb wanting to work on a newspaper."

"I think I did too." I sighed. How can a person love an inanimate thing so much? Yet I loved this newspaper. "Sometimes I wonder how it is with children. You see some kids and you know, without a doubt, that she's going to grow up to be a fashion designer or he's going to race cars or another one will be a veterinarian. And then there are other children, bright, too, who never quite find out what it is they're supposed to do. Know what I mean?"

She nodded in agreement. "I think you're one of the lucky ones."

"Oh, Mother, I don't feel very lucky right now."

She put her arm around me. "Sometimes good things come out of bad."

"This is pretty bad. I'm out of a job. The only thing I know how to do or want to do is run a paper. I'm not a kid anymore. Hell, I don't even have a car and the insurance company is trying to screw me out of paying for the Jeep."

"Got your health." This was all-important to Mom.

"You're right there. I guess I should count my blessings."

"The mortgage payment on the farm isn't punishing. If you can't get work, you can always knock around with something to make that payment and put food on the table. You've never been too proud to work at whatever you could find. You sanded floors in college."

"I'll get by." I put my arm around Mother and walked her over to the Curl 'n Twirl.

I dropped her off for her morning ration of gossip, chatted with Mr. Pierre for a few moments about yesterday's tennis match, and then returned to work. He offered hope about my future. At this point I no longer had hopes but I still had hunches.

I remembered working on the paper during my summer vacations when I was in college and working through the night on underground newspapers protesting the war and racism. I thought of myself as a rebel then. Now I was a rebel with a Mastercard and while I nursed no complaints against Mastercard, I didn't think I could buy the *Clarion* with it.

The atmosphere inside was that of a tomb. Pink slips everywhere. Charles explained to the boys in the back that there would be generous severance salaries. Roger had been offered the job of running the new *Clarion* and had accepted, as he should have. Michelle, too, was offered a raise and a promotion and to my surprise she turned it down. She said she didn't know what she was going to do next but she'd work out the week and start investigating her options.

John, half in the bag, was cleaning out his desk. Roger made a reference to John's drinking and John replied with a lilt, "They talk of my drinking but never my thirst." John left us before noon. I can't say I ever liked John but he knew how to find a story. I wasn't happy to see him go.

After lunch we revived a bit because a wire story came down about Senator Gary Hart's alleged indiscretion with an unnamed lady. I assigned Roger a background article on Hart and I specifically instructed him to place this personal stuff in context with the man's voting record and program for the future. To Michelle I assigned the more difficult task of checking sources on this story. I gave her the name of an old Florida friend and former newspaper woman, Connie Coyne. That would get her on the right track. For myself I reserved the job of writing an editorial about the private behavior of public servants, but I wanted to wait until more facts rolled in. They were not long in coming. This story was going to be a front-page smash for the next two or three weeks. It fairly took my breath away.

Before the day was out we'd had an editorial meeting with Charles and decided to go for broke and highlight every person running for President, both parties. Each day we would give background, public and private, on a candidate. Michelle, excited because this was a big hard news story, wanted us to shine the klieg lights on the sex stuff. We all agreed that was bound to sell newspapers but we at the *Clarion* had to formulate our own policy about just what is fair. Michelle had the green light to find whatever she could, but we were uncertain as to what we would use and how. We twisted and turned but arrived at no conclusion.

This was going to be our last week together but at least it would be a good one. We set another staff meeting for the next day at one. I suggested, for the first time in our history, that we include everyone on the newspaper. This issue of privacy in public life was so important that I wanted everyone's ideas. The rest of the editorial staff agreed. That was a wonderful surprise in itself.

I called Mom to give her the wire story. She was back at home and I could hear the treadmill as I spoke. A light drizzle started before lunch so Mom was walking her five miles at home. I asked her if she was jogging in a black cashmere sweater with a simple strand of pearls and she said no, that outfit belonged to Liz Rife. She got off the phone fast because I knew she wanted to call Aunt Louise and gloat. However, I found out before she hung up that she had paid Aunt Wheeze the fifty dollars.

I waited about a half hour, then called Aunt Wheeze to take her temperature on the subject. While my aunt was never one to avert her eyes from a juicy sex scandal, she was still excited about the fifty bucks won off her sister. She had promptly spent it, too. She'd bought a Marie Antoinette TV cabinet and it was being delivered tomorrow.

I asked her what kind of cabinet she could get for fifty dollars and she said that she added her winnings to the seventy-five dollars I paid for renting the Chrysler. I made a crack about putting her Virgin Mary in the bathtub next to the Marie Antoinette cabinet. I knew better than to say it but something came over me. She called me "every other inch a lady" and hung up in my ear.

35

UNWELCOME KNOWLEDGE

TUESDAY . . . 28 APRIL

A low pressure system glowered in the skies. Not a drop of rain yet but I knew it would dump buckets on Runnymede within the hour. Lolly, Pewter, and I sprinted toward the *Clarion* as though it were raining. Lolly loved it when I'd run and beg her to chase me. Chows, big teddy bears with hearts, aren't fast but they aren't dumb. Lolly ran first to the steps of the paper, thinking she'd nab me there, but I turned and dashed back into the Square and she joyously leapt off the steps. Pewter joined in for a moment or two and then, feeling that it was undignified to be seen cavorting with a mere dog and woman, bounded onto the cannon to watch us.

Mutzi unrolled the green awning over his store. The stalls were empty. The fruits and vegetables were stacked on the sidewalk. He stopped unpacking for a moment and loped over to play with us. Now Lolly had two people to chase and she didn't know whether to shit, run, or go blind, as we say on the Dixon side of the line.

We wore out before the dog did. Mutzi leaned against the cannon. Pewter's long whiskers swept forward in curiosity. Mutzi petted her and then stuck his head in the muzzle of the cannon.

"Can't see a thing." His voice echoed.

"What'd you expect?"

"Dunno." He pulled his head out. "Stay here a sec, will you, Nick?"

Mutzi crossed the street, disappeared into his store, and then reappeared carrying a huge metal flashlight.

"What's that for?" I asked. "It's eight in the morning."

"Will you shine that like this?" He shone the flashlight muzzle at an angle. "And hold her steady?"

"Sure."

Mutzi fiddled a bit to get the right angle and to keep his head out of the light. "Uh-huh."

"What?"

"There's a mess of powder in there. Damn, I must have been so drunk I poured in a quart of the stuff."

"How do we clean it out?"

"Might try a vacuum cleaner. Run the wire into the store—late, very late at night."

"Are we in danger?"

"Not so long as there isn't a ball in there and not so long as nobody touches a match to the wick."

"Let me try something." I examined the loading end of the cannon. The nub of a wick extruded. I lightly shoved it back so it was flush with the metal. It could easily be pulled out but until Mutzi and whoever, probably me, could come down in the middle of the night and clean this thing out, it ought to be safe. Anyway, the only person who played with the cannon was Mutzi.

We were so engrossed in what we were doing, Mr. Pierre scared us. Mutzi explained the situation to him but swore him to secrecy. Who knows what civic committee would descend upon us over this? Yet another committee investigation. The only good thing ever done by a committee was the King James version. Mr. Pierre agreed that a tight lip was the wise course of action and he promised to help.

When I finally got to my desk, a fresh copy of the *Clarion* was on it, as usual. The inky smell wafted to my nostrils even as the ink smeared over my fingers. We can send a man to the moon but we can't print a newspaper that doesn't smear. Mother picked on me for not dressing up for work but I didn't see the point, since I resembled a smudge pot before nine-thirty in the morning. I leafed through and beheld Michelle's article on bingo. The paper included samples of cards for the different games: regular X, railroad tracks, block of 9, champagne glass, inside picture frame, and a miniature of what a blackout bingo would look like. I read the piece, fascinated. Michelle did a fine job. She'd even included a history of bingo, which was developed in 1880 in Italy from the game of *Tombola,* a kind of lottery. Then I read in bold print the date of the blackout bingo game. May 8. That was ten days away.

Michelle, carrying a pile of *Congressional Records*, entered through the back.

Before she dumped them on her desk I was at her. "What's this about the blackout bingo game May eighth?"

"That's what Saint Rose's said."

"How come I don't know about it?" I was peeved.

"You passed out."

"Someone could have told me."

"Nickel, you've been occupied with the *Clarion*. We've all been in the dumps over the sale—who the hell has time to think about bingo?" she rebuked me.

That was the first time I'd ever heard Michelle swear.

"You're absolutely right and I apologize."

The phone rang and she picked it up. "For you."

The call made me livid. It was an Eagle agent from God-knows-where; she sounded like she was speaking to me from the bottom of a well. The appraiser had recommended a check for $64.44. I had a $200 deductible. This amount was low because I had authorized repairs before the appraiser could see the damage. I told her about my claim being erroneously given to Maryland Accident Protection by my local insurance representative, just as I had previously explained to another Eagle agent, two weeks ago. The woman couldn't have cared less. She talked to me as if I were a waterbug and she crisply said I could drop dead—in a less direct way. I jammed the phone receiver onto the cradle. Furious.

"What's wrong?"

"You don't even want to know but trust me, never insure anything with Eagle! And you can bag Richards, Hilton, and Richards too!" I thought a second, picked up the phone, and dialed Jackson. His secretary put me right through.

"Jackson, more crap and I need legal advice."

"Hey, I'm sorry about leaving the courts like that. I don't know what got into me." He wasn't immediately interested in my problem, since he had his own agenda.

"Tough loss."

"I couldn't stand the way he gloated!"

Diz had looked happy but I didn't think he'd gloated. I kept that to myself though.

"You can pound him in a rematch."

"I will but I don't have you for a doubles partner this summer. Don't you think it will be difficult being his partner? Maybe you can back out."

"I try to keep tennis separate from the rest of my life, and I can't back out."

"I suppose."

"Listen, Jack, I'm having a real mess with Eagle over my Jeep." I explained in detail what had transpired.

After carefully listening, he said, "Bring me your papers and if you've got a phone log, bring me that too. I'll take care of this. Often what they do on a large claim is, they'll try to get off cheap. You'd be surprised at how many people accept that. The insurance company figures they've got your money. They've been getting your money for years, so this Jeep accident is really paid for. During negotiations they usually relent and the claim is settled. It's a shitty way to do business but there you have it."

"Why do we take it? I mean, why do Americans just sit around like two hundred and forty million bumps on a log and get raped by these big companies?"

"Good question. The chain of accountability is removed from the customer. Theoretically, your local agent is accountable to you, but the minute there's trouble the job gets fobbed off on the major carrier. And there's no such thing as a 'clean' accident, so if the major carrier wants to, they can find 'variations' in any claim. On the other hand, there are people who gouge the companies for more money than the actual damage."

"I'm not that kind of person."

"I know that but Eagle doesn't. It's a little like the IRS. You're guilty until proven innocent."

I felt sick again. This kind of stuff upsets me. "Sometimes I think I'd like to be a hermit and never have to deal with junk like this again."

"I know the feeling. Why don't you bring me over your materials after you put the paper to bed?" He paused. "I can't tell you how sorry I am about how things are working out—everything."

"Me too. See you tonight." I hung up the phone and then remembered that it was Tuesday. Our night. I didn't want to go over to the office.

Charles had come in to work while I was on the phone with Jackson. He was a little draggy but he picked up when we had the meeting of all the *Clarion* personnel over the issue of public figures' right to privacy. What a great meeting. People contributed a lot and their comments were not shallow. How was I going to live without Arnie and the boys, the gang?

It's a funny thing. A lot of people, higher up on the social scale, stare down their noses at working people like Arnie. They figure they don't think. I know a fair number of people perched on those corporate ladders who don't think either. Some people's minds question and roam and others' don't and it has nothing to do with one's station in life. Just because someone is a laborer doesn't mean he or she is stupid. Sometimes hardships have kept an individual from an education, and sometimes temperament. A lot of people I know observe the man in the three-piece suit and they think he's choking on his white collar. For some people success is money and power or the illusion of it. For others it's quality of life. It would be nice to have it all but the older I get the more I respect the guys like Arnie Dow who love what they do, knowing full well they're "just a working man."

Well, we worked hard today. After the meeting, which lasted three hours, we had Verna bring in food for us. I returned to my desk and picked up the paper again.

In Michelle's article she had woven some funny facts. She found a place, Sullivan, Illinois, where people play Bessie bingo. They've marked out 144 squares on grass and use cow chips. If a cow chip lands on your square, which you've bought for $20, you win the prize of $1,000. The proceeds go to the forty-nine-member Sullivan High School choir, which is so good it needs the money to travel to national competitions.

As I reread her article I found myself laughing anew. The screwiest fact she'd picked up was from the *Globe and Mail,* a Toronto paper. A Mrs. Grisdale had been lost and the authorities brought in a medicine man from Ontario who prepared a sacred hut and called on spirits to help locate Mrs. Grisdale. After this ceremony they held a bingo session and raised $200. No word yet on whether they ever found Mrs. Grisdale.

Michelle leaned over my shoulder. "Not bad for a cub, is it?"

"You don't think much of yourself, do you?"

"Who's my teacher?"

She had me there. "Thought about what you're going to do next?"

"No. What about you?"

I shook my head. "You know Roger will hire you even though you turned Diz down. They'll take you gladly."

"The new *Clarion* is slashing editorial staff."

"He'd hire you anyway."

"Maybe."

"You don't want to work on the other side of the Square, do you? You ought to think about it. It's the way newspapers are run today."

"I know, but no amount of technology is going to help me bang out a good story. I learned that here."

I waited a minute. "So how's it going with you and Rog?"

"I go to bingo games with him and sometimes I go to dinner with him. Don't start sounding like your mom or Wheeze."

"I do not sound like my mother or my aunt."

"You're getting as nosy as they are."

"I am?"

Her eyes darted. "A little bit."

"I think I will assign you that story on early airport art."

I dumped out paper clips on my desk. I like the plastic kind because they're in different colors and then I can sort them out according to color. I pushed together the orange ones. "Okay, so I'm curious. Hoping for the best, that's all."

"The best meaning I have some romance?"

"Well—yeah."

"What about you?"

"Me?"

"We are having a discussion about romance, are we not, or did I miss something?"

"Don't get fresh, Michelle. Romance and I seem to be strangers."

"Every single day of your life?"

"Are you interviewing me or what?"

"No."

"Not every day of my life. I lived with a woman for three years—God, that was ten years ago. Anyway, she left me as her career prospered."

"That doesn't exactly follow."

"Yeah, it does but you have to know her. If she'd thought anyone knew she was gay she would have died on the spot. She was so far in the closet she was voted Miss Garment Bag of 1977. Anyway, I respected her wishes and we didn't go anywhere publicly together but as time went by, as time does, a few people noticed that she was in her thirties and unmarried with a roommate. When the roommate was determined to be me, the plot thickened. So she dumped me and maybe it was just as well, because I can be quiet, you know what I mean, but I have a damned hard time lying. If someone had put it to me: 'Are you Frances's lover?' I don't know what I would have said. Anyway, I'm probably not the easiest person to live with."

"Why is that?"

" 'Cause I love my cat and dog more than anything or anybody else." I laughed.

214

"That's a sad story."

"Not as sad as you think. The happiest day of my life was when Frances moved in with me and the next happiest day of my life was when she moved out."

"Not everyone is as brave as you are."

"I'm not brave, Michelle. Don't ever mistake me for someone brave. I just happen to be a bad liar. Even a child could see through me. Anyway, I think the reward for conformity is that everyone likes you except yourself."

She thought about that. I opened my drawer to push in the paper clips of colors I didn't like. On Tuesday nights I'd substitute those colors for the good colors in other people's paper clip boxes but so far no one had ever noticed.

I put the paper to bed about ten. The Hart scandal was exploding but Roger and Michelle had their fingers on the pulse and I figured they'd be in early tomorrow. I went into the bathroom and combed my hair. I was sure there was more silver in it than at the time of my haircut. Then I rooted around in the cabinet and found a tube of lipstick that Michelle must have left there, Mango Ice. After all these years I couldn't get it exactly right and left a streak of Mango Ice on my front teeth. I rubbed it off.

Lolly and Pewter led the way. Jackson was glad to see me and I was glad to see him, even if I was steamed about Eagle. On top of my car damage I'd now have legal fees. After all, Jackson couldn't work for free.

After a proper social kiss on the cheek we settled down to work.

"Jack, you've got lipstick on your cheek."

"Gives me a raffish look. I won't wash my face for days." He smiled and then gasped. Ragged pain etched on his face.

"Jackson?"

Sweat poured down his face. He couldn't answer me. His left arm twitched. His breathing was harsh. My father died of a heart attack and I knew one when I saw one. I also knew if I took him to the hospital at this hour we'd both be ruined.

I picked up the phone. He frantically waved at me with his right arm. He was thinking about the rescue squad, and on Tuesday nights Peepbean Huffstetler was in charge over there. . . .

"Don't worry, honey. I have a plan." My voice sounded reassuring and calm.

My plan involved calling Mr. Pierre so he could carry Jackson to the hospital in his car. But Mr. Pierre was out and about. Now I was in trouble. Without a second of hesitation I dialed Mother.

"Mother, come over to Brown, Moon, and Frost right away. Jackson's had a heart attack."

"Is he dead?"

"Only socially." How could I be flippant at a time like this? I always came up with smart-alec stuff when I was most scared. "Mom, I think he suffered a mild one. I can explain later."

We hung up the phone without goodbyes.

Mother arrived within three minutes. Together we helped Jackson down the back stairway to Mom's car. At this point he was more frightened than in pain, although he could have another attack, and Mother and I knew she had to get him to the emergency room fast.

Mother, cool as a cucumber in danger, whispered to me: "You go pick up Regina. Tell her I called you and don't tell her anything else. I'll have time to think of a story on the way to the hospital."

She shut her car door and took off. I could see that with her right hand she was rubbing Jackson's neck.

Regina was checking her course plans for the horse show. I had only to say, "Come with me," and she came without resistance. I explained about Jack while we drove to the hospital.

When we arrived she turned to me. "Come in with me."

"Sure."

Mother and I stayed there until Jackson was comfortably settled in his room. Mom said that she'd gone over to the office late to change her will. Evening was the only time Jackson had open today. He suffered the attack and she rushed him to the emergency room because she didn't want to wait for the rescue squad; not that the squad wasn't good—they were—but she thought she could get him there five minutes faster by herself. She said she'd called me from the emergency room so I'd go pick up Regina. Mom covered all the bases.

When she left, Mother looked tired. Memories of Dad's heart attack must have been going through her mind because her face was so sad.

I took Regina back home, once she was satisfied that Jack would be all right. I wanted to make sure she'd be all right herself. We talked with the windows down, and the sweet smells of spring perfumed the conversation. She said that every woman married to a middle-aged man was secretly braced for this kind of thing. Jackson pushed himself too hard. He simply could not admit that he was growing older. Then she smiled and said if he recovered she'd go out and buy a Porsche 911 cabriolet, white. She'd worry about paying for it later.

When I walked Regina to her door I hugged her and told her I loved her.

I drove back with Lolly and Pewter, who'd endured the whole ordeal with me. I felt as low as, maybe lower than, I did the moment I knew I'd lost the *Clarion*. I just about lost Jackson. Whoever said "Here today and gone tomorrow" wasn't kidding.

The difference between genius and stupidity is that even genius has its limits. How stupid I was to assume that tomorrow would be like today. The vicissitudes of romance were painful but it never occurred to me that Jack could die. He wasn't even fifty. I was beginning to realize that even if we all lived to be one hundred we wouldn't be who we were today. We can only imagine the future in terms of our own current emotional state, and it's well nigh impossible to imagine feeling emotions you've never felt before. Time would propel us through new situations, new emotions. The thought of Jack dying was a new, terrifying emotion.

I knew he'd be all right. I prayed that he would be all right—but now I had a vision of my life without the people I loved. Losing Dad was agony enough. No one else could go. Other people's friends could die but not mine. I needed them too much. I loved them too much. Would life be worth living without them? I knew I'd find out in the decades ahead. I felt as thought I'd been hitched to Calamity's traces and was now pulling heavy, unwelcome knowledge.

36

MOTHER DROPS
A BOMBSHELL

WEDNESDAY . . . 29 APRIL

Regina called at seven-thirty A.M. to tell me the doctor confirmed that Jackson had suffered a mild heart attack. Somehow it was consoling to have the doctor say what we already knew. He'd be out of the hospital in a few days, after they ran tests on him.

I told her to come to the stables around five. We could ride and take her mind off her troubles. She said she might.

The *Clarion* chugged along, its last week at the southeastern corner. Charles stepped with a heavy tread. The enormity of what had transpired was seeping into his pores. As it was, nobody was smiling much.

Mother called. She expected to see me after work, ready to paint and ready to talk. My hand shook when I hung up the phone.

Michelle noticed. "You all right?"

"Mom's working on my mood."

"Juts doesn't appear to be the kind of woman to mince words."

"Yeah—I know." I opened my drawer to see my penknife and my "good" paper clips, lined up. The order made me feel better. "I can't fault her this time. I've been stupid. I sat up half of last night thinking about stupidity. You know, Michelle, history is not intrinsically cyclical. The cycles only mean we haven't learned anything from the past. Therefore, one factor is not cyclical: human stupidity."

"So much for history. What about you?"

"You're getting cheeky, you know that? The bingo article was fine. Don't let it go to your head."

Michelle, when she first arrived, would have backed down with her tail between her legs. Not now.

"Who died and made you God?"

That phrase out of Michelle's mouth stopped me cold. "You've been talking to my mother."

"She took me out for breakfast last week, remember?"

I remembered. "What'd she do—tell you every sin I've committed since birth?"

"No, she advised me that your bark is worse than your bite."

"My Mother said that?" Now how was I going to scare Michelle into submission when she sprinkled adjectives with gay abandon throughout her work?

"She talked mostly about herself."

"Her favorite subject." I was a trifle unkind.

"It's everybody's favorite subject."

"It doesn't seem to be yours."

She shrugged. "What can I say? I come from a family where my father wears a coat and tie for dinner and he calls Mother 'darling' when he wants to call her 'bitch.' I'd rather deal with your mother any day."

"Sure, she's not your mother. I could probably deal with yours better than you do."

"If you can get the shot glass out of her mouth." A flash of anger illuminated her face.

"I'm sorry."

"I used to be. Now I'm disgusted. If Mom and Dad had any guts they would have gotten divorced years ago. However, their place in the social set is more important than anyone's happiness, even their own. You'd be surprised at how many people live their lives like that."

"I guess Diz and Liz do. I never thought about it much."

"I didn't either until I came here. My first few months on this paper I felt like I was in a foreign country. . . . I was. People say anything to one another. They curse and throw glue pots. Even the men cry."

I heard Lolly thumping her tail under my desk. "Actually, people don't say as much as you think. I guess we do show a fair amount of emotion, but don't be deceived. There are emotions hidden as deeply here as the ones you're talking about back home."

"I suppose if someone was a murderer they'd hide it."

"Who wouldn't? No, I mean the resentments. The old pains. You and I see the surface angers but I'm not sure I know where they started. Like the bickering between Mom and Wheezie. I don't think they know anymore."

She was considering this when I observed Roger crossing the Square. He was coming from the Bon Ton building.

"You going to blackout bingo with Rog?"

"Yes, but I'm going to tell him it's our last date. That deadline gives me time to work up my courage."

"Don't hold this against him." I swept my hand in the room, indicating the paper itself. "He did the smart thing."

"I know but I feel like I'm leading him on."

I understood and we shut up when Roger came through the door. He may have felt a bit traitorous, because he was conspicuously silent too. Breaking up the old gang was hard but we had two more days together as a full staff, so we might as well enjoy them.

Gene canceled our riding date so I scooted directly over to Mother's. Might as well get it over with.

I wasn't going to enjoy painting Mother's living room or enduring a scene over Jackson. I pulled the Chrysler up her manicured driveway. Lolly, Pewter, and I hopped out and let ourselves in the back door. The kitchen shimmered with the aroma of fried chicken, greens with fatback, and grits. Well, if she was going to lay me out to whaleshit, she was going to feed me well while she did it.

Mother was in the living room. She'd prepared everything for me. All I'd have to do would be to dip the roller in the oil-based paint. We never used acrylic paints. She'd assembled good brushes for the trim work too.

She let me get started. While I painted she rewired a lamp.

"So?"

"Mom, what can I say? I was having an affair with him. I broke it off. Last night we really were doing business—not what you think."

"It took two of you to make that mistake. What's he got to say for himself?"

"The only thing he ever said to me was that he loves Regina but twenty-two years—is twenty-two years."

She was carefully stripping off the covering of a wire. "Heard that one before."

"Mom, why don't we just fight and get it over with? You can call me any name in the book. I deserve it but I might lose my temper anyway."

"You and Jackson were like two shits that passed in the night." Her crooked smile twitched.

"Go on." My cheeks were warming up.

"I'm not mad at you."

"You're not?" I bobbled the roller.

"Careful!"

I regained control of it. "Yes, ma'am."

"It could have been worse. You could have acted like the Siamese twins of love, joined at the hip."

"Thanks." I was not enthusiastic.

"I don't care about sexist acts between consenting adults." She twisted the wires together. "I mean sexist."

"Very funny. I think I'd feel better if you let me have it."

"I can't do that. I'm not saying it's right what you did. It isn't. And I hope to heaven my sister and her big-nosed sidekick Orrie never find out. But right or wrong, it makes sense to me. You've known each other since you were kids. You liked each other. You and Jackson used to play baseball and tennis together from sunup to sundown from kindergarten through college. I thought you'd catch fire then but no, he wanted the other one. Nice girl but I've always felt you and Jackson have more in common than Jack and Regina."

"I don't think men marry women, at least when they're young, on the basis of commonality."

"You know what Cora used to say. 'Men fall in love with their eyes, and women with their ears.' And, honey, Regina is a knockout. You're good-looking but she's a magazine type."

"Kept her looks too."

"Too much makeup—but yes. I expect Jackson's flopped in that hospital bed with deep thoughts. I don't envy him." She put down her wire clippers, next to the strippers. "Would you marry him if he got a divorce?"

"He never would."

"That's not the question. Would you?"

I'd never thought about it. Not once. Which says something about my ability to push back certain emotions.

"I guess I believe that Jack belongs to her no matter what I feel for him—so, no, I don't think I would marry him."

We didn't say anything else until I finished the room. "Mom, can we eat? I'll do the trim after supper."

We ate. She told me that she'd been talking to Mr. Pierre about learning hairstyling. She'd like to make a little money. I'd heard this before. Right now, apart from social security, her small savings, and what I contributed, Mother's income came from babysitting. She got a lot of business because she was great with kids.

"Now I've got something to tell you."

"Yes?" I dug into the grits, my second helping.

"Ed Tutweiler Walters and I are going to live together."

I paused, stared at my grits, and put down my spoon. "What are you saying?"

"You heard me."

"My God. Mom, you barely know him!"

"That's why we're living together. We'll be living in sin." She beamed.

"He hardly talks."

"That's the way he is. He has a good sense of humor."

"He's going to need it," I blurted out.

"You're a fine one to talk. After what you've just gone and done."

"Oh, I don't care about the living in sin part—I think—maybe, well, I don't know."

"You don't like him?"

"No, no, I do like him. I wish I knew him better."

"You'll have that opportunity."

"What about Wheezie?"

Goodyear stirred on the floor.

"I don't know. I have to think of some way to break it to her. I've talked to Mr. Pierre. We thought maybe we could ease her into it tomorrow at the Curl 'n Twirl. It's harder for her to throw a major hissy if people are around."

"Don't hold your breath."

"If I bring her here she'll destroy the house. If I go over to hers she'll yank the phone cords out of the wall and pull the drapes down. You know how she gets."

"Maybe if Orrie's there it'll help."

"We thought of that." She placed a crisp wing on my plate. "He can't take your father's place."

"I know. I'm a little shocked, that's all. I think when it has time to settle in I'll be happy for you." I took a bite. "Mom, does this mean I won't see you so much?"

"Sometimes you act as though that would be a bonus."

I didn't respond.

After a few minutes she spoke. "Maybe you won't see me quite as much because I'll be going places with Ed."

"Are you doing this because of social security?"

"Partly, and partly because when I was young people got married. You courted and you got married and that was that. I think the freedom people have today is better. You don't really know someone until you live with him. I don't care what anyone says, I'm living with him and I have no intention of going down the aisle.

Maybe later, if it doesn't mess up money, yes—but not now. No one's telling me what to do or how to do it. It's my life."

I ate some more and thought about what she'd said. "Mom, good luck."

"You too."

"Why me?"

"Because you've lost your baby—the paper—and you've lost a romance even if it was ill-advised, and you're going to feel blue for a while."

After dinner and a dessert of white cake with vanilla and bitter chocolate icing, Mother's special recipe, I started the woodwork. I should have waited until the walls were completely dry but I'm a careful painter and I wanted to get the job done. I'd get to the other rooms another time but she did need her living room. Maybe Ed could paint the other rooms. He began to seem like a good idea.

She showed me Peepbean's work on her coffee table. It did look like marble. I was amazed that Peepbean was that accomplished a craftsman.

At eleven I decided to bag it. I was tired and I started to make mistakes. I cleaned the brushes, cleared up my mess.

I kissed Mom at the door on the way out. "Thanks for supper."

"I'll call you when we're all at the shop."

"Okay. I'll come over." I waited a second. "Mom, thank you for being understanding. I thought you'd rip me up one side and down the other."

"I'm not giving you a good-conduct medal, Nickel, but these things happen. You're in the prime of life. I don't expect you to live like a nun."

"None of this and none of that."

She smiled. "You know right from wrong but, well, you made a mistake."

"I thought you'd blow up because of my natural mother. I mean, didn't she fool around with a married man and get caught?"

Mother stiffened slightly. "You aren't at all like her, and times are different now."

"I hope so. But when I see some of the shit that comes over the AP wire, I wonder."

"Thank you for being understanding about Ed."

"It's a surprise, but you shouldn't be alone. I always thought there'd be another man in your life but it took a long, long time. Think it will take me that long?"

"Don't be thinking about time. When it's right, it's right."

I kissed her again and left. Maybe Mother was growing up too. Maybe you never stop. If this had happened to me ten years ago I think she would have killed me. Or maybe I was off base. I could misjudge Mother but I think we do that to the people closest to us. We expect more from them and we're harder on them when they disappoint us. It isn't fair, but that's the way it is. I was grateful she didn't disappoint me tonight and I hoped I hadn't disappointed her too much by my escapade with Jackson.

I did know right from wrong, dammit, but those Ten Commandments are sure easier to read off the page than to practice. Back then when people got married their life span was about twenty-five years. Until death us do part came swiftly. Now we live into our eighties and nineties and often in good health. I meet more people in one year than my grandmother met in her lifetime. Some of those people are sexually attractive. I'm not saying that the Ten Commandments are out of date but I do think it was easier to keep them for those Hebrews out there in the desert in the backward dark abyss of Time. Then I wondered about the difference between Christians and Jews. What is a Christian but a Jew with a life insurance policy.

I DROP A BOMBSHELL
MYSELF

THURSDAY . . . 30 APRIL

My editorial on the private life of public figures jolted the town. I came out strongly for full disclosure of all aspects of a candidate's life including his or her sexual life, but my reasoning was not exactly what most people's reasoning was, even if they came to the same decision. I said that politicians today were little more than another form of entertainer. Hell, they had face lifts, hair jobs, dye jobs, and makeup jobs, and of course blow jobs. They studied with media consultants, wardrobe consultants, and probably even psychic consultants. They were just another group of suntanned bullshitters, less concerned with serving their constituency than with landing a bit part on *Dynasty*. If politicians wanted to act like movie stars, then we, the public, had a right to treat them like movie stars. Their private lives were now fodder for the public they so desperately sought to dazzle. The presidential race evolved into a pretty-boy contest. I myself would rather see George Shultz as a candidate than one of the glamour boys. As for liberals, Alan Cranston was still in there fighting but he, too, was not another pretty face.

The phones jangled off the hook. Some Runnys laughed; some were furious; some agreed with me; others wanted to know why Charles would allow sexual innuendo in the paper. Innuendo. How polite of them. I laid it on the line.

Wasn't it boiling it down to sex anyway? Sex is used to sell cars, underarm deodorants, breakfast cereal, and now, politicians. And sex was destroying Gary Hart. We sat around the AP wire machine like kids under a Christmas tree. The lady's name, Donna Rice, was revealed. No one even pretended that she was part of the campaign team. When Hart issued a statement saying he was wronged by the press, he sang in every key but the right one. If the man had had any guts he would have looked America squarely in the eye and said, "Yes, I slept with her and it was great." If he had guts and was a gentleman he could have said, "I love her. I know this will cause distress for my family but I love her nonetheless." Even wispy Edward VIII had courage at his Waterloo. But maybe Gary Hart was a cold, calculating man. Maybe he didn't love her. Maybe he figured, as many people do, that he could eat his cake and have it too. He'd been married very young. I can't imagine being married as many years as Senator Hart, but putting that difference aside, it's better to come clean. Maybe the American public wouldn't vote into office a man who admitted he loved a woman who was not his wife but I think they might respect him for admitting it.

My own feeling was that there probably wasn't a representative or senator who has remained faithful to his wife unless someone's been feeding him saltpeter. There's something askew about a nation that expects its public servants to have better morals than the rest of us. Maybe the public doesn't expect its elected officials to have better morals but merely to be more clever in the deception. Curious.

While the Gary Hart scandal bubbled over, the PTL mess sank to name-calling. By the time Jim Bakker's enemies were finished with him, it sounded as though the guy went on one big fuckathon. I couldn't tell if the other TV preachers were jealous or genuinely concerned about the state of his soul. It wouldn't be his soul that I'd be concerned about.

Rarely has the AP wire provided me with so many belly laughs in a short space of time. Even Charles, grim and grave today, had to laugh at some of it.

Roger came over and told us a sick joke that was making the rounds of the Square. Nixon, Teddy Kennedy, and Hart were in a boat at sea. The boat began sinking and Nixon said, "This boat is going down. We've got to save the women and children." Kennedy replied, "Fuck the women and children," and Hart quipped, "Is there time?" Roger thought it was pretty funny. I can't say that I did, but it was an object lesson in how swiftly people can savage the fallen.

Michelle asked me if I thought a gay person could run for President.

"We've had gay Presidents," I said, "but they lied, and also it was a long time ago."

"They say that J. Edgar Hoover was gay."

"Who wants to claim him," I shot back.

"I don't see that sexual behavior affects a person's ability to be President."

"Doesn't."

"So, what's the issue?"

"Were you a Girl Scout?"

"Yes." A puzzled expression came over Michelle's face.

"Do you remember the fire ceremony we'd have when we'd go on our camp-outs?"

She laughed. "I haven't thought of that since I was a kid. Sure, I remember. There were four little fires and a big bonfire in the middle. We started out in darkness and then a Brownie would light the fire of friendship and each fire would be lit sequentially with lots of mumbo jumbo until the big fire was set off." She stopped. "What's that got to do with running for President?"

"As you got older, didn't you think the fire ceremony was pretty corny?"

"Sure."

"Same difference. You want to laugh but if you do the others will get mad at you. A man who runs for President is like a Girl Scout going around the nation setting off these fires—with a solemn face, I might add. What would happen if one of them said, 'This is horseshit'? Not only would the less imaginative campers get mad, so would the camp counselors who put together this incendiary theater for the kids. So every guy out there running has to pretend that he loves his wife, is faithful to her, loves his kids, and is just an all-around family guy with a golden retriever and a big mortgage. Family guys don't run for President, but hey, why mess up the act?"

"You ever think about running for office?"

"I think about running from it."

"You know everybody. You care about Runnymede. I think you'd be good."

"Michelle, you're a fountain of compliments and I appreciate it but we're back to your question on the local level. Is this town going to elect the Good Gay Girl Scout to public office?"

She appeared thoughtful. "Ever think about why you're gay?"

"I became a lesbian out of devout Christian charity. All those women out there are praying for a man and I gave them my share."

Michelle's jaw dropped to her chest.

"Got you that time, didn't I?" I flashed a victory "V." "And now, Brenda Starr, I'm off to the Curl 'n Twirl." The summons from Mom had come.

Pewter, Lolly, and I started out of the building. Michelle called after me: "I'm onto you, Nickel. You deflect people with your humor but one of these days you're actually going to talk to me—about you."

As I closed the door I replied, "Only if you talk about you. To get you gotta give."

Mr. Pierre greeted me with a conspiratorial air. Mother, Orrie, and Wheezie were loudly arguing the merits of my editorial, Gary Hart, and men in general. Men were taking a beating. I felt like importing three of them so there'd be a fair fight.

"You've got the town abuzz." Orrie even had the paper in her hand.

"That's my job."

"I certainly think you could have done without mentioning . . . you know." Wheezie was referring to the line about blow jobs.

"Yeah, but it got your attention, didn't it?" Mother said.

"There are less vulgar ways to do that," Louise sniffed.

"Name one." Mother put her on the spot.

"Juts, that's not Wheezie's expertise. Nickel's the expertise stripper." Mr. Pierre winked at me.

Georgette sang out, "Line one for you, Mr. Pierre."

"Excuse me, darlings." He picked up the phone and was soon immersed in ordering hair supplies.

Orrie shifted her weight on the chair. "A looker."

Mother craned her head to get a better look at the Donna Rice picture in the paper. "Maybe she knows how to sail a yacht—better rename that boat the *Titanic*."

"All tips and no icebergs." Wheezie spoke knowingly about Miss Rice as she tossed Goodyear and Lolly tiny Milk-Bones. Mr. Pierre kept a bowl of them on the counter.

"Now, who's focusing on sex?" Mother teased her.

"I wasn't upset over the sex part. I don't think Nickel should have used those—words."

"I hope the girl can count." Orrie folded up her paper.

"Why?" Mother asked.

"Because women who miscalculate are called mothers."

That set the girls off. Mr. Pierre hung up the phone. "What did I miss?"

Orrie repeated her jibe, which received fresh laughter.

Mother glanced from Mr. Pierre to me and back to Mr. Pierre again. She felt it was now or never.

"Wheezie, I have something to tell you and I thought it would be nice to hear it among friends."

"You sick, Juts?" Louise's brow furrowed.

"No." Mom stuck. Nothing issued from her mouth.

Orrie checked her wristwatch. "I've got to meet Ann Falkenroth at Mojo's in five minutes."

"I didn't know you were having lunch with Ann." Wheezie crossed her legs.

"Do I have to tell you everything?"

Louise's answer was simple and direct. "Yes."

"That's what I'm trying to do, tell you everything at once." Mom did this in one breath. "Ed and I are going to live together."

"Don't be absurd." Orrie's laughter tinkled.

Mr. Pierre impressed upon her the gravity of the situation. "It's true."

Louise stood up. "I saw him first!"

"No, you talked to him first."

Orrie, perceiving that Louise's blood pressure was spiraling upward, said, "Now, now, that's not—"

"Shut up." Wheezie put her hand over Orrie's mouth with a backhanded flick of her wrist. "You did this to spite me!" She spat the words at Juts.

"I did not. We get along and—"

"He gets along with me, too—oh, little did I think you could stoop so low. Only now do I know."

Mother got flippant. "You're just pissed because you didn't ask him first."

Louise stomped for the door, opened it, and hollered as she was framed in the doorway: "I'm tired of being the buttocks of your jokes!"

She slammed the door behind her. Mr. Pierre winced.

Orrie, a trifle pale, again checked her watch. "I think I'd better be going."

"You aren't going after her to console her?" Mother asked, her voice rising.

"She's your sister, not mine. She'll huff and puff and blow the house down and then get over it. Besides, all is fair in love and war, Julia, and it looks like you win—this time."

We watched Orrie leave. I sat in a chair and so did Mr. Pierre. Georgette called Verna to tell her the news.

Mother brazenly called out, "Tell her to put it on the blackboard. Julia Ellen Smith shacks up with Ed Tutweiler Walters."

"Mom, don't rub it in."

"I'm not rubbing it in. If it's going to be all over town by the end of lunch hour it might as well come from me."

Mr. Pierre rubbed his chin. "Wish I knew what Wheezie is going to do. She won't take this lying down."

"What can she do aside from have a fit and fall in it?" Georgette asked, now that she'd hung up the phone with her mother.

"What'd Verna say?" Mother wanted to know.

"She says Ed is old enough to know what he'd doing and so are you."

"That's it?" Mother seemed disappointed.

"That's it," Georgette promptly replied.

"I think Aunt Wheezie really cares for Ed," I said.

Mother did not appreciate my concern or my line of chat. "You stay out of this."

"You wanted me here for moral support—or is it immoral support?" I didn't like her tone of voice.

"People who live in glass houses shouldn't throw stones." Mother's eyes bored into me.

"Hey, Mom, I've graduated to being a part-time adult. When I want you to live my life for me, I'll let you know."

"Trees manage their affairs better than you do."

That did it. I left. If she was upset over her sister, she could damn well take it out on someone other than me. I burned off energy walking around the Square and decided to go into the Medical Arts building to see if my tests had come in.

Trixie motioned me into her office as she emerged from an examining room. She didn't keep me waiting.

"I was going to call and tell you to come over."

"Am I healthy?"

"You are in splendid health and I'm glad of it"—she paused and came a bit closer to me—"because you're pregnant. Since you were being cute and clever during the exam concerning your sex life, I shall assume a star is rising in the East."

"Holy shit."

Bet I drove over every back road in the county. The dog and cat fell asleep in the car. When I finally got home I called Mr. Pierre. He said he'd marry me and I shouldn't give it a second thought. He also said that I should go straight to Mother with the news.

With reluctance I did as he advised.

Mother was experimenting with her new pillows on the sofa when I walked in.

"Are bygones bygones?" she asked, her version of an apology.

I lowered myself onto the sofa as she pulled a pillow out from behind my back. She tested it in the other corner.

"The last few days have been hectic." This was a weak start.

"Never a dull moment." She stepped back to study the color combinations.

"It's not over yet."

She looked sharply at me. "Oh."

"I'm pregnant."

"What?"

"I'm pregnant. Trixie Shellenberger told me after I left the Curl 'n Twirl."

She gripped the other arm of the sofa and launched herself back on her pillows. "Oh, my God!"

"I'm going to have the baby." I repeated myself. I didn't know what to say.

"I should hope so—I want to be a grandmother, but what a mess. What a fine kettle of fish." She rubbed her temples.

"Mr. Pierre offered his hand in marriage."

"He did?"

"I don't know if he meant it or not."

"Well, if he does mean it take him up on it fast. It may be the only way to save our face—what's left of it."

"Thanks."

"You haven't exactly been conventional." I could see she was torn between elation and despair. "Why'd you talk to Mr. Pierre before me?"

"I thought he'd be more objective than either you or I," I said.

She murmured an agreeing noise and sank farther into the pillows.

"Mom, what are we going to tell Aunt Wheeze?"

"Nothing."

"She's bound to find out sometime."

"She's had one shock. Another one might put her under." She rested her hands on her cheeks.

"Are you thinking?"

"You try thinking. I'll try praying—that we get out of this one alive."

"It's not that bad—is it?"

"Have you thought about what your child is going to do when he or she grows up?" Her eyes were solemn. "She's going to write a biography of you called *Mommie Queerest*."

THE *CLARION* CHANGES HANDS

FRIDAY . . . 1 MAY

The Virgin Mary's was a planned pregnancy. Mine was not. I awoke at six-thirty A.M., my mind a jumble of conflicting thoughts, my emotions in the electric blender. I would be unemployed at five tonight. I was to deliver sometime in December a child whom I conceived without the benefit of a husband. My Jeep lay in sections at the garage. I couldn't pay to fix it and Jackson couldn't wrangle with Eagle until he was back in the office, full steam. If he was strong enough I should enlighten him about this unexpected event. Maybe I shouldn't tell him ever, but that seemed cruel. I don't sleep around. During the sexual revolution I was the only person of my generation not getting any. Now I got more than I bargained for.

Self-pity is the simplest luxury. I nearly surrendered to it, but after a punishing workout and a hot shower I recovered my good sense or what was left of it and considered the pluses. I was healthy. My mother appeared to be supporting me, and for all her bravado and wisecracks, this must be emotionally affecting her. Life wasn't turning out as she had envisioned it, but does it ever—for anyone? I had two furry souls, Lolly and Pewter, who loved me. Kenny loved me too. I lived on a fine patch of the earth. I was okay. And the more I thought about it the more excited I became. I wanted to be a mother. I was prepared to welcome this little person into the world, planned or unplanned, and do what I could to prepare her/him to survive it and occasionally triumph.

When I was fresh out of college I knew everything. Now I wasn't

certain what I knew. I had surrendered all my beliefs. I wait for the
Truth to find me.

I did know that I believed in life and I was joyous, down deep, to
be giving life. I wanted a healthy baby. As to the social stigma,
could it be any worse than being gay? I'd fight if I had to but I was
going to have this baby.

Whistling down the hill in the Chrysler, I beheld the town and it
appeared brighter to me. The water tower off the Emmitsburg Pike
loomed like an ugly sentinel of the town, but even the tower with
SOUTH RUNNY 1988 painted over it looked beautiful to me. The spire
of Christ Lutheran, gold and blue, was gleaming, and the darker
tone of Saint Rose's steeple and Saint Paul's shot up over the
rooftops. I loved this place. I wanted my child to love this place. I
reckoned someday she or he would climb the water tower, in the
depths of the night, and paint her class's year on it. David Wheeler
would sputter and then send a clean-up crew. It's not as if David
didn't do the same thing in 1970.

May ushered herself in with soft sunshine and little humidity. I
pulled the Chrysler around into the parking lot. It was still early. No
other cars rolled around the Square. Pewter, Lolly, and I strolled
around the entire Square. We took our sweet time.

I thought about being a mother and I thought about Mom.
Mothers invent our idea of love. Mother feeds us. Cleans us. Puts us
to bed at night. Mine read to me every night until I could read to
myself. Mother patches your cuts and bruises. Packs your lunch.
Puts your clothes on and teaches you how to tie your shoes. She
teaches you how to tell time too. You watch the little hand for the
hours and the big hand for the minutes. Mother not only tells you
right from wrong, she shows you. One time I stole from the old Bon
Ton a yellow yo-yo with a black stripe through the middle; it looked
like a bumblebee and I love bumblebees. Mother marched me right
back into the store and forced me to return my booty. I was seven. I
never stole again. Mother teaches you sympathy for others and
responsibility. She scolds, chides, and whacks you when she has to
but she's there. She's always there. She's the person who presents
you to the world your first day of school. Even as you depend upon
her she is teaching you to let go. Dad is beloved and in my case even
worshipped but he's not there the way Mom is. A man grows up
and expects to find some of this mother-love in his wife. A woman
has to transfer her affections to a man. She doesn't expect a man to
love her as her mother did. Already, we expect less.

I wondered about this with Lolly dancing at my heels and Pewter
madly chasing squirrels. Our entire concept of love would shift if

men cared for children the way women do. Please, this is not to fault men. They are imprisoned in the work force. Nobody gives them the choice of working or staying home with the children. They work until they drop or they've made enough to retire. And it's good to work, gives you confidence, but they're overworked. Their own children all too often are strangers to them as they work to put food in their mouths. Their lives are one big ambush as other men try to take away what they've earned, beat them into the ground for a promotion, steal their woman. Is it any surprise that so few men are truly friends with one another? Even when they are supposed to be relaxing they compete.

My Dad was smart. He was a fisherman. Dad hated competition, and by other men's standards, Chessy was not a success. He kept a roof over our heads but Mother had to work, too, and in Dad's generation that was a bad mark against him. But because he was no threat to anybody, he was loved. And because he wasn't money-oriented he spent much more time with me than other dads. He taught me about the stars, cars, and wars. He taught me how to fish even though it bored me. I never had the heart to tell him. He taught me the names of trees, countries, and every gadget in his store. He taught me to be a good baseball player. He was my first editor and he said that old man Hunsenmeir, whom I never met, used to tell him that an editor comes down from the hills after the battle and shoots the wounded. After this reminder, he'd read my efforts and make careful suggestions. My father treated me, even as a child, like a thinking person. He never talked down to me and he rarely had to reprimand me, but then he had Mother for that. Truly, I was loved by my father and far more fortunate than my friends whose fathers were more distant, yet even Dad's love was not the same as Mother's. Mother was my life force. Dad was her assistant.

My child wasn't going to have a father and I can't say that I was pleased about that. I wondered whether or not to take Mr. Pierre's offer. I was born a bastard. Most people have to work at it. However, I didn't want to inflict that taint of illegitimacy on my child. Yeah, I know movie stars have children out of wedlock and it's glamorous. Movie stars don't live in Runnymede and my nose was bloody plenty of times as a kid over this. Some sucker would call me a bastard and the fists would fly. I gave as good as I got.

By the time I'd reached the *Clarion,* I'd half made up my mind to accept Mr. Pierre's generous offer. My step faltered as I saw the sunlight slide over the picture window with THE RUNNYMEDE CLARION painted on it. How could this be the last day? I wanted my child to be a copy boy, to know the smell of lead and ink in the back room, the shake, rattle, and roll of the AP machine, the hustle-bustle of reporters and editors all yelling at once. Surely heaven was a newspaper and God was Editor in Chief.

The door opened. Charles, Ann at his side, was packing his office. He suddenly looked old to me, old and broken, but here he was a very rich man. He didn't glance up when I pushed through the door. Michelle was coming in the opposite way, through the back door. Roger hadn't arrived yet and John's desk already had the air of a cold corpse.

The honor of the farewell editorial would go to Charles. It would run tomorrow. I was to write today's editorial and I'd sat up last night, after my talk with Mom, and penned a silly one. Michelle gave it the headline, ARE WE HAVING FUN YET?, and it was about Washington's annual survey of hospital emergency rooms and how people got there. Twenty-six thousand people landed in the ER because of dancing. Billiard injuries produce a steady stream of ravaged bodies, due less to the game than to the fights that ensue. Playing a musical instrument keeps the ambulance crews busy, as kids chip their teeth on trumpets, saxophones, and the occasional tuba. One child tried to stuff baby brother into the tuba. Moving pianos produces a variety of broken toes, crushed ribs, and other fractures. Large-scale fun, like amusement parks, provides a bumper crop of injuries, with roller coasters being the prime culprit, Ferris wheels following at a close second, bumper cars trailing at third. Over six thousand people fell off of barstools last year and had to be rushed to the hospital. Fortunately, most of them were so plastered the damage to their persons was not as bad as it could have been. Of all the forms of having fun the least dangerous was fish watching, although there was a case in Portland, Oregon, of a man being bitten by his pet piranha.

Reading that editorial produced the only flicker of a smile Charles allowed himself. When five o'clock arrived we stood together in the front room, deep afternoon shadows falling across the Square and the statues, and Charles bid us goodbye and good luck. Quietly we went our separate ways. I felt as though someone opened the end of a kaleidoscope and the colored bits flew out.

Michelle and I didn't say goodbye, because she said she'd be seeing me at bingo tonight. I went over to Mojo's with Pewter and Lolly. Verna was depressed about the end of the *Clarion* as we'd known it, as Runnymede had known it since 1710. She sat down in the booth with me and consumed chicken-fried steak, mashed potatoes swimming in gravy, biscuits—really fabulous biscuits—broccoli, a salad with ranch dressing, and a stupendously large piece of cherry pie, her favorite. After this gargantuan repast she dabbed her mouth with a napkin and said, "If only I could figure out a way to have a supper like this and not get fat."

"That's easy," I replied. "Eat all you want—just don't swallow it."

For a minute there she believed me.

I helped her close up the restaurant, then we walked across the Square to Saint Rose's. Her children would already be there.

"Vern, I'm not playing tonight. Tell Mom and Aunt Wheezie I went home. I feel so bad I'm not fit company."

"Ah, honey, come on—make you feel better. You might even win the pot."

"Not tonight. Anyway, I'm going to win next week, the big one."

"Okay, I'll tell them. You take care, hear?"

"Thanks." I watched her bulk disappear down the little sidewalk along the edge of the church property. She turned the corner to go into the back entrance. Fat though she was, she was beautiful to me then. People who care for you inevitably become beautiful.

I drove over to the hospital. The dog and the cat crabbed about being stuck in the car. I left the windows down a bit and told them both to stay. Then I opened the door to the small hospital. The odor of disinfectant assailed my nostrils. I hate hospitals.

Jack, room 418, was reading a book.

"Hi."

"Nickie!" He put his book down and held out his arms.

I hugged him. "I'm so glad you're all right."

"I'm fine. It wasn't much of a heart attack. The doctors are making a bigger deal out of it than it has to be but you know, they're like lawyers—they have to justify their existence."

"How long do you have to stay in here?"

"Tomorrow. I could have gone home yesterday but those blood-suckers are running every test known to man. Gene says this is what happens when you don't get checkups. Apparently my cholesterol level is over the moon but the doctor said I'm in great shape. The exercise probably saved me—that and the fact that I'm not a smoker. So-o-o, no butter and no rich fats and yeck." He made a face.

"How do you feel now?"

"I feel fine. In a way this is my first real vacation, because even when I'd go on vacation I'd call in to the office. I considered myself the indispensable man."

"You are."

He patted my hand. I was sitting on the edge of the bed. "Thanks for the flowers. Thanks for everything. You and your mom were wonderful. She came by and brought me this." He held up an electronic puzzle. "Damned hard, too. She said you'd be by."

"She did, did she?"

"We had a good long talk about you." He lowered his voice. "I didn't have anyone to talk to about you, and I don't know, Juts sat down and I started talking. God, I feel so much better. She's very understanding and she loves you. We both love you."

"Did she say anything else?"

"No."

"How's your heart feel right this minute?"

"It feels fine, Nickie. I'm fine."

I leaned over and whispered in his ear, "I'm going to have a baby."

He wrapped his arm around me and held me next to him. He didn't say anything. He rocked me back and forth, then whispered in my ear: "Are you happy? Because I am."

"I am happy but I don't know what I'm going to do next." I moved a bit away from him so I could see his face. "I'm still in shock. That and the paper."

"Yeah, I know. Loved your editorial." He squeezed my hand. "Maybe Regina would divorce me so I could marry you. And you could come live at our house or I could become a Mormon and marry you both."

I laughed. "I don't know how she'd take it if she knew, but I think Winston and Randolph wouldn't be thrilled. They're at that difficult age." I picked up Mom's electronic puzzle. It made beeping tones. "We can't get married, Jack, because Mr. Pierre has consented to marry me."

"Him!"

"It's a great kindness on his part. The child will not be illegitimate."

"The child will grow up with a father who wears more makeup than his mother."

"So—she or he will learn early how the rules of society often violate the rules of the heart. I don't think it's so bad. Mr. Pierre is a warmhearted and responsible man."

"He is that." Jack chewed his lip. "You're going to have the baby? You wouldn't—"

"Never."

"I'll provide for the child. I'm not going to leave you in the lurch, especially now."

"Unemployed and prospects dim."

"Not dim—undisclosed, to be discovered. I'll set up a trust fund. Does Mr. Pierre know I'm the father?"

"I'll tell him." What I didn't say was that someday, when the time was right and I was strong enough, I'd tell Regina.

"Think you should?"

"The man is going to give my baby his name. He's going to try and be as good a father as he can—and without the enjoyment of making the thing, I might add. He deserves to know, but then he knows anyway. He knew we were carrying on. Who else could it be but you? I haven't formally told him, that's all."

"I'll always be a part of you."

I looked at him, my eyebrows coming together in concentration. "But you were always a part of me. We grew up together. We'll grow old together. We belong here."

"It's different now. We made something, somebody special, I hope. Hey, she's got you in her, she's going to be special."

"How do you know this baby's a girl?"

"I have two boys. I want a girl." He smiled. "I'm as close to you as I can get. We're bound for life." He held up his hand to stop me from speaking. "From us comes new life. Think of it as the ultimate heterosexual experience. Those are more your terms. You'll see me in this baby every day of her life. And when I see her I'll see you. I hope she's got the best of us because if she does, she's off to a hell of a good start."

These sentiments, unknown to me, rested in my mind. I didn't know what he was talking about. I heard him. Intellectually I understood him, but I didn't feel it. Perhaps he was right. In the birth of the child and the raising of it, I would understand emotionally what he was trying to convey to me. "You sound as though you want to be a father and you can't. That belongs to Mr. Pierre."

"I'm going to be a very loving uncle."

"Regina will figure it out, you know."

"People see what they want to see." He took a breath. "But I'm going to talk to her. I don't know when. But I am. I'm happy. I want her to share in that happiness even though according to convention she should be furious at me. Knowing you, I don't know how she could be."

Where was Miss Manners when I needed her? She'd have an answer to this. Confusing as the social aspect of my pregnancy was, conflicted as I was about Regina, I felt at peace, happy, excited. I didn't understand how I could feel that way under the circumstances but I did. In a funny way my feelings reminded me of when

I realized I could love a woman. I was fifteen. The world told me it was wrong, but for me I knew it was right, and I was content. I knew I couldn't be a full person if I didn't follow my instincts. My instincts were telling me to have this baby and let the chips fall where they may.

We caught up on gossip, but we'd interrupt our gossip to dream about the baby. Jack wanted to know what Mom said and I told him she was worried but essentially happy to be a grandmother.

"I'll call you tomorrow." I got up to leave.

"Can't come by?"

"It's the annual Delta Delta Delta fund-raising horse show."

"I'm fence crew—" He looked more disappointed than he really was. Jack didn't like splinters in his hands any more than I did.

"Got a replacement."

"Who?"

"Diz."

A flicker of anger crossed his features. "Is he practicing the common touch?"

"No. I called him at his office to congratulate him on his acquisition of the paper and then I hit him with the fence crew. Being as how I was magnanimous in defeat, he graciously agreed to a day of manual labor."

"I never will like that guy."

"You're both bulls with long horns, that's why." He started to purse his lips in a question but I continued. "You're two very masculine men, lots of androgen in those bodies, and you both want to lead the herd. Even if you hadn't been rivals as children you'd be rivals as adults. It's chemical." I closed with a flourish of my hand. I half believed what I'd said and I half didn't, an interesting predicament.

"Smith's endocrinic view of the universe."

"You got a better one?"

"At the moment, no. If anything, my hormones are catching up with me."

I kissed him on the cheek again. "They sure caught up with me."

39

URSULA HUMBLED

SATURDAY . . . 2 MAY

May opened her luscious arms for the horse show. Azaleas blazed, the robins returned in squadrons, and the light shimmered and danced. Our annual show was held at the indoor ring of The Barracks, a high-powered show-jumping stable owned by Claiborne Bishop. Claiborne was an inactive Delta Delta Delta alumna but she made up for it by donating the ring, her expensive jumps, and the announcing system.

At The Barracks at the crack of dawn, the field crew trudged through the deep soft footing to set up the first course. Regina, designer of our course, directed us from the spectators' platform, which ran the length of the huge indoor arena. Michelle, Mr. Pierre, Diz, and I sank up to our ankles in the brown loam as we hauled around rails, standards, brush, and potted plants. Even at that early hour, children and adults trotted and cantered in the schooling area off the main ring.

Kenny, shining and braided, lounged in his stall and so did Regina's horse. It wasn't enough that we worked this damned show, we had to ride in it, too; Ursie wanted the classes jam-packed. She huffed and puffed that Tri-Deltas must be out in force to combat the Kappa Kappa Gammas, Kappa Alpha Thetas, Chi Omegas, Delta Gammas, Alpha Delta Phis, and whatever other sorority alumnae showed up to ride or to push their children into it. Ursie's devotion to Delta Delta Delta, misplaced though it might be, was genuine. We would outshine those other "girls" no matter what.

Verna BonBon was our ringside announcer. Verna didn't go to college but we'd made her an honorary Tri-Delta last year because she possessed the best voice in town. Also, Verna gave out a lot of free food to hungry people over the years and this was our chapter's small way of thanking her for community service that we should have done ourselves.

Ursie, staggering under the weight of her crystal fox-head jewelry, actually wore her Delta Delta Delta pin on her expensive Valentino dress. A crescent moon with a trident passing through it snagged holes in the silk pattern but Ursie was beyond caring. This was a small price to pay to be the center of attention. The audience area, decorated with silver, gold, and blue bunting, our sorority colors, must have taken Ursie and her daughters half a day's work.

"Welcome, ladies and gentlemen, to our eleventh annual Delta Delta Delta horse show. A big round of applause, please, for Ursie Yost for her spectacular organizing. She vows this year's show will run like clockwork. Take a bow, Ursie." Verna's rich alto crackled over the loudspeakers.

Ursie, in high heels, cheerfully plunged into the middle of the show ring. She took her bows at nine A.M. on the dot.

"If she bends over too far she isn't going to get back up." I smirked.

"You're jealous of the jewelry," Diz commented.

Our little ground crew stayed at the ring level behind a swinging door. The setup was a bit like what you see in the bullring. The clowns have a place where they can hide from the bulls. We were the clowns.

The first class of the first division was Small Pony Hunter, which meant the little kids would be up. We'd get the worst spills out of the way immediately. The low jumps discouraged bad accidents but little ones do get pitched over ponies' heads, slide off the sides, or dismount in terror. As the tots popped over jumps I scanned the audience. The turnout was the best ever, helped by the good weather. Our Runnymede gang showed up: Mom accompanied by Ed, Louise sulking, Orrie, Mutzi, various BonBons, Muffin Barnes and Gloria Fennell from our stable, Elliwood Baxter, Shirley McConnell, and our entire hunt club. Hunt clubs from Virginia, Maryland, and Pennsylvania showed up for the adult classes. Jill Summers, M.F.H. of Farmington Hunt, brought her kids and adults. Jake Carle, II came in with Keswick, a wild and woolly bunch. The Maryland clubs like Goshen Hunt came splendidly appointed, along with Green Spring Valley, Iron Bridge. Mr. Hubbard's Kent County Hounds were easy to spot: The men wore scarlet with an orchid collar. Apart from Farmington Hunt Club and Keswick, the other Virginia clubs that crowded into the area were Deep Run, Middleburg, Orange County, Warrenton, and Piedmont. From Pennsylvania we drew Rose Tree, Plum Run, Mr. Stewart's Cheshire Foxhounds, Beaufort, and Radnor. We even had a visitor from Roaring Fork Hounds near Aspen. She wanted to observe how we did things to see if she could run a similar event for the club back home in Colorado.

Ursie's cleverness was in combining two upscale groups of people, fox-hunters and sorority alumnae, to garner funds. The turnout even stunned Ursie, by nature an optimist.

The morning clicked along right on schedule. Clockwork. Tiffany won a blue ribbon for Large Pony Hunter. Harmony came in a disappointing third in her division but as she was entered in some afternoon classes her hopes remained fresh.

Michelle, smudges on her face, big gloves on her hands, took a lunch break while Diz and Mr. Pierre and I kept working. We'd need to stagger our breaks. Lolly and Pewter sat with Mother and Goodyear. Mom made herself conspicuous by cheering when I'd drive the tractor. I waved my baseball hat at her.

"Amateur owner over thirty years. Next class. All aboard." Verna's voice rang out.

"Mr. Pierre, I'm in this one. Can you handle it?"

"Is Michelle coming back?" he sensibly asked.

I pointed to Michelle, eating on the run, already moving toward our holding pen.

"All right, darling, I'll brave it without you." He winked at Diz, who winked back.

Riding in a competition is my idea of hell. I become self-conscious and lose my rhythm. Fortunately, Kenny's a push-button horse and he packs me around when I begin to falter. I put on my hunting coat, gray with the gold facings and the B & G hunt buttons. Our club was unusual in that you could wear a black coat or a dark-blue one or a gray one. The club was formed by veterans of the War Between the States, and they kept their colors. The worn elbows on my coat shone like peach stones. My cap was nearly bald but if you didn't peer too closely at me, I looked properly turned out.

Regina brazenly wore a pink coat and top boots. As Master of Foxhounds she could do what she wanted, although traditionally pink coats were worn only by men who have earned their hunt colors. Regina's one rebellion caused chatter whenever people from other hunt clubs beheld her. I loved it and thought she looked sexy, kind of like when Marlene Dietrich wore a top hat and tails. The mixture of sultry femininity with masculine attire is a high-voltage combination.

Regina rode before me, even though as course designer she shouldn't have. We figured Ursie could eat a fig. Let Regina have her moment in the sun or under the fluorescent lights.

My turn came next and my throat tightened. Kenny pricked up his ears and trotted out. I cut my teeth on two-and-a-half-foot jumps; actually, it was more like extraction. By this time, theoretically, I knew what to do. Well, I made it around and looked ridiculous. I quickly untacked Kenny after my turn, whipped off my jacket, and hurried back to my post.

A few luncheon drinks enlivened the crowd. Verna got cute on the P.A. system. Ursie swanned about. A perfect day. A perfect show. Mr. Pierre, Michelle, Diz, and I, physically weary, became punch-drunk. We laughed at everything. One of the lessons a show like this teaches you is that the hunt seat is not superficially acquired. There's lot to laugh at.

We were down to the last class and the biggest, Green Working Hunter. *Green* referred to the horse, not the rider. It was a coveted class because people wanted to take their young horses and get in the ribbons. If selling the horse was a future goal, those ribbons would be important.

By now, happily filthy, our little fence crew leaned behind its protective enclosure. Eleven green hunters cantered by us. A fence was chipped here or there, a rail down, but so far so good. The twelfth horse, Tallulah, groomed to perfection, was ridden by Harmony. Harmony's hands, soft and responsive, nudged up on the animal's neck as they cleared the first fence. Ursie commanded the center box in the audience. From out of the corner of my eye I thought I saw movement by the far wall of the ring.

"What's that?" Mr. Pierre pointed.

Michelle, with her twenty-twenty vision, laconically said, "Looks like a skunk to me."

"It is a skunk." Diz began laughing, which set off the rest of us.

The animal had endured as much of this show as she could possibly take and had decided to emerge from her carefully concealed hole to put a stop to it. She scolded. She sat up on her hind legs. Harmony didn't see her. The horse did and refused the fence. Properly taught by Muffin Barnes, Harmony collected the horse, got into a rhythm, made a small half-circle, and again approached the jump. Dutifully, the horse approached the jump, again perceived the mephitic animal on the other side. Harmony sailed over the jump. The horse didn't. The chestnut mare wheeled and thundered around the ring. By now the audience had spied the source of excitement. The field crew tore out to Harmony. Apart from her pride she was fine. Harmony beat a hasty retreat. The horse continued to circle the ring. Ursie held her hands over her eyes like a visor and grasped the situation.

"Nickel, get that skunk out of the ring!"

This order displeased me but I had an idea. "Lolly, Pewter, come here." Pewter rushed into the ring, caught sight of the skunk in full regalia, and rushed right back, the craven coward. Lolly, having encountered this type of creature before, merely stood next to Mother and wagged her tail in cheery encouragement. She had no intention of helping me.

The horse walked up to me. She'd tired of her escapade.

"Tallulah, good girl." What else do you call a flaming chestnut mare? Tallulah let me lead her to Diz, who walked her into the schooling area.

By now Ursie was fit to be tied—or as Mother would say, "All beshit and forty miles from water."

"Do your job!" Ursie bellowed at me, her antique-rose lipstick framing her cavernous mouth.

I moved toward the skunk, who wisely scampered away and, as I carefully pursued from a distance, decided to circle the ring. Her tour was accompanied by flicks of her terrible tail but no action as yet.

"Can't you do anything right!" Ursie vaulted into the ring and as she did, the skunk returned to her nest. Ursie, sweating, stumped up next to me. "There, that takes care of that! Honest to God, you tick me off. Standing here in the middle of the ring. Doing nothing. We're behind schedule. Do you hear me? Behind schedule! I want this show to run like clockwork!"

Mr. Pierre came alongside me, and Michelle took up a position on the other side.

"Ursie, that'll do." Mr. Pierre's voice conveyed the message that she ought to lay off.

"Oh, shut up, you silly faggot!"

Before we could recover to reply, the skunk made a reappearance, this time with four little heads sticking out of the hole. She turned, gave a signal, and the skunklets followed. By now Ursie no longer teetered on the brink of hysteria—she plummeted over the edge. Up to her ankles in loam and horse droppings, she made a beeline for the skunk. The stands cheered the skunk, not Ursie. The skunk stood her ground and shooed her babies back into the nest. She waited with cool precision for the arrival of this rabid human.

Ursula Yost received a blast at close range and fell on her knees screaming, "I'm blind! I'm blind!"

Momma skunk, with dignity, sauntered back to her hole and disappeared.

I was laughing so hard I feared all my Mother's potty training would go out the window. Diz sat in the turf, tears rolling down his cheeks as he screamed with laughter. I glanced up in the stands. Mother and Aunt Louise were propping one another up as their sides heaved with wrenching howls. Ed had his arms around both of them and the three of them leaned like the Tower of Pisa. I hoped Aunt Wheeze wouldn't break a hip if they went over.

I noted that Ursula's two darlings made no effort to rescue their mother. Foaming at the mouth, Ursie crawled around the ring on all fours. She was unintelligible but I heard a reference to Braille.

Finally the fence crew pulled themselves together. We jogged over to Ursie. Our eyes watered from the potent perfume. I hauled her up.

She could see enough to snarl at me, "Get your hands off me. I never want you to touch me—you—you—"

I let her drop. Mr. Pierre and Diz picked her back up. They turned their faces from her but the aroma was not to be escaped. Michelle reached into her shirt pocket and wiped Ursie's eyes with a red farmer's hanky.

Ursie, half sobbing, half growling, lunged at me. "You're behind this, Nickel Smith, I know you are."

Michelle in a firm, gentle voice, said to Ursie: "Jesus loves you but the rest of us think you're an asshole."

Out of the mouths of babes. Mr. Pierre and Diz nearly dropped their unwanted burden again. The laughter made them weak.

Michelle Saunders had learned more at the *Clarion* than how to churn out good copy.

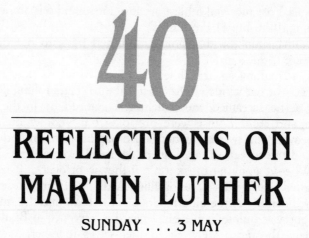

REFLECTIONS ON MARTIN LUTHER

SUNDAY . . . 3 MAY

The message of Christian foregiveness fell upon deaf ears. The pastor droned on. I avoided Mother's eye because we'd giggle. She'd make references to yesterday's debacle and that would set me off. Also, Carolyn Chapman, impeccably dressed and sitting in the pew ahead of us, had forgotten to take two curlers out of the back of her hair. We couldn't look at the pastor without looking at her. That would set us off again. Her husband, Ken, must have been half asleep this morning. You'd think he would have seen the pink sausage-shaped rollers.

Mother and I endured the eternal sermon with downcast eyes. Perhaps our retinas would suffer the reverse of the damage done to Michelangelo's eyes as he painted the Sistine Chapel. He suffered for art. I suffered for hair curlers.

Oh, well, since suffering is such an important part of Christianity, some people feel it their duty to spread it around. Those people manage to run huge TV evangelical empires. There's a delicious perversity in having people send in contributions to be told that, one, we are by nature sinful and unclean; two, we're going to die any minute now so get ready; three, some of us (read in: those who don't send money) are going straight to hell.

If I went to hell I'd know they had lowered their standards. Actually, I rarely thought of hell. Where there is no faith, devils are a necessity. Despite my faults I had faith, planted and nurtured by Mom and Dad until today it was unshakable. Therefore, why talk about it?

Our pastor sure could talk, but to his credit, he didn't pound on hellfire and abuse. His topics were drier: church dogma. I was proud of Martin Luther nailing his ninety-five theses to the door of the Palast Church in Wittenberg on October 31, 1517, but why refight the battle every seven days? Thank you, Martin Luther, but I need something I can live by today. The selling of indulgences by the Catholic Church did not rivet my attention.

Mother teased me. She said I was a lukewarm Lutheran. What I really was lukewarm about was organized religion. As soon as the followers of Christ collected money and erected edifices to God— to their egos is closer to the truth—troubles began. Still I went to church. Being with Mother and listening to Bach is not a bad combination. Then, too, a church is a place for faith to gather and therefore is joyful, but a church won't save you. What you do in this life will save you.

It seemed to me that there were millions of Americans not doing a damn thing with their lives except servicing their greed. The wages of sin appear to be success. Christ's message would be easier to embrace if we didn't see the shysters, con men, and power brokers ever advancing up the ladder of proud capitalism and political office.

When I was young and knew everything, I used to think the beauty of Christianity is that no one is in danger of practicing it. It's too austere and difficult.

Now I believe that no matter how austere and difficult, it's better than the alternative and we've got to try to love thy neighbor as thyself.

So far, no halo shines over my head. Maybe I was better off not being Saint Nickel, but then I was slipping and sliding with the rest of the human race and I was preparing to bring another soul into this confusing conflagration called life.

41

BLUE MONDAY

MONDAY . . . 4 MAY

After working out, Lolly, Pewter, and I drove over to the barn. Kenny, glad to see me despite my poor performance yesterday, endured a bright early morning ride. The dew covered the grass like a wet blanket, which made it heaven for Lolly because the scent was down low.

Following my brisk ride I repaired to the tennis courts, where I encountered ladies who do not work. I forget about those kinds of women. They tend to be a generation older than I, and they've made a simple, straightforward bargain with their men: You work in the outside world and I'll raise the children and keep a good home. Those that hadn't gotten dumped for younger women seemed quite content as they scurried around the courts. An oddity about this type of woman is how preoccupied she seems with her femininity. Here they were banging away at the tennis ball, hair frosted to a woman and wearing fetching designer tennis togs as well as those awful socks with the pompons on the back. I had trouble taking them seriously. They spoke in voices a half-octave higher than their normal range and they were relentlessly upbeat. I felt suffocated in their presence.

I was being unfair and I knew it. After I squashed three of them in a row, two sets apiece, I left. On the one hand I respected them for keeping their end of the bargain. On the other hand, couldn't they talk about something other than their tennis games, their children, and one another?

248

It wasn't until I parked behind the *Clarion* building and beheld the silent press that I realized I was homesick for the paper and I had taken some of my unrecognized misery out on the "gal group." They were no different from the corporate clones who dressed alike and spoke exhaustively about business, the stock market, and sports.

My loss preyed on me. Every day of my life since college I was surrounded by the events of the world. War, famine, pestilence, political power struggles, the arts, and fascinating stories about individuals chugged out of the AP wire. I covered local car accidents, the rare murder, tax and zoning battles, fiftieth anniversaries, and high school sports. Everybody covered everything at the *Clarion*. I was used to living in the center of events and now I'd been banished to the tundra.

I wanted to parade by the old Bon Ton and peek inside but I couldn't bring myself to do it. I went over to the Curl 'n Twirl instead. Mother was getting a manicure.

"Hi, Mom."

She turned and smiled. "Hi back at you." She raised her voice. "Mr. Pierre, my one and only child is here."

"Be out in a minute, Juts."

"What's he doing?" I asked.

"Ordering a new color line from the supplier. There're going to be a lot of cool blondes this spring and summer."

"Want to have lunch with me?"

"Thanks, honey, but Ed and I are going antiquing."

"You never cared about antiques before."

"I didn't say I cared about them, only that we're going out looking."

"Are you going to study Eastern religions too? Omm." I hummed the mantra.

"I most certainly am not. Anyway, Ed's just curious. He likes to know about things. He's not some religious nut. Wheezie, per usual, overstates things."

"I'm glad to hear Ed has a curious mind. He doesn't talk enough for me to know he has much of a mind at all."

"What an ugly thing to say." Mother jerked her hand, causing Kim Spangler to mess up her nail.

"Julia, put your hand back here," Kim demanded.

"Sorry." Mother put her hand down. "Ed's not a chatterbox. He belongs to the older breed of men, quiet and strong. Just the way I like them."

"He'd have to be quiet around you."

"What's wrong with you? You're a whistling bitch this morning."
Mother frowned.

"I guess I am. I apologize."

Mr. Pierre emerged from the back room, escorted the salesman to
the door, and then greeted me. *"Divina!"*

Georgette rolled her eyes. "Nickel?"

"If you've got any compliments to give me, give them to me in
English."

He appraised me shrewdly, "That kind of day, is it? Darling,
you're at sea because you're not working. Now my appointment
book is busy, busy, busy, but how about if I take you to dinner
tomorrow night? Better yet, I'll cook."

"That's a deal."

"We have things to talk about." His voice carried hidden meanings.

Mother glanced up at me. "Is that it? The paper? Poor baby, no
wonder you're out of sorts."

I sat in the chair next to her. "Well—yeah."

Louise swept through the door. Lolly, Goodyear, and Pewter
surrounded her. She gave everyone a pat and then pushed me out of
the seat.

"You're too young to sit down. I need a breather. I ran over
here as fast as I could." In the background I heard a siren. I started
for the door. "Don't bother," Louise said. "Mildred Foster ran off
the road. She's languishing on the sidewalk of Baltimore Street."

"Bet you ran her off the road," Mother teased.

"Well, I did but it was quite by accident. Mildred never looks
where she's going. But that's not why I hurried here. I heard on
good authority that when they got Ursie Yost to the hospital, Trixie
Shellenberger had to sedate her. Still haven't gotten the smell off
her either." A wicked grin spread over Louise's carefully scrubbed
face.

We allowed ourselves a laugh at Ursie's expense. David Wheeler,
looking very official, came through the door.

"Here for a wash and dry?" Mr. Pierre's voice was singsong.

"No, I am here for Mrs. Trumbull."

Without batting an eye, my aunt pointed a finger at me. "She did
it. She's driving the third Chrysler, you know."

"I was nowhere near Baltimore Street!"

David towered over Louise. "Mildred saw you. Now let's get this
settled as painlessly as possible."

"Mildred can't see two feet in front of her face!" Louise spat.
"That's why she's parked on the sidewalk. She doesn't look where
she's going."

"How would you know she's on the sidewalk if you weren't there? Come on."

Louise let out a wail.

"Aunt Wheezie, I'll come with you."

I spent two hours straightening out Louise's mess. Mildred Foster was no picnic either. If this was how I was going to spend my time, I needed to find a job fast.

FATE

TUESDAY . . . 5 MAY

I repeated my format of yesterday. I worked out, rode Kenny, and played tennis. Today I felt more inclined to like the pompon girls. I crammed my time with errands which ate up most of the day and then I descended upon Mr. Pierre's for dinner. He grilled lobster and I stuffed myself with this new treat.

Afterwards we sat at opposite ends of his huge 1930's sofa, our feet just touching, shoes on the floor. After a fabulous meal, catching up on gossip, making predictions for our friends' futures, he tactfully inquired as to my health.

"Great. Those old wives' tales about pregnancy are true. I'm chock-full of endorphins. My body feels wonderful."

"What about the rest of you?"

"Wretched about the paper. It would be easier if I could hate Diz, or even Charles for selling it in the first place, but I can't."

"Fate. Be patient. I absolutely believe that everything happens for a purpose and you will come out of this ahead."

"Do you really believe that?"

"I do and it's a source of comfort to me." He inhaled. "Plus, *ma cherie*, I've seen it happen. I've seen good things come out of bad and I've seen miracles."

"Name me one miracle." I smiled and pushed his foot with mine.

"You."

"Me?"

He nodded. "You were dumped in an orphanage in Pittsburgh. Gas rationing was in effect. The war, remember."

"I don't remember a thing."

"Chessy took up a collection of gas coupons and drove from Runnymede to Pittsburgh over those awful roads. Juts had pneumonia, so Louise accompanied him. They lied to get you out, said they were your parents. They liberated you and on the way home a blizzard hit. You weighed five pounds, which must have been what you weighed when you were born, and you'd been in that place about a month. The orphanage doctor told Chessy not to take you, you wouldn't live, and Chessy said, 'By God, she will live!' You had to be fed every three hours. All across Pennsylvania and Maryland your dad and Louise pulled into gas stations, farms, wherever there was a light. Total strangers gave you milk and heated it. That, my dear, is a miracle. Your mom and dad got up around the clock with you for three months after they brought you home and you lived—triumphantly, I might add. Fate—and miracles."

"You're right and I forgot."

"I don't remind you to make you feel guilty but only to reassure you. You have been blessed and loved and you've grown into a productive, responsible citizen."

"You're being sweet to me." I smiled. "Tell me a miracle that doesn't involve me. A miracle about you."

He thought awhile. "Let me tell you something I never told anyone but Bob. You know I was in Korea."

"Yes. How come you didn't say you were a homosexual to get out of the army?"

He tossed his lilac head. "Just because I'm a homosexual doesn't mean I should be excused from service to my country. I'll have none of it. The armed services are so wrong on that subject I scarcely know where to begin. I just lied. I never admitted to being gay and at that time I wasn't quite as willowy as I am now, my sweet. Anyway, I was shipped over and assigned to combat." He reached over and sipped his after-dinner liqueur. "One night I was on guard duty and it was colder than a witch's tit. The snow crunched underfoot and you know how crystal-clear winter nights are. The stars were brilliant and a half moon shone overhead. My feet tortured me but I kept pacing. A little gust of wind came up and a swirl of snow enveloped me, then dropped as quickly as it had risen. I saw not fifty feet in front of me a Korean soldier. He must have been my age, about eighteen. We simply stared at each other in disbelief and then he raised his rifle and I raised mine. I don't know who started firing first but we emptied our rifles and neither one of us hit the other. I was so scared I peed myself and I will not admit that to another human being. Once our rifles were empty we stared at each other and then he ran away. It was a miracle we didn't kill each other, and I had a great revelation that night. If human beings cannot find a way to settle their differences without resorting to violence, then we deserve to die. There is nothing noble about killing another human being because he's in a different uniform, because he worships a different God, because you're squabbling over real estate, and isn't that what wars are about? It's grotesquely wrong, Nickie, so wrong that anyone, anywhere on earth who attempts to justify it is serving dark gods."

His face, impassioned, changed before my eyes. His protective, queenie mannerisms melted away. Mr. Pierre was a man, a real man. I'd never seen him that way before.

"What are you staring at?" he asked.

"Nothing, nothing—I was thinking about what you said. I think I agree with you but if someone walked through that door and tried to hurt us, I'd kill him if I could."

"So would I, but I'm not talking about deranged individuals. I'm talking about organized violence which the state justifies under the umbrella of patriotism. When one whole group of people subjugates another, whether by the gun or the club or more sophisticated techniques, it's evil. I could have killed that boy in Korea—hell, he probably didn't know why he was there any more than I did. I'd have his soul on my conscience to this day."

"But would he have your soul on his conscience?"

"I don't know, but if his conscience is less than mine, it still doesn't make killing him right."

"I'm not arguing, but you said you didn't want to be excused from serving in the army."

"I don't. Until the entire human race matures enough to realize that war is more than evil, it's the road to total extinction, we've got to have a standing army. I think there should be universal draft across the board, no exceptions, men and women alike. Serve two years, from eighteen to twenty, and then get on with your life. It would certainly be one way to get people to learn about one another. I met men in the service I would never have met in civilian life and I acquired a little discipline and self-confidence in the process." He crossed his feet, warmed by cashmere stockings. He was warming along with his feet. "I don't get it. I just don't get it. We, the collective 'we,' operate on the crisis mentality, and what bigger crisis is there than war? It gives people a single, overriding common purpose. Why can't peace be a single, overriding common purpose? Why do we wait for a crisis to pull us together? Let's pull together for peace. Let's control events instead of letting events control us."

"I'm glad that Korean kid didn't launch you into eternity."

"I'd miss the opportunity to marry you. You *are* going to marry me, of course."

"Let's talk about that. Are you expecting that we'll live together?"

"You can't raise the baby alone. Besides which, darling, someone's got to redecorate your house. My house is paid for, so we'll rent that out and the income will pay for your mortgage."

"Mr. Pierre, I can't take your money."

"What else am I going to do with it? How many trips can I take? How many cars can I buy? How many times can I redecorate the shop or this house? You'd be doing me a favor. I wouldn't be squandering my money. Let's say I'd be investing in the next generation." I didn't say anything so he continued. "Nickie, as husbands go we know I shall leave a great deal to be desired. But as fathers go I won't be found wanting. And I'm alone. My life has never been the same since Bob died. For a while there I lost the reason to live. I plodded along by rote, if you will."

"That's what Mom says too."

"It takes years for your heart to heal after the death of your mate—and I miss him. I'll always miss him. But again, Fate—the Fates—are kind. They saw two alone people—and note I said alone, not lonely—and they gave us a baby, a reason to make a family. Someone to worry over and dream about. Two someones. You and the baby. People don't have to sleep together to be a family. They only have to love one another and I already love you."

"I love you too. I don't think I'm going to be much of a wife," I said quietly.

He waved his hand. "I know, darling. I'll be a better wife than you will."

How kind of him not to fuss. I was beginning to look forward to life with him.

"Well—when do we get married?"

"As soon as possible, so we're close to nine months when our cherub arrives."

"I don't want a big wedding. I don't think I could stand it."

"We've got to have your mother and Louise. We'll ask Louise at the last minute so she doesn't have the time to work up a major tantrum."

"Okay."

"Sunday."

255

"This Sunday?"

"Twelve noon on the dot."

"Can we get the church?"

"I've made every arrangement. We only need to get our blood tests and Trixie will do a rush job."

"Okay." I gulped.

"You know the first thing I'm going to do after we're man and wife?"

"What?"

"Take a blowtorch to your wardrobe."

OVEREDUCATED AND UNEMPLOYED

WEDNESDAY . . . 6 MAY

Kenny was being shod, so I couldn't ride him. I did go down for my blood test. That took five minutes. I ran more errands. I got vitamins for Kenny, a new collar for Lolly Mabel, catnip for Pewter. I bought a load of mulch for my garden and arranged delivery. That was before lunch.

At lunch I zipped into Mojo's. Arnie Dow and Michelle were sitting at the counter. When I came in we grabbed a booth. We opened our conversation with lots of banter but as lunch wore on, so did we. We were utterly miserable without our paper.

After lunch I whipped myself into a frenzy gathering items for the Blue and Gray Hunt Club newsletter but it wasn't the same as putting out a real paper.

This was going to be harder than I thought.

GIN

THURSDAY . . . 7 MAY

"I'm going to win. I give you fair warning." Louise peered over her cards.

"Ha, dream on, Wheeze." Mother pulled another card off the top of the deck.

Since they lost their tempers without shame, playing gin was risky. I was painting Mother's dining room. If Ed was going to live with her I didn't see why he couldn't do it, but painting was better than moping around the Square so I went ahead. The double French doors stood open from the dining room to the living room which allowed me to see and hear everything. Aunt Louise surprised me. After her initial sulking, pouting, and raving, she'd calmed—quickly, for her. I was sure that when Ed moved in she'd provide us with some spectacular displays of pique. Still, it was unnerving that she was so in control of herself.

"Ursie joined the PTL Club." Mother discarded.

"Ursula Yost?"

"Pass the 'ludes." Mother said.

Where did my Mother hear such things? I didn't even know she knew about Quaaludes.

"Ha. Ha." Louise pronounced this in a manner to suggest she thought it unfunny. "I was the one who told you about sedation. She's out and about." She turned toward me. "And if you know what's good for you, Nickel, you'll lay low."

"I will."

"How much money did the show make?" Louise brushed away Pewter, who stuck her paw in the peanut bowl. The cat managed to get one peanut out of the bowl and proceded to knock it around the room.

"That cat is so noisy. Julia, don't you think Pewter's a noisy cat?"

"Eleven thousand four hundred and twenty-eight dollars," I answered.

"You made that much?" Mother was impressed.

"Does the skunk get a cut?" Aunt Louise was in good form today.

"No, but I'll invite her back for next year."

"I never saw anything like that in my life." Louise threw down a card. She wasn't paying much attention to the game. "Do you remember the time the possum crawled onto the altar in church?"

Mother laughed. "That was something."

"How old were you?" I called down from the ladder.

"I can't speak for my sister but I was nine." Mother gleefully threw down a card and her hand. "Gin!"

"Nickie distracted me. That hand doesn't count."

Mother marked her game pad.

"I said, don't count it."

"Oh, come on!"

Louise pushed the cards together and shuffled. "You can count it but I'm not." She made a notation on her own pad. "Saw Charles Falkenroth today. He looks bad." Her voice dipped into her toes on "bad." "Have you seen him?"

"Not since last Friday," I replied.

"Are you going to deal or what?" Mother rapped the table, making Lolly and Goodyear bark. Pewter huffed her fur.

Louise doled out the cards. "He looks bad, I tell you. Any word on Jackson Frost?"

"Regina called and told me he's working a half day today."

"So soon," Mother drawled. Her eyes never left the cards. Mother could remember which cards were pulled and which stayed in the deck from hands she had played sixty years ago.

"It was a mild heart attack."

"Scared him plenty, though. He felt Death's sour breath on his neck." Aunt Louise was in her element when there was a medical prediction or a tragedy to be reported.

"Pay attention."

Louise returned her concentration to the game. I painted in peace until Wheezie shattered it with a too-loud "Gin!"

The games continued, with Mother winning more than losing and

Wheezie getting steamed but still holding on to her temper. I was proud of her.

Louise bent the tip of a card. "Hear what happened last night at the North Runnymede town meeting?"

This caused a pang. If I'd been working I would have gotten a full account last night from the reporter who covered the meeting, and it would have been replete with details we couldn't print.

"Bucky Nordness gave a report on the condition of the police force with a lengthy recap of his service. He oozed humility. Millard Huffstetler said, 'Don't be humble. You aren't that great.' "

"Millard said that?" Mother smiled. "Good for him."

"Birds do it," Louise sang.

"Bees do it. Even overeducated fleas do it." Mother picked up the next line.

They sang and played cards. Seeing those two white heads bent over their cards, I imagined them as children, singing and playing cards at the kitchen table. Each sister, a coincidence of the flesh, became the other's reality check. Over the decades they shared experiences, associations, the geography of the town itself. Mom and Aunt Wheezie weren't mirror images of each other but it was impossible to imagine one without the other. When they were this peaceful, they were adorable.

45

BLOWOUT BINGO

FRIDAY . . . 8 MAY

The parking lot at Saint Rose of Lima's overflowed at six o'clock. By seven, game time, the stragglers who came in said there wasn't a space left at the *Clarion*'s old parking lot and even the side streets were packed.

The Fourth of July parade got crowds like this, and for Father Christopolous this was the Fourth of July. The good priest bought a blackout bingo card for himself, a huge sheet with four cards to it, and he sat up front by the door.

Those people able to walk or be carried squeezed into the hall.

David Wheeler was there, as was Bucky Nordness. Bucky was already being a pest by insisting that this gambling was on Pennsylvania premises. As though we didn't know.

Our gang, dressed to the nines, filled up one long table: Mom, Ed, Wheezie, Orrie, Mr. Pierre, Michelle, Roger, Thacker and assorted BonBons, Ricky, Decca, Sonny and Sister, Georgette—I think BonBons rose from the dead, there were so many of them— and Max, Georgette's boyfriend. Also at our table, to my delight, were Regina and Jack and, to my astonishment, Diz Rife. He was seated next to Louise. Mom and Mr. Pierre saved me the seat on the other side of Louise. Arnie Dow and the boys from the back room were there. Even Ursie and Tiffany and Harmony were there. Said they needed the money. Peepbean quickly pressed his fiancée into service as a card counter because of the huge number of players. Millard volunteered to help also.

Goodyear lay under Mom's feet. Lolly crawled on her belly under the table until she touched noses with her dad. Pewter, even before the game started, prowled up and down our table in search of tidbits. No flies on Pewter. She knew the BonBons were loaded with food and the children couldn't resist her. Her purrs were deafening until Mutzi took over the microphone.

"Pot's already seven thousand and twenty dollars!" He placed the .38 beside him if for no other reason than to irritate Bucky. The money was on the Ping-Pong ball table. The glass Ping-Pong ball machine, lid off, sat on top of the table and the money was next to it. Mutzi showed us the pot to whet our appetites. "Now you regulars know the rules, but for you newcomers, welcome to Saint Rose of Lima's Friday night bingo. Here's how blackout bingo works. In order to win you must black out *all* twenty-five numbers on one of your four cards." He held up a sheet which demonstrated the concept. "Naturally, this game can take some time but we've got plenty of that. Are you ready!"

We shouted in unison, "Yes!"

"Okey dokey, smokey." He turned on the Ping-Pong ball machine and snatched the first ball. "Number twenty-nine, number twenty-nine, to win is divine."

Ed dabbed twenty-nine. We each examined our cards nervously. I was surprised, delighted, at Aunt Wheezie's behavior. Granted she was being ooey-gooey to Ed Tutweiler Walters, but she wasn't snarling or attacking Mom with her dab-a-dot. In fact, she was almost ooey-gooey to Mom.

"One. The number one will give you fun." Mutzi's voice betrayed his own excitement.

Verna played three sheets. She paid twenty dollars apiece for those sheets and when you figure in the children, the BonBons had invested a lot of money in this bingo game. I could see Diz on the other side of Wheezie. He seemed to be thoroughly enjoying himself. It occurred to me that Diz had probably never been to a bingo parlor. Michelle was bent over her card in total concentration. Roger wasn't looking up either.

"Fifty-eight, fifty-eight, win this card and be my date," Mutzi sang out.

Forty numbers must have been called. My sheet had dots sprinkled over it but so far I was nowhere close to winning.

Ed's card showed promise and Mother's, too, but Mom was generally lucky in cards and games. Mutzi, to celebrate the blackout bingo game, wore a green Day-glo string tie. Even Peepbean was dressed better than usual. He'd changed from his painter's pants into chinos. Goodyear began to snore under the table and Mom gave him a light shove with her toe. The dog grunted and stopped. I heard Lolly's tail thump. She was happy about something. I ducked my head under the table and saw the reason: Decca BonBon was feeding her part of her hot dog and Verna was too engrossed in the game to notice. As no one had fussed over Mom and Ed, I guessed that no announcement had been forthcoming as to their intentions. The BonBons knew; Orrie, Mr. Pierre, and I knew, which is to say that everyone in the room knew but had been told to keep it a secret. They were probably wondering, would Juts spill the beans tonight?

"Two, the number two. 'Tea for two and two for tea, me for you and you for me.' " Mutzi would have continued except the deafening silence of the hall, bursting to the seams with people, warned him that everyone wanted to get on with the game.

"Got it!" Wheezie smacked down her dab-a-dot, leaving a clear blue circle. She leaned over Diz's chest. "Nickie, I have to powder my nose. Will you play my card?"

"Okay," I whispered.

Diz slid the card over to me and Wheezie hurried to the ladies' room. It must be killing her to miss even a second of this game.

"Give me thirty, give me thirty, I want to see children clean and never dirty." Mutzi swayed at the microphone.

The lights cut out. We were plunged into darkness. You can always tell the hypochondriac in the room because Sister BonBon shouted, "My eyes! What's happened to my eyes!"

Mutzi spoke clearly into the mike. "Just a minute, folks. Don't lose your place. We'll have light restored in a second. Peepbean. See to it, will you?"

True to his word, within a minute or two the lights came on.

A furious Wheezie sputtered as she stumbled out of the ladies' room. "What's the big idea? You pulling a fast one, Mutzi?"

"Now, Wheezie, you know I wouldn't do something like that to you."

Wheeze glowered at him and scurried back to our table. She leaned over Mom. "I'll get you for that, Julia!"

"Can it, Wheezie. Every time something goes wrong I am not behind it."

"Let there be light," Mutzi jovially said, then remembered Father Christopolous was in the room, and coughed. "Ready, steady, go." The Ping-Pong balls bounced upward again. "Twenty-three, twenty-three, Wheezie had to—hmmm, let me see."

At that the room roared with laughter and Aunt Wheeze bent her head over her card. She glowed crimson.

"Okay, seven, lucky seven and— Hey." Mutzi's voice trembled as he plucked a ball out of the machine. "Hey, is this a joke? The money's gone!"

Peepbean hustled over and inspected the table.

"You see anything?" Mutzi's Adam's apple spiraled upward.

"Nope. Gone."

Millard joined Peepbean. This was a family affair. They got under the table. Nothing.

Mutzi fought for control over himself. "Ladies and gentlemen, we are going to have to suspend play until we find the pot."

Bucky, the big cheese, sashayed up there. He, too, looked around. David Wheeler stayed in his seat. Damned if he'd help Bucky until asked, and Bucky would never ask.

Bucky pushed Mutzi aside and boomed into the microphone so that it squawked: "Don't nobody move! I will inspect every purse and every pocket and go over this place with a fine-tooth comb. Peepbean, you're my deputy for the night."

Peepbean, no fan of Bucky's, did what he was told.

Bucky started at one end of the tables and Peepbean at the other. Michelle, quick-thinking, was writing down everything in sequence as it happened.

"You free-lancing, Michelle?" I asked.

"This might be a good story."

"I'll buy it." Diz smiled but he cast his eyes about the room, sweeping, searching.

Aunt Wheezie clutched her heart. "My angina."

"Oh, Aunt Wheezie, not now," I moaned.

Diz put his arm around her. "Let me help you."

He rose to help her up and she wobbled to her feet with his assistance. Mom leapt up and got on the other side of her. "Come on."

"Sit down!" Bucky bellowed.

Diz, with authority, replied, "She's sick, Bucky."

"I don't care. Nobody moves."

Aunt Wheeze swooned. Ed rose to help Mom and Diz. He tried to take Wheezie's pocketbook off her arm. She held it closer.

"She sleeps with her pocketbook, Ed. In fact she has the first dollar she ever made."

"I hate you!" Louise hissed at Julia.

"You're ill, Mrs. Trumbull." Diz was polite.

"I'm sick of *her* is what I am." Wheezie began to revive quite miraculously from her angina attack.

"I told you all to sit down." Bucky's face darkened.

"Goddammit, Nordness, we've got to call an ambulance." David Wheeler, fed up, mixed into it.

"You stay south of the line, you dumb redneck. You're in Pennsylvania now and you'll do as I say."

As these two bitched at each other, Diz, Ed, and Mom helped Wheezie over to the door to fresh air. I walked over to help too.

"Sit down, Nickel!" Bucky shouted at me.

I quite forgot myself. "Fuck off, Nordness!"

A few people clapped. Others snickered. When my head was turned to yell at Bucky, Louise dashed out the door. Mutzi saw her first. He picked up the .38 and fired a warning.

"Louise!" Mutzi shouted as he discharged the gun.

Goodyear howled, screamed, warbled the most godawful sounds, and then flopped down.

"The dog's been shot!" Michelle screamed. She crawled under the table to revive Goodyear, whose tail was already wagging.

"Shot!" The word was repeated at faraway tables where people couldn't see Goodyear.

Lolly started barking. Mutzi fired again. Then asshole Bucky pulled his revolver and peppered the ceiling. It did not quell the panic; it agitated it. People burnt the wind getting out of there. Tables were knocked over and the last I saw of Pewter, she charged over debris and leapt over chairs.

Mutzi, still at the mike, hollered, "Mayday! Mayday!"

Verna shouted back, "Of course, it's a May day, you silly twit."

That was all I saw inside because I was running as fast as I could to get into the Square. I had to find Aunt Louise before anyone else did, most notably Bucky Nordness.

Someone was running with me neck and neck. To my amazement, it was Mother. Right on my heels were Mr. Pierre, Diz, and then David Wheeler, who edged past us. Unfortunately, Bucky used the parking lot exit and as we spilled into the Square he came around the side of Saint Rose's, his revolver pulled, firing into the air.

Aunt Louise had reached the cannon. I could see her breathing was labored, and with an afterburner burst of speed I pulled away from the others and drew closer to my aunt, whose face was dangerously mottled.

"Stop or I'll shoot!" Bucky ordered.

I twisted my head and witnessed the gun leveled straight at me. I didn't stop.

Mother ran between me and the line of fire. She was waving her arms like a crazy woman. "Don't shoot! You'll kill the baby!"

Wheezie, collapsed against the cannon, crabbed at Julia: "She's not a baby. She's forty-two years old."

"She's going to have a baby," my mother screamed at the top of her lungs. She was still waving her arms as Bucky advanced upon us both.

"What?" Numb with shock, Louise dropped her purse, and the bingo money fell out of it.

Bucky caught up with us and started to put Louise in handcuffs. Lolly sprang at him and bit him in the leg right about the same time that David Wheeler tackled him around the waist. Goodyear streaked across the Square toward Mom. Mr. Pierre and Diz reached Louise. Diz picked up the money and stuffed it in his pockets as he mumbled to Louise, "Keep your mouth shut."

"Is that how your family got rich?" Louise was just plain outrageous. What had gotten into her? She swooned for an instant.

"I'm going to say I stole it. Now shut up, Mrs. Trumbull," Diz commanded. "I realize this will be difficult for you."

I started to laugh. Mother was taking Louise's pulse and Ed was fanning her with his handkerchief.

"Why'd you do such a fool thing?" Mother growled to her sister.

Ursula Yost, nailed to the spot, had her hand covering her mouth. She appeared to be in shock at the disclosure of my pregnancy. Shock would soon turn to righteous indignation.

By now Mutzi was with us, too, as was most of Runnymede. The grunts and groans of Wheeler versus Nordness were frightening. I pulled Lolly away because she was going to bite Bucky again. Goodyear was eyeing his other leg.

"Why'd you steal that money?" Mother wouldn't let up on Wheezie, who was enjoying, the tiniest bit too much, the attentions from Ed, Mr. Pierre, and Diz. She was oblivious to the situation she had created.

"I wanted a face lift."

"Why?" I dragged Lolly back to her side.

"Because Ed wouldn't've fallen in love with Julia except she's younger."

"Huh?" Ed was puzzled. "You told me she was your older sister."

"Well—I—" Wheezie blushed. She didn't mind stealing the money; she minded getting caught in the fib.

The fight between David and Bucky escalated. None of the men dared separate them, and they were doing each other bodily harm.

Mutzi fished out the wick on the cannon. "Diz, jam the ball down the cannon muzzle."

Diz, next to the cannon balls, heaved one up and set it on the lip of the muzzle. With a shove it rolled into the barrel. Diz Rife was having the time of his life.

"Got a ramrod of some kind?" Mr. Pierre asked.

Wordlessly, an umbrella was passed over to Diz. We never did see where it came from. Diz wiggled the umbrella around. "Best I can do."

Mr. Pierre lit a match. "Stand back."

Everyone jumped out of the way except for David and Bucky but it didn't matter because they were rolling around on the ground. Mr. Pierre touched the match to the wick and within seconds a tongue of flame unfurled from the mouth of the cannon, followed by a roar. Michelle put her hands to her ears. A crash of glass and splintering of wood greeted our ears. Falkenroth, Spangler & Finster again. The cannon produced the desired effect. It broke up Bucky and David. They scrambled to their feet.

As they did so, David adroitly shoved Bucky over the Mason-Dixon line. "Stay on your side, asswipe!"

Lip bloodied, police shirt ripped, Bucky swayed on his feet, trying to decide what to do. He warned, "I'll get you Wheeler, just you wait." Then he wiped his mouth and saw the blood on his shirt.

A moment of quiet followed this pandemonium. Aunt Wheezie abbreviated the silence as she said to me: "Are you really pregnant?"

"Yes." I spoke as loudly as I could under the circumstances.

"In that case I want my car back! And I'm not refunding any of the money. Our family has been through this before and—"

"Shut up, Louise!" Mother said.

At that Goodyear howled, screamed, and flopped over dead again. The dog twitched with happiness at being able to perform his trick twice in one night.

Aunt Wheeze observed this in horror. "What's wrong with the dog?"

"Nothing," Mother lied.

"Don't take me for a fool, Julia. That dog does that on purpose." She walked over to Goodyear, who hadn't gotten back on his feet again. "Louise." She enunciated perfectly.

Goodyear, since he was already on the ground, couldn't fall down, so he howled and rolled over. The bystanders, caught between laughter and shock at everything that was going on, put their hands to their mouths. This was not lost on my aunt.

"Julia, does everyone know about this?" Her face was empurpled.

"Well—" Mother waffled.

"You don't have much room to be superior. I don't think this is funny. I don't think you're funny. You're a rotten mother but then what could anyone expect? You never gave birth. You don't know what real mothering is about. You took in this bastard here." She pointed directly at me. "And now she's an unwed mother too. More little bastards!"

Mr. Pierre opened his mouth. "Just a minute—"

Louise cut him off. "Pariah!" She pointed at me again.

"What's a pariah?" little Decca BonBon asked.

"That's something like a martyr with more suffering and less class." I tried to salvage this family debacle with whatever humor I could dredge up.

"Shut up!" Louise wheeled on me. "If you hadn't invaded our family, none of this would have happened." She looked from me to Mother. "I've done Jesus one better. He had one Judas. I've got two!"

"Just a minute, just—" Mr. Pierre tried again.

This time Mother cut him off. "You listen and you listen good, Louise." Goodyear started to howl. "Shut up, Goodyear!" Mother meant it. The poor dog put his tail between his legs and lay down. Lolly lay down next to him. "You blab, blab, blab about being a mother." Louise moved back a step. "Your daughter Maizie threw used sanitary napkins at passers-by in the Square. They had to take her away. Don't talk to me about being a mother. You did a piss-poor job of it!"

Louise's eyes looked like poached eggs. She attacked Juts with a fury. As she swung her purse more money fell out of it. The sisters were on the ground rolling around, an older distaff version of David and Bucky. Eight decades of hate rolled around with them.

Diz surveyed the situation and then put another ball down to the muzzle. "Mutzi?"

Mutzi nodded his head. "Yo!"

Mr. Pierre touched off the wick, and boom! Falkenroth, Spangler & Finster was being reduced to rubble. Mother and Louise sprang apart, and that fast, Ed grabbed Mom and Diz pinned Louise. They dragged them apart in opposite directions, Orrie tagging along after Louise. I was left with everyone staring at me. I opened my mouth but Mr. Pierre stepped beside me.

He put his arm around me. "Ladies and gentlemen, we had hoped to announce this under different circumstances but the present seems the time. We're going to get married."

Not one person believed that Mr. Pierre was the father of my child but that was beside the point. Everyone cheered.

Diz called out that he would be taking Louise home and Ed said the same about Mother. It was a good thing because none of us could have withstood another bombardment.

When I walked into the bingo hall Michelle came with me, as did Lolly and Goodyear. Arnie Dow, Jackson, and the men were already righting tables.

"Are you going to marry him?" Michelle asked.

"If you have a better answer, tell me."

Regina walked up behind me. "I'm happy for you, and the hell with public opinion."

The three of us searched for Pewter. My kitty loathes loud noises and I feared she was cowering somewhere or, worse, had been trampled in the melee. I did notice as I continued the search that not a scrap of food was on the floor, nor on any of the tables. As the dogs had run out with me, suspicion began to fall on Pewter, wherever she was.

"Found her," Michelle called from the other end of the room.

There was Pewter, in the Ping-Pong ball machine. The cat had eaten so much she couldn't move. Even though the air current was on to push the balls in the air, none of them were moving. Closer inspection revealed that each Ping-Pong ball had fang marks. Punctured, they couldn't rise with the air.

That was it for blackout bingo, May eighth. Blowout, as it was instantly christened, if braved again, would have to be scheduled for another time. I had no intention of stopping at my mother's. I wasn't mad at her but I figured she was being ministered to by Ed. As for Aunt Louise, I could wring her neck. So Goodyear, Lolly, Pewter, and I drove home. Pewter burped the whole way, the little pig.

THE BIRTH OF
THE MERCURY

SATURDAY . . . 9 MAY

Strong coffee with chicory brewed in my coffee maker. Lolly and Goodyear shared a bowl of doggie crunchies drenched in warm meat broth. Pewter ate a light breakfast. Small wonder. The old railroad clock on the wall read seven forty-five A.M. I was on my second cup of coffee when I heard a car pull up behind the old Chrysler. I cursed because I needed the time to myself to sort out what happened last night. I was also praying that jackleg police chief Bucky Nordness would not press charges against Louise, even though she richly deserved it. And what if he vented his spleen on Lolly? I didn't look out the window because I was sure it was Mother or, worse, Wheezie. A rap at the door dispelled that notion.

"Come in."

The front door swung open and Charles Falkenroth stepped into the front hall just as I was coming in from the kitchen.

"Nickel, I hope you will forgive this intrusion at an early hour but I know you're always up at the crack of dawn and I must speak with you."

His face, ashen, worried me.

"Let's talk in the kitchen. I've made chicory coffee and I have the best bran muffins this side of the Mississippi."

"You didn't make them." He smiled weakly and followed me into the kitchen.

"Mom did, Thursday, but I've kept them in the fridge."

He observed the large muffins. "Thanks, no. I'm off my feed. Take coffee though."

270

As I poured the coffee he soaked in the atmosphere of the place. Lolly trotted over for a pat. "Nickel, the memories I have of this house and Cora . . . I used to love to come up here as a boy. I think every kid in Runnymede did. She was a wonderful woman, your grandmother."

"Did you know she couldn't read or write?"

"No, I didn't know that."

I put the coffee before him and he thanked me. "She was born in 1888—no, it was 1878, I think. They didn't have much money and Cora went to work early. Schooling wasn't wasted on girls."

He shook his head. "Maybe the good old days weren't so good."

"They never are."

"Nickel, I've made a terrible mistake. I can't sleep. I can't eat. I've barely said two civil words to Ann. I should never have sold the *Clarion*. What was I thinking of? If I retire I'll die. I called Diz but he won't sell me back the paper—and I don't blame him. I've come to ask for your forgiveness and for your help."

"There's nothing to forgive. You did what you thought was right and you sought the best deal for all of us. By the way, what are you going to do about Morningside? Ann had her heart set on it."

"We're hoping to winter there. Ann's talked with Orrie and I think we'll buy a house together. It's too expensive now by ourselves."

"Orrie likes her sunshine and I think she's off Fort Lauderdale since the coconut robbery."

"Let me tell you what I want to do. I want you to run the paper."

"We don't have the paper—"

He held up his hand to quiet me. "I've bought back the building. Diz was good about that. Took an arm and a leg off me though." He laughed. "He's a businessman. He charged the bank valuation for the press—which is to say, nothing. So we have our old press. We have the building and we have the AP wire. This Falkenroth needs a Hunsenmeir."

I could have jumped out of my skin with excitement. "You mean it?"

"I mean it, and I mean it fifty-fifty, which right now, kid, is fifty-fifty of nothing."

I heard a wild screech. A slam, two slams. Louise and Orrie tromped through the back door.

"Where is she?" Wheezie demanded. "Oh, hello, Charles. What are you doing here at this hour? Say, are you the father of Nickel's baby?"

"Wheezie." Orrie was appalled but titillated.

"I beg your pardon." Charles's bow tie trembled.

"That brat—not my blood, I remind you—is having a baby and she's not married. Well, I lit a candle for her and a candle for the baby. Imagine having her for a mother."

I almost expected her to say a pregnant lesbian was a contradiction in terms.

"Nickel?" Charles was incredulous.

"It's true. I am, however, to marry Mr. Pierre so my esteemed aunt's objections will be handled properly. The baby won't be illegitimate."

"How you got pregnant wasn't proper," she snapped.

"Congratulations." Charles leaned across the table and kissed me.

"You newspaper people are all alike. Liberals," Louise sniffed. "Where is she? Where's my baby sister? I'm going to kill her for last night."

"She's not here."

"She's not home either," Orrie informed us.

"Did you try Mr. Pierre's?"

"You think I'm a dunce? That's the first place I looked, and the Curl 'n Twirl too." You could almost see the smoke creeping out of Louise's ears.

Another car pulled into the driveway. A door slammed. Yet another.

"Yoo hoo!" Mom cheerfully opened the back door, Ed in tow. She beheld Louise. "Oh, it's you."

"I am not speaking to you—now or ever."

"That's a relief." Mother brightened. "Hi, Charles. Hi, Orrie." Mother didn't seem surprised that Charles was here at such an early hour. However, after last night we were bombproof. Nothing would seem bizarre.

Ed came over and slapped Charles on the back. He was the most expansive I've ever seen him. "You missed a good show last night, buddy."

"I'm beginning to get that feeling."

"Look, everybody. I'll make up more coffee and we'll have an impromptu party—even though some of us are not speaking."

"That includes you, you—well, I can't say it." Louise flounced into a chair.

"Charles and I are starting another paper. So let's drink to it after I get the coffee made."

As I was measuring out coffee and Mom was rummaging under the cabinets for Cora's old samovar, I called out to Charles: "Why don't you ring up Arnie Dow and see if he'll come back to work?"

"What am I going to pay him with? I mean, Nickie, I'll whip

through what Rife gave me if I pay at the old rate, which wasn't much to brag about anyway."

"Advertising will take care of that and we could profit-share, you know. Call him."

Charles did. "Said he'll do it. Said he'll come up the hill to celebrate. Asked if you're okay. Told him he could see for himself, although you looked fine to me."

Within minutes Arnie was through the door. Hellos were exchanged.

He threw his arms around me. "Are we crazy or what?"

"We're crazy."

"Would you have it any other way?" Mother found the samovar. "Orrie, will you tell my sister to mix up some biscuits?"

"Louise, will you mix up some biscuits?"

"Why?"

"She wants to know why?' Orrie repeated.

"Because Nickel can't cook and because my beastly sister makes the best biscuits in town, second only to Verna."

"I resent that! Mine are better than Verna's! And don't get the mistaken impression I was talking to you because I was not. I was speaking to these lovely people here and Ed." Louise reached for the spatterdash mixing bowls and went to work.

"Let's call Verna and tell her about the paper." That fast, Orrie was on the phone.

Pretty shortly thereafter, Verna, Georgette, and Decca chugged up the hill, and Verna, bless her heart, brought more food.

"Charles, what do you think about Michelle? I think she's turning into a real reporter."

"Off to a slow start. I didn't know if that one would make it but she is turning into something special. Why don't I hire her—is that what you're saying?"

"You got it." I passed out mugs and cups to everyone.

Charles dialed Michelle. When he returned to the kitchen he was smiling. "She's ecstatic. Says she'll be here in a minute. Hope you don't mind."

"The more the merrier," Wheezie sang out as she beat the batter. "Except for some people, of course."

Mother chose a prudent silence for a change.

Michelle breezed up the hill and knocked on the front door. Arnie got the door. They kissed and hugged, which was a surprise considering Michelle's reserve, and then she kissed and hugged me. More surprises. Verna, counting out eggs for omelets, put Michelle to work before the woman even had time to sit down.

Mr. Pierre flew through the front door. "Where is everybody? I've been all over town looking for you girls!" He bowed to the ladies and nodded curtly to the men. Mr. Pierre had a standing truce with men. At the sight of me he jubilantly said, "Mom *cherie*."

"I'm Mom *cherie*," Mother said.

"Now you are *grand* Mom *cherie* and Nickel can be *petite* Mom *cherie*."

"Speak English," Louise said. "I'm tired of this French shit."

As my aunt had never uttered the word "shit" before, conversation came to a halt and then slowly, like a train on a hill, moved forward again.

"I was saying"—Mr. Pierre dropped his voice to a lower register—"that Julia is Big Momma and Nickel is Little Momma."

"*Cherie* isn't Momma," Orrie said.

"Don't be a stickler, Orrie. It works on my nerves," Verna requested.

"All right, all right, but we've got a houseful of newspaper people here and they like to get their facts just so," Orrie defended herself.

"What are we going to call the paper?" Charles untied his bow tie and made himself comfortable by the table.

"How about *The Courier*?" Ed spoke up. "We got a *Courier* at home."

"The *Tribune*." Decca joined the conversation. "In olden times the tribune was the voice of the people. That's what Uncle Sonny tells me 'cause he knows everything."

"Not a bad idea," I said.

"I've got the most marvelous idea." Mr. Pierre had the phone in his hand. "Let's call Diz Rife and ask him."

"You're going to call Diz?" Michelle couldn't believe it.

"Why not? You all are going to be strange bedfellows. Think about it." Mr. Pierre reached Diz on the phone and a spirited discussion developed which I couldn't hear because Louise had the bad grace to call my mother a trollop and Mother replied that Louise was a tart. Then Louise said that she wasn't speaking to Mother and Mother was becoming paranoid thinking everything was being said about her and everyone was talking about her— either she was paranoid or she had a big head. This was said distinctly and with vigor to Verna, who was noncommittal. Mother said that as long as we were on a psychological tack, some people had persecution complexes: They persecuted other people, meaning herself.

Diz Rife's splendid Aston-Martin Volante circled the farm. He couldn't find a place to park at the house and pulled over on the side of the road.

Before he could knock on the door Mr. Pierre opened it and invited him in.

"Diz, you like omelets?" Mother asked.

"I like anything you make, Julia."

Mother, charmed, applied herself to the omelets with renewed energy. As she beat the eggs Verna tossed in cheese and whatever else she'd cut up on the butcher block.

"Nickel, can Pewter eat raw egg?"

"I don't know why not. She eats everything else."

That got a laugh from the group. Diz was handed coffee by Louise, ushered to a chair by Ed, and immediately buttonholed by Decca, who wanted to know if he really was the richest man in the world.

"Diz, we're starting another paper." Charles met the issue head-on.

"That's what Mr. Pierre mentioned over the phone."

"What do you think?" I called over my shoulder. Louise had me cutting out biscuits.

"I think competition is the life of trade," he said. "You can't use the name *Clarion,* though, and you can't say founded in 1710."

"No, but we can say, 'In the same two families since 1710,' " Charles parried.

"Yeah, I guess you can. Can't call it the *Trumpet* either, since the *Trumpet* was incorporated into the *Clarion.* What are you going to call it?" He leaned back in his chair, his hands behind his head.

"Why not *Mercury*? He is the god of communication, is he not?" Mr. Pierre offered us the idea.

"I like that!" Arnie was enthusiastic.

Charles shrugged. "Why not?"

"Okay by me," I said.

"Me too," Michelle chimed in.

Louise cast her vote. "It's sacrilegious."

"Why?" Verna wanted to know.

"Pagan stuff." Louise's lower lip jutted outward. She was wearing her cerise lipstick shade again which ran up the cracks of her upper lip. "All those naked statues." She shook her head.

"We're talking about a newspaper, not sculpture," Arnie laughed.

"I had my say-so and that's that." Louise was really pouting now.

"Mercury it is." Charles was final.

Before Wheezie could create a scene, I said, "You know, Aunt Wheezie knows everybody and everything. She ought to have some kind of social column in *The Mercury*."

Charles, blindsided by the suggestion, hemmed and hawed.

Diz, teasingly, said, "Maybe the *Clarion* should have her." He was enjoying the idea of having a rival.

Wheezie fluttered, but before she could say anything else Mother whispered, "Exhale, blowfish."

Louise, batter bowl in hand, threatened: "I am not speaking to you. And you will never be mentioned in my column."

"Uh, Mrs. Trumbull"—a formal note in his voice, Charles held out the palm—"I think you belong at *The Mercury*. The Hunsenmeirs and the Falkenroths are a team, you know."

"Why—yes." Louise was as happy as I have ever seen her.

I knew in my heart that she would dictate that damned column to me, but I'd had worse assignments in my day.

The breakfast party lasted the whole day. Verna, Mother, and Pierre ran down to Mutzi's for more food for lunch and supper, and then Mutzi joined us too. We called David Wheeler and he showed up with his wife, who kindly brought a covered dish. Diz made a trip to the liquor store and that was a huge success. The whole Frost family came over and I wasn't as nervous as I thought I would be about that. By nighttime, we gathered around Cora's upright to sing. Mother suggested a game of Crap on Your Neighbor for those not interested in singing.

I don't know what came over me but I asked Diz if he would be my baby's godfather. He said he would and that he was deeply sorry he wasn't the baby's father. I also asked Jack, for obvious reasons and for the not-so-obvious reason that it would force him and Diz to cooperate about one thing in their lives.

Mr. Pierre, many martinis later, confessed he was nervous about marriage.

Decca asked her mother: "Why do people get married?"

Verna answered, "So they don't have to eat alone."

Mr. Pierre cleared his throat. "This is as good a time as any. Nickel and I will be married tomorrow, high noon at Christ Lutheran."

"Why didn't you tell me?" Louise shrieked.

"We thought it might upset you—this being a hasty courtship," I fibbed.

"Hasty? You've known him half your life. There's no time to have a shower."

"I thought you were against this marriage?" Mother said.

"I am but that's no reason not to give a party and I am not speaking to *you*!"

Michelle came up to me and whispered, "Are you going through with it?"

I nodded and whispered, "It'll be okay." Louise thumped to one side of the room and Juts to the other, thereby creating two camps.

I clapped my hands for silence. "Mother, Aunt Wheeze, in honor of my marriage, I want you two to make up now. I refuse to have you all spoil the wedding."

"Why'd you wait until the last minute to tell? I'm kept in the dark about everything." Louise was close to tears.

"Darling," Mr. Pierre crooned, "it's been so hectic and unexpected. We didn't mean to slight you."

"When did Julia know?"

"Yesterday," Mom replied, "so I haven't known that long." She lied, as we'd told her Wednesday morning.

"Don't rush me. I haven't made up with you yet!"

"Aunt Wheezie, come on."

Louise turned to Mr. Pierre. "And why are you marrying her? You don't even know her bloodlines. What if she has hereditary insanity? You could have married *me*!"

Eyes focused on Mr. Pierre. He gallantly walked over to her. "When I met you, you were married to Pearlie Trumbull. You were off limits. Fascinating. Magical looking. Those bones." He indicated her facial bones. "But off limits. Then as years went on we became as sister and brother. How could we get married?"

Louise was having none of it. "Easily enough! Julia trapped Ed and now Nickel trapped you with the oldest trick in the business."

"I was not trapped." Ed spoke with such authority he startled everyone. "A person can't explain these things. Julia's the girl for me. It's a feeling. It doesn't mean I don't like you."

Louise would have preferred that Ed remain strong and silent—especially silent. She wailed, "No one's going to marry me. No one's going to love me."

Naturally, everyone except Mother crowded around Louise. At the edges of the gathering people racked their brains for a man, any man still breathing, who could be produced for Louise.

Jack edged over to me. "Damn you! I don't want to share the baby with Diz."

"You're going to. I know what I'm doing—for all of us. You two have got to bury the hatchet."

"In my back. That's where it will get buried."

"O ye of little faith." I touched his shoulder but he remained mad.

HERE COMES THE BRIDE

SUNDAY . . . 10 MAY

As the eleven-o'clock-service worshippers filed out, the wedding party filed in. I thought this would be a tiny wedding with myself, Mr. Pierre, Mom, and Louise, but everyone from the paper came, the bingo gang, my stable and hunt club buddies, and many of Mr. Pierre's customers.

According to tradition I had not seen my groom since last night. Regina volunteered to be my matron of honor. We sat in one of the back rooms rehashing Louise's extraordinary confession. We both felt sorry for her, even if she was being a pill.

Decca BonBon stuck her head in the door and told us that Ursie Yost was in attendance. So were Pewter, Lolly Mabel, and Goodyear. They were as close to me as my human friends. The pastor balked but I won him over. If God made all creatures, then those creatures should be welcome in his house of worship.

Regina and I laughed over Mother leaving Goodyear on the Square the night of blackout bingo. I'd taken the dog home with me. It was an indication of Mom's emotional state. She hadn't been separated from her dog since the minute he was born.

The longer we waited the more nervous I became. I thought I was doing the right thing but how do you know? All decisions are based on insufficient evidence.

"Stop pacing. You're making me dizzy," Regina said.

"Was I pacing?"

"Here, sit down next to me. There's something about ceremonial

278

moments in life that bring out the best in people. Do you remember my wedding?"

"I was your maid of honor and I told you I was scared for you. I should have kept my big mouth shut."

"You were honest. I was scared too. The social pressure around a wedding is enough to make anyone nuts. It's supposed to be the happiest day of your life. I was glad to get it over with. My one regret is that I didn't finish college, but I've never regretted marrying Jack. He's not perfect but neither am I and neither are you. We muddle through somehow." Her cheeks glowed. She could have been the bride. "Now is there anything you want to tell me?"

A bolt of fear ripped into my side. "Like what? You know everything there is to know about me."

"Like who is the father of the baby. I'm not dumb, you know. It's one of the two godfathers and I think it's Jack. You have a logical mind. You would reason that the natural father would want to spend as much time with his baby as he could without arousing suspicion. If you named one man the godfather, that would be too obvious. Two will keep them guessing." Her tone of voice was matter-of-fact.

"You aren't giving me any credit for trying to build a truce between them."

"Oh, yes, I give you credit for that but I don't give you credit for not telling me the truth."

"How could I?!" I blurted out. She had me. Why try to back out of it?

"You know, the funny thing, Nickie, is that I'm not really hurt by the fact that you slept with Jack. I'm hurt by the fact that you didn't tell me."

"I feel terrible. I was wrong to start up with him in the first place but I don't see how telling you would have made it any better or easier. Why rub your face in it? Why cause you pain? I never lied to you. I didn't say anything, that's all. If the situation were reversed, what would you have done?"

"I don't know. I'd like to think that I'd tell you."

My hands were shaking. "You're taking this with more good grace than I could muster."

"Well." She paused for a long time. "Men are different from women and I know that and I know Jack. This is going to sound odd but I expect less of men than of women. Jack hasn't been one hundred percent faithful over these twenty-two years. I don't applaud him for that, mind you, but he's got his frailties. He tries to do the right thing, and most times he succeeds."

"Why didn't you tell me about the affairs?"

"They didn't seem that important. I chalked them up to his fear of getting older, and—forgive me for sounding conceited—I never thought he'd find a woman to replace me. But you—you were something else again. Apart from your history, there's the element of conquest. You know how crazy men get around lesbians. I never thought he'd leave me for you but I knew this affair wasn't superficial for him. I knew he was torn."

"Do you hate me?" My voice was barely audible.

"No. I can understand how any woman would fall for Jack. What hurts me is that you did it behind my back. If you had come to me we could have worked it out. It would have been painful but it would have been clean."

"I'm sorry. What can I say except I'm sorry? I told Jack and Mr. Pierre that I would tell you. I figured after the baby—sometime." I breathed deeply. "Does Jack know you know?"

"I told him last night after the party. He was stunned but he didn't back down. The difference between you and Jack is he didn't say he was sorry. He profusely apologized for the other woman but he didn't apologize for you. He said that he's in love with you and that he's in love with me. He also said that you broke it off and you're sticking to your guns." She sighed. "It's confusing, isn't it? I'm not mad at either of you, really. Maybe I'm too old for that stuff. Maybe I've gotten to the point where I don't believe that love is a controlled substance. You can't outlaw it or confine it within the bonds of matrimony. It wasn't as if you stole anything from me. I don't own him. I don't want to own him. You didn't do this to get even with me and neither did he. It happened. These things happen."

"What do we do now?"

"We don't do anything. We go on. I'm disappointed that you didn't tell me but I'll live. It's not the end of the world. Don't do it again."

"I won't."

"I don't just mean sex. I mean about telling me the truth. When people withhold emotional information, invisible barriers go up. You should be able to tell me anything and I should be able to tell you anything—infuriating, insulting, painful, absurd. It doesn't matter. What matters is that we share and we heal wounds before they cut too deep."

Shaken to the core, I nodded my agreement, and at that moment Decca arrived to tell us we could go out.

I received my second shock of the day. Mr. Pierre had washed out his lilac rinse. His hair was steel-gray and he'd cut it short.

The wedding proceeded without a hitch. Mother and Louise were civil to each other. They both cried, for different reasons.

I'll remember my wedding day for the rest of my life, because my friends came together to wish us well and because my best friend taught me a lesson. She taught me that deep love is more complex and subtle than I'd realized. She taught me that conventional responses are for conventional people. She revealed my own arrogance to me. I thought I knew what her response would be. I thought I could control the situation and spare her feelings. I underestimated her. I kept trying to fit a round peg into a square hole. I kept trying to make life rational. And I kept trying to cover up my own emotional cowardice. Because I was smart and physically brave I could sweep under the rug my emotional shortcomings. Regina showed me myself. It wasn't so much that she showed me my failures, only that she showed me who I was. If I wanted to change something, it was up to me. So often the truth is told with hate, and lies are told with love. She told me the truth with love, more love than I felt I deserved at that moment. I was beginning to understand that I would and could change emotionally, that anything could happen—I wasn't dead yet. I hoped I'd be up for the adventure.

48

HER MOTHERSHIP

MONDAY . . . 14 DECEMBER

Two new guests arrived at the party on planet Earth. Twins. By the time I gave birth, Trixie had told me I was going to have twins. Since I know very little about my own bloodlines I had no way of knowing that I might bear two children. Twins generally skip a generation, so that meant that my grandmother or grandfather was a twin. I did not use the Lamaze method. Dr. Lamaze is a man. He wouldn't be suffering the birth pain. Women since B.C. would have given anything to ease that pain and I ordered Trixie to hit me up with Demerol.

Julia Ellen Smith arrived first by eleven minutes. She was followed by Grayson Chester Smith. Mr. Pierre's real name is Peter Gerald Grayson which I never knew until we were married. As I kept my maiden name, I named the boy after his "father." I would have given little Gray my dad's name first but I don't think Dad liked Chester. Chessy he could endure. I figured wherever Dad was, he'd understand.

Mr. Pierre wore out the floor in the waiting room. I told him he could come in if he wanted to but he declined. However, when those two tiny babies with curly black hair were presented to him, he went to pieces. He cried. He kissed me. He cried some more. He said it was the happiest day of his life and what a blistering idiot he was to have waited so long to be a father. The fact that these two little ones were not of his loins mattered not a bit to him. It was love at first sight. He also gave me a fantastic pair of ruby and diamond earrings. I know a man is supposed to present his wife with a major piece of jewelry when she presents him with a child, but I was happily surprised when Mr. Pierre gave me the earrings. Once he made certain that I was fine, he paraded around the Square, cold as it was, stopped in every shop, gave out cigars, and bragged, bragged, bragged about the astonishing beauty of his daughter and son. He had Peepbean paint a huge sign with blue and pink ribbons which he put in the front window of the Curl 'n Twirl.

I found out sometime later that he also paid a clandestine call on Jackson Frost. Mr. Pierre, behaving like a gentleman, relieved Jack of any financial responsibility for the twins. Jack thanked him but said that he'd set up a small trust and it was going to stand. Both men agreed that if Pierre died, Jack would step forward and assume the masculine responsibilities toward the children.

Diz Rife wanted that job too. He proved an attentive godfather, because he showed up about two hours after Julia and Gray were born. Already she was dubbed Little Juts. I think he bought out F.A.O. Schwarz. Diz had no children and although he didn't speak of it, it must have stung him, for he was the first Rife not to reproduce. Apparently he, too, had a heart-to-heart with Mr. Pierre, so my babies, born to an emphatically unwealthy mom, had the good fortune to have three men step forward to assist them through this life.

Diz and I competed like two crazed heavyweights up until the time of my birth. He—I should say Mid-Atlantic Holding Shares— poured a ton of money into the new *Clarion*. There were color photos on the front page, colored weather maps, lots and lots of entertainment gossip, and a big special real estate section. Our *Mercury* kept the old front-page layout and concentrated on hard news plus expanded local coverage. To our shock, Aunt Louise's column, "I Remember," took off. Before the column was two months old it had been syndicated. The column reeked of nostalgia, that residue of pleasure. She dictated the column to me and I put it down as she spoke. Aunt Louise became a star. The fan mail for Wheezie arrived by the truckload. Her success mellowed her to the point that she forgave me my pregnancy and hasty marriage. She was less quick to forgive her sister, now living in sin.

Blackout bingo was outlawed north of the Mason-Dixon line. Whatever Diz said or did to him, Bucky dropped the charges against Aunt Louise, me, Lolly, and most of the town, whom he accused of obstructing justice. The bingo pot went to fix the Falkenroth, Spangler & Finster law offices. Mutzi, furious at being denied blackout bingo, instituted a new practice called Nevada cards. This didn't supplant the actual bingo game but accented it. The cards were like miniature slot machines and Runnymede went wild for them. I won a hundred-dollar pot on a Nevada card the week before the kids were born.

Mother came to the hospital off and on most of the day. She was down in the cafeteria when little Julia arrived. One of the nurses paged her and she hurried back upstairs in time for Grayson. After Mr. Pierre left she came into the room. I must have looked awful because she combed my hair. I was exhausted. I could barely lift my arm. As the drug wore off I felt pain. The nurse told me I'd have to sit in a rubber doughnut for a while. The indignity of it all!

Upon seeing her grandchildren, Mom said, "Why, they look just like me."

"We're not related by blood, remember?" The painkiller was really wearing off now.

"Who cares?" She oogled the babies.

"You do—or you did."

"You're too sensitive. You take things personally."

I scooched up so I could lean on the pillows. I'd been lying flat on my back, and tired as I was, I didn't want to be lying down for this conversation, since it had taken me forty-three years to get to it. "Mother, I don't ever want to hear about being adopted again. I don't ever want to hear that my bloodlines are not your bloodlines. I have heard it so many goddamned times I know it word-for-word by heart, and I expect you to pass on this message to your media star sister."

Mother appeared stunned. "What's wrong with you?"

"I have two beautiful babies and I never, ever want them to feel what I have felt every single day of my life."

"What's that?" She forced herself to ask the question though I knew damn well she didn't want the answer.

"To be loved but never to belong. It's a form of punishment."

"I do love you." Her I'm-a-tough-bird face began to crumble.

"I know you do, but you kept me at bay. You kept me under your thumb—maybe that's a better way to put it. Every time I did something wrong, you or Louise would tell me I was an orphan or that I might be like my natural mother, and after today I don't know how any woman could give up her babies. I couldn't. I never want to hear that shit again. So this is the end of the line, Julia."

"Don't you dare call me Julia!"

"I will call you Julia until you agree to drop this subject. Then I'll call you Mom again."

She put her face in her hands and sobbed. The only time I'd seen my mother cry like that was when Dad keeled over dead at the store and Wheezie was the one who had to tell her. She cried so hard she couldn't speak and I am sorry to say my heart did not go out to her—not until she spoke, anyway.

"You don't know what it's like not to be a real woman. You're on the other side of the fence now." She cried anew.

"What are you talking about? A woman's a woman."

"I'm not a real mother. I didn't bear you. Some bitch got to know you for nine months before I did, and Louise rubs my nose in it. I wanted babies."

"You had me."

"It's not the same!" She grabbed the Kleenex so hard the box tumbled on the floor. "Now you're a mother and you're even further away from me."

"Mother—" I had to wait while she blew her nose. "Mom, I think mothering is in the raising, not the bearing. You've got to get over this. You've hurt yourself with it and you're hurting me and I don't want you to hurt Juts—"

She interrupted. "Little Juts. I'm Big Juts and don't forget it."

"I don't want you to hurt Little Juts or Grayson. You don't realize how children see these things. When I was small I didn't have adult emotions. I couldn't put this stuff in perspective. I used to lie awake at night and wonder what did I do wrong that my natural mother would throw me away. And if I was bad, would you throw me away? Do you know, the only person who never said a word about this was Daddy? I really was his daughter and if it weren't for his unqualified love I don't know what I would have done."

"Are you saying I was wrong to tell you?" She was trying to understand.

That in itself was a victory, since Mother couldn't admit she was wrong.

"No, it wasn't wrong, but once would have been enough. If I had questions over the years I would have asked you. Now I am going to tell my two kids, some day when they're old enough, that I was adopted. If they want to ask me questions, they can. If they want to ask you questions, they can, but let them decide when to ask and how much to know."

"All right—if you feel that way." She wiped her eyes. "What about Jack?"

"I'll cross that bridge when I come to it. I think as far as the children are concerned, Mr. Pierre is Daddy."

"Has he been back since this morning?"

"No."

"He's put up a sign in the store window with the babies' names and times of arrival. He'll bankrupt himself if he gives out any more cigars."

She was gliding away from painful knowledge. I suppose I couldn't blame her, and as her spirits were restored she chattered on. Her faults, in modified or maybe even worse form, were my faults, and I guessed in some ways they'd be Little Juts's and Gray's faults too. We were fighters, not criers. We stiff-armed the anguish of our own limitations, our own labyrinth of fears, even as we grasped more tightly at life with the other hand. I knew I'd struggle with that tendency for the rest of my days.

I slipped back down in the bed. Strange as it may sound, this brief conversation with Mom took more out of me than bearing the children. She got up to leave and kissed me on the cheek. I must have been dozing because I was startled.

"I'll see you later tonight."

"Bye, Mom."

"Nickie—"

"What?"

"I'm sorry I threw out your paint set."

With that she left and I knew I'd won, at long last.

49

FLYING A KITE

FRIDAY . . . 25 MARCH

Aunt Louise turned eighty-seven today, although we pretended she was eighty-one. The *Today* show came to Runnymede in honor of her birthday and to show the rest of the nation this little town, bisected by the Mason-Dixon line, which Wheezie had catapulted into fame.

When they initially approached her they wanted to fly her to New York City, but after lengthy discussions with her and out of deference to her age they decided to spotlight the town. Aunt Louise gave an idiosyncratic tour of the town, with the accent on the *idio*. She flirted outrageously with Bryant Gumbel, horned in on Willard Scott's weather report, and nearly caused Jane Pauley a nervous breakdown. Before the camera, dear beloved Louise threw out her script, evaded Ms. Pauley's questions, and went off on a toot. Her crowning moment was when she was walking around the Square and she pointed to the Hanover Street corner and said, "And here is where George Porterfield, a distant cousin of George Spangler's, exposed himself to me in 1931. Reasons as to this unnatural act are still debated." Fortunately, the Hunsenmeir sibling rivalry flickered in front of the camera but did not explode into emotional flames. Louise allowed a shot of herself and Mom but then kept edging in front of Mother, who finally reached back and grabbed the fabric of her coat so she couldn't move, smiling wildly all the time.

The staff of the *Today* show left town more exhausted than the

Ancient of Days they sought to protect by coming here in the first place. However, the ratings shot through the roof and I feared that television would return for more of Wheezie. Visions of my aunt rubbing shoulders with stars danced in my head. Not only would she rub shoulders with them, she would gleefully tell them how to live their lives and they'd learn more of *her* life than they ever wanted to know.

Mother tolerated Louise's fame as well as she could, although she did say loudly enough to be picked up by audio, as the camera moved in for a close-up of Louise at the Confederate statue and cannon: "Lifelike, isn't she?" Apart from that and pulling back at her coat, she restrained her competitive juices, but then she had Ed. Mom was happy.

After the excitement of the morning I returned to the paper. We were holding our own and then some. Mr. Pierre and I took turns taking the babies to work. He'd have them one week and I'd have them the other, but on the weeks that I would have them at *The Mercury* he'd run in and out of the office. He then would return to the Curl 'n Twirl to announce to anyone who would listen the wondrous feats of his babies.

Michelle doted on the kids too. Pewter did not. While she did not dislike them, she suffered no bouts of enthusiasm either. Once she discovered she could lick the formula bottles she showed more affection, and one morning I found her curled up in the crib, although when I came into the room she turned her back on me as if to say it was an accident that she'd fallen sleep here.

Lolly, like my husband, was a goner. She kept within two feet of the babies. If they'd gurgle, she'd cock her head and wag her tail. If anyone she didn't know came near them, she'd bare her fangs. Sometimes I'd watch her watching them. I think she thought they were hairless puppies. One thing was certain: She knew they belonged to her.

I envied the babies because they'd grow up in a newsroom. Eventually, when they got bigger, Mr. Pierre and I would have to figure out day care, although I hoped we could manage them at our places of work until kindergarten. I found myself, like Lolly, staring at them. It was hard to believe they came from me.

Jack and Regina visited the babies, if not once a day, then every other day. Jack melted at the sight of them and so did Diz, who found marvelous excuses to walk across the Square to *The Mercury* or to drop by the house.

Mr. Pierre—I should call him Pierre, because I dropped the "Mr." after the wedding—transformed the interior of Bumblebee Hill. He ransacked the countryside for falling-down barns and houses. He brought home a truckload of old blue boards last week and neatly stacked them by the shed. When I asked him why, he said they'd make beautiful siding for the addition we'd build. When I said what addition, he said the children would need their own rooms when they got bigger and he had it planned to the last nail.

Pierre had changed. He'd become more aggressive with other men, more direct. He used to fight back with his "fairy act," as we called it between ourselves, but now he dropped it. He remained the best-dressed man in town but his style changed. He wasn't wearing shocking colors. He turned to designers like Alan Flusser. The faggot jokes ground to a standstill. Who knows what people say about him behind his back, but to his face men's attitudes have changed. He is who he is. He isn't pretending to be Mr. Butch, but in a way, the real Pierre is emerging. The children have transformed both of us.

And, as he promised, Pierre transformed my wardrobe. He finds me comfortable clothes that enhance whatever attractiveness I've got. He drags me into stores and fusses over me and I let him do it because he knows more than I do. I even like the way I look.

The biggest surprise is that Pierre is learning to ride and play tennis. He says that the best thing for a family is to enjoy a common activity. By the time the children are on horses he'll be a good rider. He's quite disciplined about it.

The other thing is that Pierre swears Michelle has a crush on me. He can be wicked that way because he knows he'll make me self-conscious. I don't think that she does, but if she does, I wouldn't know what to do about it. I've banished romantic love from my mind. It seems like such an overrated emotion. If I had to choose between a great, overpowering passion and the love of good friends, I'd choose the love of good friends.

I glanced up at the wall clock, its brass pendulum swinging. It was time for Louise's party up at our house. I called to *The Mercury* people. We hurried to finish up our jobs and then left.

Louise, still high from her morning's television triumph, preened at her party. Her cake bore the usual thirty-nine candles, which she blew out in one try, provoking comments about being a windbag.

Goodyear's training had been reversed so that he no longer fell dead at the sound of her name. Pierre and Ed fixed people drinks and Verna and Mom organized the covered dishes, since everyone had to bring food. Ed didn't talk any more than when I first met him but I'd become accustomed to his friendly silences. Pewter was making a pest of herself in the kitchen.

The children slept upstairs. They slept a lot but Mom told me to gird myself because once they start crawling around on the floor, they sleep less and so do you.

By the time the food was served, we were starved. I adore covered-dish parties because you get to sample everyone's cooking. Verna brought macaroni and cheese as well as her biscuits. Jack and Regina cooked a perfect Virginia ham. Mother whipped up her usual baked beans with bubble gum. Salads, vegetables dripping with sauce, spoon bread, and a list of desserts that was sinful completed the menu. You can tell when you're at a good party because the talking rolls like waves. Everyone was talking, laughing, congratulating Louise on her performance.

After dessert Mom and I took a breather. We walked outside in the deepening light. The early daffodils swayed in the sharp wind that cut down from the north.

She put her hand over her eyes as the sun began to set. "Good kite weather."

Her red kite, which she'd been flying this windy March, was in the car. She took it out. An idea seized me. I reached in my jacket pocket and retrieved a small notebook. Then I wrote a note to Dad. I tied it on the kite tail.

"Mom, let me do something. I want to let this kite go as far as it will go. I'll buy you another one."

"I've had that kite for years."

"Please, I want to do this."

"If it's so important to you—go ahead."

I ran with the kite but I couldn't get it aloft.

"Here, gimme that."

Mother ran with the kite, expertly playing out the line, and a stiff gust of wind lifted it up.

"Let it go," I told her as another blast of wind pushed the red kite farther upward. "Let it go to God."

She turned to me, a quizzical look on her face, then smiled and let go the string. The kite soared until it became a red speck, and then we could see it no more.

The note read:

Dear Dad,

You're a grandfather now.
I wish you were here. I hope you're happy wherever you are.

Love,
Nickel

P.S. You were right. Life is too important to be serious.

ABOUT THE AUTHOR

RITA MAE BROWN was born in Hanover, Pennsylvania and grew up in Florida. She earned a degree in Classics and English from New York University, and a doctorate in Political Science from the Institute for Policy Studies in Washington, D.C.

She has published several books of poems, a translation of six medieval Latin plays, seven novels—*Rubyfruit Jungle, In Her Day, Six of One, Southern Discomfort, Sudden Death, High Hearts* and *Bingo*—and a writers' manual, *Starting from Scratch*. She has been twice nominted for an Emmy, for her scripts *I Love Liberty* and *The Long Hot Summer*.

She lives in Charlottesville, Virginia.